**Paula Gosling** was born in Detroit and moved permanently to England in 1964. She worked as a copywriter and a freelance copy consultant before becoming a full-time writer in 1979. Since then she has published thirteen novels, has won both the John Creasey and Gold Dagger Awards from the Crime Writers' Association, and has served as the Association's Chairman. When she isn't committing murders by typewriter, cooking or reading, she can be found in her sewing studio, creating abstract embroideries and patchwork quilts. She has a wonderful husband, two beautiful daughters, one lovely cat, and a pet overdraft which she is grooming for Gold in the Banking Olympics.

*By the same author*

A RUNNING DUCK
ZERO TRAP
LOSER'S BLUES
WOMAN IN RED
MONKEY-PUZZLE
THE WYCHFORD MURDERS
HOODWINK
BACKLASH
DEATH PENALTIES
THE BODY IN BLACKWATER BAY
A FEW DYING WORDS
FAIR GAME
THE DEAD OF WINTER
UNDERNEATH EVERY STONE

# DEATH AND SHADOWS

Paula Gosling

WARNER BOOKS

A *Warner* Book

First published in Great Britain in 1998
by Little, Brown and Company

This edition published by Warner Books in 2000

Reprinted 2001



A CIP catalogue record for this book is available from the British Library.

ISBN 0 7515 2548 0

Typeset by Palimpsest Book Production Ltd
Printed and bound in Great Britain by
Mackays of Chatham plc, Chatham, Kent

Warner Books
A Division of
Little, Brown and Company (UK)
Brettenham House
Lancaster Place
London WC2E 7EN

www.littlebrown.co.uk

*This one is for Max Who*
*lives on in Blackwater Bay*

# ONE

THE GIRL IN THE WHITE uniform hesitated.

Was there time to get down to the mailbox and back again without anyone noticing she'd gone? She glanced at her watch. Maybe – if she hurried.

The intertwined branches of the forest clacked and clattered overhead. The wind was damp and there was thunder in the distance. She shivered and began to walk faster, picking her way with difficulty over the rough, steeply canted path. Twice she slipped and pebbles rolled down the slope ahead of her, bouncing off the roots of the trees on either side of the path. It made it seem as if someone else were walking with her.

She paused.

Was that someone else? Ahead? Behind?

The pebbles skittered, the branches of the trees whispered together and all around her the woods were filled with moving shadows. Don't be silly, she told herself. You've been down this path a hundred times, you know the noises well enough – small animals, insects – the hill was alive beneath the massive oaks, maples and birches.

She hurried on, a little edgy now and laughing at herself for it. Ahead and below, between the trunks of the trees, she could see the olive-green surface of the deep, slow-moving river, glinting under the last shafts of sunlight. The storm clouds were massing, trapped by the surrounding hills, darkening everything steadily, inexorably.

'You're going to get wet, you dunce,' she muttered to herself. 'Why didn't you accept that lift, after all?'

But she knew why.

Her ankle turned, traitorously, at a drop in the path and she caught at a birch tree to steady herself, the white bark papery under her palm. As she took a breath, startled by her sudden loss of balance, she heard the sound again. Not an animal. Not insects. Not the wind. Not pebbles.

Footsteps.

Lightning brightened the shadows for a moment and she saw the point of it dipping into the hills on the horizon, a great sword of fire that made the subsequent shadows seem even darker. And colder.

She hurried on, making for the open part of the path that ran along the riverbank to the bridge. There she'd be in full view of the cars on the highway and the houses on the opposite bank, where the town touched the river. Thunder came more loudly now, deep, but with a whip-crack edge. It rumbled away reluctantly, preparing to come again.

Her breath was getting tight in her chest and the fresh air she dragged in was icy in her throat. She made a sound – half whimper, half gasp – and began to run.

She was just ten yards from the end of the woods when she was caught.

Her name was Juli[illegible]alinsky.

She was not the f[illegible]

# TWO

IT HAD BEEN A LONG week's journey from Omaha. Laura Brandon's old car had fought her all the way from the recently shorn wheatfields of the sunny west to the autumn-touched hills surrounding the Great Lakes. She had expected to find glorious arboreal displays when she reached the area around Blackwater Bay, but instead had entered another world, a world of ghostly shapes and shadows that loomed up and then disappeared in a heavy fog. The town itself had been oddly quiet, with condensation dripping from the eaves of the old houses and the new shops. It looked like a nice town, possibly even a friendly town, but the fog lent it a mystery that did not make her feel welcome. The late-September colours of the trees were shrouded in grey clinging wraiths that swirled as she drove through, making it seem as if the pavements were peopled by ghosts. It wasn't wet enough for umbrellas, but her spirits were definitely dampened as she crossed the bridge over the Black river and peered through the windshield, trying to penetrate the mist to find the turn-off to the Mountview Clinic.

She almost missed it.

The sign was discreet, even modest, and did not prepare her for what she saw at the end of the long rising drive.

'Wow.'

So this was Mountview, her uncle Roger's little goldmine and her new place of employment. It was a huge old building, all pink brick, white columns and ivy, but its beauty was somewhat obscured by the folds of fog that curtained it. Lights glowed behind the windows, but in enclosing it the fog somehow gave it a look of smug disdain. We are content, it said. We do not require your presence. Kindly leave us alone. Deliveries at the rear. Ordinary people need not apply.

'You'll have to admit, it's a change from Caspar Street,' she said over her shoulder. The Largest Black Cat In The World was curled on top of the pile of boxes and suitcases that filled the rear seat. He opened one green eye, but admitted nothing.

She put the car back into gear and cautiously circled the left wing of the building, passing through a gap in a high dark hedge that prevented passers-by from seeing anything so distractingly modern as a row of automobiles.

Other concessions to the twentieth century had also been relegated to the rear. Behind the old building was a very modern annexe. Although there was no compromise in the long straight lines of the extension, they were softened by extensive plantings of Virginia creeper that had turned red, now dripping drearily.

She parked the car in an empty slot and took a moment to stretch. Now that she was spared the distractions of travelling she felt strong misgivings. Had this been the right thing to do? She rested her forehead momentarily on the steering wheel.

When her friend Julie Zalinsky had gone to work for Uncle Roger she'd been really pleased for her. (And also relieved that she'd yet again got away with not taking the job herself.) The pay and conditions seemed ideal and Julie had wanted to 'settle' after a long spell of moving from one hospital to another. Uncle Roger, of course, had always wanted Laura to come to Mountview, but she hadn't felt comfortable with the idea of working for her father's brother. She'd wanted to succeed on her own merits.

Unfortunately, hers hadn't been a success story. More a tale of hard work unrewarded, plus a marriage that had benefited only her ex-husband in the end. She had supported him through medical school, only to watch

The girl who had been working at the computer looked up and smiled as Laura came across. An older woman, filing something in one of the many grey metal cabinets that stood against the walls of an inner room, put her sheaf of folders down and came out. 'May I help you?' she asked.

'Hi. I'm Laura Brandon. I've just—'

The woman's expression changed from polite enquiry to friendly welcome. At least it was *intended* to seem friendly, but there was something in the bright-blue eyes that said otherwise. Uh-oh, Laura thought. Tread warily here.

'I'm Mrs Cunningham, your uncle's personal assistant. We've been expecting you since yesterday. He'll be *so* pleased you've arrived at last.'

In other words she was late. She opened her mouth to explain how she'd had to nurse her rather elderly foreign car along the highways between here and Omaha, but Mrs Cunningham flowed on.

'I'll go through and tell Dr Forrester you're here. The double doors on your left are his.' She turned to the typist. 'Will you finish filing these, Beth? I don't want them left out.'

'Yes, Mrs Cunningham,' the girl said, getting up obediently. But as the thin, blonde figure of Milly Cunningham passed through the door behind the counter, the girl flashed a look of intense dislike after her. She reddened as she caught Laura's eye. Laura grinned sympathetically. Obviously Mrs Cunningham was a Force To Be Reckoned With. Challenge One, and she'd only been in the place for two minutes. She'd nearly reached the double doors when they were flung back and Roger Forrester strode towards her.

'Laura! At last! I was beginning to worry!'

Her heart twisted in her chest. She'd forgotten how much alike they were.

Aside from the fact that Roger Forrester had lived three years longer than his twin brother and was consequently a little greyer and a little more lined, it could have been

Laura's late father, Richard Forrester, standing there. Although, she admitted ruefully to herself as she was swept into a bear hug, her father's blunt hands would never have been so perfectly manicured, nor would his suit (on the rare occasions he'd ever worn one) have fitted as flawlessly. Richard Forrester had run more to bandaged thumbs and plaid flannel shirts, to sporting an assortment of screwdrivers and drawing instruments in his pocket rather than a perfectly folded Irish linen handkerchief, and to getting himself into a muddle over business rather than making a brilliant success of it as his twin brother had done.

'You're thinner,' her uncle said as he released her and gazed down with a frown.

'And you're not,' she shot back, poking an affectionate finger at his midriff.

His frown changed into a sheepish grin. 'I told you I had good cooks here.'

'You told me that all right. What you didn't tell me about was all this,' she said, gesturing around at the entrance hall. 'It's so beautiful it makes me feel guilty just to walk through it.'

'Now, why guilty, for heaven's sake?' he asked, puzzlement not quite obscuring the pleasure in his voice.

'Well, if you'd warned me I'd have stopped to change into a ballgown or something. Shame you have to clutter it up with sick people, isn't it?'

He chuckled. 'Oh, we keep them all chained to their beds so they won't spoil the décor. In fact, the rotunda is very inefficient – we should have closed it off, built across on each floor, but I couldn't bear the thought of destroying it.' He beamed down at her. 'Come on, you look as if you could use a restorative. Good bourbon, for instance.'

She followed him, passing through a small outer office (presumably Mrs Cunningham's domain) into the spacious room beyond.

Her uncle Roger was at a side table pouring drinks.

She guessed this was technically an office because there was a massive partner's desk placed diagonally across one corner, but it was more like a sitting-room. There were two deep chintz-covered couches facing one another across a low table in front of the fireplace. Books lined the walls between the windows. The colour scheme was green and gold.

The colour of money.

Her uncle turned, two glasses in his hands, and smiled. 'Welcome, Laura,' he said, coming across. 'I hope you'll be as happy here as I am.'

'You do live here, then?'

'Oh, yes. Bedroom, dressing-room and bath through there,' he said, nodding towards a door in the wall beside the fireplace. 'We'll do the full tour after you've relaxed a bit. Sit down – you look exhausted.'

She sank gratefully into the depths of one of the couches and he sat opposite, putting his drink down on the table and reaching for his cigar case. 'Tell me how it's been.'

She grimaced and shrugged. 'I've managed.'

'You didn't *have* to "manage".'

'Yes, I did.'

'Only because you're too proud for your own good. Just like your father.'

She looked up quickly and for an instant, no more, met the grief in his face. So he missed her father as much as she did. The pain was as real and fresh in his eyes as it was in hers whenever she caught sight of herself unexpectedly in a mirror. He lit his cigar and the flame obscured his expression. When he shook out the match, the look had been extinguished too.

'You know what divorce is like,' she tried to explain. 'It leaves you wanting to prove something, that you haven't gone down under it, that you can survive. Or maybe it's different for a man.'

'Not really,' he said softly. 'But I certainly don't think *I* would have immersed myself in the hellish emotional demands of working with the disadvantaged and refused alimony if I'd been in your position. It was Mike who destroyed your marriage, after all.'

'It takes two to ruin a marriage.'

'Or, in Mike's case, three or four.' His smile was wry.

'He's not a bad person, just a weak one,' she said quickly. Why she was bothering to defend her ex-husband was beyond her – what he'd done was indefensible. She was not going to think that way any more.

'Then you're still in love with him?'

She considered the question seriously, as she often had over the past year, whenever Mike's letters or telephone calls came. 'Actually, you know, I'm not,' she finally announced, to herself as well as to him. 'The wound has been successfully cauterized, doctor.'

'I'm glad, and I'm glad you're here where I can look after you. But I can't say this is an ideal locale at the moment.' His face was suddenly bleak.

He meant Julie, of course. 'Have they found out yet who killed her?' She was relieved that he had brought it up before she'd had to work it into the conversation. She could hardly admit she'd come here predisposed to suspicion and mistrust. He was her uncle, her father's brother, after all. And yet . . . and yet . . .

Forrester shrugged. 'There's been no progress. The sheriff seems an able man, far more intellectually qualified than he needs to be as sheriff of a small county like this, but perhaps that's not enough. He's been up here almost every day since it happened, questioning the staff, doing just about everything he could. Even so, he's apparently come up with nothing. She was a nice enough girl, no secrets to her, no reason we can come up with for her being killed like that. It was so sudden, so eerie, somehow.'

'How do you mean, "eerie"?'

'Well, it's thrown everyone, as you can imagine. Some of the patients were very upset, especially those who are here for emotional or mental reasons. We lost a few, of course.'

'You mean they . . .'

He glanced at her, then shook his head. 'No, no – I mean they left and went elsewhere. But the staff have been very unsettled. We've had several of our local employees quit, as a matter of fact. Said they just didn't feel "comfortable" here any more. Considering the employment situation locally it seems odd that they'd give up a good job and good pay for no real reason. But it's sort of changed the way we look at everything. Before, the woods were beautiful – now, they're a little intimidating. The town seemed close – now it seems far away. We feel our isolation, in more ways than one. Before the murder you could best describe Blackwater as a pretty ordinary town – with a few eccentricities, I'll admit, but finding its way forward, just the same. Now "spooked" would be closer to it.'

'I can imagine,' Laura murmured. The way Julie had been 'spooked'? she wondered.

But he shook his head. 'No, funnily enough, I don't think you can. I've never come across anything like it. One of the GPs in town told me the other day that he'd had an absolute flood of hypochondriacs in his waiting-room. They complain of insomnia, headaches, gastric upsets, breathing difficulties – all stress-related complaints from people he hasn't seen for years except for the odd cut finger. I mean, it's not as if Blackwater hasn't seen murder before, but this time it seems different. And I don't know *why*. It's strange.'

'At least it's given them something novel to gossip about,' Laura said carefully.

The bleakness in his face tightened to something more like anger. 'I think they blame me. Or Mountview, somehow.'

'Why would they do that?'

'We're outsiders, you see. And she was one of ours. She worked here and lived here. Not one of them, you see.'

'But surely—'

He shook his head. 'It's nothing overt, nothing you can exactly put your finger on . . . shops going silent when I come in, nobody nodding to you on the street any more, that kind of thing. Not ostracized, exactly, but—' He shrugged. 'They seem sort of . . . wary of me. It's very uncomfortable.'

'I'm sorry,' Laura said. It was also very interesting. What was the local gossip, then, about Mountview? How could she find out? To give him his due, he seemed genuinely upset by it.

'Oh, we'd always have been outsiders to some extent,' he said in a more practical tone. 'But since we've brought employment to quite a few local people, I thought we'd eventually be accepted. I expect it will be all right in time.' He forced a smile. 'Anyway, no sense in depressing you the minute you arrive, is there? Come and have a walk around. I've been looking forward to showing off.'

'I'm already pretty impressed,' Laura said, standing up and putting down her glass. Even a few sips had left her feeling rather unsteady. She cleared her throat. 'Aren't you curious as to why I suddenly agreed to come here after all this time?'

'No,' he said quickly. 'I don't question good fortune. That has a habit of making it go away. I just accept things as they come along and try to remember to say thank you whenever I can.' He smiled at her. 'You see, I'm a lucky man. I always have been, although I've never known why. Things do have a way of working out for me. It almost seems unfair, sometimes.' He chuckled, opening the door for her. 'But not enough for me to feel guilty about it.'

Oh, really? she thought.

And scolded herself for doubting him.

After all, he was family.

And Julie could have been crazy.

Couldn't she?

# THREE

THE MEDICAL WORLD HAD BEEN astonished when Roger Forrester had turned from a successful career administering massive hospitals in places like San Francisco, Denver, Chicago and Boston with conspicuous style, to creating his own little oasis in the mid-west. Forrester stick to a one-horse operation? The man who moved through society as smoothly as he did through the stock market, accruing friends, patrons and profits with equal ease?

Ridiculous.

Laura, too, had had doubts, remembering her uncle as the man in the Gucci loafers, the doctor who always smelled of aftershave rather than antiseptic and who always seemed to have at least one beautiful woman trying to snare him. (One actually had, but not for long. Despite being an Italian countess of impeccable breeding, her morals had proved to be less noble than her bloodline and the marriage had soon ended.) Indeed, a good deal of Roger Forrester's social success had stemmed from the fact of his being – and staying – a highly eligible male.

Now, however, as he showed Laura over Mountview, she was getting an entirely different picture from the one adolescence had given her. Common sense should have told her that all the style and charisma in the world wouldn't have made her uncle a success in hospital administration. That could only have come about through ability and hard work, for big hospitals are unforgiving when it comes to incompetence. They can't afford mere figureheads.

He knew his job. It was evident in everything he said

and in every detail he pointed out on the tour. Apparently there was something different about looking after your own.

'Mountview is small because I want it that way. After all those years of corner-cutting and compromise, I wanted a place where what came first was keeping the patients happy, not the Board. And, incidentally, to give the best possible care.'

'For which they pay through the nose.'

He grinned. 'Indeed. It is a business, after all – a kind of retirement hobby for me, in that the administrative side is child's play compared with what I used to do. I have a lovely place to live and I can, occasionally, make a kind of contribution to medicine.' He pushed open a door as they returned from the annexe to the main building. 'If you're still hankering after a little do-gooding, it might interest you to know that we also maintain a free clinic in Hatchville.'

She stopped and stared at him. 'You never told me that.'

'You never asked. We actually have two young physicians working for Mountview – David Butler and Owen Jenks. They alternate between here and there.'

'Julie wrote me about both of them.' Laura had to smile at the recollection. Julie had been quite taken with both the young medics – David Butler because he was handsome and charming ('maybe a little *too* charming' Julie had been careful to say) and Owen Jenks because he was so very dedicated ('he has a real vocation that I find quite inspiring'). One week she would rave about David, the next about Owen.

Roger smiled. 'I expect she did. Owen works mainly at the clinic in Hatchville and David mostly here, but they trade off as it suits them and take turns with being on night call. There isn't much of that, as it happens, which is fortunate. They are both good, so I leave their scheduling to them – although it is David who usually assists at any surgery done here. Owen is better at general medicine.

Aside from those two, you could call this Old Crock's Manor. Martin Hambden, Aaron Stammel and Clifford Gantry all have an affiliation with us. A few others, too.'

'Martin *Hambden*?'

'I thought that might impress you, though in his case I have to admit it was more good luck than design. He's a native of Blackwater Bay and still maintains a home here. In a few years he plans to give up the Grantham end entirely. He has several patients with us at the moment.'

Laura had never thought that finally accepting her uncle's offer would mean she could work with one of the mid-west's most outstanding orthopaedic surgeons. It was an unexpected bonus. 'That's marvellous.'

They entered the east wing of the main building. An occasional open door gave a glimpse of the patients' rooms, each individually furnished to a standard and style one might expect of a five-star hotel rather than a medical clinic.

The annexe was the main working area of the clinic, housing kitchens, laundry, a small surgical complex of X-ray, operating theatre and intensive care recovery room. Laura's office, the gym and the treatment rooms were at the far end, overlooking the hydrotherapy pool. There was also an occupational therapy room. 'You'll be kept pretty busy. We have several patients recovering from joint replacements, thanks to Martin. And there are others with complaints in addition to their main reasons for being here – arthritics, mainly. We have quite a few older patients.'

'They have the money,' Laura said.

He looked at her. 'Public medicine demands a lot, Laura. More than I could give, in the end. I got tired of all the fighting for money, beds, equipment – my health was beginning to suffer.'

'I didn't realize that.' She was stricken to think that she hadn't considered that possibility. Roger and her father had been twins, and Richard Forrester had died three years ago, after leading a much less pressured life than his brother. 'You're . . . all right now?'

'Oh, fine, fine. Mountview was exactly what I needed.'

They continued down the hall towards the nursing office.

'All the patients are on the same floor, I see.'

'Yes. If we're full we have forty in-patients. Most stay in for less than two weeks, although we do have some long-term cases. Usually things like nervous breakdowns or depressions, which take a long time to improve. Our psychiatrist, Harlan Weaver, oversees their treatment. You'll like him. He comes in several times a week for regular therapy sessions, but is local so is always on call should there be an emergency of any kind. Obviously we don't take severe psychiatric cases which require confinement or anything like that, nor do we treat addiction. Those are very specialized areas, something we might get into at a later date. But there are many people for whom a short period of pampering and escape can do wonders. Being "sick" gives them an excuse to dignify retreat. When their natural strengths return they continue treatment with their own physicians or psychiatrists.'

'A country club for neurotics?' Laura teased him.

He chuckled. 'You might say that – but some of these patients are high-powered business or creative people who need special understanding. Harlan is good at that – particularly with creative types. Not every psychiatrist can cope with those, you know. Creativity is a sensitive thing and needs equally sensitive handling.' They moved on. 'Before the annexe was built we took only convalescents, but now we're doing some surgical work as well. Nothing too ambitious – you do need full facilities for that. Most patients are diagnosed before they come to us and we liaise with their own doctors. We don't do emergency work, obviously – we're more about peaceful after-care than ER excitements. Of course, one day I'd like to expand. The top floor could be converted to more patients' rooms instead of staff accommodation and storage, which is what it's set aside for now, but that kind of expansion takes money. And a big commitment, too. I do have a splendid long-term development plan, but it will have to wait for quite a while.' He knocked on the door at the end of the hall and opened it. 'Get your hand out of that chocolate box, Shirley,' he said as he went in.

'That's not fair,' objected the nurse behind the desk. 'I'll have you know I haven't had a chocolate in . . .' She looked down at the watch pinned to the front of her uniform. 'In two hours. I must have lost *pounds* by now.'

Forrester smiled. 'Laura, this is the real boss of Mountview, my chief nurse, Shirley Hasker. They just keep me around for show. Shirley, this is my niece, Laura Brandon.'

Shirley Hasker was a tall, heavily built woman who could have seemed motherly were it not for the lines of tension around her mouth and the cool aura of natural authority that surrounded her. When she took Laura's small hand in her plump one there was real strength underlying the soft flesh. 'I'm glad you're here, Laura. The agency physio we had really wasn't much good with the patients.'

'From what Uncle Roger has said, they'd hate just about anybody after Miss Zalinsky,' Laura said with a smile.

Nurse Hasker's face clouded. 'It was a terrible thing to lose her like that. Terrible.'

'Now, Shirley, you mustn't dwell on it.' Forrester's quick professional cheer rang a little hollow.

'I'm not dwelling on it,' Shirley said defensively. 'But we can't pretend it didn't happen, can we? She was a lovely girl and she was dreadfully murdered. It was more than a crime, it was a tragic waste of a young woman's future. She could have done so well.'

'Yes, well—' Roger Forrester seemed oddly discomfited by this display of passionate outrage. Shirley Hasker's eyes blazed with indignation on which his cajoling tones seemed to have little effect. 'I'm sure we all agree on that. Laura and she were good friends, of course, so she especially misses her.'

Shirley Hasker looked at Laura, startled.

'Julie and I trained together and we were working at the same hospital before she came here,' Laura explained, taken aback by the sudden enmity in the older woman's face. Why was it unwelcome information that she had been acquainted with Julie?

'I see,' Nurse Hasker said stonily.

Forrester spoke hurriedly. 'What is important is that Laura is here, now, and I'm delighted that she is.' He beamed at his niece and she felt even more awkward.

'Even nicer if Julie were here, too,' murmured Nurse Hasker, looking at Laura with faint reproach.

'Indeed,' Forrester said uncomfortably. 'Indeed, well, we must get on, Shirley. I just wanted Laura to know where she could come for guidance on the patients, that's all.'

'If I'm not here someone else will be.' Shirley glanced down at the papers on her desk as if eager to get back to them. 'Nurse Pink is my deputy, but all our nurses are more than competent to deal with any difficulties or questions you might have.' She looked again at Laura. 'Our main concern is the patients, of course. That's what we're here for.'

'Obviously,' Laura said rather crisply. No wonder Julie had been unhappy. First Milly Cunningham, now Nurse Hasker – both obviously prepared to dislike her from the start. Well, fair enough. She didn't have to be loved to do her job. But it was odd.

It was almost a relief to close the door on Nurse Hasker's piercing blue eyes, yet Laura felt that rudeness was not natural to the big woman.

Her uncle's next words confirmed it. 'She was dreadfully upset by Julie's death. She was very fond of the girl. Perhaps too fond.' His glance met hers, then moved away, as if embarrassed by the contact. 'I don't mean to imply there was anything unhealthy in their friendship, of course—'

'No, of course not,' Laura murmured dutifully. They continued on their tour. He'd introduced her to so many people that she had lost track of the names. It's fortunate that everyone wears name tags, she thought wryly, otherwise I'd be in real trouble. Mountview seemed to have no shortage of staff despite what her uncle had said about losing people after the murder.

She looked at his averted profile as they descended to the ground floor again and saw a flush of embarrassment on his cheek-bones. Or was it annoyance? 'I'm sure Nurse Hasker didn't mean to make me feel unwelcome.'

He stopped at the foot of the stairs. 'Nevertheless, you do feel it, don't you? I'm sorry, my dear. After all, you have more right to be here than anyone.'

'What do you mean?'

He frowned slightly, then smiled. 'Never mind, I know how you feel about that. The point is I needed a new physiotherapist and you happen to be a very good one. I've always wanted you here with me in the "family business" as it were, so it's all worked out well, hasn't it?'

Laura tried a laugh. 'Maybe she thinks you killed Julie so I could have her job.' She was horrified to see his face go suddenly pale. 'Hey, that was a joke.'

'Of course. You'll have to forgive us, Laura – Shirley, myself, the others you've met – all of us. We're still not ourselves. As time passes and the memory of all that fuss and suspicion diminishes, I'm sure you'll find Mountview a pleasant place to work.'

'Suspicion?'

'Oh, yes. We all had to produce alibis and so on, the usual thing, I suppose. It's pretty dreadful to have someone look at you and wonder whether you're capable of murder. It's as if your whole existence were suspect, suddenly. Where were *you* at eight o'clock last night, for instance?'

'In my motel room, watching television, I suppose.'

'Can you prove it? Do you have any witnesses?'

'Only my cat.'

'There you are, then. That's what I mean. We don't live our lives prepared to account for every minute of them, do we? There are many times when we're alone, when we can't remember what we were doing . . .'

She saw his hand was white-knuckled where it gripped

the newel post. 'You can't mean they seriously suspected *you*?'

'Oh, indeed. They suspected – they *suspect* – everyone. It needn't even have been a man, you see. A woman could have done it, a fairly strong woman, anyway. Anyone can lift a rock and—' He shivered. 'I had to identify her.'

'I'm sorry. You must forget it, you know.'

His eyes glittered. 'How can we? Until they arrest someone, we're *all* murderers.'

# FOUR

'THIS BUILDING USED TO BE the stables,' Roger Forrester said, as he opened the door at the top of the outside stairs. 'I hope you'll be comfortable here.'

'Oh, but it's wonderful!' Here, too, was a contrast to the misty world outside. Bright rag rugs dotted the polished surface of the wide old floorboards and cheerful plaid curtains framed a view of the clinic, just visible through the fog. One side of the room had been separated off as a small but well-equipped kitchen and there was a real fireplace.

'Bedroom and bath through there.' He looked around in a rather disapproving way. 'It's not luxurious, but you'll have it to yourself. If you don't want to bother cooking there's the staff canteen, of course—'

'I never expected this,' Laura said, amazed. 'I presumed I'd have to get a place in town – because of Solomon.'

'Yes, well, I remembered that monster would be coming with you.' Forrester smiled. 'This was where Julie lived – I hope that doesn't bother you.'

'Not at all.' She glanced around. 'What happened to her things?' she asked, trying to sound casual.

'Oh, I expect Milly packed them up and sent them off someplace,' her uncle said vaguely. 'I don't believe there was any family, so what was useful probably went to some charity or other. Why?'

'Oh, I just wondered,' Laura replied. 'She had something of mine – a cashmere scarf – and . . .'

'Sorry. If we'd known . . .'

'It really doesn't matter,' she said hurriedly. So much for her first attempt at 'detecting'. 'Who lives downstairs? I noticed as we came up the staircase that it was furnished too.'

'Our two residents share it. Owen has been at the Hatchville Clinic today, but you'll meet him soon enough. David is probably still on duty – I'm surprised we didn't run into him during our tour.' He glanced at his watch. 'Good Lord, they'll be here any minute. Ever heard of Gilliam Enterprises?'

'I think so.' She had vague recollections of old mining money diversified into electronics, steel and plastics.

'The youngest Gilliam son is a new patient of ours. He's been here for a couple of weeks now and I'm about to be quizzed about his progress.'

'You don't look too pleased.' She was investigating the cupboards in the kitchen and her voice sounded rather hollow.

'I'm not,' he admitted. 'Frankly, his progress has been nil, but it's not our fault. He's a real stinker of a patient.' He looked at her apologetically as she emerged from what had proved to be a broom closet. 'And I'm afraid it's you who'll be getting the worst of it. It's a sciatic axonotmesis.'

'That's not *so* difficult to treat.'

'I didn't say the case was difficult, I said the *patient* was difficult,' he said with a grimace. 'Anyway, don't worry about it now, Monday is time enough. You have the weekend to settle in. I'll get Michaels to bring your things up.'

'Thank you.'

'When you've unpacked, come over. We can have dinner together and talk.'

'I'd like that.'

'Good.' He put his hands lightly on her shoulders. 'I'm glad you're here at last, Laura Forrester Brandon. Mountview is as much yours as mine and we need you here. *I* need you here.'

'Are you handing me the keys of the kingdom?' she asked, a little disconcerted by his formal speech.

'No – only to the liquor cabinet.'

'Then I'll be over as quickly as I can.'

He chuckled. 'If he did nothing else, Richard at least taught you to appreciate the finer things in life.'

'He did everything for me and you know it,' she said, suddenly on the defensive. 'It wasn't easy for him.'

'I don't imagine it was easy for either of you,' he commented. 'Both being pigheaded mavericks with no one around to act as a go-between. If your mother had lived I'm certain she'd have been worn to a frazzle just keeping the peace. She was the only person I ever knew who could handle Richard – without him realizing it, I mean. And that includes me.'

'He was very proud of you.'

'And I was proud of him. I guess it would have been better if we'd let it show now and again, instead of arguing all the time.'

'He didn't like being told what to do.'

'And neither do you? I'll try and remember that.' He smiled.

He left her to explore her new home. She was investigating the controls of the cooker when a figure appeared in the open doorway, laden with an armload of firewood. He was stringy and pale, and had a way of poking his head forward so that he resembled a curious weasel sizing up a chicken house.

'Oh – thanks,' she said, as he marched across the room and dumped the logs unceremoniously beside the fireplace. One rolled a little way away, but he made no move to retrieve it. He eyed her as he came over to lean against the breakfast bar and she felt instant discomfort. The impulse to cover herself up was almost overwhelming.

'You like the place?' he asked in a nasal voice that bespoke adenoids or the end of a cold. There was a trace of Maine in his words too, so perhaps he was a displaced down-easter.

'It's lovely.'

'Last girl lived here had her head bashed in.'

'So I understand.'

He seemed disappointed. 'Don't that scare you?'

'Not particularly. I have no intention of walking alone in the woods at night. And since I've only been here an hour or two I don't *think* I've made any enemies.'

He laughed at that, revealing small white pointed teeth. 'Maybe you had a few before you even came, ever think of that?'

'Now how could I have?' she asked, annoyed at herself for being drawn. The wiry little man seemed so full of malice it was almost visible in a haze around him, yet it had a curiously objective quality. He was the kind of man who would never pull the wings off flies, but would delight in watching someone else do it.

'You met Miss High and Mighty Cunningham yet?'

'Yes.'

'Well, there's one for a start. She don't think much of your uncle bringing you here and that's the truth. Wants to keep him all to herself, don't want anyone else horning in on her territory, taking up his time, sort of undermining her influence you might say. She's the queen bee all right, and you have to keep on her good side to survive around here. She never liked Miss Zalinsky, neither.'

'Perhaps her mother was frightened by a physiotherapist,' Laura suggested.

He seemed to resent this. 'Laugh all you like, girlie. This place isn't as pretty as it looks.'

'That's probably because nasty things keep popping out the woodwork,' she responded snidely.

'Maybe.' He laughed abruptly, ignoring the implication. 'Something popped out of the woods for Julie Zalinsky, that's for sure. I'm only trying to give you a friendly word of advice. Up to you whether or not you take it.' He cast her fate to the winds with a wave of his bony hand and, as he did so, the light caught a glint of red from a large ring he was wearing. For a moment she thought there was blood on his hand, but the light left the ring and it was revealed as simply a large and vulgarly ornate lump of male self-indulgence. Michaels was obviously proud of it, for he used his hands a great deal as he spoke, so no one could miss seeing it. It was ugly, but looked expensive.

'My uncle said you would help me bring in my things,' she said.

'Don't you want to know who else to watch out for? I'm maybe the only one around here who'll give you the straight goods. Or are you too—'

'Excuse me, is this yours?' came a voice from the still-open doorway and Michaels jerked around. Behind him stood a young man who looked like an ad for pipe tobacco, all lean lines and noble cheek-bones, but the effect was spoiled somewhat by his efforts to avoid being savaged by an outraged Solomon who dangled from one hand and was attempting to reduce his captor's tweed jacket (or better still, the captor himself) to shreds.

'Good heavens, how did he get out?' Laura asked, going over to relieve him of his burden. Solomon gave one last snarl, then settled into her arms like a baby, blinking his big green eyes innocently and commencing to purr loudly, as if he were no more dangerous than a kitten. Nobody was fooled, least of all Laura, who had been through this kind of thing before.

'He was hanging half-way out of a car window, trying to snare a sparrow,' the man said. 'I was going to call the zoo to see if any panthers had escaped, but then I remembered your uncle saying something about your having a rather large cat.' He grinned. 'I'm David Butler. Welcome to Mountview.'

She had guessed this was the gifted young resident her uncle had been praising so highly, and that Julie had alternately worshipped and deprecated. Bet he goes down well with the rich widows and hungry divorcees, she thought wryly.

'Thank you.' She put Solomon down on the couch and looked up to see Michaels staring at him in absolute terror. 'He's not as dangerous as he looks,' Laura tried to reassure him. 'He just has a pituitary condition or something – doesn't know when to stop growing.' Since Solomon weighed something in the region of twenty pounds and had not an ounce of fat on him, she quite understood people being a little leery of him, but Michaels's fear seemed to go deeper than that.

'Can't stand cats or dogs,' he said in a thin voice, edging towards the door. He caught the contempt in Butler's eyes and spoke defensively. 'Allergic to 'em, see? Sets off my asthma even to be in the same room. You'll have to get your own things in . . .' He rushed out, giving a large and not very convincing sneeze as he scuttled down the outside stairs.

David and Laura looked at one another, then began to laugh simultaneously. 'He's a disgusting specimen. God knows why your uncle keeps him on,' David spluttered.

'For contrast, I imagine.' She turned towards the kitchen. 'I think I saw a jar of instant coffee in one of the cupboards. Would you like a cup? I'm dying of thirst.'

'Sounds fine. I'll bring your things in from the car while you're making it.'

'Oh, you don't have to—'

'I know I don't have to. I'm trying to impress you with my chivalrous manners and rippling muscles. Are you impressed yet?'

'Not yet.'

'You mean you wouldn't buy a used car from me?'

'Let's see your hands.'

Obediently he held out his hands for inspection. They were long-fingered and square-palmed, strong and smooth. 'Well?'

'Not a chance.' She laughed. 'Those hands wouldn't know a crankshaft from a carburettor. Go peddle your used cars somewhere else.'

'You've crushed my spirit now,' he complained over his shoulder. 'I may need *two* cups of coffee to recover.' He went down the staircase, his tread firm and solid after Michaels's fretful flight.

Well, well, she thought. Such men are definitely dangerous. Laura did not particularly care for handsome men – they usually thought their looks were sufficient unto the day and made no effort otherwise.

As he brought in the last of her boxes she waved the sugar bowl at him. 'Sugar?'

'Just half a spoonful, thanks.'

She stirred the mug and handed it over. 'Sorry about the instant coffee and powdered milk.'

'It's fine.' He glanced around. 'This layout is different from ours downstairs. We've got more rooms, but you've got more light.'

'I never expected to be staying right at the clinic,' she admitted. 'Because of him.' She indicated Solomon, who was steadily and quietly investigating every corner of the little apartment.

'A pet is a luxury I've never had,' David said. 'I seem to have been living in dormitories and hospital accommodation for ever. Coming here was a real pleasure, I can tell you. But I'll hold off on the child substitutes until I've really settled down. I'm more of a dog man, actually.'

'That's probably because you've never known a cat,' she said. 'He might convert you.' She didn't like dog people either – it was a war of personalities, always.

'If he doesn't eat me first,' David said, eyeing Solomon warily. 'We didn't exactly get off to a good start.'

'Oh, he's very forgiving. Feed him a few times and he's yours for life.'

'At least you're assured of not being bothered by Michaels.' David smiled. 'He used to drive Julie crazy, hanging around.'

'Oh?'

'Yes. I think he had a crush on her, or something like that. He's a hard worker and can turn a hand to most things about the place, which I suppose is why your uncle keeps him on, but he's a nasty piece of work, in my opinion. Sly and nosy, and all too ready to pass on unpleasant gossip.'

'He doesn't seem to think much of Mrs Cunningham.'

David's face shifted into neutral. 'She's very efficient.'

'And you don't like her, either.'

'I didn't say that.'

'You didn't have to.' She went to the window and looked over at the main building. 'She's been with my uncle a long time.' She turned back to him. 'Is that the problem?'

'Perhaps. It's hardly my place to say.'

'My, you're discreet,' she teased.

He had the grace to smile and put down his empty mug. 'How about joining me for dinner tonight? To get acquainted.'

'That would have been nice, but I'm having dinner with my uncle.'

'Oh, of course. I should have realized. Maybe another time.'

'Sure.'

'Great.' He glanced at his watch. 'Hey, I've got evening rounds. Thanks for the coffee. See you—' With a grin and a wave he was gone. She stared at the empty space of the open door and smiled. Well, well – the beautiful David Butler wasn't used to being turned down, was he? Or had he thought she was putting him in his place by reminding him that Roger Forrester was her uncle and he was, technically, the hired help? Good heavens, she thought remorsefully, I hope not. After all, she was only hired help herself, really. And while she was not prepared to fall instantly for his all-too-obvious charms, she had no intention of alienating him either. It was clear she was going to need friends at Mountview.

Her assessment of her position was underlined that evening by Milly Cunningham. The woman didn't actually say or do anything that was overtly unfriendly, it was simply the exaggerated manner she maintained throughout the meal and afterwards as they sat with brandy before the fire. She wanted to know all about Laura's work in Omaha, how she had lived there, what her apartment had been like, who her friends had been.

She's being *so* nice to me, Laura thought cynically, she's doing all the polite and acceptable things, making the right conversation, just the way the Lady of the Manor would do with a new governess before relegating her to the nursery.

She watched as Mrs Cunningham laughed at something her uncle Roger had said. She'd heard about the super-efficient Mrs Cunningham for most of her adult life, because Milly had been Roger's assistant in several hospitals, moving with him up the professional ladder.

Until now, however, she had been no more than an apocryphal figure, often referred to but never seen. After hearing all the panegyrics about dear Milly's efficiency and organization, Laura had expected to meet a spectacled machine in skirts. Earlier, Milly had worn glasses and a severe suit, and had appeared quite formidable. Now her golden hair was loosened to spill across the shoulders of her brilliantly coloured Italian silk dress, and gold glinted at her throat, wrists and ears. It was a transformation clearly designed to impress the New Girl, and it had – although perhaps not in the way intended.

She's his mistress, Laura thought, and in more ways than in bed. He's besotted with her. He hadn't let it show earlier today, but that was his professional face. She didn't like it. No, she thought suddenly, I take that back.

I don't like *her* and she doesn't like me.

But Milly and Laura went on smiling and talking equably, because of Roger Forrester. He beamed at them, switching his focus from one to the other, obviously wishing them to be dear friends. It would never happen.

It was not clear to Laura how much of her automatic dislike had been engendered by the various degrees of antipathy the girl at reception, Michaels and David Butler had each revealed towards Milly Cunningham. But she didn't need other opinions to form one of her own.

'It's a shame you couldn't have come to us long ago,

Laura,' Milly was saying. 'It will do Roger good to have family around him. But, of course, you had your own life to lead, didn't you?'

In other words, Laura had kept busy by messing up her marriage. Thanks for the reminder, Laura thought. She knew she was being defensive, but she also knew she was right about Milly Cunningham. She probably killed Julie, she thought resolutely, knowing it was nonsense, but taking pleasure in the thought that she had immediately solved 'the case'.

Forrester returned from refilling their glasses. 'At least you don't have to worry about driving home, do you?' he said jovially. They'd had two bottles of wine with dinner and he was very merry. Both Milly and Laura were stone cold sober.

'No – only about falling on my face in the parking lot,' Laura agreed. She sipped her drink and cleared her throat. 'By the way, thank you for getting my apartment ready and stocking me up with the basics,' she said to Milly. 'Everything was in place, the bed made . . . everything.'

'One of the nurses, I expect,' Milly said negligently. 'I left it to Shirley to organize. Of course, I had a look around to make sure everything was in order, but . . .'

But the actual *work* had been done by someone else. Of course. How could Laura have thought anything else? 'And was it you who took care of Julie's things?' she asked, trying to make it sound like casual curiosity.

'Why, I—' Milly began with a frown.

'Apparently Julie had some things of Laura's – a cashmere scarf, wasn't it, dear?' her uncle explained.

'Yes,' Laura said. 'It isn't important, really.'

'But how could she have had something of yours?' Milly asked, looking puzzled.

'They were old friends,' her uncle answered. 'They worked together in Omaha. Don't you remember, it was she who recommended Julie to me.'

'Oh, yes . . . I had forgotten all about that,' Milly said

faintly. She looked across at Laura and there was something behind her eyes that made Laura want to shiver. 'So you were close, then?'

'Yes. We kept in touch.' Laura watched her as she spoke.

'Oh.' Milly's face was expressionless as she took in that piece of information. After a minute she turned to Forrester. 'You know, we should have had David and Owen in for dinner too, Roger,' she said brightly.

'Oh, no – plenty of time for that. I want to get acquainted with my niece before anyone else does.' Roger bent to kiss Laura briefly on the cheek before resuming his seat opposite. As he sat down next to Milly, Laura suddenly realized why she was reacting so strongly to the other woman and felt ashamed.

She was simply jealous.

It was the twin thing. It was like seeing her father sitting there with another woman. Because Laura had been the only woman in her father's life from the age of twelve and her mother's death, she'd felt a more than normal possessiveness about him. It would have taken a very special woman to win over the watchful wary child she had been. Fortunately or unfortunately, he'd been too absorbed in his work to feel the need of a wife, so she had been both daughter and mother to him as she grew up, gradually taking over the running of the house even while she was pursuing her studies. Although they did have help in the house, it was she who oversaw his diet, ironed his shirts, tried to make sure he got enough sleep and protected him from the day-to-day details of life. It had been a burden she gladly bore, knowing he appreciated it, that she was necessary to his happiness and well-being.

That did not give her the right to extend that relationship to her uncle merely because he *looked* like her father. But the resemblance had been causing her great difficulty ever since she'd arrived. Intellectually she knew it was foolish, but every time he smiled a certain way, moved a certain way, turned his head a certain way, her heart contracted. She missed her father so much. Perhaps she was being unfair to Milly. Maybe Julie's unhappiness here had simply been a clash of personalities with Mrs Cunningham. I must try to like her, she told herself. I must really try.

'I met David Butler earlier,' she said. 'I liked him.'

'He and Jenks are both excellent physicians.' Her uncle nodded. 'The resident we had before the annexe was built was – well – unsatisfactory.'

'He drank,' Milly said coldly.

'We never knew that for sure, Milly,' Roger protested.

The old story of brother doctors sticking together, Laura thought, and saw from Milly's expression that there, at least, they were in agreement.

'*I* was sure,' Milly said firmly.

There was a brief silence.

'Well, I'd better get back to my little home,' Laura said brightly, standing up. 'Solomon will think I've deserted him for ever.'

Milly shivered slightly. 'I saw him standing in your doorway this afternoon. He's enormous, isn't he?'

Obviously another cat hater, like Michaels. 'There have been suggestions that he's part panther,' Laura said. 'I think of him as a little old man in a fur coat, because he's so grumpy and—'

They both stared at her. Oh, God, she realized, I'm getting an attack of the whimsies. Time to go home.

'I'll walk you over.' Her uncle stood up too.

'No need,' she assured him. 'I brought a flashlight.'

'Even so—'

'Oh, Roger, don't fuss. It's only a few yards,' Milly said. 'It's not as if she were going near the woods, after all. Our nurses are in and out of that parking lot all the time and nothing has ever happened.'

'I'll be fine.' Laura spoke firmly and made her farewells.

* * *

When the door had closed behind his niece, Roger Forrester turned to Milly Cunningham. 'Well?' he asked. 'What do you think?'

'I think she is a lot brighter than I expected,' Milly said, frowning. 'And why didn't you tell me she was a friend of the Zalinsky girl?'

'I did,' Roger protested. 'I'm sure I did.'

'Well, it's too late now.' Milly stood up and carried her glass over to the window. She moved the heavy brocade curtain aside, then rubbed the glass with a finger and tried to look out. 'Do you think you can convince her to do it?'

'Oh, I think so,' Roger said confidently. 'She's bright, but she's still very vulnerable. She'll take my advice, I'm sure.'

Milly turned. 'I wish I agreed with you. I think she's going to be awkward, Roger. She seemed a little too interested in the Zalinsky girl.'

'What do you mean?' Roger was suddenly uneasy.

'Oh, I don't know.' Milly came away from the window, allowing the curtain to fall back into place. 'She kept going back to it. Asking questions. She seems very curious.'

'Well, they were friends . . .'

'Hm.' Milly refilled her glass from the brandy decanter. 'And you really think that's why she suddenly agreed to come here after all these years? Just because she and that awful girl were friends?'

'Why not?'

Milly sighed. 'You really are an innocent, Roger, where women are concerned.'

He stiffened. 'I don't know why you say that.'

'Because she's going to cause trouble and we haven't much time left for trouble. Two months, Roger, that's all we have. Two months. Unless . . .'

'Ah.' Roger smiled. 'There's always "unless".'

The fog had persisted. Low floodlights, designed to illuminate the front of the clinic, made gigantic blooms of brightness within the grey. But when Laura rounded the corner of the building and went through the gap in the hedge to the parking lot she was plunged into darkness. She took the flashlight out of her coat pocket and clicked the switch.

Nothing.

She stopped dead and tried it several more times, shook it, clicked it again. Still nothing. It had been working perfectly when she'd packed it and she'd put in fresh batteries only last week. She hesitated, then resolutely went on. No sense in giving Milly the satisfaction. Now that her eyes had adjusted to the dark it was sufficient in fits and starts to get her across the gravelled lot to the far hedge. She moved between the cars, touching them lightly to guide herself, but when she got to the outside hedge there was nothing for it but to walk straight ahead and hope for the best.

After one close encounter of the prickly kind she found the gap in the hedge she was looking for and passed through, comforting herself with the thought that she'd left the lights on in the apartment when she'd departed. And she had – but they were fuzzy and faint, and no help at all. Cautiously she began to move towards the foot of the stairs that went up the outside of the old stables, her feet crunching on the drive that led to the garages further back, the mist touching her face with chill, ghostly fingers.

What was that?

She stopped. It stopped. At least, she *thought* . . .

She started walking towards the stairway again . . . and again imagined she heard other footsteps on the gravel behind her, in the shadow of the hedge.

'Hello?' she asked idiotically. No answer. What had she expected – 'Good-evening, I am your local rapist, may I escort you to the nearest dark alley?'

Suddenly frightened, she ran towards the stairs and started up them, tripping and falling in her haste. She thought she heard a low, malevolent laugh in the darkness, then she was at the top, fumbling at the door and practically falling through it. She slammed it behind her and stared at Solomon, who stared back with wide green eyes.

Solomon's ears were pricked forward, but he didn't seem uneasy. She thought he might have been if there were really someone outside and surely he would be looking out of the window. But he was staring intently at her, apparently wondering why she was out of breath and leaning against the door. Maybe he wasn't such a coward after all. Things were not what they seemed out here.

It had been her imagination and the wine, she told herself. Not being used to the darkness and the noises of the country, she'd spooked herself. It had probably been the wind, or some branch rubbing against another, or a small animal rustling in the hedge.

There was a sudden shriek from the woods at the rear of the grounds and she nearly jumped out of her skin. After a moment there was another shriek in the distance and belatedly she recognized it as the cry of an owl. She gave a self-conscious laugh as Solomon jumped down from the window-sill and came over to butt his head against her shins.

'We city folk have to learn country ways, chum,' she told him, leaning down to lift him up and hold him close. He felt warm and solid and familiar. After a moment he became bored with this and began to struggle.

'All right, all right.' She put him down. He twitched the fur along his spine, then sat down and looked up at her questioningly.

'I have had too much to drink,' she informed him. 'I have been hearing things that aren't there. And thinking things that shouldn't be thought.'

He got up and walked towards the kitchen – uninterested in her problems and ever hopeful of a snack.

As she took off her coat she heard a car engine start in the parking lot. She went to the window, but couldn't see anything, even when she cupped her hands on either side of her face. The fog was just as thick as it had been all day, but it didn't seem to bother the person driving the car, for the headlights didn't come on until it was nearly at the foot of the drive. The faint beams looked like hazy caterpillars. Milly, presumably, going home after a last nightcap with her precious Roger. There, she thought. Maybe she *had* been wrong about the woman. Maybe she'd assumed too much.

She undressed, fed Solomon and had a quick shower. What with travelling and then having to maintain a bright and lively front during dinner, she was exhausted and the bed looked very inviting.

There was a lovely quilt on the bed, what she thought was called Double Wedding Ring in design, in white with blue and touches of bright pink, fresh and delightful. She remembered that Julie had been interested in needlework and wondered whether she had made it – it certainly looked handmade. With a sigh of pleasurable anticipation, she turned back the covers and climbed in. Lying cosily curled up with Solomon tucked behind her knees, she ran over all that she had seen, the people she had met, the facts she had learned, and realized she knew little more than she had when she'd left Omaha. No startling revelation had been made, nobody appeared to have the word 'Killer' tattooed on their foreheads and everything seemed pretty straightforward. All right, there were a few personality conflicts, but that was true in any office, hospital, school, whatever. Maybe her motives in taking Julie's place had been mixed, but the result was the same. As a friend and as a detective she was a dismal failure. In Omaha it had all seemed so obvious, so uncomplicated, so easy. But now that she was here and facing the reality of Mountview and its population she knew she was out of her depth. She could never satisfy her curiosity. She didn't even have an idea where to begin. So she would take Julie's place and do the job until they found a replacement, then she would move on. Of course she would. There, that was settled.

She snuggled down. The bed was cosy.

But sleep would not come.

# FIVE

LAURA HAD PURPOSELY ARRIVED ON a Friday so she'd have the weekend to settle in. Unfortunately, it had not taken her more than an hour on Saturday morning to distribute her few belongings – she had sold all her furniture before leaving Omaha, shedding the last remnants of her marriage like a skin, feeling her heart lift with the new freedom.

Now, after a restless night making and then unmaking up her mind, she still had questions.

Why was Nurse Shirley Hasker so unfriendly?

What was Michaels hinting at when he talked of 'enemies'?

And why did everyone except her uncle seem to dislike Milly Cunningham?

And what, if anything, did any of this have to do with Julie's death?

When she stepped out of her door, she saw that the fog had dissipated and the world was bright and light and lovely. Even the clinic looked friendlier and the trees in the woods surrounding it were rich with the colours of autumn, glowing now in the sunshine. She felt better, stronger and a little foolish for having wasted half the night in pointless conjecture.

She drove into town and parked in the centre, delighted at the ease with which she found a parking space. Not at all what she was accustomed to in the city. She took a load of clothes into the laundromat, had a quick wash and blow-dry at a surprisingly fashionable beauty salon, hoping to catch some gossip, and explored some of the more attractive stores. There was an air of old-fashioned peace about the place.

After lingering in a really lovely art gallery and being tempted by a fabulous abstract quilt that hung there, she managed to find the local newspaper office: the *Blackwater Bay Chronicle*. And, standing there, she knew that for all her resolutions in the night, she was still troubled about Julie's death.

She went in and introduced herself to the girl who sat at the desk nearest the counter, who said her name was Emily Gibbons and what could she do for her?

'Well—'

'You want to place a lonely hearts advertisement?' Emily Gibbons twinkled.

'No, of course not.'

'You have a terrific sofa you want to sell?'

'Uh – no. I—'

'You want to announce a wedding, birth, death?' She grinned, counting them off on her fingers. She was very attractive, with big dark eyes and a quirky smile, and Laura took to her immediately.

'No,' she said, still unsure about how to phrase her request.

'Do you like string?' Emily suddenly asked.

'Very much,' Laura said. 'Particularly the brown fuzzy kind you get around big packages.'

Emily laughed. 'You'll do,' she said. 'Now come on – out with it. You'll find I'm really hard to shock.'

'Oh, hell.' Laura capitulated. 'I want to look at your back issues. I'm interested in a murder.'

'Ah,' Emily said, abruptly more serious. 'Recent or ancient?'

'Recent,' Laura said. 'Julie Zalinsky. She . . . she was a friend of mine and I want to know what's been done so far to catch her killer.'

Emily tilted her head to one side, apparently not shocked at all by what to many would seem a rather morbid request. 'That's pretty succinct,' she said. She lifted a portion of the counter and beckoned Laura through. 'Come this way.'

She showed her to the computerized files and produced sheets for the microfiche. 'It's all here,' she said and, with a slightly quizzical glance, left her to it.

Laura went through the papers that covered the story. Julie had been killed in the woods between the clinic and the town. She had been bludgeoned and her throat had been cut. She had not been assaulted sexually, nor had she been robbed. Day after day, story after story, the same thing was said: 'Investigation continues' – apparently without result. She sat back and sighed. Nothing.

Emily came over and sat down beside her. 'Did you know her well?' she asked.

'Yes,' Laura admitted. 'We trained together and worked together before she came here to the clinic to work.'

'Ah, yes – The Clinic,' Emily said.

Laura looked at her curiously. 'What does that mean – that tone of voice?' she asked. 'What's wrong with the clinic?'

'Oh, nothing,' Emily said hastily. 'It's just that it's a bit exclusive, a bit beyond most people here in Blackwater. And there's some resentment that they didn't put the free clinic here but over in Hatchville.'

'My – Dr Forrester said Blackwater didn't have as many poor people as Hatchville.'

Emily sighed. 'True – but that doesn't mean we don't have *any*, does it? It's just that local people feel like there was a bit of politics involved . . . you know how people get. And there's a lot of rivalry between Blackwater and Hatchville. They should have taken that into account.'

'Who's "they"?' Laura asked.

Emily shrugged. 'The money people behind the clinic. The Town Council. People like that.'

'Oh.' Laura fiddled a little with the microfiche. Emily Gibbons seemed inclined to talk and she was happy to listen. 'What have the local police done about the murder?' she asked.

'The sheriff, you mean? Just about everything he can do,' Emily said. 'He doesn't have a big staff and there weren't many clues or anything. It rained that night, you see. But he's a good man, he'll get there in the end.'

'Doesn't he have any suspects?' Laura enquired. 'Any at all? It's been almost a month, now, since she . . . died.'

Emily shrugged again and seemed suddenly less friendly. 'He's doing his best. There are . . . problems.'

'What sort of problems?' She seemed a better source than the newspaper stories.

'Well, apparently the people up at the clinic aren't exactly co-operative,' Emily said. 'They claim it's nothing to do with them. And the town thinks it's nothing to do with *us*. Everybody wants to think it was some kind of tramp passing through or something. And maybe it was.'

'Nobody wants to get involved,' Laura said rather bitterly.

'I suppose you could say that,' Emily agreed. 'Really it's more like nobody wants to think about it. Nobody wants to believe there might be a killer in the town. I mean, we have our phantoms and our fears like anywhere, but the tramp theory seems to be the most appealing. Her death does seem so random, so pointless, and nobody knew her very well, so they don't really . . .' She noticed Laura's expression and stopped, looking embarrassed. 'I'm sorry, I forgot you said she was your friend. But shit happens, you know? Bad things happen all the time. Everywhere – even in a nice town like this one. No place is immune. Nobody is immune.'

'I guess not.' Laura stood up. 'Thanks for the chance to look through the stories.'

'Open access, that's us. Did you find anything? Do you know anything that might help Matt find her killer?' Emily asked eagerly. 'Maybe you ought to talk to him about it.'

'Oh, no,' Laura said hastily. 'He might think I was criticizing him or something. I mean . . . what do I know about investigating crime?'

Emily seemed disappointed. 'Well, you knew the victim.

Sometimes that can be helpful. It would be worth a try, wouldn't it?'

'Maybe,' Laura said. 'Maybe.' She didn't want to commit herself to anything just yet. She thanked Emily again and went out into the street, which was now quite busy compared with the way it had been the previous fogbound afternoon. People nodded and smiled, and everything seemed normal. There were already Hallowe'en displays in the windows of the shops, grotesque masks and all the ghastly paraphernalia of that bizarre ritual so loved by children.

She decided to head for the local library. It wasn't difficult to find – it was quite big and part of it appeared to be brand-new. Apparently Blackwater Bay people liked to read.

When she entered she realized it was more than just a library; it also functioned as a social centre, with chairs placed for easy conversation as well as for study. There was a section where people could rent videos or CDs, and a large area set aside for children where several were enthusiastically painting as well as playing or choosing books.

Despite all this activity, however, the place had a quiet atmosphere. The librarian behind the horseshoe desk was a big, soft man with a sleepy expression. When she handed in her completed application form, however, she felt herself being examined, evaluated and filed away in what was obviously a very well-organized brain.

'Welcome to Blackwater Bay, Ms Brandon,' he said.

'Thank you.' She noticed a small wooden sign next to the blotter: Mitchell Hasker, Chief Librarian. 'Oh – are you Nurse Hasker's husband?'

'Brother. Shirley never married,' he said with apparent satisfaction. 'She looks after me as well as any wife – but without the complications.' This was apparently meant to be amusing, for he raised his eyebrows and lowered his chin, waiting for her smile. When it came, rather uncertainly, he bestowed upon her a small one of his own design.

'I was hoping to find something here on local history,' Laura said.

He beamed approvingly. 'Very sensible when moving into a new town. I can recommend several.' He came out from behind the desk and went to a nearby shelf, his walk duck-footed and heavy. Drawing two books out, he handed them to her. 'The Beveridge is the most authoritative, but I think Rapp's has more flavour.' As she took the books he went on, 'We have quite a lurid history, in a way, especially during Prohibition, but the town goes back much much further than that. There was a settlement here even before they built the fort in what is Grantham now. People seem drawn to live by water and we had settlers here living right along with the Indians. I'm the President of the Blackwater Bay Historical Society, as a matter of fact. If you're really interested, perhaps you'd like to come along to one of our monthly meetings.'

'Perhaps – when I've settled in,' Laura said guardedly. 'I understand you've had some recent excitement too. A girl, murdered in the woods?'

'Yes.' It was his turn to look guarded. 'A great shame.'

'Did you know her?'

'She was a regular patron,' he said briefly. 'She read a lot.' He sniffed. 'Mostly romances.'

'Ah.' Laura gazed at him with what she hoped was innocent enquiry. 'I suppose the town is pretty upset about it.'

'Naturally,' he snapped. 'We like to think we are a law-abiding community. Of course, it didn't happen in the town, as such. Outside of town, it was. In the forest on the other side of the river. On the Mountview estate. Not really anything to do with Blackwater itself.' Again, Laura thought, that dismissal of Julie's death as something foreign, something to be ignored.

He went back to the desk and stamped three books for a young woman with a little boy and two for an elderly lady who stared at Laura with open curiosity.

'You're the new physiotherapist at the clinic, aren't you?' he asked suddenly. 'You ought to know all about it by now.'

'But I don't,' Laura said. 'Nobody wants to talk about it.'

'Understandable,' was his only comment. He changed the subject. 'Shirley's been looking forward to your coming.'

You could have fooled me, Laura thought, but smiled.

'It was a terrible thing that happened to your predecessor,' Hasker said, leaning forward and lowering his voice. 'I hope it hasn't put you off.'

'No, not at all.'

He nodded and began to fiddle with some file cards. 'Shirley was very upset. Well, *everyone* was, naturally. I hardly saw a soul in here for days.' His face was wistful and Laura recognized the withdrawal symptoms of a gossip addict cut off from his main source of supply. She suspected current history held as much fascination for Mitchell Hasker as that of older days.

'It seems quite busy today.'

He looked around and beamed. 'Yes, it does, doesn't it? Well, it is a kind of community centre, now, ever since we had the new extension built. I knew they wouldn't stay away for ever. I told Shirley that. "They'll be back," I said. "They'll get over it."'

'Not over it yet,' the elderly woman said from beside Laura. She'd been pretending to look over some leaflets while listening to their conversation. Her bright eyes blinked up into Laura's from beneath her rather unfortunate red hat. 'They know He's still out there, waitin' for another chance.'

'Oh, Mrs Hattie—' protested Hasker.

The old lady ignored him. 'You mark my words, young woman, He'll strike again. Doesn't like strangers, does he? Doesn't like new folks pushing in on his territory.'

Laura looked from the old woman to Mitch Hasker in puzzlement. 'Who doesn't?'

'The Shadowman, that's who,' said Mrs Hattie, her voice filled with ghoulish satisfaction. 'That's who.'

'Now, Mrs Hattie,' Hasker admonished her. 'You'll frighten Ms Brandon.'

'Who on earth is the Shadowman?' Laura asked, with only half-concealed amusement.

Mrs Hattie sniffed self-righteously and clutched her books to her scrawny bosom. 'Nobody to laugh at, that's for sure and certain. He doesn't like being laughed at.' She looked Laura up and down. 'Doesn't like snippity young girls, especially. You be careful.'

Everybody seemed intent on warning Laura about something. She turned to Mitch Hasker with a question but didn't speak. He was watching Mrs Hattie stomp off, muttering. His face wore an odd expression, knitted together with both embarrassment and satisfaction. He turned to Laura with an apologetic smile. 'You mustn't mind her. She's not – quite right.'

'You mean senile?'

'Oh, no, quite *compos mentis.* I meant she wasn't quite right about the Shadowman. She delights in old superstitions, but like many poorly educated people she gets them wrong. The Shadowman is a long-standing myth, dating back practically to colonial times. It's degenerated into the local version of the bogey-man – mostly used to scare youngsters into behaving themselves. That's part of a much older tradition, of course, dating back to the caveman, in my opinion.'

And she could see she was lucky to be getting his opinion.

'Actually,' Hasker went on, 'I'm writing a book on the entire subject of folklore and superstition in the area. Salem wasn't the only town to have witch trials and burnings, you know. We had two, right here in Blackwater Bay.' From his tone, they'd only swept up the ashes yesterday.

'Then there's no such thing as the Shadowman?'

Hasker frowned slightly, as if this were not the approved attitude. 'Not . . . as such.'

'As what, then?'

'I mean to say – not some mythical being hundreds of years old who comes out at night to murder people. That, of course, is a quite different tradition, middle-European in origin.' His distaste was obvious. My goodness, Laura thought, so there's such a thing as a tradition snob.

He was looking reflective. 'I would go so far as to say there may be *something* in the area. Something that hides behind the myth of the Shadowman. The black arts still hold their fascination today, especially in rural areas, I'm afraid.'

He didn't seem afraid, he seemed delighted. 'There have been things,' he continued portentously. 'Quite unpleasant things that have happened even in this town, over the years. I remember hearing of them as a boy. And more recently, too.'

'You mean murders?'

'Oh, no. Good heavens, no. But animals have been killed, or sickened and died, houses and barns have caught fire mysteriously – that sort of thing. Always with an element of ritual in it, always . . . a question behind it. It's fascinating how ingrown and petty these small communities can become. As I said, I'm writing a book on it.'

It was the second time he'd mentioned the book. 'I look forward to reading it,' she said dutifully.

'Ah, well – it's a lifelong project, really. I have so much research still to do and my constitution has always been delicate.' He sighed heavily. 'But the work fills the long hours. I press on.'

She caught the look of a born obsessive in his eye, and decided rather suddenly that she had to get back and feed Solomon. Why, the poor thing must be starving. It was clear that once Mitch Hasker got going on his pet subject he could continue for hours. 'Yes, well – I wish you well with it.' She started to turn away.

'You read those books I recommended and then come back to me and we'll go on from there. You rely on me – I'll see you follow the right paths.'

'I'll do that,' Laura said in a *very* cheery voice. 'Thank you.' And made her escape.

She took a deep breath of the crisp autumn air when she got outside. The sight of the blue sky and perfectly ordinary people walking up and down the street restored her sense of humour. For a minute there she'd begun thinking Blackwater Bay was a bag of mixed nuts, but it was just an ordinary small town. Kids on bicycles, dogs and cats, supermarkets and churches – all standard issue.

Nobody in their right mind could believe in witch's covens meeting behind the lace curtains of those lovely old houses she'd spotted. The sudden image of Blackwater Bay matrons dancing naked in the prim cemetery of the Methodist church she'd passed earlier nearly made her laugh aloud. The silly old fool with his Important Book and his superstitions, she thought.

As she drew near the place where she'd parked, however, her laughter subsided. A tall, rugged-looking man in uniform was standing next to her car, writing.

'Oh, dear – have I overstayed the limit?' she asked with specious innocence, coming up to him. 'I didn't see a sign anywhere.'

The uniformed figure turned and smiled. 'No limit except in high summer, ma'am. Plenty of room for everyone at the moment and we like to welcome visitors. I'm Sheriff Gabriel. I was just going to put a note under your wipers – you've got a bald tyre, left front, could go any time.'

'Oh, have I?' Laura asked, peering down as if she hadn't known that for weeks.

'If you're travelling far it's a risk I wouldn't take, myself,' he added, closing his notebook. He was a big man in his late thirties, with a relaxed air that belied the alertness and penetration of his blue eyes.

'I'm not travelling far – I live here,' she said. He glanced down at her Nebraska licence plate. 'That is to say, I've just moved here. My name is Laura Brandon, I'm working up at the Mountview Clinic.'

'Oh?' His glance was sharper still. 'Nurse?'

'No, I'm the new physiotherapist. I'm taking Julie Zalinsky's place.' She watched to see his reaction. His face tightened and the blue eyes lost their friendly warmth.

'You must be Forrester's niece, then.'

'That's right.'
'Living in town, are you?'
'No. Up there. Why?'
'I like to keep track of things, that's all. Hope you enjoy living here.' He started to move away.
'Sheriff?' He stopped and looked at her. 'Have you – are you any closer to finding out who killed Julie?'
'We're following up several leads,' he said impassively.
'Somebody said . . . something about a Shadowman.'
He looked disgusted. 'So you've already had your ear bent on that one, have you? Pay no attention, it's a lot of damn nonsense.' He glanced down and saw the library books. 'Been to the library, I see. So it must have been Mitch Hasker running off at the mouth again. You look too sensible to waste your time over that.'
'Actually, it was Mrs Hattie who said it.'
He grinned, suddenly, and it transformed his rather stern face into something very likeable. 'Mad Mattie Hattie?'
'They don't call her that, do they?'
'Kids do. Well, she was fool enough to marry Jack Hattie with a first name of Matilda, and when she started going a little strange, folks apparently couldn't resist it. Like I say, kids mostly. She doesn't like kids – otherwise she's harmless.' He nodded again and moved away. 'You get Jake Miller to change that tyre for you, Ms Brandon. It's very dangerous.'
More warnings.
Her uncle Roger had said that Sheriff Matt Gabriel was an able man. It seemed to her he was a great deal more than that. He hadn't been writing her a note about her bad tyre when she'd come up, he'd been writing down her licence number, which meant he'd noticed a new car in town within an hour or two. The warning about the tyre had been quick, easily offered and a perfect cover-up.
'If he's so smart, why hasn't he caught the killer yet?' she muttered to herself, getting into the car.
He obviously wasn't trying.

# SIX

ON MONDAY MORNING SHE ENTERED the pool area through the double doors at the end of the long corridor that bisected the annexe. The warm dampness and the smell of chlorine enveloped her, and she was momentarily blinded by the reflection of light from the surface of the water.

'Well, good-morning,' said a voice from the pool.

She blinked and saw someone gliding towards her with a lazy sidestroke. 'Good-morning,' she said, surprised.

When he pulled himself out she was confronted by Ichabod Crane – or at least, a man who could have played the part to perfection. Tall and skinny, but beautifully muscled, he had gangling long arms and dark hair that flopped limply over his bony forehead. He cleared his throat, causing his pronounced Adam's apple to bounce up and down. 'Hello,' he said, extending a large-knuckled hand. 'I'm Owen Jenks.'

'Well, hi,' Laura said, shaking his hand, which was surprisingly warm considering his build and the fact that he was soaking wet.

'I hope you don't mind,' he said, looking embarrassed as he towelled himself down. 'Julie was always saying we should take advantage of the pool and the gym whenever she wasn't using it.'

'Of course,' Laura said. 'I agree completely.'

'Good. I like a swim before I start work. Gets the blood circulating.'

'Yes. I understand you spend a lot of your time at the free clinic in Hatchville.'

'That's right.' Having been 'caught' using the facilities, he seemed anxious to please. 'We see mostly people who can't afford insurance or HMOs. Homeless, indigent, or just plain poor. It's very interesting.'

'I should think it's very depressing,' Laura said.

His eyes brightened as he picked up his glasses and put them on. They gave him an owlish, intellectual expression, quite at odds with his rather flamboyant swimming trunks. 'Oh, no – they have some fascinating diseases, you see. And you can make quite a difference.'

'I know what you mean. I used to work in that kind of environment.' She leaned against one of the ladder uprights.

'Well, then you know how good it can feel,' Owen said enthusiastically. 'Of course, Dr Forrester sees it mainly as a tax deduction, but—'

'A *tax* deduction?'

He shrugged and bent down to pick up a heavy terrycloth robe. 'Well, it is one, of course, but that doesn't mean he doesn't have good intentions. And it does wonders for our relations with the local communities.'

'That's not what I heard,' she said.

He looked surprised. 'Really?'

'Someone told me there was some resentment because it wasn't set up in Blackwater itself.'

'Oh, that. I think setting it up over in Hatchville was a condition of the change of use for Mountview. It's just a store-front operation, nothing fancy, and I can only do the most basic kind of medicine, but – it helps people. Maybe they thought it would lower the tone of the town. Blackwater is a bit . . . well, a bit . . .'

'Snooty?'

'No. They're friendly enough. But sort of self-conscious. You see, for some reason they get a lot of coverage in the city papers. There have been some unusual crimes here and the media seem to think it's kind of a crazy place. Eccentric, I guess you'd say. Whenever anything happens they run all kinds of stories and the local people resent that.'

'I suppose they would,' Laura said slowly. No wonder they didn't want to be connected with Julie's death. Especially if there was this daft story about a Shadowman lurking around. It would make them look crazier than ever.

'Anyway, as I was saying,' Owen continued. 'We see some interesting cases over in Hatchville. Stuff you'd never see up here. Butler hates it, but I love it. He says he has to shower nine times after working there for a day, but—' He frowned. 'I don't smell, do I?'

She laughed out loud at his earnest enquiry. 'No, you don't smell – except of chlorine.'

He seemed gratified. She found his whole awkward demeanour very pleasing. This was definitely not a man with airs and graces, but one who would be honest with you and who could listen to the most embarrassing details without judgement. A great asset in a physician, and one which both her ex-husband and David Butler lacked. They were social animals, glib and practised, which was fine as far as patients were concerned, but it always made her uneasy. On first impression, Owen Jenks was completely upfront, for good or ill, and very dedicated. It was probable that the pampered Mountview patients infinitely preferred David Butler's suave manner to that of the forthright Dr Jenks. And it was probably their loss, although she had yet to have an opportunity to observe the individual skills of the two young doctors. Julie had thought them both to be effective.

'Have you been shown around the place?' he asked, after a moment's silence.

'Oh, yes, Uncle Roger gave me the five-dollar tour. I met David Butler on Friday.'

'Oh.' Owen's voice was a bit flat.

'He seemed very nice,' she said neutrally.

'Oh, he is. Very nice. And a good doctor, too,' Owen acknowledged reluctantly. 'But . . . we have different points of view. We don't see much of one another, being on opposite schedules, sort of. It works out better that way.'

'Why?'

'Well, I like him. And I admire him. He's just ... different from me.' He paused. 'I'm not very good with rich people,' he finally blurted out. 'I can't do all that jolly "how did you enjoy the charity ball last week?" kind of stuff. He can. I'm more a "have the headlice cleared up?" sort of doctor.'

She laughed and after a moment he did, too.

'I know Uncle Roger thinks he's lucky to have both of you,' she said.

'Does he?' He seemed inordinately pleased to hear it. 'I worry sometimes that ... well, that I'm kind of a last one chosen for basketball kind of thing. My qualifications weren't all that good. I was lucky to get the job – and I came cheap.' He smiled to take the sting out of the comment.

'And you work hard,' she guessed.

'I try,' Owen agreed. 'You seem to have the same attitude.' He indicated the armful of files she was carrying. She'd come over the previous morning to take out the current patient files and familiarize herself with them. Between reading the files and glancing through the books of local history that Mitch Hasker had recommended, she had passed a quiet and contented Sunday afternoon by the fire, with Solomon curled up beside her on the sofa. This morning she felt fresh and full of energy. 'Oh, these. I just wanted to know what I'll be up against.'

'Good for you,' he said approvingly. 'The chronic cases have kind of got stacked up in a holding pattern over the last few weeks.'

'Most doctors find chronic cases a bore.'

He tied the belt of his robe tightly around his spare middle. 'It seems to me most doctors would benefit from being sick once or twice themselves. It would give them a whole new insight on what it's like from the patient's side.'

'Are you volunteering as a guinea pig?'

He shook his head. 'Don't have to. I had chronic bronchitis as a kid. Spent every winter hacking and wheezing, and watching other kids have fun in the snow.'

'You seem to have got over it.' She found it hard to keep her eyes off his slim but well-muscled body. It was such a pleasure to see a healthy whole male for a change.

'My family moved to Colorado when I was eleven,' he explained. 'Either the mountain air cured me or I just outgrew it. The point is, I remember only too well what it was like to lie there convinced nothing would ever change.' He glanced up at the clock on the wall. 'Well, I'd better get dressed and start morning rounds.'

'Who was on duty last night?'

'Oh, I was. David was away for some weekend conference or other – he does a lot of that. And your uncle was here, of course. Theoretically he's always on duty – it's his hospital, after all.'

'But Uncle Roger hasn't practised medicine for years,' she said in surprise.

'Oh, ye of little faith. He's kept up, all right. If anything dire had happened I was here. Roger's quite capable of prescribing a sleeping pill or oxygen – but if they start to bleed . . .' He saw she looked shocked. 'Hey, listen, this isn't a fully operational hospital, remember, despite all the equipment. Most of our patients are chronics or convalescents. If we upgrade then we'll need another resident, but for the present we make do just fine with nurses and paramedics.'

'Then you're wasted here.'

'I hope not,' he said, looking a little put out.

'I meant it as a compliment.'

'Oh.' He considered it. 'I'm not, really. Some of the cases are interesting and I've met quite a few top specialists. And then, of course, there are all the rich widows. One of them might decide to set me up in practice.' He gave her an innocent look, then grinned. 'Go on, admit it. That's what you've been thinking about David and me, isn't it?'

'Of course not.' She felt herself blush.

'Well, it's not so far from the truth,' he admitted. 'It's still hard for a poor boy to get into private practice, what with the cost of equipment and the price of malpractice insurance, especially with those student loans to pay back as well.'

'I see.' She knew only too well about student loans and how much it cost to set a doctor up in practice – it was one of the things that had destroyed her marriage. Mike had never understood why she wouldn't touch her trust fund for him.

It had been a great bone of contention between them. By ordinary standards she was the equivalent of a rich widow herself, for her father's inventions and patents had made him wealthy. They had also killed him. When her mother had died so unexpectedly, Laura had taken on the duty of making her father sleep after days spent in his workshop obsessively working on some 'revolution' or other. It was she who had carried out coffee and sandwiches at two in the morning, thrown blankets over him when she found him slumped asleep over his drawing board and helplessly watched him destroy himself. She hated the money because it symbolized all the time that had been stolen from her and from her mother and – in the end – from him.

She stubbornly refused to admit it even existed. Her uncle and a set of lawyers and accountants administered it. She was sent yearly reports that went into a drawer only half read. She'd been convinced that if she'd given it to Mike it would have taken him away from her too.

Of course, in the end, it had been a blonde who had taken him away. The money probably wouldn't have made any difference.

'So you're putting in your time and saving your money, is that it?' she asked Owen.

'That's it. You see, what I *really* want to do is go into public medicine, but there isn't much money in that. So if I can save up enough to pay off my loans and give me a nest egg, then I'll be in a better position to take whatever work interests me most.' He looked at her earnestly. 'Does that seem terribly mercenary?'

'It sounds very sensible.'

He looked relieved. 'Well,' he said, 'I'd better get dressed and over to my clinic. It was nice meeting you.'

'And you.' And it had been. The serious, rather shy Owen Jenks made a nice contrast to the super-smooth David Butler.

He went out of the double doors with a wave and she climbed up the metal staircase to her office, which overlooked the pool, trying to think about the work ahead instead of the two attractive young doctors who were to be her colleagues.

It wasn't easy.

Julie had kept meticulous records, all very correct. The agency physio who had temporarily replaced her while Laura worked out her notice had been far less correct and therefore was far more helpful to someone coming in cold.

There were some forty patients currently at Mountview, but she would have no more than a cursory contact with most of them, aside from advising on post-operative exercises now and again. There were six with whom she would be doing daily corrective or rehabilitative work.

Mr Bledsoe was a prolapsed cervical disc, according to Julie's records. The temporary physio (a Mrs Blackett) had described him as 'glum but docile'. Mr Dorrington was down as a periarticular fibrositis, or 'crabby old bastard'. Mrs McAllister was a chronic asthmatic with a weak heart recovering from a nasty pneumonia according to Julie, a 'whiner' according to Mrs Blackett. Mr Vankosic was a thrombo-phlebitis and also had 'roving hands'. Mrs Strayhorn had arthritic knees and hips and was a 'blabbermouth' too. For the record, Mr Gilliam was a sciatic axonotmesis who had arrived after Julie's death and Mrs Blackett had only one word for him: 'Impossible'.

Laura was still puzzling over this emphatic (triply underlined) assessment when there was a knock at her open door and she looked up to see a tall elderly man standing there.

'Ms Brandon? How do – I'm Martin Hambden.' He came

in, holding out his hand. She shook it, noting both his firm grip and the enlarged knuckles, and regarded him with interest. So this was one of the foremost orthopaedic surgeons in the country. She never would have guessed it – he looked more like a rawboned farmer. To start with, his suit didn't fit. It might have, once, for it was a beautifully made soft Harris tweed, but he had apparently lost weight since it had been tailored for him. Either that, or it had been made for his father who'd been a much larger man. It looked old enough.

In contrast, he wore brand-new shoes. Trainers. *Red* trainers. And a purple and white striped baseball shirt with two buttons missing. Grey hairs poked through from his chest, as if checking to see if the coast was clear.

'Roger said you were starting today, thought I'd come by and see if you had any questions about Mr Gilliam. He's my only difficult case here at the moment.'

Wordlessly, she held out the page with Mrs Blackett's comment. He read it and began to chuckle drily.

'Does she mean impossible to cure or impossible to treat?' Laura wanted to know.

'The latter.' He waggled his quirky grey eyebrows and sat down in the chair beside her desk. 'Haven't you met him?'

'I tried to introduce myself yesterday, but he was asleep. I was just on my way up to talk to all the patients about their treatments.'

'I'd either leave him till last, so you can run away, or take him first, when you've got plenty of energy. He's a son-of-a-bitch and enjoys it. Thing is, the boy doesn't want to get better. Doesn't give a damn.'

'According to this record, the "boy" is thirty-two years old,' she said drily.

'Yes – but he's acting like about fourteen at the moment.' He took a long thin cigar from his jacket pocket, looked at it wistfully for a second, sighed and put it away. 'Look again under "occupation",' he suggested, stretching out his long legs and tapping his toes together.

'Good heavens – he was a police officer,' she gasped. 'I thought he was one of *the* Gilliams.'

'Is. Didn't always like to be, though. Bit of a maverick, youngest son and all that. Always a handful at school, liked speed. Cars, motorcycles, so on. Classic rebel, but bright. Took a law degree, sailed through his bar exams without even breathing hard. They expected him to join the firm, same as the other brothers. Didn't. Became a cop, instead. They like to spit vinegar they were so disgusted with him. I'm told he was a good cop, by the way. Until this.' He tapped the folder. 'Good cop.'

'How do you know that?'

'Went to see his precinct captain.'

'My goodness, do you take that trouble over all your patients?'

'No.' He seemed disinclined to elaborate on this.

'The file says impact injury. What happened?'

'Fell from a height during a chase, broke his pelvis and both legs. Crush injury to the sciatic nerve, but fortunately the sheath was intact. Fractures have healed just fine, and the nerve is coming along slow and steady as you'd expect. But he refuses to make an effort. Seems to be planning on spending the rest of his life in a wheelchair and if he doesn't start working he'll have a self-fulfilling prophecy all right. His muscles are wasting badly.'

'We'll see about that,' she said resolutely.

He grinned at her. 'He has a mean mouth.'

'So have I,' she told him. It wasn't really true, but she wanted to impress him with her determination. 'And I have no time for slackers.'

'Well, you might get him moving at that,' Hambden said approvingly. 'You—'

'Ms Brandon?'

Laura looked up. A tall, slim nominee for Miss Universe stood in the doorway, wearing a nurse's uniform. 'Yes?'

'Miss Hasker sent me down with these.' She came into the office and handed over a pale-green envelope of X-rays. 'Somebody left them behind.'

'That was probably me,' Dr Hambden said, in such an odd voice that Laura turned to look at him. 'Sorry to give you extra steps, Nurse Janacek.'

The full force of the girl's smile was turned on him and it was almost indecent to watch his dissolution. 'Why that's all right, Dr Hambden. No trouble, really.' She turned back to Laura and the wattage of her smile diminished measurably. 'Miss Hasker says if you want to do your rounds, would you please make it some time between ten and eleven, as that's when most of the patients will be free.'

'I'll try.' Laura glanced at her watch and saw it was already past ten.

'Nurse Hasker runs a tight ship,' Hambden said in an idiotic voice that matched his idiotic expression. Really, it was getting embarrassing the way he was staring at the girl.

'Very commendable,' Laura said crisply. 'I'll try not to start a mutiny on my first day.'

Nurse Janacek stared at her for a moment, as if thinking of something else, then nodded and went out.

Hambden cleared his throat and spoke in a husky voice. 'Hard to believe she's a good nurse, isn't it?'

'A little,' Laura admitted. 'I thought perhaps the interior decorator had supplied her along with the Chippendale chairs and silk wallpaper.'

'Clarissa is *very* popular with the patients,' Hambden said with some pride, as if she were a pet. 'And very efficient.'

Well, bully for her, Laura thought to herself, but murmured a few sounds of being impressed, to please him.

He was regaining his composure and seemed to realize, suddenly, that he'd been rather obvious. 'Anything else I can help you with?' he asked, after they'd discussed Gilliam's treatment and the rest of his patients.

'You could tell me what you thought of Julie Zalinsky,' Laura said.

'There's not much to tell.' Hambden looked puzzled. 'She was a nice girl, good at her job. I was very pleased with what she did.'

'Did everyone like her?'

'Why, yes, I think so. Why do you ask?'

'Well, she was murdered,' Laura said flatly. '*Somebody* didn't like her.'

He looked surprised. 'You mean you think someone who knew her killed her?'

'Don't you?'

'Why, no. I assumed – I think everyone here assumes – that she was killed by some psychopath or something. She was kind of neutral, you see.'

'Neutral?' That wasn't how Laura remembered Julie at all, but then, she had been her friend. You don't always see your friends the way others see them.

'Yes. By that I mean she didn't have a strong enough personality to be loved or hated. She was liked, of course, but that was about the extent of it. She was just unlucky – someone in the wrong time and place. You think otherwise?'

Laura shrugged. 'I don't know what to think.'

'What's your interest?' he asked.

'Just morbid curiosity, I suppose,' she answered carefully. 'It is kind of a dramatic thing, someone being murdered. You can't help but wonder.'

'I don't wonder,' he said. 'I don't think of it as anything more than one of the terrible things that happen at random in life – and it just happened to happen near here. I certainly don't think anyone I know killed her. I don't *want* to think that. I suggest you forget it, Ms Brandon, and get on with the work at hand.' He stood up abruptly. 'Well, I think that's all I can tell you about Gilliam and the other patients of mine you'll be treating. There'll be another disc prolapse coming in next week, but it's perfectly straightforward. Use your judgement – you seem to have a fair measure of it.'

'I haven't maimed anyone yet,' she said lightly.

'I wish I could say the same.' He spoke with regret. 'I really do.' And with that he went out, only remembering to call a perfunctory goodbye when he was half-way down the hall. It echoed thinly over the squeak of his trainers on the tiled floor.

Was Hambden's attitude one that reflected that of other people at the clinic? She had noticed that the one thing they didn't refer to without being asked was Julie and her death. Maybe they didn't want to frighten her. Maybe they were ashamed of it. Or maybe they were hiding something.

It was very odd.

Taking Martin Hambden's advice, she saved Gilliam for last because she wanted to see how much time the other patients were going to require in the course of each day. When she knocked lightly and went in, she found his blinds were still drawn. He was lying there, a shadowy figure, eyes closed, hands unmoving on the coverlet, for all the world like a corpse. She could tell by his breathing, however, that he wasn't asleep. She crossed the room and put up the shade. Through the window she could see the steps going up to her own flat and Solomon, in the window, watching something down below.

'I don't want it up,' came a growl from the bed.

'Tough,' she said, turning round. 'I do. Maybe you can see in the dark, but I can't.' Now that the room was light she saw that it had a feature she hadn't noticed in the other rooms she'd visited. A bookcase – not large, but overflowing with both hardcover and paperback volumes. She noted also a book and a pair of glasses on the bed beside Gilliam's hand. Apparently he had been reading earlier. It looked like he did a lot of reading.

His eyes opened and he turned his head on the pillow, squinting at her against the light. 'Who the hell are you?' he demanded.

'I, the hell, am in charge of window shades around here. I like them up. I like patients up, too. How about it?' Laura moved to the foot of the bed and leaned her crossed arms on the metal railing. They eyed one another, she with curiosity, he with resentment.

She decided he would have had a nice face if it weren't so deeply lined and so marked. There was a small jagged scar that ran through his left eyebrow, giving him a look of permanent scepticism, and another across the bridge of his nose – but it was no more than a line. His hair was too long, he hadn't shaved for several days and his eyes were a cool, unfriendly green. What had probably once been a fairly athletic body had been softened by his months of immobility and the incipient beard could not disguise an equally incipient double chin. His hands were battered and marked with scars from all those motorcycle crashes Hambden had told her about. He might have been a beautiful baby, but he wasn't beautiful now.

'You're new,' he said.

'That's right.'

'You're not a nurse, you're not wearing a cap like the others.'

'My, my, aren't you the observant one, Lieutenant Gilliam. They teach you that in detective school?'

His eyes went from her capless head to her physiotherapist's badge. He grunted, closed his eyes and dismissed her. 'I'm too tired for games today.'

'So am I,' she said firmly. 'Didn't Dr Hambden tell you what your treatment was going to be?'

'He said his piece, then I said mine,' he informed her, his eyes still closed.

'Gee, I bet he was impressed.'

'Not really. Neither was I. It was just the same old things in the same old way – but louder.'

'And you said all the same old things, too – only more pathetically.'

His eyes opened at that and he struggled up on to his elbows to glare at her down the length of the bed. 'Look, lady. I'm a cripple,' he announced. 'I've had a dozen doctors playing jigsaws with me for nearly a year. They loved it. Put in a pin here, a bolt there, they said okay, Mr Gilliam, you're a man again, get up and walk. But I couldn't. I can't. And I never will. *I've* accepted that, so why the hell can't everyone else? You want to do your little healing thing, fine, but go and do it somewhere else.'

She glared back. 'Well, they say a patient becomes his disease, but it was never so obvious to me before. You've become your disease all right, Mr Gilliam – one big pain in the ass.'

He blinked.

'You've had your say, now I'll have mine,' she went on.

'Not interested.' He lay down and closed his eyes again.

'Well, then, all you have to do is get up and walk out on me, isn't it?' she said pointedly. His mouth tightened, but he was silent. 'I've worked with a lot of men like you, Mr Gilliam. Vietnam veterans, some of them, but plenty of civilian casualties too and most of them a lot worse off than you. Legs blown off, spines crushed, all kinds of things. The ones who tried hard always improved, but the ones who lay back and felt sorry for themselves always got worse because they *wanted* to get worse. They wanted to pay back the world for putting them where they were, they wanted the world to wait on them, apologize to them, feel sorry for them. It was the price they put on themselves and it was pretty cheap, if you ask me. No doubt life was always easy for you – what a smile didn't get you, money would. But you can't buy back the ability to walk and you can't dream it back either. You have to *work*, Mr Gilliam. You have to work your fat little ass off. All that's wrong with you now is a slowly healing sciatic nerve plus muscle wastage, which you've brought on yourself, and that wasn't very clever, was it? I hear your lunch coming now, so I'll leave you to enjoy it. Unless, of course, you want me to cut it up and chew it for you. I have other patients who are willing to work. If you're man enough to match them, fine. If not, you can lie there and cultivate your bedsores. Frankly, my dear, I don't give a damn.'

She went to the door, shaking, then turned. 'What made you become a cop, anyway? Was it just for the shiny buttons and the badge?'

'No,' he said in an even voice, his eyes still closed. 'It gave me the right to shoot people legally. I wish I still had it. What made you become a physiotherapist?'

'I like beating up defenceless old ladies,' she told him. 'And children, like you.' Before he could answer she was out of the door.

Tom Gilliam opened his eyes and stared up at the ceiling, cursing quietly and steadily to himself. Well, he'd done it again, still batting zero as Patient of the Year.

Of course, it was that girl's own fault, she'd come in there with a chip on her shoulder and caught him on the raw. He'd got so used to the cooing of sympathetic doves in white uniforms. He knew, in a corner of his mind, that the little physio had been right. And shrewd. To come on like that probably wasn't natural to her – it cried out 'premeditation'. No doubt in collusion with that flinty old bastard Hambden.

Restlessly he shifted in the bed and winced as a shaft of pain momentarily impaled him. After a few seconds he breathed again and it began to fade.

The things she'd said were true, but it didn't make them any easier to bear. What was the point of trying? He'd made his gesture, tried to contribute to society and all that crap. And what had it got him?

This.

Oh, he'd intended to make a fight of it in the beginning. But then he woke up one morning and found that circle of family faces around his bed and he'd turned sour. It wasn't the pity in their eyes – not that there was much of that. It was the smugness. See? those eyes said. This is what you get for going off on your own, for not joining the family firm, for being so rebellious and independent. We Told You So.

God, he hated them with their pompous assumption of superiority and virtue. He'd met people on the street worth fifty of either of his brothers or their wives. If he'd done what they expected of him, become an executive with the company or even joined some fuddy-duddy law firm, he might have turned out just like them. He hoped not. But on the other hand, if he'd done the expected thing he'd at least be on his feet now – instead of lying here like a damn parcel.

Oh, the place was lush enough, every possible comfort provided, but it was still a chintz-lined coffin. He was dead, he just hadn't stopped breathing yet. The only advantage of being at Mountview was that it put him out of Their reach. Unless they decided to drive up from Grantham – and he knew they wouldn't. Out of sight meant out of mind and cheap at half the price. God knew there was enough money in the Gilliam coffers to keep a cripple in comfort for ever. He'd rest up here and when he got tired of it he'd move into a decent apartment and hire a male nurse to look after him. He'd find something to fill the empty hours – maybe he could take up knitting helmet covers for the motorcycle division.

It was about all he was good for.

The sunlight was in his eyes, making them water. Damn that officious little physio, hadn't he made it clear he wanted the window shade *down*? Was everyone in this place totally incompetent?

He reached over his head for the call button and pressed it, relishing the noise of the buzzer outside – but it cut out after a few seconds, leaving only a light burning to show the nurse which room required attention.

Well, where were they?

Damnit, he wanted someone to yell at right *now*!

# SEVEN

LAURA NEARLY COLLIDED WITH HARLAN Weaver as she marched down the hall, head lowered and fists clenched. He was the consulting psychiatrist to the clinic, a nice, comfortable man with a sweet disposition and a penchant for plaid shirts and tweed jackets.

'Whoa, there,' he said. 'You look ready to murder someone.' He took hold of her arm and steadied her. 'What's wrong?'

'Gilliam,' she managed to get out through clenched teeth.

He chuckled. 'Never mind. Even Nurse Hasker has trouble with him.'

Laura sniffed and looked up. 'She does?'

'Yup. And as for me, he calls me Dr Freud and makes rude suggestions about my pipe. He says I have a secret desire to be a locomotive, puffing away.'

She started to smile. 'Oh, that's ridiculous.'

'Of course it is. And so is letting yourself get upset by Tom Gilliam. I've been trying to motivate him. The professional side of me says this is a frightened man, but he makes it tough to maintain your objectivity. His attacks are only self-defence, but—'

'I attacked him first,' Laura admitted.

'Did it work?'

'Not that I noticed.'

'Didn't work for me either.' He put an arm around her shoulders and squeezed them comfortingly. 'Forget it, get some lunch, think about all the other nice people there are in the world.'

'Like you?' She smiled. He was very reassuring and calming. She guessed he was pretty good at what he did – it was certainly working for her.

'Especially like me.' He grinned down at her, then went back into his office.

David came up as Weaver closed his door. 'Look out, Laura,' he said teasingly. 'He's sneaky. He'll charm your guard down and then pounce on your neuroses.'

'You should talk,' she retorted. 'I like him.'

'Of course you do. It's his business to be likeable. But you can't deal with nutcases all your life and come out unscathed. There are hidden depths to Dr Weaver, you mark my words.'

'Rubbish,' she chided him. 'You're just jealous.'

David raised an eyebrow. 'Then why did his wife commit suicide?'

'She did? How awful for him.' Laura was shocked, both by the fact and by his casual way of mentioning it. Handsome he might be, but obviously not above a little malicious gossip.

'Not very nice for her, either,' David said conversationally. 'I'm not saying it was his fault, just pointing out that people aren't always what they seem. I, for example, look quite sane, but in fact I am a starving man, ready to eat the nearest horse. Is that normal?'

'No, but there is a cure.'

'Exactly. Lunch, applied internally. This way for instant relief.' She laughed and followed him towards the stairs. As they went down the hall, she noticed Sheriff Gabriel coming out of the nursing office. He glanced at her as they passed by, but gave no sign of recognition.

'Is he still investigating Julie's murder?' she asked David.

'I suppose so,' he answered, opening the door to the staff cafeteria for her. 'He hasn't been around for a while, but I heard he was back questioning people.'

'Has he talked to you?'

'Not today. I suppose my turn will come.' He seemed completely unbothered by the prospect.

They collected their food and sat down at a table near the windows that looked out over the front lawns. There were quite a few nurses eating quick lunches, some orderlies and – over in a corner well away from everyone else – the handyman Michaels glowered around ferally as he consumed his food. His gaze momentarily met Laura's and she shivered. The man was not nice, not nice at all.

She gazed across the table and wondered again about David Butler. It wasn't his fault he was physically attractive. Simple genetics, that's all. She should be prepared to overlook it as a drawback. But something in her rebelled, even as she granted his charm.

'It seemed like such a good approach when I discussed it with Dr Hambden.'

'What did?' David was attacking his salad with all the surgical finesse of an orang-utan.

'Being aggressive with Mr Gilliam. According to Dr Hambden everybody in his family fluttered around him, catering to his least whim and all the rest of it. If I were a man who'd become a cop, I guess I'd have found that infuriating after a while.'

'That's fair enough as far as it goes. But from conversations I've had with him, his family only pretended to be concerned. He thought they were almost glad he'd been hurt – as if it proved they had been right all along about him going into the family business instead of something as outrageous as law enforcement. There's a lot of family tension there. A lot of resentment. Also, you've got to remember that in these cases a lot of patients equate loss of mobility with a loss of masculinity. According to Weaver, he feels as if he's been castrated. You must have seen it before.'

She glanced up as Clarissa Janacek went by with a tray, followed by a small, dark nurse who seemed more of a shadow than a second person. Janice Goodfellow, that was it. Laura remembered meeting her when she was touring the clinic on Friday: a soft-voiced, sly girl. She hadn't taken to her much.

'With nurses around like Miss Janacek, I'd have thought he'd soon get over *that* misconception,' Laura said.

David glanced over at the two girls, blonde and dark heads bent together conspiratorially, sending occasional glances their way. 'I think she'd like to help him to do just that, but from what I've seen, Gilliam isn't buying,' he said. 'She is a great flirt, but I don't know if she's anything more than that. People talk, but I think it's mostly jealousy.'

'Maybe she's not his type.' Laura caught his wry look. 'All right – she's any man's type. I always used to resent women like that, until I realized it was rather like resenting the Grand Canyon or Niagara Falls. They're a natural phenomenon.'

He chuckled. 'Maybe. I dated her for a while when I first came here.'

'Oh?' She felt a sudden cramp in her stomach and started eating.

'Mm. But I wasn't exactly what she has in mind for herself. Poor boys don't interest her, except as momentary distractions, of course.'

'Do I detect a trace of bitterness?' Laura asked lightly.

'Hell, no. She wasn't what I had in mind for myself, either. Wait until you get a flash of her real personality, the one that lurks under that flawless exterior.'

'How do you mean?'

'I'll leave you to discover that for yourself. I wouldn't dream of spoiling the fun,' David teased. 'Aside from Mr Gilliam, what do you think of your patients?'

With a final glance at Clarissa and Janice, who were still staring at her with cold eyes, Laura began to discuss her cases with David. It seemed a good time for a general consult, for he had been treating most of these people for some time, and knew their personalities and their conditions better than she could glean from Julie's notes. Her uncle Roger had encouraged her to talk to Owen and David about the patients – 'let them bring you up to speed,' he had said. David had several helpful suggestions to make and she found herself relaxing at last. She toyed with her dessert spoon. 'Did you know Julie Zalinsky very well?'

He put down his coffee cup. 'Yes, pretty well. Why?'

'Do you have any theories about who killed her?'

He looked at her oddly. 'Why should that interest you?'

'Oh – I knew Julie,' she replied. 'We trained together and we were working together in Omaha. I recommended her for this job.'

'Oh, I'm sorry. I didn't realize you were close friends,' David said, looking surprised.

'Not close, exactly. But friends.'

'So is that why you came here to take her place? Because you were friends?'

'Sort of. I feel kind of . . . responsible. If I hadn't recommended her she would be alive now.'

He reached over and touched the back of her hand. She could feel the electricity of him even though the touch was light. Damn him. Really, one shouldn't be so susceptible, she told herself. Just because he's attractive doesn't mean you have to fall for him. It's not an automatic requirement, even though *he* might think so. She moved her hand away. He gazed into her eyes, which was almost worse. He had the eyes of an earnest boy, dark-brown and gentle. 'Look, Julie's murder was just one of those things. One of those terrible things that happen these days. She was unlucky, she was in the wrong place at the wrong time.'

'That's what people keep saying.'

'Well, it's true.'

'I wonder,' Laura said slowly. 'I mean . . . she wasn't happy here. She wrote me that she thought something was wrong—'

'She wrote to you?' He seemed oddly taken aback.

'Oh, sure – we kept in touch.'

'What did she say was wrong?' he asked, frowning.

'That's just the trouble – she *didn't* say. It was all kind of vague – and she was prone to dramatize things.'

'Oh, yes – that she was.' David nodded. 'It was kind of appealing, if you like childishness. Personally, I don't.'

'Didn't you like her?'

'Oh, I liked her all right. But after a while I learned never to believe half the things she said. She was fine with the patients, but when you got to talk to her outside work, well—'

'I know, I know.' Laura smiled. 'At least if you called her on it she'd have the grace to laugh. It was an old habit she'd pretty much grown out of, exaggerating things. So I probably am just being silly, but—'

'But what?'

'Well, what if there *is* something wrong here?'

'Like what?'

'I don't have the least idea,' she admitted sheepishly.

'What does your uncle say?'

'Oh, I haven't said anything to *him*.' She suddenly realized she'd probably said too much to David already. 'I mean, he's so proud of Mountview and everything—'

'He has a right to be,' David said.

'I know, I know.' Now she felt embarrassed. 'Forget I spoke. You're right, I'm just being morbid, looking for things that aren't there.'

'In which case there's nothing to worry about, is there?' He grinned at her.

She smiled. 'I guess not. I just feel bad about Julie.'

'Tell you what. If you get to the end of the week without murdering one of your patients or anyone on the staff, I'll take you out for a lobster dinner. What do you say?'

'I hope I survive. I love lobster.'

She was discovering that adjusting to the patients wasn't nearly as difficult as adjusting to the staff. The salaries paid at Mountview were among the highest in the area and the working conditions were excellent. As a result, Roger Forrester could pick and choose, and many travelled a fair distance each day for the privilege of working there. Shirley Hasker, of course, who ran the nursing staff with a firm hand and little humour, lived in Blackwater. But if she took a motherly interest in her nurses, as her brother and

Uncle Roger had indicated, Laura saw little sign of it. She was humourless and bossy, and saw no one's point of view but her own.

However, Laura soon found favourites among the nurses. There were 'the Bobbsey twins', Merry and Cherry Bartlett. They were not, in fact, twins – just sisters. But they both had short blonde Dutch-boy bobs, round china-blue eyes, and an intense way of taking and carrying out instructions. In contrast, Marilyn McNeilage was red-haired, plump and bouncy, while her friend Kay Pink was tall, angular, wryly funny and extremely efficient. Janice Goodfellow was dark and quiet, and shared a house in town with Clarissa Janacek, whom she patently adored.

In this she was alone.

Why Clarissa had gone into nursing was beyond Laura. She was efficient enough, and most of the patients thought she was wonderful because they were too ill and self-absorbed to see beyond her exceptional beauty to the ego within. Now that David had mentioned her underlying personality, Laura was more wary of the girl.

In contrast, Terry Soames was a jolly, hearty occupational therapist who came in three times a week and harassed the patients good-humouredly into producing bad paintings, uneven tapestries and lopsided ashtrays. They liked one another immediately and were soon talking like old friends. Laura chanced to mention Clarissa.

Terry was pounding clay in preparation for the day's activities and her strong, capable hands dug into the sticky grey stuff with a little extra force as she spoke. 'She's out for a rich, weak husband, that's all. What better place to find one than here? Either it will be some divorced or widowed millionaire down with haemorrhoids, or the husband of some patient who conveniently dies and who will be very open to consolation.'

Laura was startled – was this what Julie's letters had been referring to? 'What do you mean, "conveniently" dies?' she asked cautiously. 'Are you saying she'd actually—'

'Oh, no.' Terry slammed the clay down on the marble

slab to remove the air bubbles. 'At least, I don't *think* so. I just meant that if ever a woman snuffs it here whose husband is at all a reasonable catch, there you will find Clarissa offering consolation. Although she did make a play for David Butler.'

'He doesn't seem to think so much of her.'

'No. It's Owen who has the crush now. Poor sap. She hardly gives him the time of day because she knows he'll never be a rich doctor, whatever happens. Owen will always be the guy in the free clinic somewhere.'

'That's not a bad thing.'

'I didn't say it was. I think he's great, although he does have his moods, too. I saw him put his fist right through a window once.'

'Good heavens.'

'Yes, well . . . it was because of someone's stupidity – more frustration than rage,' Terry continued. 'The thing about Mountview – or any small hospital – is that everything gets blown out of proportion because everyone sees the world as existing only in here. It doesn't, believe me. You want to be careful about that, Laura. Living up here and everything – be sure you get out every once in a while. Don't let people like Clarissa or Shirley or Milly Cunningham make you think they're important. They're not.'

'I know. My uncle said that Julie's murder has made the staff edgy,' she ventured tentatively, thinking of how she'd seen the sheriff talking to one of the nurses earlier. Terry snorted.

'For about a week, maybe. Any difficulties you meet now were here *before* Julie was killed. Milly was always a pain in the neck, Clarissa was always a bitch and—' She paused. 'No, I take that back. Shirley Hasker *has* changed. I used to like Shirley, but I must admit she's making it kind of hard at the moment.' She went back to cutting and pounding the clay. 'Maybe she'll settle down soon. She used to be a lot of fun.'

'Oh, really?'

Something of Laura's dislike of the chief nurse must

have come through, for Terry glanced at her with wry amusement. 'Yes, really. She's got a right to be sour on life, you know, but she never used to show it.' Thud, thud went the clay. 'That brother of hers – he made sure she never married so he'd have her there to wait on him for the rest of his useless life, the old fraud.'

'Fraud?'

Terry wiped a sleeve across her face, leaving a smear of grey clay under one eye, obscuring some of her freckles. 'Sure. You met him, didn't you say?'

'Yes.'

'How many times did he mention his damn book?'

Laura laughed. 'Only once or twice.'

'You got off easy. He's been living off that book ever since he had to leave college because of his "delicate health" – a cover-up for flunk, if you ask me. Or worse. Rumour has it they threw him out because he drank too much one night and got into some kind of trouble, if you can believe it of the prissy old poop. Anyway, here he's been ever since, making life hell first for his parents, who died of exhaustion no doubt, and now Shirley.'

'You're a mine of information,' Laura said with a grin. 'How much should I believe?'

Terry giggled and scratched her nose, leaving yet more clay on her face. She looked about ten years old. 'Oh, I could tell you a tale or two about this town all right. What do you want to know?'

'Tell me about the Shadowman,' Laura suggested impulsively.

Terry's face paled, making the freckles and the smears of clay stand out in strong relief. 'Oh, that,' she mumbled and turned back to her work.

'I'm sorry – I didn't mean to upset you,' Laura said, startled at this reaction. Everyone else she'd mentioned it to had either laughed or told her to pay no attention. The more they did that, the more curious she had become.

Terry sighed. 'Some things really get you when you're a kid. I had a dog, not much more than a puppy he was – I'd got him for my birthday at the beginning of the summer and I'd played with him all day, every day – it was a real relationship, you know? My parents were having some trouble with the store – they ran a hardware store then – and I didn't have any brothers or sisters, just Smokey, my dog. And then one night he disappeared out of the backyard. There was a big storm, and I was afraid he'd get cold and wet and sick.' Abruptly her shoulders hunched, and her fingers dug deeply and savagely into the clay mound on the slab. 'Jeez, you'd have thought I was over it by now, wouldn't you?'

'I'm sorry,' Laura said, upset by the distress Terry was obviously feeling. 'Don't—'

'Oh, it's all right.' Terry sniffed and resumed her work on the clay. 'The next morning we found him strung up on a tree branch. His throat was cut and his lovely tail was gone.'

'Oh, my God, how awful.'

'My mother screamed and said it was the Shadowman, and my dad told her to shut her mouth and made her take me inside. He cut Smokey down and buried him quick, so I wouldn't remember. But I did. They bought me another dog right away, and it was a really nice dog and I got to love him, but he wasn't Smokey. He was just a dog, that's all.'

'And that's what he does, this Shadowman? Kills children's pets?'

'Or sets fires or turns livestock loose – whatever will hurt the people most. Been going on for years. Some will tell you it's been happening for centuries. I don't believe that, though.'

'But it was always property, or animals, never people.'

'That's right.'

'Until Julie.'

Terry shrugged. She cut the worked clay into four sections and placed two of them on waiting potter's wheels, wrapping the balance in damp cloths. 'I don't really think there's any connection and I'm sure the sheriff doesn't either.'

'But he – oh, damn, I've got to go. Maybe we can talk more later.' Laura had her own ogres to face and she could hear them approaching. She left the Occupational Therapy room and went into the hall.

They were arriving in convoy, Mrs Strayhorn's loud, penetrating voice as good as a fanfare of trumpets, Mrs McAllister's whine an obbligato beneath it.

They had become great friends and insisted on doing everything 'together', including their physiotherapy sessions. Laura took a deep breath and received them with a smile. She almost meant it.

Mrs McAllister was a small woman in her forties with a hairstyle reminiscent of Claudette Colbert and a pinched little face made over-bright with inexpertly applied make-up. Mrs Strayhorn was a big-boned woman with a bird's nest of grey corkscrew hair and large protuberant eyes that darted about taking in every detail.

'Now – who wants to go first?' Laura asked brightly.

'Oh, dear,' Mrs McAllister whimpered, shrinking down into her cashmere shawls. 'Not me.'

'We'll be back in an hour,' Clarissa said from the door.

'Better make it an hour and a half,' Laura said with a grunt. Mrs Strayhorn was no sylph.

'Can't be all that difficult,' Clarissa drawled. 'Just two of them, after all.'

'How true,' Laura said tightly. 'Maybe I should take in laundry part-time, to fill the empty hours.'

'I didn't say that,' Clarissa murmured. 'I'm sure your *uncle* wouldn't want you to overdo things.'

'Now, look—' Laura began, straightening up, but the doorway was empty. Their voices floated back down the hall, like malicious sparrows, laughing.

Mrs Strayhorn raised an eyebrow. 'My, my – she doesn't like you very much, does she?'

'Probably because I don't like her very much,' Laura said.

'Nothing to do with it.' Mrs Strayhorn spoke firmly. 'She just doesn't like the way Dr Butler has been paying you attention. She likes all the men to look at *her*.'

'She's so pretty, I don't see how they could help it,' Mrs McAllister commented, taking out an inhaler from beneath her shawls. 'Quite the prettiest girl I've ever seen.' Psst, went the inhaler. She used it so often it had become a kind of punctuation for her.

'Now Mrs McAllister, you must stop using that. You're far too dependent on it. If you'd practise your exercises you could easily do without it.' Laura wheeled out the heat lamp and positioned it over the treatment table and Mrs Strayhorn's knees.

'Oh, I don't think so,' Mrs McAllister said dubiously. 'I had an attack only last night, you know. A bad one.'

'The exercises might have prevented it.' Laura's voice was brisk. She'd heard all about the attack from Kay Pink. Mrs McAllister was a true asthmatic, but she compounded her condition with the conviction that she was 'high-strung' and sensitive. And so she was – when it suited her. Last night's attack had been typical of the self-induced variety, coming on when she'd learned that Dr Butler had changed her sleeping pills. Dr Jenks had tried to calm her down and convince her the new pills were preferable, but feeling that she had been dismissed too lightly by one of the Bartlett girls, she'd worked herself into a full-blown anxiety attack and they'd eventually had to put her on a nebulizer.

'Oh, I *do* try to do them,' Mrs McAllister whined. 'I do. Everyone thinks I don't, but I do. I want to get better, but I get so tired and I need to sleep—'

'You have to give the exercises time, you must make them second nature,' Laura insisted. 'It's all a matter of control and relaxation.'

'Oh, yes,' came the terribly weary reply. 'That's what Dr Butler says, too. I think he was just a teensy-weensy bit cross with me this morning.'

'I am very, *very* cross with you,' came David's voice from the door, but he was smiling at her as he spoke. Mrs McAllister shot him a startled look, then dissolved into a flurry of blushes and dimples as she drew her shawls into a more becoming halo around her shoulders.

'That's right, bully her, it's the only way,' came Mrs Strayhorn's commendation from the treatment table.

'I have no intention of bullying her,' David said, laying a hand on Mrs McAllister's shoulder. 'But I do want her to help me make her better rather than fight me and Dr Jenks.'

'I do *try*,' murmured Mrs McAllister, ignoring the derisive snort from her friend. 'I do *want* to help.'

'I know you do,' David said, giving her shoulder a gentle encouraging squeeze. 'But you must go on trying, mustn't you?'

'Why, yes – I . . .' she fluttered vaguely.

'Laura, have you any free time this afternoon?' David asked, giving Mrs McAllister a final gentle pat on the shoulder. 'I've been in to see Gilliam and I think you should pay him another visit. He might be more receptive now.'

'What did you do to him?'

'I carried on where you left off,' David said. 'And I think your uncle had another word with him, too.'

'Well, if you think it's worthwhile.' Laura sounded doubtful.

'A moustache,' said Mrs McAllister suddenly.

'What?' David asked, momentarily disconcerted. Even Mrs Strayhorn turned her head on the pillow to stare at her friend.

Mrs McAllister blushed but held her ground as she gazed up adoringly at David. 'I think you'd look very good in a moustache,' she said with a terrible flirtatiousness. 'I don't know why, but I can just see you in a moustache. Isn't that odd?'

Laura looked at him with her head on one side. 'You know, she's right. It would suit you.'

'Nonsense,' said David, embarrassed.

'Ever kissed a man with a moustache, Myra?' Mrs Strayhorn queried in clarion tones from the treatment table. 'Might do you a power of good. Always did me. Mr Strayhorn had a splendid moustache,' she confided to Laura, turning her head back. 'Lovely and curly it was.'

David was recovering himself. 'You mean I should deprive the world of this face by covering it up?' He struck a pose. 'Never! Never say I!'

'Oh, shut up.' Laura laughed.

'You grow a moustache and then give Myra a kiss,' directed Mrs Strayhorn. 'Probably cure her asthma instantly.'

'Oh, Nellie!' wheezed Mrs McAllister, her chest apparently seizing up at the very thought.

The silly old fish has a crush on him, Laura thought. They probably all have, come to think of it.

'Well, I promise if I ever grow a moustache you'll be the first girl I kiss, Mrs McAllister,' David promised lightly. Laura could see that although he was going along with the joke, he found the conversation unsettling. He glanced over Mrs McAllister's head at her. 'Are we still on for tonight?'

'Yes – I'm looking forward to it.'

'Good. I'll clear it with Roger, then. Owen has gone into Grantham about some damn thing or other. He's always hiving off when he could be most useful. Claims to be doing some kind of research on "community medicine".'

'Well, maybe he is,' Laura said. Owen Jenks had impressed her with his intense devotion to his work. He seemed like a little boy obsessed with railway trains or butterflies or stamps – but he was a good doctor with a heavy dedication driving him on. Sometimes he was a little distant with the patients at Mountview, which they resented. She had come to realize it was just because he was thinking about some poor soul at the free clinic.

'I suppose he wants to publish,' David conceded. 'But I don't know what he expects to get out of it.'

'Does he have to be getting something out of it?' Laura asked.

'Certainly. Why else spend time on it? It's not as if we have all that much time to spare around here,' David said impatiently. 'And he'll never *get* published – he hasn't got the communication skills.'

'Perhaps he just wants the knowledge,' Laura suggested, feeling oddly defensive on Owen's behalf.

'And I want high-button shoes,' David said. 'Equally useless.'

'Well, I think it's admirable,' Laura said firmly.

He looked at her suspiciously. 'You do?'

'Yes.'

'Oh.' He seemed nonplussed. 'Well, it may be admirable, but it's not very convenient. Not tonight, anyway.'

When he'd gone, Mrs McAllister turned in her wheelchair to look up at her. 'Are you going out with him?' she asked.

'As a matter of fact, I am,' Laura admitted.

'Watch out, you'll make Myra jealous,' Mrs Strayhorn warned.

'Oh, Nellie, don't be silly,' Mrs McAllister protested.

'Probably come after you with a shotgun,' Mrs Strayhorn continued, unabashed. 'Dr Butler is Myra's own private preserve, you know. She didn't like it when that little Zalinsky girl took a shine to him and look what happened to *her*!'

There was a moment of silence.

'Oh, Nellie,' said Mrs McAllister in a horrified whisper.

'Well—' Mrs Strayhorn spoke defensively, realizing she'd gone too far. 'I was only teasing.'

'You mean Dr Butler and Miss Zalinsky were friends?' Laura asked slowly. 'Close friends?'

Mrs Strayhorn looked uncomfortable. 'I know Miss Zalinsky thought they were. I'm not sure what *he* thought. But she took an interest, that's for sure and certain. Always asking about him, talking about him. Like she thought he was some kind of movie star or something.'

'You shouldn't joke about things like that,' Mrs McAllister said, her breath beginning to catch in her throat. Out came the inhaler again. Psst-psst. 'That poor girl, murdered like that all alone—'

'Take it easy, Mrs McAllister.' Laura left Mrs Strayhorn

to come over to the outraged little figure in the wheelchair. 'Remember the exercises . . . breathe from the diaphragm—'

'She . . . you shouldn't have said that, Nellie,' Mrs McAllister said, when she could breathe again. 'I can't help it if I think Dr Butler is a fine young doctor. He reminds me of some other doctors I knew.'

'God knows you've known enough of them,' Mrs Strayhorn commented. 'Professionally, that is.' She cackled suddenly. 'Fell in love with every damn one of them, too, I'll bet.'

'Didn't.'

'Did. Bet you did.'

'Didn't.'

'Now, ladies—' Laura said in a soothing voice, feeling like a playground monitor.

'Well, I can't help it if the doctors are interested in my case. I'm unusual, you see.' Mrs McAllister smiled to herself at the thought.

'You mean you're rich,' Mrs Strayhorn snorted. 'And you're so dumb you believe everything they tell you, trying this new treatment and that new treatment—'

'I'm allergic to antibiotics and all kinds of things that cure most people, so treating my symptoms is *very* complicated, very difficult,' Mrs McAllister said in a small, hurt voice. 'They do their best. They've always done their best.' She sighed heavily, in a reverie of physicians past and present who had bent over her, solicitous and sympathetic to her every need. 'Oh.' She blinked and reached for the inhaler to ease a sudden shortness in her chest.

'She'll never learn,' Mrs Strayhorn said in a dramatic whisper over the psst-psst. Raising her voice, she added with salacious glee – 'They're all alike, these sex-starved women. Always falling in love with their doctors.'

Mrs McAllister looked at her reproachfully. 'Oh, *Nellie*!'

# EIGHT

LAURA BRACED HERSELF AND ENTERED Tom Gilliam's room. She was surprised to see that someone had cut his hair. Although it was far from being neat, it was a reasonable length. He seemed more vulnerable for having been shorn. He was wearing his glasses and his finger was holding a place in a thick book that lay on the bed.

'Hello.'

He'd been gazing out of the window and turned his head to regard her warily. 'Your fan club has been giving me a hard time.'

She came across to the bed. 'My what?'

'First the boy wonder, Butler, tells me I should co-operate with you because you are such a nice girl. Jenks then gangles along in the middle of the damn night and says more or less the same thing. Then that shrink Weaver drops in to see whether I'd like to talk about my aggression, then your uncle comes along and says if I'm going to be paying for it I might as well take advantage of your expertise. That was his word, not mine.'

'I can see it wouldn't be one of yours,' Laura said drily. 'Nobody's an expert on Tom Gilliam but Tom Gilliam, right?'

'Right. Of the various approaches I think I favour your uncle's. Value for money. It's something the Gilliams have always esteemed.' His tone was ironic.

'Then you've decided to co-operate?'

'I've decided to *think* about co-operating.'

She couldn't help smiling. 'Where's the fun in instant capitulation, is that it?'

'Right.'

'I've discussed your case with Dr Hambden—'

'I'm not a "case", I'm me.'

'Obviously. But you're not the only man – or woman – who's ever sustained this sort of injury. I've worked on similar problems.'

'Did you make them walk again?'

She met the green eyes square-on. 'Yes.'

'All of them?'

She had to be honest. 'No.'

'Can you make me walk again?'

'Only you can make you walk again. It takes hard work—'

'I knew there was a catch.'

The sarcastic tone was back in his voice and it had her on edge immediately. That's all it takes, she thought, just that razor in his voice and she was on the defensive. Is it a cop's trick? Was she supposed to be confessing to something? 'I need to examine you to assess your range of movement,' she said and proceeded to do so. She knew by the changes in his breathing that she was hurting him, but he said nothing. 'You're allowed to utter an occasional "ouch",' she told him. 'It might help.'

He was pale as he glanced back at her. 'How about snivelling, whimpering and sobbing?' he gasped.

'In moderation only.' She helped him to turn back over. 'Your pain is worse, isn't it?'

'Must have been the trip in the ambulance.'

'Nothing to do with it.' She glared at him. 'Don't you know that your pain means the nerve is alive? If you didn't have any pain you wouldn't have any hope. That nerve came within millimetres of being severed, but it wasn't. If it had been you would be quite free of pain – you wouldn't have any sensation or control, either. Do you understand?'

'Hooray for pain?' He didn't believe a word of it.

'Temporarily, yes.'

He gazed up at the ceiling. 'Son-of-a-bitch.'

'I know that hurt you. I'll see if you've been written up for pain-killers.'

'I don't want anything.'

She put her hands on her hips. 'I don't give a damn whether you want it or not, Mighty Mouse. If you keep pulling that stiff upper lip routine we won't get anywhere. Fighting pain can only increase it, wear you out and make you feel lousy. Hasn't anyone ever told you that?'

'Nope.'

But she knew they had, must have done, dozens of times. He just hadn't listened, that was all. 'Well, if you insist on playing hero we can forget the whole thing. It's going to be hard enough as it is, seeing the state you've got yourself into. Either you do what I say or forget it.'

'I thought this was supposed to be a rest home.'

'If you'd planned a life of martyrdom, wheelchairs and self-pity, you've come to the wrong place. This is a clinic. If you're prepared to give up the sad-boy routine we might just get your act together.'

'I didn't "come" to Mountview, I was *put* here by my loving family.'

'Oh, yes?' she asked brightly. 'Drugged you, sewed your lips together and everything, did they? Crap, Mr Gilliam. You came here to get away from them, and you know it.'

He regarded her in some surprise. 'Now that's interesting. How did *you* know it?'

She turned at the door. 'You talk in your sleep.' She went out, then stuck her head back in. 'Shame about Rosebud, wasn't it?'

She was relieved to see Kay Pink behind the desk at the nursing station. It would have been too much to face Shirley Hasker in her weakened state. She flopped into a chair. 'Whew.'

Kay grinned. 'What's the matter? You look like you've gone three rounds with Mike Tyson.'

'With Gilliam.'

Kay shrugged. 'Same difference.'

Laura laughed. Kay's wry the-hell-with-it attitude was a tonic not only to her but for all the patients as well. Like her uncle, Laura recognized gold when she saw it. 'I must say, Mountview isn't what I expected,' she confessed. 'I thought all the patients would be sitting around on satin cushions demanding caviare and pedicures.'

'It's as good a hide-out as any.'

'Hide-out?'

'Sure. Take Mrs Williamson, the gall bladder in sixteen. I'm not saying her gall bladder didn't need taking out, it did, but it wasn't urgent. Dr Stammell took it out because what Mrs Williamson really needed was a legitimate excuse to collapse. Her damn round of parties, club meetings, tennis lessons, French lessons, charity dos and lovers was driving her into the ground. Also, while she's in here, she won't be sniffing coke up that elegant nose of hers. She knows it's a bad habit, but so is being in fashion. Her operation will give her an excuse not to compete for at least a year, if she wants it.'

'I see.'

'Mr Tucker is hiding from his ex-wives and Mrs Panotis from her present husband, who's one of those hairy-chested types who can't understand why she won't worship him the way he worships himself. Mrs Strayhorn can either stay here and gossip with her buddy Mrs McAllister, or go home to an empty house and a string of paid companions who're about as much fun as a stuffed frog.'

'Are you saying none of them is really ill?'

'Nope. They all have legitimate complaints and they need medical care – that's the *real* price they pay for coming here.'

'You sound as if you feel sorry for them.'

'I do. Don't you?'

'Let's hear it for the ailing rich?'

'Right. But not too much.' Kay grinned. 'I got troubles too, but I couldn't afford this place.'

'Did you know Julie Zalinsky very well?' Laura asked casually.

'No more than anyone else,' Kay said. The abrupt change of subject didn't seem to bother her. 'When she first came she was very chatty – we got on just fine.' Kay smiled, then the smile faded. 'But in the last few weeks before she died she changed, you know. It was odd. She didn't stop being friendly, but she kept herself to herself a lot more. And I used to find her in the oddest places, late at night or early in the morning, as if . . .'

There was a step behind them and Clarissa came in. She went over to the mirror and, after a minute inspection of herself, tucked in a wisp of pale-blonde hair. 'By the way, I gave the last of the Xanax to Mrs Jackson – you'd better get some more up.'

'There's another bottle on the lower shelf,' Kay said.

But Clarissa shook her head. 'No, there isn't. I looked. This *was* the second bottle.'

Laura glanced at Kay and saw she was frowning. 'That's funny, I'm sure I—'

Cherry Bartlett stuck her head round the edge of the nursing office door. 'Can you give us a hand with Mrs Armstrong, Kay? She's running a fever and I think she's delirious. She keeps moaning about her husband building her a hospital of her very own.'

'Oh, no. I thought she looked paler this morning – she said she had a sore throat. But she's always got some complaint. Damn, I should have listened.' Kay hurried out.

After a minute Clarissa turned from the mirror and looked at Laura as if she were a case of something virulent. 'I hear you're going out tonight with David Butler.'

'I didn't realize it had hit the papers,' Laura murmured.

'Well, don't get your hopes up,' Clarissa advised. 'He'll give you a rush, then drop you flat like he did all the rest.'

'Oh? You too?'

Clarissa smiled a very small smile. 'I didn't give him the chance. I dropped him. But if I decide I want him back he'll come back. I just thought I'd save you being disappointed, that's all. You look like the kind of girl who would get hurt by that sort of thing.'

'Thank you very much,' Laura said icily.

'I suppose you think I'm conceited,' Clarissa continued.

'It *was* one of the words I had in mind,' Laura admitted.

'I'm just realistic. I get what I want because I make people want to give it to me. Everybody's out for what they can get, they just won't admit it to themselves or anyone else. *I* admit it.'

'To everyone?'

Clarissa's expression became derisory. It did nothing at all for her looks. 'No, of course not to everyone. But I don't think I'll be wanting anything from you, so it doesn't matter.'

Laura stared at her. Presumably Clarissa had a brain, for she was a registered nurse and that meant passing exams. Presumably she did her job well, or Uncle Roger would have fired her long ago. So how could she stand there and talk like that?

Kay came back in and sat down with a sigh. 'Clarissa, I want to set up barrier nursing for Mrs Armstrong. David thinks it might be a staph infection.'

'Oh, great,' Clarissa said. 'Nothing like closing the barn door, is there?' she tossed over her shoulder.

Kay glared after her, then glanced at Laura and grimaced as she fished a fresh cigarette from the pack on the desk and lit it. 'Which Clarissa is she today?' she asked as she shook out the match.

'I beg your pardon?'

Kay chuckled again. 'Dr Weaver once said that Clarissa was the first example he'd ever come across of someone who'd actually made schizophrenia work. According to him, Hollywood's loss is our questionable gain. She has at *least* two personalities and what's more, she knows she has them and uses them. She uses them very well.'

'That's a little frightening,' Laura said.

'Not really. She'll get her come-uppance one of these days.'

The end of the week had arrived and as Laura hadn't murdered any patients – it had been a close-run thing in Mr Gilliam's case – she was going out to dinner with David Butler. When she was ready he hadn't appeared, so she went over to the patients' lounge. She was still feeling compelled to work her way through the minefield of opinions and information about Julie and her time at the clinic, and had quickly learned who her most likely sources would be and where to find them.

Needless to say, the current joint rulers of the roost were Mrs Strayhorn and Mrs McAllister. By unspoken command the space directly in front of the television set was kept clear for their wheelchairs and other patients arranged themselves as best they could. Neither Mrs Strayhorn nor Mrs McAllister could be rated as medical miracles, for theirs were chronic illnesses, but in sheer staying power and decibel level Mrs Strayhorn overcame all aspirants to her place at the top. As her shadow, Mrs McAllister was tolerated. It was Mrs Strayhorn who chose what was to be watched.

They were both in place well ahead of time tonight, for the designated programme was a thinly fictionalized account of a scandal that had taken place in a hospital that Mrs McAllister had actually been *in*, although – to her eternal regret – not at the relevant time. She was, nevertheless, looking forward to giving her opinion on the authenticity of the piece. 'I'm sure they'll get it all wrong,' she said happily, looking forward to several hours of tsk-tsking, oh-dearing and generally criticizing with 'authority' all that Hollywood had done. After all, she *knew*.

'Now, I intend to enjoy this, Myra,' Mrs Strayhorn said in a warning voice. 'I don't want to hear a running commentary on every little damn thing in it, is that clear?'

Mrs McAllister was slightly hurt at this pre-judgement. 'That's not fair, Nellie,' she said in her thin, reproachful voice and psst-psst went her trusty inhaler. 'After all, I *was* there.'

'And don't we know it?' Mrs Strayhorn said indulgently.

Mrs McAllister took this in good part, although she

wouldn't have done from anyone else. 'Oh, Nellie, you make it sound like my illness was a career or something.'

'Do I?' Mrs Strayhorn's eyes twinkled. 'Well, what do you know about that?'

Mrs McAllister sniffed and was about to allow herself to be deeply hurt by this evidence of mistrust on the part of her friend, when she saw Owen Jenks appear in the hall outside the door. She waved, then frowned as she watched Clarissa Janacek come up to him and put her hand on his arm, while speaking in low tones. 'Little hussy,' hissed Mrs McAllister.

'Who?' Mrs Strayhorn craned her neck with difficulty. 'Oh – her. She certainly enjoys making him suffer, the poor sap. Worships her like some goddess or something.' The two in the hall were joined by a third and Mrs Strayhorn grinned as Clarissa turned her attention to the new arrival, leaving Owen Jenks standing there with his mouth open. 'Dr Butler, now – he's different. She can't make much headway with *him*. He's got his eye on Ms Brandon, here. Miss Gorgeous had her chance and muffed it, if you ask me.'

'Really?' Mrs McAllister was instantly intrigued.

'Oh, of course, you weren't here then, were you?' Mrs Strayhorn gloated. She rarely let her friend forget that she was the 'senior' patient at Mountview by more than three weeks. 'Oh, yes – she had her chance at him just before Miss Zalinsky came along.'

'Was he dating Miss Zalinsky?' Laura asked, surprised. Julie definitely hadn't mentioned anything like that in her letters.

'I think they were *friends*,' Mrs Strayhorn said slowly. 'But he plays it very cool, that one.'

'What do you mean?' Mrs McAllister instantly suspected implied criticism of her precious Dr Butler and would have none of it. 'He's marvellous.'

'Exactly. So he isn't going to settle for any Jane, Zsa-Zsa or Harriet, is he?' Mrs Strayhorn said. Noting her friend's rapt expression, she went on reprovingly, 'And it won't be *you*, either.'

'Well, I never thought it would be!' Mrs McAllister registered outrage, but not very convincingly.

'Hah! Don't kid me! I've seen your beady little brain weighing up the possibility of setting Dr Butler up in practice instead of endowing this place like you said. Go on, admit it, you'd love to be his "interested patron".'

Mrs McAllister drew herself up. 'Well, so what if I would? It would be a good investment. I happen to believe Dr Butler is an excellent physician. But as it happens there are other reasons why I might just do it, so there.'

'Such as?'

'Never you mind. Maybe you'll find out, maybe you won't.'

'Good Lord, you don't mean you're finally thinking of divorcing that no-good gigolo you married and chasing after the beautiful young doctor?' Mrs Strayhorn seemed only half surprised. Laura took another look at Myra McAllister. She was quite a bit younger than she appeared and a couple of million dollars in the bank could make some men overlook a lot of things, although Laura seriously doubted David could manage it in Mrs McAllister's case.

'I never said that.' Mrs McAllister's hands went to her hair, as the two doctors entered the lounge.

'Good-evening, ladies,' David said, coming across with a smile. 'Just thought we'd look in before I went off duty and Dr Jenks took over for the night. Everything all right?'

'Everything's just nifty,' said Mrs Strayhorn wryly. 'We're considering rolling back the rug and having a jitterbug contest as soon as you're out of sight.'

'She's only kidding.' This from Mrs McAllister.

'He knows that, Myra,' Mrs Strayhorn said acidly.

'We're going to watch a movie about the scandal at the St Charles Hospital.' Mrs McAllister leaned forward. 'You remember—'

'I don't believe I do,' David said, frowning.

Mrs McAllister looked surprised. 'But you must. Surely—'

'Myra forgets not even doctors know as much about hospitals as she does,' Mrs Strayhorn observed. 'She's the only woman in the US who has an intern in every port and a resident in every capital.'

'It's the one where that doctor was stealing drugs and selling them to pay a blackmailer,' Mrs McAllister told Dr Butler eagerly. '*You* know. And somebody else got the blame?'

'Sounds dreadful,' David said with mock disapproval. 'I don't know if I should permit you to watch such shocking stuff. Might give you the wrong idea about the medical profession.'

'I doubt it.' Mrs Strayhorn's voice was dry.

'I think I remember something about it,' Owen said, as Clarissa came up with a tray of coffee. 'Didn't he get away with it in the end – or am I thinking about somewhere else?'

'Get away with what?' Clarissa asked, putting down coffee for the two ladies.

'Stealing drugs and selling them,' Laura said. She remembered the case all right and it had been an ugly one.

Clarissa's hand jerked and she spilled some of the coffee on to the table. 'Damn,' she muttered.

'Personally, I think it was all a frame-up, myself,' Mrs McAllister went on, watching Clarissa mopping up the mess. 'You see, I *know* the doctors involved. They talked to me. Told me things. There was someone *else* behind it all, someone they never caught. Probably not a doctor at all.'

'You're too innocent, my dear,' Clarissa said. 'Believe me, if you knew some of the things that doctors get up to your hair would stand on end. They're not saints.' She looked up at David and winked. He didn't wink back, contenting himself with a raise of the eyebrows.

'Don't call me "dear".' Mrs McAllister sounded petulant.

'Most doctors are decent,' David said mildly. 'It seems to me evil is in the eye of the beholder, in your case.'

'And I've beheld quite a lot.' Clarissa gave a harsh laugh. 'Believe me, a *lot*.'

'Well, I don't believe you,' snapped Mrs McAllister. 'I think you have a nasty mind.'

'Oh – you've cut me to the quick.' Clarissa twisted her body provocatively, pretending to look at her back for an invisible knife. 'Am I bleeding, Dr Butler?'

'Not much,' David said dismissively, with a smile at Mrs McAllister. He nodded towards the television screen. 'I think your programme's starting.'

'You watch it, you'll see. It was somebody else all along.' Two bright spots of red rose on Mrs McAllister's cheeks and her breathing was quick and wheezy. 'I *know*.'

'Don't get so het up, Myra.' Mrs Strayhorn was a little worried by her friend's over-reaction to Clarissa's teasing. 'She didn't mean anything.'

'Didn't I?' enquired Clarissa of no one in particular.

'Are you sure you wouldn't be better off watching this in bed?' David asked Mrs McAllister. 'You've been up most of the day, you know. We don't want you having another attack.'

'I'm fine,' Mrs McAllister wheezed, with a poisonous glance at Clarissa's shapely back as the pretty nurse joined Dr Jenks and bent solicitously over Mr Cobbold. 'Or I would be, if some people would mind their own business.'

'Well, I admit to being guilty ... of keeping a lady waiting.' David gave Mrs McAllister's shoulder a last pat. 'Are you ready, Laura? Have a good evening, all,' he said to the room in general.

'You, too, doctor,' came the dutiful chorus, but all eyes were now on the television screen, where the drama was unfolding before them, other people's problems and other people's fears, beguiling distractions in Technicolor.

They'd had enough of reality, thank you.

* * *

It was a pleasant dinner. Laura learned a lot about David and his hopes and dreams. What she didn't learn was much about Julie. David admitted he'd taken her out 'a few times', but said it was more pity than attraction. He seemed disinclined to say more and, rather than harp on a subject that seemed to worry him, she left it alone. But his resistance intrigued her.

They got home late and had to stifle their giggles in the parking lot. It wouldn't do for the patients to think they'd been having a good time – after all, the medical profession is supposed to be above such frivolities. One less drink and they'd have been quite calm, one more and they'd have been edging into inebriation. As it was, they giggled. Or rather, Laura did. David contented himself with a choked chuckle that struck her as even funnier than her own.

'Watch out, the Shadowman might getcha!' David's voice was sepulchral, close to her ear as they passed through the hedge into the deeper darkness beyond.

'Idiot,' she said indulgently, starting up the stairs to her apartment. Suddenly she lost her balance and clutched at the handrail, pressing on it more heavily than usual – and found herself without support. With a faint crack the rail began to give way. As she lurched after it, David's arm came around her, pulling her back against him. Her thin, startled shriek was cut off almost before it started, although her heart continued to pound.

'I believe you need some coffee,' David said into her ear.

'The rail,' she managed to say.

'What about it?'

'It's loose – didn't you hear it crack?'

'No.' Still holding her gently with one arm, he reached out and touched it. As he pushed against it there was another, louder crack, followed by a crunching sound as the rail fell away completely and landed on the gravel below. 'Good God!' he gasped. 'I thought you'd just missed a step in the dark. You could have broken your neck!'

They edged their way up to the door. David made her stand on the last but one step as he tested the platform outside, then took her key and unlocked the door. Once inside, they stared at one another, surprised into sobriety. 'Are you okay?' David asked.

'Yes, I'm fine, really.' She was a little shaken, but no more.

He looked angry. 'Have you got a flashlight? I'd like to look at that rail.' He took the light and went outside. Laura heard him crunching around on the gravel below as she put the coffee-maker on and got out mugs. He was gone some time – the coffee was ready when he came back in, looking even angrier.

'I was trying to find something to fix it temporarily, but Michaels has put a lock on his precious shed. The wood on the support rails was rotten. When the middle two went, the rest broke under the strain. It's stupid – Michaels should have noticed that when he was painting them last month. I'd give him hell about it in the morning if I were you. Or I'll do it myself, if you'd rather.'

'No.' She smiled at him, amused by his protective anger on her behalf. 'I can give people hell when I have to – just ask my ex-husband. The Forrester temper is legendary, when roused.'

He smiled back, eventually. 'Why do I get the impression it's difficult to rouse?'

'Because we're all such lovely people,' she said. The effect of the wine hadn't *quite* worn off and he did look sweet, all angry on her behalf. 'Haven't you noticed how trusting and innocent we are?'

His smile became wry. 'You, maybe. Not Roger.'

'Well, it's me you're with at the moment. Why not take off your coat and have some coffee?'

He did.

# NINE

THE NEXT MORNING LAURA HURRIED across the parking lot and had to skirt an ambulance that was backed up to the side entrance of the annexe, its rear doors standing open. She glanced inside, but saw no one. Michaels was standing inside the entrance, looking sour as usual.

'New patient?' she asked.

He grinned maliciously. 'Nope. Garbage collection.'

He rocked back and forth with his hands in his pockets, enjoying his little joke. She opened her mouth to tell him about the rotten railing that had failed the previous night, when the service elevator doors opened and her uncle Roger stepped out, followed by a man wearing dark clothes and a sombre expression.

'You can go up now, Michaels,' Forrester said. 'Use the special trolley, move quickly, bring it down in the service elevator – you know the routine.'

'Yes, Dr Forrester.' Michaels was all duty and attention now, every trace of unpleasantness hidden under an obsequious demeanour. He scuttled into the service elevator and stabbed a bony forefinger at the controls. Just as the doors closed he sketched a broad wink at her and drew his fingers across his throat, which fortunately her uncle didn't see. He was talking in a low voice to the dark-suited man.

'Very unfortunate,' Uncle Roger said, half to himself, as the other man waited by the ambulance for his passenger.

'Mr Cobbold? Mrs Armstrong?' Laura asked sympathetically.

'No. Mrs McAllister. She passed away last night.'

She stared at him. 'You're joking.'

'I'd hardly joke about a thing like this,' Roger snapped. 'Be sensible, Laura.'

'But . . . she was perfectly fine yesterday.'

'She had a weak heart.' He turned away abruptly. 'Continuous asthma attacks, emotional outbursts, a history of congenital illness . . . we knew it was on the cards. But Butler thought he was making real headway with this new drug regime of his.'

'I know – he was so pleased. I can't believe it.'

'It's not a matter of belief, but of fact. We have to accept it and move on.' He spoke brusquely and she realized he was more upset by the loss of Mrs McAllister than he was prepared to admit. Although he had long been out of regular practice, he still retained the physician's hatred of death, as a soldier hates an enemy, named or unnamed, who snipes at him out of the darkness. Darkness confers such an unfair advantage.

Laura watched him stride into the building, then turned and slowly climbed the service stairs to the upper floor. Mrs McAllister was to have been her first patient this morning. Mrs McAllister *and* Mrs Strayhorn, of course. 'Oh, Lord,' she murmured to herself and turned, going down the hall and round to the nursing office.

When she got there she was startled to see Shirley Hasker still behind the desk. By rights she should have gone off duty at eight. She sat slumped in her chair, dark circles under her eyes, staring dully at the patient file on the blotter.

'Are you all right, Miss Hasker?' Laura asked, concerned by the older woman's appearance.

Shirley looked up. 'Why shouldn't I be?' she asked in a flat voice.

'Well, you've been up all night, and what with Mrs McAllister and all—' Laura turned at a footstep behind her.

Kay Pink came in. 'Time you went, Shirl,' she said briskly.

'Go on, off you go. Your brother's downstairs in the car, waiting.'

'He'll have to go on waiting, then,' Shirley said. 'Dr Forrester told me to stay here until he came back.' The board beside the desk buzzed briefly and her eyes went to it. With a sigh she heaved herself out of the chair and smoothed down her uniform. 'There he is.' She went out, walking heavily, and they stood in silence, listening to her slow progress down the hall.

Kay glanced at Laura and raised an eyebrow. 'And what can I do for *you*?' she asked.

'Nothing for the moment,' Laura said with a forced smile and went out. She walked after Shirley and was about to go into Mr Gilliam's room, which was opposite the late Mrs McAllister's, but some devil made her hesitate. She unashamedly eavesdropped on the conversation in the late Mrs McAllister's room.

Roger Forrester asked, 'Did it buzz?'

'Yes,' Shirley answered.

'So there's nothing wrong with the system, is there?' he said pointedly.

'I'm sorry, Dr Forrester. I know we were busy last night, what with Mr Cobbold vomiting and Mrs Panotis having more nightmares, and Mrs Armstrong's delirium, but we would certainly have responded if Mrs McAllister had called for help.' Shirley's voice was dull as she made her explanation. She sounded as though she were on automatic pilot.

'She must have called for help, Shirley. Didn't Nurse Janacek say the bedclothes were in a tangle when she found her?'

'Yes, but—'

'Then the attack must have lasted several minutes, anyway, before her heart went.'

'She didn't ring,' Shirley insisted in that dull voice.

'I see.' Uncle Roger sighed in exasperation. 'All right, then. Did she eat a normal dinner?'

'Yes. Although she did rush it a bit – there was something

on television she wanted to see – but it was all according to her diet sheet.'

'She had her sleeping pill as usual?'

'After the usual argument, yes.'

'Argument?'

Laura heard Owen Jenks's voice, then. Farther away, but in the room. 'David has been trying to wean her off barbiturates. She didn't need anything as strong as the stuff she'd been getting, but she insisted that the new pills weren't helping her to sleep properly. They were, but she refused to admit it.'

'Were there any contra-indications with the new drug?'

'None whatsoever.'

'And she took it, in the end?'

'Oh, yes, she took it,' Shirley said. 'I stood over her until she did.'

'And when did you make your last round?'

'I checked her at midnight,' Shirley answered. 'She was asleep and breathing normally at that time.'

'You're sure?'

'I'm *absolutely* sure. That was why I wasn't too worried about missing my two o'clock check because of Mr Cobbold. I should have sent one of the other nurses, of course – I realize that now. But at the time—'

'You're certain the call was within her reach when you came in?' Uncle Roger asked.

'Yes, I told you,' Owen said. 'Nurse Janacek called me and I came over at once. This was about four or just after. Mrs McAllister was lying on the bed and the bell-call was hanging quite near her. I used it myself to summon Nurse Hasker when I'd made my examination.'

'I see. And aside from making your examination and attempting resuscitation you touched nothing else until I came up?'

'Why should I?' Owen asked irritably. 'I was more concerned with my patient than with your damned electronics.'

Uncle Roger sighed. 'Well, the physical signs are clear.

An acute asthmatic attack leading to heart failure. Her heart simply couldn't take it. I'm not sure we could have done anything for her even if we *had* heard a call.'

'She didn't call,' Shirley said stubbornly.

'Yes, yes, all right, Shirley.' Uncle Roger sounded impatient. 'Owen, you'll have to sign the death certificate.'

'But—?'

'You were the physician on call at the time,' Uncle Roger pointed out.

'I'd like a post-mortem, first,' Owen said.

'But *why*?'

'Exactly – *why*?' Owen's voice was perplexed. 'I'd like to know why it happened. There was no reason for her to have an attack of such severity – she was actually *improving*.'

David Butler suddenly spoke. Laura hadn't realized he, too, was in the room and she jumped at the sound of his voice, which was very near the door. 'I agree with Owen.' His voice was firm.

'I'm afraid I can't allow that,' Roger Forrester said.

'Why not?' David asked. Laura was wondering the same thing.

'I think you know why not. For the same reason I want to be sure everyone did all they could to prevent this. We can't *afford* it. You know what that woman's estranged husband is like, David. He was in the other week, oozing around her, demanding money. She was very upset and one of the orderlies had to make him leave. He's the type who would just love to have a case for negligence to slap on us. And you certainly don't expect me to bring the coroner in on this? It would be asking for trouble.'

'Even so . . .' Owen said reluctantly.

'No, I'm sorry.' Forrester spoke flatly. 'If you won't sign the death certificate, then of course I will.'

'We were *not* negligent,' Shirley Hasker said emphatically, her voice sharper and more defensive. 'We had no reason to suspect Mrs McAllister would have any difficulty of any kind last night. When she was watching that thriller on TV with Mrs Strayhorn and the others she was in fine spirits. You saw that yourself, Dr Forrester.'

'Yes – she was in good shape when I looked in on them around nine-thirty,' he conceded.

'Exactly,' Shirley said. 'She could hardly bear it when the commercials came on, she was enjoying it so much. One of those special crime reconstruction things. She said it was almost like it had happened to her, didn't she, because it was so real and she had been in that particular hospital. In fact, they were all lapping it up.'

'So they were,' Roger said absently.

'Is there anything else, Dr Forrester?' Shirley asked. 'My brother is waiting—'

'Oh, I'm sorry, Shirley. No, that's all.' Roger cleared his throat. 'You look all in. It must have been rough last night. How *is* Cobbold?'

'Sleeping like a god-damned baby,' David growled.

Owen spoke. 'You should have called me sooner, Shirley – there was no need for you to put up with all his nonsense.'

'Well, we kept thinking each time was the last and that he'd settle down,' Shirley said. 'I knew it wasn't blood, no matter what he said. It was chocolate-covered cherries – he'd got somebody to sneak them in for him. I didn't want to call you out just because he'd eaten too much again.'

'It's what I'm here for,' Owen said, not unkindly.

'That's what we're both here for,' David added.

'It's all right, Shirley.' Roger's voice was gentle. 'Go on home and get some sleep. We can't do without you and you know it, but if you'd like me to get someone else in tonight—'

'No, no – I'll be in,' Shirley said. 'I'll be fine.'

She came out and gave Laura a vague, distracted glance. Laura had opened the door to Mr Gilliam's room, but still stood there obviously listening. When Shirley didn't make any comment, but just went down the hall, she stayed on, still listening.

After a minute, her uncle spoke. 'We can't take the risk.'

Somebody sighed – she couldn't tell if it was Owen or David. 'We realize your position, Roger. All the same—' It was David's voice.

'You don't like compromising your ideals.'

'I don't know whether I'd put it as high as all that. But as none of us was actually in the room when she died . . .' Owen began.

'Perhaps not, but you were here soon after. The fact remains that medicine is not an exact and infallible science. Win some, lose some. I know it sounds hard, but dead is dead. The signs were unmistakable – heart failure following acute asthmatic distress, pure and simple.'

'I know. Our concern is with the living. Maybe you're right.' Owen didn't sound convinced.

'It's not a matter of being right, it is simply more efficient. I'm aware of how callous that sounds. I'll get Kay to clear out Mrs McAllister's things and I'll take care of the death certificate and contacting that husband of hers. You'd better get on with your rounds, David, the patients will have long since finished breakfast. And Owen – aren't you due at the clinic this morning?'

'Not until this afternoon,' Owen said. 'I already called in and told them I had to get some sleep.'

'Are you sure you're all right?' Roger asked.

Owen sighed again. 'Sure. It's just that once they *did* call me . . .'

'There was nothing you could do,' David said.

'Yeah. I tried, but – she just didn't respond.'

'Fair enough. You did all you could.'

'It's never enough, though, is it? We haven't lost many patients here . . . I've sort of got over the habit of closing it out. And she was a nice old girl. A bit silly and so on, but she was okay.'

'Yes, she was,' David agreed. 'And not as old as she looked, either. Which makes it even more odd . . .'

'A post-mortem would explain it,' Owen said. 'I really think we should . . .' And all of a sudden the three of them came out of the room..

Laura was shocked by her first sight of Owen Jenks. Yesterday he'd looked full of life and bright-eyed. Now his face was drawn and his eyes looked dead. 'Owen—' She reached out and touched him as he went past. He stopped and stared at her as if he'd never seen her before. Nobody seemed to question the fact that she was standing there in the hall. David and Uncle Roger went on, leaving Owen with her. 'I'm sorry – about Mrs McAllister,' she stammered.

His eyes focused, finally, and he managed a slight smile. 'Thanks. I just feel so damned . . . useless.'

'I know,' she said softly. 'Truly, I know how you feel.'

He stared at her. 'Do you? Then I feel sorry for you.'

She started to speak again, but he walked quickly away and she watched until his tall lean figure disappeared through the double doors at the far end of the hall. This is why he's at Mountview, she thought to herself. Maybe he and David, both. Like Uncle Roger, perhaps he found death a slap in the face every time it occurred. Maybe he couldn't stand up to it either. She remembered that her father had told her once that his brother Roger had moved into administration because he was too sensitive.

Pressing her lips together, she knocked on Tom Gilliam's door.

'So come in, already. How long are you going to stand there?' he called out. When she went in, he fixed her with a sharp and knowing eye. He'd been reading a different book this time and his glasses had slid down his nose. He looked alert and foxy. 'What's going on across the hall?' he demanded.

'Nothing. Now.'

'Okay – what *did* happen?'

She glared at his persistence. 'An old lady died, that's what happened.'

He leaned back against his pillows and smiled in satisfaction. 'That's what I thought,' he said.

'You don't have to look so pleased about it.' She was annoyed by his smug tone.

'I'm not pleased about it,' he retorted. 'I'm pleased that I deduced from the amount and kind of activity out there this morning exactly what happened. Call it personal satisfaction. I never met the lady, remember. I'm sorry she's dead, but not *very* sorry if it means she's out of a lot of pain, for instance. You, on the other hand, seem a bit angry about it, if you don't mind my saying.' His eyes were on her, questioning.

'It was an unexpected case of heart failure and she was one of my patients, so naturally I'm upset,' Laura said.

'What were you doing with her?'

'She was a chronic asthmatic. Asthma can be partially controlled through posture and breathing – oh, it doesn't matter. The point is, instead of treating her and Mrs Strayhorn this morning—'

'Strayhorn. She's the one with a voice like Gabriel's horn bringing down a glacier? I've heard *her* over there often enough.'

Laura smiled briefly. 'Yes. She was Mrs McAllister's best friend and she's very distressed. They've put her under sedation, which leaves me with an entire morning to devote to you.'

'Oh, great.' He didn't seem overly enthusiastic about the prospect.

She regarded him thoughtfully. 'Do you often lie there and make deductions about what's going on outside your door?'

'Sure. You can only read so many books a day, you know.'

'Did you hear anything going on last night?'

'No, unfortunately. Something woke me around one o'clock, but then I went back to sleep. It was all the activity around four this morning that I noticed. The fact that people were going in and out of the room across the hall, but every time the door opened I did *not* hear that whiny little voice of hers. Then, a little while ago I heard men's voices instead, several of them. Not only your uncle and Butler and Jenks, but someone else, too, with a very flat voice. And then a trolley came, running light on its wheels going in and heavy coming out. That meant she was either on her way to an operation, or on her way out. I guessed dead, because they were all just in there having another conference and she wasn't back. See?'

'Very impressive. And how far did the parsley sink into the butter, Holmes?'

'Ah, that was it, you see. The butter did nothing in the night-time. That told me everything, Watson.'

She came across and sat down on the chair next to his bed. She'd never done that before and he was instantly on his guard. Whatever was coming, he didn't think he was going to like it.

It took her quite a while to formulate what she was going to say. It wasn't until he'd begun talking about working out what had happened to Mrs McAllister during the night that his profession had actually registered with her. Here was an expert, indeed, an objective expert. He might be able to guide her in finding out what had happened to Julie and whether or not it had anything to do with the clinic. Listening to Uncle Roger prevaricate about doing a post-mortem on Mrs McAllister had worried her. What was he afraid of? Hadn't Mrs Strayhorn said something the other night about Mrs McAllister endowing the clinic? Did that mean she was leaving it something in her will? The thought that Uncle Roger could have done something to speed Mrs McAllister's death was almost too awful to contemplate, but the thought niggled at her. Was this the kind of thing that Julie had meant?

What about that woman she'd mentioned in her last letter – the one who died unexpectedly? Had others left money to the clinic? Had she discerned a pattern? Did that have anything to do with her being killed? It was a horrible thought, but it was one that Laura couldn't dismiss outright. She had to deal with it, even if it meant harming the clinic and her uncle. He would be furious if he knew she had been harbouring these thoughts and she did feel bad about it – but she couldn't stop herself. He might have been her father's twin brother and she couldn't imagine her father ever doing anything like that – but there *was* a streak of implacability in the Forresters. It was what was driving her on now. She looked at Tom Gilliam, wondering. He looked back at her, apparently questioning whether she had momentarily lost her mind. Would it be doing him a favour, too? Giving him a sense of self-worth, of usefulness? It was a gamble – life was a gamble – but frankly, she didn't know where else to turn.

'If you're so hard up for mental stimulation, maybe you could use your deductive brilliance on another problem they've got around here.' She heard herself say 'they' instead of 'we' and realized she still didn't feel a part of her Uncle Roger's 'family'. Something was keeping her outside, especially since hearing the conversation in the late Mrs McAllister's room. Was it self-preservation? Or just natural caution?

'Oh? Somebody stealing bandages, are they?' Gilliam asked.

A flicker of a smile, but she didn't meet his eyes. 'No. At least, not that I know of. But somebody did get murdered.'

'In here? How reassuring you are, Miss Nightingale.'

She glanced up. 'No, not in here. In the woods, between here and town. The girl I replaced, in fact. Her name was Julie Zalinsky.'

'And when did this happen?'

'About four or five weeks ago.'

'And you think I can just lie back and exercise my little grey cells, do you? I can't visit the scene of the crime, I can't talk to the people concerned, I know nothing about the investigation – and yet I'm supposed to lie here and be inspired to come up with an answer to whodunit? I must say, I'm flattered. You must think I have supernatural powers.'

She glared at him. 'No, of course I don't. Sorry – I didn't think it through. It's just a puzzle to me, something unfinished, something that still upsets people I like. And you were a policeman, a detective . . . aren't you a *bit* curious?'

'Nope.'

'Not even—'

'Not even a little bit. Sorry.'

She stood up. 'All right. Then we might as well get started with your treatment. I want—'

'No.'

'What?'

'No. I've decided I don't want any treatment, thank you. I just want to be left alone. I thought I had made myself perfectly clear on that point.'

She very much wanted to hit him. 'But you said that—'

'I believe I said I was thinking about it. I have thought about it and decided not to bother. Think of all the free time that gives you. You could take up a hobby.'

They glared at one another. She had seen the momentary flare of amusement and interest in his eyes, then the closing down, the anger, the bleak recall of his condition.

'We have a very nice hydrotherapy pool here. How about a swim?' she suggested.

'No, thanks.'

'It would ease the cramps, relax the—'

'No, thanks. Really.'

She sighed. 'Why on earth *are* you here, Mr Gilliam?'

'I've been wondering that myself,' he said. 'When I come up with an answer, I'll let you know.'

There was no help here for her dilemma. She stared at him in frustration and simply walked out. She was still on her own and more confused than ever.

And now somebody else was dead, too.

# TEN

LAURA HAD A DECISION TO make.

She'd been at the clinic for over a week, now. She had read the newspaper reports about Julie's murder. She had talked about her to both staff and patients. She had tried to be discreet, but brought up the murder whenever she could, without any tangible result. It was clear that what Emily Gibbons had told her was true – nobody wanted to think about it. So as a detective she was a complete bust.

She wondered if she should just forget it and get on with her life here. The clinic was beautiful. The surroundings were beautiful. The patients were, for the most part, reasonable and friendly. Ditto the staff, with a few marked exceptions. Her situation was an ideal one in every respect, with her apparently loving uncle as an employer, work that was interesting but not exhausting, a pleasant place to live on her own, and people like David Butler to flatter her and take her out to dinner now and again. What girl could ask for more?

And yet . . . and yet.

There was Julie's face before her when she went to sleep. There were the letters. There was this local nonsense about the Shadowman. There was now a terrible suspicion in her mind about her own uncle. And there was Tom Gilliam.

Her tentative approach to him had been brusquely rejected, yet it seemed to her that if he could become interested in something outside himself it would be very beneficial to his physical improvement. He spent far too much time sulking and feeling sorry for himself. Everybody had tried bullying him, reasoning with him, becoming exasperated with him and ignoring him. Nothing had worked.

But what if he were made to feel *useful*?

Might that have an effect?

And might that not help her, too?

It was not with an impartial interest in the improvement of her patient that she drove into town that afternoon, but a feeling of complete frustration and failure.

Knowing what she should do and actually doing it were two different things. So she chickened out and went into the Grey Art Gallery that was just up the street from the sheriff's office. It was peaceful in the art gallery and she needed a few moments of quiet before she tossed herself at the feet of the rather forbidding Sheriff Gabriel.

A little old lady – no other words for her – was sitting at the desk that stood to one side of the gallery, sewing on a quilt block. She looked up and smiled as Laura came in, then went back to her work.

Laura stopped in front of the beautiful abstract quilt she had noticed the previous week. 'This is absolutely breath-taking,' she said, her voice rather echoing in the open space.

'Why, thank you,' the little old lady said. Laura turned to look at her more closely. She was round and placid, and had fluffy white hair.

'Did *you* make it?' Laura asked.

'Yes, indeed I did.' She smiled.

'But that's wonderful.' Laura hesitated and surreptitiously glanced at the label below the hem. 'Mrs Toby?'

'That's right, dear. And you're wondering why a little old lady like me would make such a wild design, isn't that right?'

'I didn't mean . . .'

'Of course you didn't,' she said with a smile. 'I used to make traditional quilts. I'm making one right now.' She held up the block she'd been sewing. 'I teach classes in it and I like to keep my hand in – but my real love is what is called the art quilt. There's a group of us in town, here . . . call ourselves the Blackwater Bay Magpies, because we pick up fabric from everywhere. You interested in quilting?'

'I've never had much to do with it,' Laura admitted. 'But I had a friend who used to love it. I think I have one of her quilts on my bed up at the clinic.'

Mrs Toby looked at Laura more closely and put down her sewing. 'Double Wedding Ring, mostly blue and white?'

'Why, yes.'

'That would be Julie's first quilt,' she said softly. 'I wondered what had happened to it.'

'You knew Julie?'

'She was in my Saturday quilting class,' Mrs Toby answered. 'She was a lovely girl.' She gazed at Laura with bird-bright eyes. 'You would be the new physiotherapist, then?'

'Yes – my name is . . .'

'Laura Brandon,' Mrs Toby supplied with a smile. 'I'm glad to meet you, Laura Brandon. What happened to Julie was horrible, cruel. I still can't get over it. You said she was your friend?'

'Yes. We trained together, worked together.'

'And now you've taken her place with your uncle.' Mrs Toby seemed to be remarkably well informed. Presumably the Blackwater Bay Magpies picked up a lot more than fabric in their flights around town. Laura came over and sat down at the far side of the desk. Mrs Toby picked up her sewing again and began to stitch while she spoke. 'Very fancy place, your clinic. Julie enjoyed working there.'

'Not towards the end, she didn't,' Laura said, before she could stop herself. She realized abruptly why Mrs Toby knew so much – it was impossible *not* to talk to her. She seemed so . . . receptive.

'No,' Mrs Toby agreed. 'Not towards the end. It was funny, really, in a way. Not ha-ha funny, but . . .' She paused and looked down at her needle. 'Her stitching went all to pot,' she finally said. 'Normally she had a fine hand – even, steady – she was one of my best pupils. But in the last week or two before she died she was all over the place.' She frowned. 'And she did say one odd thing I remember, now.'

'What was that?'

She gazed at Laura over the top of her glasses. 'She said – in a very bitter voice, I recall – she said, "I hate liars, Mrs Toby. I hate them more than anything."'

'That was it?' Laura had momentarily hoped for more.

She shrugged. 'For what it's worth. Maybe it meant nothing at all.'

'She did write to me—' Laura began.

Mrs Toby stopped stitching and looked up. 'She wrote to you? Told you why she was unhappy?'

'No, not exactly. Just that she *was* unhappy and thinking of leaving. She felt kind of guilty about it because . . .'

'Because it's your uncle's place,' Mrs Toby finished for her, cutting off a thread with a snap of her little gold scissors.

'Yes. And now I don't know what to do.'

'What do you *want* to do?' Mrs Toby asked, not unreasonably.

'I want to find out who killed her,' Laura blurted out. 'But I don't know how to go about it. I've talked to people at the clinic, but—'

'You should be talking to the sheriff,' Mrs Toby said. 'Tell him what you think, what you know. He'll be glad to listen.'

'Will he?'

Mrs Toby smiled encouragingly. 'He's a real *good* listener, Ms Brandon. Better than he is a talker. That's why we all have to work so hard to get him re-elected every few years. He won't brag about himself a bit. Very exasperating when you're trying to win him some votes.'

Laura was getting a whole new impression of the man she'd met that first morning, when he was looking at her car and noting down her licence number, and whom she'd seen around the clinic, grimly questioning members of the staff. Mrs Toby certainly seemed fond of him. 'All right, I will.'

Mrs Toby picked up her sewing again. 'Good for you,' she said. 'And come back on Sunday – we're opening a show of photographs taken by local schoolchildren and my friend Mrs Norton is baking cookies to serve. She bakes fine cookies. You'll like them.'

Mrs Toby had made Laura feel much less isolated, all of a sudden. She stood up. She *would* speak to the sheriff. She *would* tell him what she thought and what she knew.

And what she didn't know.

It couldn't hurt. Could it?

The sheriff's office was a new-looking building of red brick with white trim and had wide windows facing the street. In one of them a very large ginger cat sat with paws folded, viewing the passing scene with lively interest. Laura wondered if he was a deputy. Surely a sheriff who kept a cat couldn't be *all* bad?

The day was quite warm, a period of Indian summer having followed that first foggy weekend, but within the office the air was cool and fresh. A long counter ran across the room, and behind it there were desks and computers and other office machines, including a very large coffee-maker. Beside it there was a big basket lined with paper napkins and containing doughnuts. Cliché after cliché, she thought. Do all policemen function on coffee and doughnuts? Apparently – although the men on *NYPD Blue* often seem to have Danish and canoli as variants. She realized she was approaching the coming interview with all her preconceived notions intact.

Most of the desks were empty. On the corner of one lounged a husky blond man in uniform with big blue eyes and big bulging muscles, behind another sat an overweight lady (quite close to the doughnuts, Laura noted) with her hair done up in an elaborate French twist with embellishments, and between the two on a large wheeled office chair sat the sheriff himself, drinking coffee but without a doughnut. She was aware of other people moving around the room doing various tasks, but it was these three who held her attention.

'Hello,' she said.

'Well, hell*o*,' said the muscular blond man with a rather boyish and inoffensive leer.

'Ma'am,' said the sheriff, putting down his coffee mug. 'What can we do for you?'

'I . . . my name is Laura Brandon,' she began.

'Miss Brandon.' He nodded and waited.

'I would like to talk to you,' she said, glancing warily around. 'Privately.'

'No problem.' He got up, smiled and she felt herself relax a little. 'By the way,' he went on. 'This is Tilly Moss, our station manager, and my Chief Deputy, George Putnam.'

They murmured their hellos and she murmured back, suddenly shy. Coming here had suddenly made everything seem very 'official'. Wondering and imagining and playing at finding out was one thing, but actually talking to people who wore guns at their hips and had badges and uniforms and books of rules and powers of arrest was commitment. Perhaps it was the fact that for her Julie's death had been a distant event, in a way unreal, and as such it seemed almost an intellectual and emotional problem rather than brutal reality. Like something she'd read in a book.

But these people had seen Julie's body. They had seen other bodies, other crimes, victims and criminals, all the harsh truths of human frailty. They *knew*; she only imagined.

Deputy Putnam held up the flap so she could go through, smiling as she passed. Miss Moss smiled too. She managed to smile back, but it was an effort. She was shaking inside.

The sheriff closed the door of his glass-walled office and gestured to a chair, going around to take his own place behind the big desk. He had reddish hair with quite a bit of grey in it, a square jaw and crinkles around his eyes, as if he stared into the sun a lot.

'Well, Miss Brandon? What can I do for you?' Sheriff Gabriel asked in a very gentle voice.

'It's about Julie Zalinsky,' Laura said. 'About who killed her.'

He raised an eyebrow. 'Do you know who killed her?' he asked.

'No . . . oh, no,' she answered hurriedly. 'And neither do you, yet, do you?'

'As you say . . . neither do I,' he acknowledged.

'Oh, I don't mean to criticize.'

'You'd be one of the very few, then,' he said. 'People around here seem to think I've been sitting on my hands about this one.'

'Have you?' she blurted out, then felt herself going red.

He smiled forgivingly, which was nice of him, she thought. She was handling this about as badly as she could without 'How Not To Do It' lessons.

'No,' he said. 'I haven't. I have questioned everybody at the clinic and everybody in town who knew Miss Zalinsky – not too many of the latter, she kept herself pretty much to herself up there. I have gone over the scene of the crime several times and made use of the extensive forensic facilities offered by the State Police.' He gave the last rather grimly.

'You didn't like doing that?'

'We like to handle things ourselves if we can,' he said. 'I have truly tried everything I can, Miss Brandon. By the book and any other way I can think of, and I am no closer to finding Miss Zalinsky's killer than I was two days after it happened. I am not happy about it, but there doesn't seem to be an answer so far.'

'Maybe I could help,' Laura said.

He didn't laugh. He just waited.

'This is very difficult for me,' she went on.

'I can see that. Take your time.'

She cleared her throat. 'I am a physiotherapist. I trained with Julie, some years ago, and we were working in the same hospital in Omaha. I recommended her for the job at my uncle's clinic – Mountview. My uncle was always asking me to work for him and I didn't want to—'

'Why not?'

'Because it was too easy,' she said. 'I have too much pride for my own good, Sheriff. I wanted to stand on my own two feet. Does that make any sense?'

'Absolutely.' He nodded. 'Go on.'

'Well, when he asked the last time I recommended Julie, as I said, and she got the job. We wrote to each other and at first everything was just fine. But then her letters changed. She seemed to be uneasy, unhappy.' Laura scrabbled in her handbag and produced the last few letters Julie had sent her. 'I kept these because they kind of worried me.' She gave him a minute to glance through them.

'She never actually *said* what was worrying her,' she went on after a minute. 'I think she was about to tell me, but—'

'But she was killed.'

'Yes.'

'And you think she was killed *because* of what she was about to tell you? Whatever it was that was worrying her at the clinic?'

'Yes.'

'What was she like, Miss Brandon?'

He had gone right to the heart of it. 'She was inclined to be a little melodramatic, I admit,' Laura said slowly.

'Yes, I had received that impression from people at the clinic.'

'But then they would say that, wouldn't they, if they were hiding something?' she blurted out.

'To be honest with you, Miss Brandon, they didn't say much,' he told her with a sigh and put the letters down on his desk. 'For me this has been what I call a Teflon case. My questions slide off the people up there; I can't seem to penetrate their reserve or their defences, whichever it is.'

'I know,' she said. 'I've been trying too. Mrs Toby says it's because nobody wants to think about it.'

He grinned. 'You know Mrs Toby?'

Laura smiled back. 'I just met her. She's . . . quite remarkable.'

'Oh, she is that,' he agreed. 'Knows everything about everybody. She knew Miss Zalinsky through her quilting classes. She was a big help in giving me a picture of what your friend was like.'

'She just told me something Julie said a little while before she was killed. Something about "hating liars".'

Again, the eyebrow went up. 'That's interesting.'

'Yes,' Laura agreed. 'But she didn't say *who* was lying.'

'Couldn't you just spit?' he said sympathetically.

She was rather taken aback. It seemed a rather unlawman-like thing to say. 'I beg your pardon?'

'To be so close to an answer and not get it?' he explained. He sat forward in his chair and banged the desk with the flat of his hand. 'I *know* it's something to do with the clinic, I've felt it all along. But nobody agrees with me, not even my own deputy out there. And I can't give you a reason, Miss Brandon, why I feel that, but I do. They all smile, and say how much they want to help and so on, but they give me nothing . . . nothing at all.'

'Maybe they prefer to think it was the Shadowman,' she suggested.

'Damn!' he exploded, leaning back again. 'So you've heard that nonsense as well, have you?'

'Yes. It does sound kind of crazy.'

'It is. It is. Shadowman legends have been crawling around this town for years. My father was sheriff here before me and he had to put up with the same kind of ridiculous maundering. George, out there, he's convinced of it. He went back into the files and found an old murder case that is more or less the same thing as your friend's. Unsolved, too. A young teenage girl killed in the woods up by Mountview, her head bashed in and her throat cut. Happened about thirty years ago, now, in my father's time. Everybody in town called it the Shadowman Killing. And there are stories of other similar killings in the last century, also unsolved. That's where all the flak is coming from. So far I've managed to hold Emily down, but . . .'

'Emily?'

'Emily Gibbons over at the *Chronicle*. She wants to run stories about the Shadowman, mostly because of that nut Mitch Hasker who is President of the Historical Society and thinks it's somehow "romantic" for a town to have such legends attached to it. He's writing a book . . .'

Laura smiled wryly. 'I've heard about the book.'

'Yes, just about everybody has. For years we've been hearing about that book, but it never appears. Meanwhile, every damned thing that goes wrong in this town gets blamed on the Shadowman. It's enough to drive you to drink.'

'You're a realist,' she ventured.

'I am,' he agreed vehemently. Owen Jenks had told her that Blackwater Bay had acquired some kind of reputation for eccentricity in the media. If that was the case, something like the Shadowman would be meat and drink to the Sundays and the Weird and Wonderful departments of the TV stations. They'd have Robert Stack down there in no time, wandering and wondering all over the place. No wonder the sheriff was trying to keep that kind of conjecture out of the local paper. After a minute he looked up. 'Well, thank you for your help, Miss Brandon, but . . .'

'There's more,' she said quickly.

'Something you've found out?' he asked hopefully.

'No. A favour. And maybe . . . help.'

'Go on.'

'I have a patient at the clinic. His name is Thomas Gilliam and he is a police detective in Grantham. Or, he *was* until he had a bad accident. He's a temporary paraplegic, more through his own disinclination to try to get better than for any medical reason. He could be made to walk again, but he's too busy feeling sorry for himself to make the necessary effort. He can be pretty unpleasant.'

'If he can't walk then he couldn't have . . .'

'Oh, he wasn't here when it happened. But I think you could help him.'

'Me?'

'If you were willing to let him work on Julie's killing.' There, she had said it.

He frowned. 'I don't understand.'

'Well, you said you had trouble talking to the people at the clinic. I would guess that's because of your position and people's natural antagonism towards the police and anyway most people hate being suspected and . . .'

'I see where you're heading, Miss Brandon. You think this Gilliam could find out things that I haven't been able to because he's just a patient and nobody would realize what he was doing.'

Laura sighed. 'Yes. I mean, he's a trained detective and—'

'Just a minute.' He held up his hand like a traffic cop. He picked up his phone and dialled a number, asking for somebody named Stryker. 'Hi, Jack, this is Matt Gabriel. Got a question.' He paused, listening, and grinned. 'Nice talk, very nice talk for a grown man,' he said. 'Do you know a detective on your force called—?' He looked at Laura.

'Tom Gilliam,' she said.

'Tom Gilliam,' he repeated. He explained the situation and what she had suggested, then listened again, nodding. 'No kidding. Yeah . . . yeah. . . .' This went on for some time. 'Okay, Jack, thanks. When are we going to see you up here?' He listened again. 'I'll look forward to that. Bye – and thanks.' He hung up the phone and looked at her. 'He says Gilliam probably wouldn't help me. Says he's turned sour since his injury.'

'That's true enough. But—'

'But he also says the guy is very good. Smart. A lateral thinker, that kind of thing. And rich. Must be, to be up there at your uncle's place. Unusual, a rich cop.'

'His family has money. But he still became a policeman,' Laura pointed out. 'At least they knew he couldn't be bribed.' Not, perhaps, the most diplomatic thing to say to a police officer, but he let it pass.

'I don't know, Miss Brandon. It seems kind of a way-out thing to do.'

'What are your alternatives?' she asked bluntly.

'Jack says Gilliam is bed-ridden,' the sheriff said.

'Only through choice. He can use a wheelchair. He can get around if he wants to.'

'But making him want to is your problem,' the sheriff said. 'And letting him help me is my problem.'

'Yes.'

'It's an interesting proposition,' he said, half to himself. 'I can see where one thing would influence the other – that making him work at one thing might make him work at the other—'

'Exactly.'

'Because it would make him feel useful again,' he concluded.

'*Exactly*!' This was going to be easy.

'I'll have to think about it, Miss Brandon.'

'Oh.' Too easy.

'There are questions of jurisdiction, confidentiality, that sort of thing. And how do we know that he will go for it?'

'We don't,' she admitted. 'But until we try—'

He nodded, thought for a moment, then stood up. 'Thanks for coming in, Miss Brandon. Like I said, I will definitely think over what you have suggested – and I'll get back to you. How's that?'

'I guess . . . that's fine,' she said, also standing up. She reached into her handbag and got out a piece of paper. 'That's my office extension.' She wrote it down. 'And that's my home extension.'

'Both come through the central system?' he asked.

'Yes. Why?'

'Just asking. I'll be in touch, Miss Brandon. Thanks again.'

'Thank you, Sheriff.' Unless she wanted to ask him about the cat or the state of his health or the crime rate in Blackwater Bay, that was it.

So she left.

* * *

That afternoon, Mrs Strayhorn seemed older, quieter and infinitely smaller than she had a few days before, but she had refused a tranquillizer that morning. 'One thing to grieve over losing Myra, another to turn into some kind of dope addict,' she said to Laura. Her eyes filled with tears as she looked around the physiotherapy room. 'So damn quiet – not the same coming down here without her.'

'I know. I'm sorry,' Laura said gently.

'Are you?' Mrs Strayhorn glared at her, then her suspicious expression slid away, as if she didn't have the strength to hold on to it. 'Oh, I guess you are at that. She couldn't help being the way she was, her parents always indulged her because of the asthma. Guess complaining got to be a habit.' She grunted as Laura massaged a particularly painful spot on her knee. 'Only way she could get attention, she thought. Never *tried* any other way. Except promising people money in her will, of course. She was big on that all right.'

'She was difficult,' Laura conceded. 'But we did like her, you know. We didn't mind.'

'Not everybody here's as kind-hearted as you. Some of them are as hard as nails. That blonde bombshell, for instance.'

'Nurse Janacek?'

'I guess that's her name.' Mrs Strayhorn frowned. 'I don't think it's good for a girl to be that beautiful. Must twist something inside.'

'Oh, I don't think so . . .' Laura murmured, while silently agreeing with her.

'Mmmmph. That's because you've never been really beautiful,' Mrs Strayhorn said uncompromisingly. 'I reckon she killed her.'

'What?' Laura was nonplussed.

'I say, I reckon she killed her,' Mrs Strayhorn repeated a little louder. 'You going deaf or something?'

'You don't mean that.'

'I do.' Mrs Strayhorn clasped her hands across her

middle, delighted with an opportunity to vent her dislike of Clarissa. 'That last night she kept teasing Myra, getting her goat. She only did it out of spite – I tell you, she as good as murdered Myra by doing that.'

'Now, to be fair, Mrs Strayhorn, Mrs McAllister did get worked up rather easily.'

'And that Nurse Janacek knew it,' said the old lady flatly. She paused, then looked at Laura slyly out of the corner of her eyes. 'She carries on, too. I saw her myself. So did Myra, come to that.'

'What do you mean?'

'You know what I mean. Carries on. With men. She's a bad girl.'

'She's beautiful, and young, and single . . .'

Mrs Strayhorn snorted again. 'Oh, hell, girl, I got nothing against today's girls, what they get up to. But *that* one is different. She was messing around with that Mr Panotis in the linen closet last week.'

Laura wheeled over the heat lamp. 'You should know better than to listen to hospital gossip.'

'Wasn't gossip – I saw 'em myself, I told you. He had his hand right on her perky little backside and as for *her* hands . . . well!'

'Now look—'

Mrs Strayhorn twisted round so as to see Laura's face the right way up. 'No – now don't *you* assume, young woman. I'm not making it up and I'm not making a mistake, either. I'm reporting what I actually saw. I've buried two husbands and there's nothing shocks me any more. I *saw* her – and that nice little Mrs Panotis was only down the hall . . .'

'How could you see them if they were in the linen closet?'

'Catch is faulty,' said Mrs Strayhorn in glee, delighted at having sprung her trap at last. 'Door opened up a crack and I was going past. Tyres on my chair are very quiet, you know. I can sneak up on a lot of people, hear things, see things. Only fun I have these days.'

'That does it,' said Laura firmly. 'It's the Jacuzzi for you.'

Mrs Strayhorn, enjoying this new game enormously,

quailed. 'That's not fair. Myra saw it too – I went down to the day-room and told her about it and she rolled right back there and had a look for herself, so there. What's more, I think Nurse Janacek saw her looking in, so she probably *wanted* her to die. She felt guilty.'

'I doubt that. She's not the type to feel guilty about anything,' Laura said, before she could stop herself.

'Hah!' crowed Mrs Strayhorn. 'See?'

'Mrs Strayhorn, whatever Clarissa may or may not be in her private life, she *is* a very good nurse and she's not stupid.'

It was Mrs Strayhorn's turn to frown. 'Maybe,' she allowed.

'And for you to imply that she agitated Mrs McAllister sufficiently to cause a fatal asthma attack is simply irresponsible,' Laura continued. 'You mustn't do it.'

'I mustn't, hey?' The old lady pretended to be chastised, but retained a defiant glint in her eye.

'No.'

'How about how she was always going off in a corner whispering with that slimy bastard who was married to Myra? How about that? Maybe he put her up to it. He was trying to stop Myra going ahead with the divorce, but he wasn't having any luck, so maybe he figured if she died while they were still married – which she has – he would get her money. Well, he's got a hell of a shock coming when they read her latest will out, that's all I can say. Serve the bastard right, too.'

'What do you mean?'

Mrs Strayhorn flounced, as much as she was able to when lying down on the treatment table. 'She was going to leave a lot of money to this place. And maybe some to that nice Dr Butler, too. But not a penny for that husband of hers. Well, maybe *one* penny, but no more.'

'Are you sure about that?' Laura asked her.

'She told me herself,' Mrs Strayhorn said.

Laura was shocked. Here was a clear motive for her uncle to have . . . no, it was impossible. *Impossible.*

It had to be.

And now she had alerted the sheriff to there being something wrong at the clinic, he might take another look. A closer look.

What had she done?

# ELEVEN

LAURA SAT WITH SOLOMON IN front of the television set, toying with her dinner. She felt too worried to eat, but kept telling herself it would be all right. The sheriff would see Julie's letters for the melodramatic outpourings of a bored woman looking for a reason to change her job. He would know there couldn't be anything wrong here at Mountview.

It would be all right.

She paused with her fork half-way to her mouth.

Somebody was coming up the outside staircase. Somebody large. Oh, Lord, she thought, it's the sheriff. Or the Shadowman. But it wasn't.

When she opened the door Tilly Moss, the fat woman from the sheriff's office, was standing there, carrying a briefcase, a handbag, a quilt and a large bag of fabric scraps. She was out of breath and looked cross. A strand of her elaborate hairdo had come adrift and hung over her nose. She puffed ineffectually at it. 'He sent me,' she said, blowing at the recalcitrant curl again. 'Can I come in?'

Laura stood back and she entered, looking around curiously. 'Nice,' she said. 'Very nice.' She turned back and looked at Laura as she closed the door. 'Didn't expect to see me, did you?'

'Well – no,' Laura admitted.

'Mm.' She nodded, went over to the sofa and sank on to it with a relieved sigh. Like many overweight women, she had small feet and appeared to be wearing even smaller shoes. It looked a painful combination. 'He didn't want to come himself or send George because somebody might spot them and get curious. I was the next best thing. I am a member of the Magpies – the quilt and the bag of scraps are my cover. I told the girl at the reception desk you were planning to take up quilting, you see, and she sent me round here. She didn't think it was odd, we're always trying to recruit members. You can return the quilt and the scraps at your own convenience.'

'Oh,' Laura said. This did not bode well. 'Would you like a cup of coffee? Or tea?'

'No, thank you. I have to get home and make dinner for my mother and myself.' She put the briefcase on the coffee table next to Laura's unfinished dinner. 'Those chops look nice,' she observed. 'Maybe we'll have chops instead.' Instead of what she didn't specify.

Laura sat down in the rocker and waited.

'Matt and George and I discussed your suggestion,' Tilly said.

'But—'

'Don't look so surprised,' she admonished. 'We talk over most things. I worked for Matt's father before him and I know more about procedure than the two of them put together. George thinks it's crazy, but I think that's because he's jealous of anyone else helping out on a case. Matt is desperate. He thought all afternoon about it and he called up that crazy friend of his, Stryker, and they talked about it, and the result is – here I am. I have no opinion one way or the other, except than it is legally acceptable to use informers and your Mr Gilliam could be classed as an informer – at a stretch. He could also be sworn in as a deputy, but to do that Matt would have to come up here and talk to him, and as he has no legitimate reason for talking to him, seeing as he wasn't here when the murder was committed, people might get curious. As to sharing confidential information – I know nothing about it. All I know is that Matt asked me to bring you this briefcase. That's all I know. Do you understand?'

'That's all you know,' Laura repeated stupidly.

'That's right. Don't shoot the messenger, I believe the saying is.' She stood up abruptly. 'You do understand about confidential information, don't you?'

'I understand it's confidential, which means I should shut up about it,' Laura said, rallying slightly.

'You got it,' Tilly confirmed. She looked Laura up and down. 'It could be that George is right, this is crazy. But Matt makes judgements about people in his own way. He's a smart man – he used to be a university professor, you know. Taught philosophy.'

'He did?' It seemed incongruous, yet there had been great intelligence in those blue eyes. And patience.

'He did. Took the job of sheriff because he thought it would be easy and he could do a lot of reading. Hasn't been able to finish a book since.' She went to the door and turned – she must watch *Columbo* too, Laura thought wildly. 'We've got the Howl coming up, *and* the election. He's got enough to think about without all this.'

Without all what? What was the Howl?

'Be careful, he told me to tell you. Be damned careful. His numbers are inside the briefcase. And if it doesn't take . . . that was his word, "take" . . . if it doesn't take, he wants the briefcase back intact. Got it?'

'Got it.' Laura stifled an impulse to salute.

Tilly opened the door and stood there, looking around at the clinic and the grounds. 'Fancy place,' she said with a combination of envy and disapproval. 'Not happy, though. Shame.'

And with that parting shot she clumped down the stairway and made her way to a car parked on the approach road beneath. Laura watched her drive away, then turned to stare at the briefcase sitting beside her plate of congealing chops. Solomon was extending a tentative paw at one of them and she almost let him get away with it. Then she picked up the plate, carried it to the kitchen and cut up the cold chops to put in his dish. At this rate she would be down to a size eight and he would be up to fifty pounds.

* * *

She went the back way, not wanting to pass Reception or the nurses' station. Across the parking lot, up the service stairs and then a quick right to the corner rooms. It was quiet in the hall, the lights had already been dimmed for the evening. She slipped into Gilliam's room.

'Good God, even the nurses knock,' he said, staring at her in surprise. 'I could have been on a bedpan or something, for crying out loud.'

'So what? I've carried bedpans before. Are you?'

'No,' he said sulkily. 'What's that?'

She looked down. 'Why, for goodness sake, it's a briefcase. Now how did that get there?'

'Very funny.' He closed his eyes. 'What do you want?'

'I want you to help me.' She pulled a chair over beside the bed and put the briefcase on her lap.

'I never loan money to strange women,' he said, still with his eyes closed.

'I don't need your money, I need your brain,' she told him briskly.

'What – for medical research? Isn't it polite to wait until the person is dead?'

'No comment. I went into town today and—'

'And bought a new briefcase. Lovely.'

'No, I went in to talk to the sheriff.'

'Parking tickets?'

'No – murder.'

His eyes opened at that. 'Who – the McAllister woman?'

'No!' She didn't want to get into that. 'My friend, Julie Zalinsky.'

His eyes closed again. 'Never heard of her.'

'Yes, you have; I mentioned it yesterday. She was the physiotherapist here before I came, and she was murdered in the woods between here and town.'

'Oh, yes, I remember – you wanted me magically to solve the case. Which, of course, I so easily could do if I wanted to. I just don't want to.'

'This briefcase is from the sheriff,' Laura said, tapping

it. 'I believe it contains all the case notes on Julie's murder investigation.'

'He gave that to *you*?' His eyes were open again. He looked horrified.

'No,' she said evenly. 'He sent it for you. He needs your help. He talked to somebody in your department in Grantham—'

'Who?'

'Somebody named Stryker?'

'Oh, God.' He seemed both amused and dismayed. 'And?'

'And the upshot is, here is all the information the sheriff has on the killing. Apparently this Stryker person also thinks you could help. You see, it's like this.' And she explained about how Sheriff Gabriel was having trouble getting anything out of the people at the clinic and how he, Gilliam, could find out things through being nosy that Gabriel couldn't. He had the perfect 'cover' because he hadn't been here at the time of Julie's murder, he had already built up a reputation for being difficult so nobody would be surprised if he asked rude questions and his was a fairly serious case, which gave him status among the other patients.

'Gee, I'm just the ideal guy, right?' he asked, when she had finished.

'Yes,' she agreed, starting to undo the briefcase.

'If only I gave a good god-damn,' he said.

She could have strangled him. 'All right, then, *I'll* do it.' She opened the briefcase. On top of the folders within there were two envelopes, one addressed to her and one to Tom Gilliam. It would have been fine if, when she picked up her envelope, she hadn't caught sight of a photograph of Julie lying dead on the ground, her throat gaping and her eyes staring upwards. Laura whimpered and crumpled up the envelope with her name on it, staring down at the terrible black-and-white scene.

'Oh, for crying out loud,' he said and pulled himself upright in the bed. 'Give it here.'

'She was my friend,' Laura managed to say in a strangled whisper. 'I didn't know . . .'

He was looking at the picture and frowning. 'No blood,' he muttered.

'It rained that night,' she said miserably. 'Everything was washed away.'

'Oh, great. That's a *big* help.'

She looked at him through her tears. 'Then you'll do it?'

'I didn't say that,' he said. But he hadn't said no, either. He picked up the envelope with his name on it, opened it and began to read. She did the same.

> Dear Miss Brandon [the sheriff had written]
>
> After giving your information and suggestion considerable thought, it seems to me there would be no harm and possibly a lot of good in allowing your patient, Tom Gilliam, to look over the results of our investigation so far. He is a professional and I have ascertained that he can be trusted. Whether it will produce any results – either for me or for your treatment – I cannot say. But I am willing to try if he is. Frankly, I have no other option at the moment. I would suggest, however, that you procure a mobile phone for him so that he and I could talk freely about the case without worrying about being overheard.
>
> Yours sincerely
>
> Matt Gabriel

'He says I should get you a mobile phone,' Laura said.

'Mm,' Gilliam replied. 'He says that here, too. As it happens, I already have one.'

'What else does he say?'

He glanced at her sideways. 'Nothing much,' he answered. 'Asking me to look over the stuff, grateful for my opinion, that sort of thing.'

'And?'

He refolded the letter and put it back in the envelope. 'I'll have to talk to Jack Stryker about this guy first,' he said.

'Who *is* this Stryker that everybody wants to talk to him?' Laura demanded. 'The sheriff called him about you, too.'

Gilliam smiled. It was the first time she had seen his smile and it was quite a revelation. All the battering and the scars and the double chins seemed to disappear – he was transformed into a real person at last.

'Jack Stryker is my boss – or was – down in Grantham. He is a good cop.'

'That's *it*?' she asked, amazed. 'He's a "good cop"?'

'That's enough.' He looked at her. The smile was gone and the stony, stubborn expression he usually wore had been reinstated. 'You think you're pretty damn clever, don't you? You think by getting me interested in this I'll feel more positive, more like working at getting better, like a whole man again.'

'I—'

'Oh, it's a reasonable supposition,' he said offhandedly. 'At least checking out a live case would be more interesting than the crap I've been reading lately.'

She stood up. 'Damn you. If it helps you, fine and dandy. I hate the thought that *you*, of all people, might be *bored*. But I am more interested in finding out what is going on in this godforsaken place. I will do anything, *anything*, including spending time with you, in order to find out why my friend was killed. It's not an attractive prospect, but I'm willing.'

'Bully for you.' He tapped the briefcase. 'Thanks for the occupational therapy. Good-night.'

She glared at him, too furious to speak, then turned and left. She thought, as she went down the hall, that she heard him laughing.

But that was unlikely.

Two hours later Gilliam closed the briefcase and listened to the night wind howling around the eaves of the building outside his room. Being on the corner was nice when the weather was nice, lousy when it wasn't.

He switched off the reading light and looked at the dark window. In the distance he could see the yellow squares of Laura Brandon's apartment above the line of the hedge and wished – not for the first time – that he'd asked someone to bring him a pair of binoculars. He could always say he'd taken up bird-watching to pass the time. It wasn't that he was a Peeping Tom, of course.

He sighed. All right, he was a Peeping Tom.

It was probably the effect of being out of society for so long, he told himself. Of being lonely and vulnerable, and in pain, and bored out of his mind. Coming to this after a life filled with incident and contrast was a shock. He wasn't himself – but who he had turned into he couldn't say and didn't recognize. He'd got fat and soft and stupid, bit by bit, until now he was like a dependent child, eager for the least bit of stimulation, coveting and crooning over each new element introduced into his life. He couldn't pin-point exactly when he realized he was interested in Laura Brandon as a woman rather than as one more adversary in the medical troops arrayed against him. Or why. She was attractive, but quite a few of the nurses here were attractive. He thought it might be because she was so belligerent. She made him respond despite his determination not to rise to any challenge. When the doctors chastised him it had no effect, but when *she* got going – it pissed him off. She got under his skin and that alone intrigued him. Why her? Why now? Was it because he *was* healing, as they said, and his body was beginning to make normal responses to things he had been too ill to notice before? Was he finally bored enough with himself to give in? Or was it just that she was so damned aggravating she'd got past his defences? Probably it was a chemical thing, he decided. Pheromones, wasn't it? Sure, that was it.

He'd read through everything in the briefcase, just trying to distract himself. The girl was right. Damn her. At first it had seemed a pointless, even silly suggestion. But as he'd lain there thinking about it, he realized that he might be useful to the sheriff at that. Which was a whole new feeling, something he thought he would never be again. Even if he made no contribution, even if he came up with nothing, it would give him an interest, something to consider outside of his own miserable existence. So, now he knew all the sheriff knew – except he was a stranger and the sheriff was local. Maybe that would be a help – no ties, no barriers. A cold look at the facts. And what were they?

From what he had read, he thought there *was* the possibility that they were looking for a long-term psychopath. Either a local resident, or a regular visitor to the area.

The more he thought about it, the less he liked the cuts made to Julie Zalinsky's throat. They'd only nicked the jugular. There had been blood loss, of course, but according to the coroner, death actually had been caused by the blows to the head, with exposure being a probable complication. So why cut the throat?

To match this superstition that the sheriff's deputy, one George Putnam, had mentioned in his reports? What was it again? Ah, yes – the Shadowman.

According to Deputy Putnam, conversations about the Shadowman were quite common in the local bars – anybody might have picked up the details of the Shadowman legend. As bizarre as it sounded, it was something that should be explored. There were signs to look for when a psychopath was at work. Someone who perhaps *thought* he was the Shadowman?

But was Julie Zalinsky's death just an escalation of a previously established pattern? Was the present Shadowman – if there was such a person – still acting out a compulsion, going for bigger and bigger thrills? Had Julie just come along at the wrong time, been a random choice after all?

If it was a local psychopath, then the thing was – in effect – out of his jurisdiction. Following that line was up to the sheriff and he didn't envy him the task, for it meant endless footwork and paperwork, painstakingly pin-pointing and then eliminating suspects, getting people's backs up and generally exhausting all possibilities, as well as himself and his staff.

All Gilliam was in a position to investigate was Mountview itself and the people in it. Unless and until the sheriff came up with something else, he might as well continue working on the basis that Julie had been killed deliberately by someone who specifically wanted her dead.

Someone here.

He had to admit the sheriff had been very thorough.

He had covered pretty much everyone at the clinic, from the great to the small, and the interviews were all in the file. He had even done a timetable of movements and alibis, such as they were. Unfortunately, the forensic evidence and the ground being dry under the body put the time of death at between approximately five and six o'clock, before the rain started. And that was a time of shift change-over. To make it worse, individual schedules were staggered to ensure good medical cover, although the fact that the patients were eating dinner then made things marginally easier. Departing staff served the dinner, arriving staff cleared away. There was, subsequently, a great deal of to-ing and fro-ing in the corridor and nobody had a really complete alibi for the period.

Forrester and Mrs Cunningham had been in his office and had eaten their evening meal there at about six-fifteen. Before that they'd been 'freshening up'. Whatever that meant. Probably that they were not together the whole time, for Mrs Cunningham used the staff facilities and Forrester those in his own apartment. Unless they had been showering together, of course – an interesting image.

Dr Weaver, the psychiatrist, had not been at Mountview that day, but had been seeing patients in his office at home. However, he'd had no patient at the relevant time and had no one to alibi him either, as his secretary had left at four, as usual, and he was a widower who looked after himself.

Butler the boy wonder had eaten a light meal in the staff dining-room somewhere around five-thirty, he said.

A couple of nurses verified seeing him there, although they'd been intent on their own conversation and couldn't say exactly when he'd entered or left.

Dr Jenks had been at the free clinic in Hatchville and had left at five, not reaching Mountview until seven, in time to take over for the night from Dr Butler. That was an interesting gap, as the distance between Hatchville and Mountview could have been covered in twenty minutes or so. What had he been doing the rest of the time?

Nurse Hasker had been in her office until five-fifteen, then had gone down to wait in the foyer for her brother to collect her. She couldn't remember when he'd arrived – around six she thought, as he finished at the library at five-thirty and would have taken a bit of time to get to his car and drive up to the clinic. She'd been seen waiting in the lobby by people passing through, but no one had been able to verify she'd been there the entire time.

Michaels, the porter and odd-job man, had been cleaning up in the operating theatre until five-thirty. He'd complained about the mess, which was, according to Gabriel's notes, fairly common for him. Sheriff Gabriel didn't like Michaels – very few did – but he couldn't prove anything against him. He claimed to have left the premises at quarter to six, arriving home at six, but had no wife or partner to verify that. And he was a very unpleasant man – nobody had a good word to say about him, except that he worked, or appeared to work, hard.

The theatre had been used by Drs Hambden and Butler, who'd performed a relatively straightforward knee cartilage operation, starting at four, assisted by an anaesthetist and two nurses. The surgery had been completed by quarter to five, after which they'd all scrubbed up together. The anaesthetist, who was not a local man but had driven up from Grantham, had stayed with the patient in the recovery suite until he had begun to come round, then left the clinic, turning over his charge to the high-dependency nursing staff, all of whom alibied one another. The patient had been returned to his room by eight o'clock that night and the operation was a success – he had left the clinic a week later.

Nick Higgins, the groundsman, had been working in the gardens all afternoon and was seen by several people putting away his tools at six or so. Again, the alibi wasn't tight and it wasn't complete, but then, very few alibis ever were.

The Nurses Janacek, Goodfellow and McNeilage reported for duty at five o'clock, five-thirty and six o'clock; the Nurses Bartlett (Cherry and Merry) and Pink, arrived correspondingly. All other nurses could more or less be accounted for.

The clerical staff – two – left the building at five o'clock. The cleaning staff only worked mornings. The catering staff had all been involved in producing the evening meals. For the moment he discounted them, pending anything new the sheriff and his team might turn up.

All of which meant that almost any of them could have killed Julie Zalinsky by working quickly, taking risks and having great luck. But then, premeditated murder often required exactly that.

It wasn't going to be proven by opportunity alone.

Or by means – the forest was full of rocks, apparently, and knives were everywhere.

So it would come down to motive and that meant finding out as much as he could about all of them.

It would mean getting out of bed. It would mean talking to the other patients. It would mean being *active.* And there was such a lot of ground to cover.

He sighed.

Despite appearances, Mountview was anything but a closed world. Specialists and family doctors came and went, visiting their patients and/or treating them. Cooks cooked for them, laundresses washed for them, delivery men dropped and collected for them. It was a wonder anyone got any sleep at all, much less got well. The place was a god-damned beehive.

People had arguments. And misunderstandings. And

bad days. And secrets. And ambitions. And grudges. And money problems. And a lot of them didn't feel very well – not only the patients. A few of them were afraid.

And one of them could be a killer.

He couldn't be certain of anything.

He could only lie there.

Thinking.

# TWELVE

THE NEXT MORNING, AS LAURA passed the glass doors of the day-room she glanced in and stopped cold in astonishment.

At the far side of the room, half hidden by the green leaves in the planters, she saw Mrs Strayhorn playing chess and chattering a mile a minute across the board.

Her opponent was Tom Gilliam.

'Well, I'll be damned,' she breathed and hurried on to the office. She didn't even take time to say hello to Kay. 'Mr Gilliam's in the day-room playing chess with Mrs Strayhorn!'

'You have some objection to his being there?' Kay asked with a twinkle.

'No. No!' Laura sank down on to a chair. 'I just never thought I'd live to see the day, that's all.'

Kay laughed. 'Well, I don't know if it was you or David or Owen or Dr Weaver, but *something* shook him up. He was determined to get into that chair right after breakfast this morning.'

Laura's mind spun without getting any traction. Had she done it? Did this mean that crabby, stubborn Tom Gilliam was taking on the challenge of finding Julie's killer? She was afraid to believe it – and yet, there he was.

'Mrs Strayhorn is delighted,' Kay went on. 'It's a god-send, something to take her mind off Mrs McAllister's death.' She glanced at Laura and smiled. 'Jealous?'

'Hardly. Moving pieces around a chess board isn't exactly rehabilitative exercise.'

'No, but it does show some kind of effort. Don't rush him,' Kay advised. 'Let him get used to being with people first. Then maybe he'll start *wanting* to walk.'

'It would make a change,' Laura agreed. She stretched, then said casually, 'Mrs Panotis seemed a little down this morning.'

'Of course she is,' Kay said grimly. 'Her husband's due for his weekly visit.'

'I would have thought that would cheer her up.' Laura got up to fetch herself a cup of coffee.

'Have you met Mr Panotis?'

'No. I think I've seen him, though. Big, dark, handsome man.'

'Right. Very big, with the shirts open to the navel and gold necklaces on his hairy chest. Mucho macho crap. He'll storm in here wanting to know why she isn't well yet.'

'She seems so . . . fragile.'

'She just can't cope with him, that's all. It's one of those ethnic things. He went back to the land of his fathers or whatever to find a bride and he found her. Zap, she comes to a strange country, big house, servants, flashy people speaking a language she hardly understands. He gives her charge accounts, tells her to get on with it, and goes back to his business and his blondes same as before. She's basically there to get pregnant and give him a son. When he can be bothered to screw her, that is, when he's drunk or between blondes. What's the matter, he wants to know, why do you cry all the time, haven't you got everything a poor girl ever dreamed of? The bastard.'

'But . . .'

'She *loves* him,' Kay said gently.

'Oh.'

'Yeah – "oh". The only way she can find to excuse her misery is to be sick, so she's sick. Except she isn't, not really, just worn out with hurting.'

'She's Dr Weaver's patient, isn't she?'

'Yes, fortunately for her. He's very good with neurotics.'

'And here's one now,' said a voice from the door and

Owen Jenks came in, looking weary but far more cheerful than he had the other day.

'Are you feeling neurotic?' Laura asked him, grinning.

'It could be that. Or hypoglycaemia,' Owen said with a smile, as he poured himself some coffee and added three spoonfuls of sugar to it. 'How are things going for you, Laura?'

'Fine,' she answered.

'We were talking about Mrs Panotis,' Kay said.

Owen nodded. 'I've just found a Greek-speaking nurse in Hatchville who's enough on the ball to give Mrs Panotis the help she needs. An older, unbeautiful nurse, of course. When we've got Mrs Panotis built up enough to go home, the nurse will move in. She'll look after her – but, more important, she'll spend most of her time teaching the poor woman how to deal with life in wonderful America.'

'And Mr Panotis?'

'If she stops crying, he'll feel the bills are worth it. Mind you, if she learns to stand up to him he might have second thoughts,' Owen said, looking amused. 'I feel a bit like an infiltrator, but that man really gets my goat. I hate to see women get pushed around, especially vulnerable women like Theresa Panotis.'

'I didn't know you were such a feminist.'

'You don't have to wear a bra to identify with a woman's troubles,' Owen said seriously. 'Besides, I feel just as sorry for Mr Cobbold. Have you met *his* wife?'

Laura started to laugh. 'The Scandinavian Valkyrie with the electric-blue eyeshadow?'

'Yes – it's no wonder the old boy's got chronic ulcers and a bad case of drooping dick,' Kay said. 'She's enough to cut the balls out from under any man. He shouts at us, but he's a lamb to the slaughter with his wife.'

'Maybe we ought to introduce her to Mr Panotis,' Laura suggested with a grin.

'I don't think this old building could stand it.' Owen chuckled. Laura finished her coffee quickly and left them to their medical discussions. She had learned that gossip often took precedence over professional conversations in the nurses' stations, and had long ago stopped being shocked by the fact that nurses and doctors freely discussed patients when they were alone. In many instances this was a good thing – a nurse might pick up a sign that a busy doctor had missed, some casual word about a new pain or symptom, a lesion or rash spotted during a bed bath – that kind of thing. And doctors did well to share information, as sometimes dual prescribing could lead to crossed wires and contra-indications between drugs. It happened in the best of hospitals. So it could happen here too.

Ahead of her, the door to the linen closet opened suddenly and Clarissa came out, tucking her hair into her cap. Laura took no notice until she saw David Butler emerge a moment later, looking furtive and slightly flushed. Her steps faltered briefly, then she set her jaw and walked on, giving David a big smile as she passed him.

'Laura – hey! What's the rush?'

'No rush – I'm just hungry.'

'Me too. Eating downstairs?'

'No – I have to go back to the flat.'

'Oh. *Wait* a minute.' He took hold of her arm. 'Are you angry with me or something?'

'No, why should I be?' She smiled at him, oh, so brightly.

He rubbed the back of his neck. 'I don't know.' He looked like a little boy. 'People are acting pretty oddly around here if you ask me. Clarissa was just telling me some cock-and-bull story about the drugs book and your uncle's shot off to Grantham without telling me—'

'Why should he tell you?'

'Because I was *supposed* to have the afternoon off,' he said pointedly. 'I was hoping you and I could go somewhere if you could rearrange your schedule.'

'Oh.' She glanced past David's shoulder. Further down the hall she could see Mr Panotis talking to Clarissa. He had hold of her arm and as he spoke he shook her slightly, as one would shake a naughty kitten. Beyond them, Laura saw Mrs Panotis standing in the open doorway of her room, clutching her bathrobe around herself and watching her husband with Clarissa.

Mrs Panotis's black eyes were blazing in her white face and she looked much less fragile than she had earlier when Laura had given her an aromatherapy massage. The small woman had winced at the least pressure. Her body had been so thin and tense that Laura had found it very difficult to relax her muscles.

'I guess that's out of the question, now,' David said mournfully, distracting Laura's attention from Mrs Panotis's taut white face. 'Owen is completely booked up at the clinic. How about tomorrow instead?'

'What?' Laura stared up at him, wondering what he was talking about. So many questions were knocking around in her head that it was filled with a kind of clanging noise.

'I *said*, what about tomorrow?'

'What were you doing in the linen closet with Clarissa?'

He stared at her for a long moment, as if trying to catch up with her thought processes, then looked even more exasperated. 'I was having a wild, passionate affair with her, of course. There's nothing like making love on a pile of incontinence sheets – we must try it some time.' She just stared at him. 'My God, the *minds* you women have,' he said, half in amazement, half in disgust. 'I just *told* you, she had some crazy story about someone altering the entries in the drugs book.'

'Why would she say that?'

'Clarissa would say anything she felt like if it meant getting some attention,' David said and his cool tone unlocked something that had been knotted in Laura's chest. 'I suppose she didn't want anyone to hear what she had to say.'

'Poor David. Always getting cornered by women.'

'Yeah. Lucky me.'

She looked down the corridor again and saw Clarissa going into Mr Cobbold's room, while Mr and Mrs Panotis were nowhere to be seen. The drama – if it had been a drama – was over. And Tom Gilliam was coming towards them, pushing his wheelchair with unpractised but determined jerks. As he passed them it slewed suddenly sideways, pushing Laura into David's arms. Gilliam looked at them with amusement as they disentangled ourselves. 'How, now, fair maid – why dost thou dally with boy scouts and striplings?' he asked in a mischievous voice.

'I'll dally with whom I like, Mr Gilliam,' Laura said, meeting his green eyes with a rush of defiance. 'Also where I like and when I like.'

Gilliam smiled and pushed the wheels of his chair forward. 'I hear the linen closet is the in-place, these days,' he said over his shoulder. 'Have fun, children.'

Somewhere in the distance a door closed.

A storm started to rise at about three that afternoon. At first there was only a random agitation of the forest around the clinic, as if some giant's hand were sweeping the nearly naked branches back and forth, irritated with the last few leaves for hanging on for so long. Then the clouds covered the sun and the wind play took on a more violent, savage quality. You could sense the rain, you could smell the rain, but it seemed reluctant to fall.

Laura stood in Tom Gilliam's open door and saw him in his wheelchair, gazing out at the scene. The light beyond him was a curious greyish-yellow and it made his face, when he turned towards her, look pinched and taut. 'You never told me there'd be days like this,' he said.

She smiled sympathetically. 'I know – your leg aches.'

'Everything aches,' Gilliam growled.

'It will ease when the rain actually starts – you'll see.' She'd been giving the same assurances to Mrs Strayhorn and the other patients in the day-room, all of whom were complaining about their various aching joints.

'Oh, sure. And are you going to tell me to take two aspirin and call you in the morning?'

'That would be a good idea. Aspirin is actually a specific for inflammation.' She saw he wasn't really listening. 'I saw you earlier playing chess with Mrs Strayhorn. I'm glad to see you up at last.'

'I bet you are,' he said sourly.

'Does this mean . . . ?'

'It means I'm not lying in bed,' he said, then sighed. 'And yes, it means I have started thinking about your friend's murder. Why everybody seems to imagine I can make any difference is beyond me, but hey – I haven't got anything else to do.'

'Except get on to your feet again.'

'Very funny.'

Laura went over to the window, then paused, as she saw the wild bowings and scrapings of the trees and the dark scudding clouds that raced by, seemingly low enough to become entangled in the scrabbling branches that were clawing the sky. It was her first real glimpse of the approaching storm – she'd been busy until now – and she was startled by the beauty of it as well as the violence.

Near the hedge on the far side of the parking lot she saw a sudden movement and a flash of white. The wind had whipped back the dark cloak of a nurse standing there, talking to Nick the gardener. She clutched the cloak around her and was once again almost invisible against the dark hedge, except for her pale hair. Laura was pretty sure it was Clarissa Janacek, her blonde curls whipping around her face. That girl certainly gets around, she thought.

From Nick's posture, however, she didn't think Clarissa was getting around him. There was no mistaking the anger in the forward thrust of his head and the set of his broad shoulders. He suddenly threw his rake down and reached for Clarissa, but she was too quick for him and ducked away. They stood several feet apart, apparently shouting into the wind. The whole thing could have been a silent movie and as such would have needed no subtitles. It was the classic scene of boy loses girl.

'Quite a storm,' Gilliam said softly.

She jumped. She'd almost forgotten he was there. 'Yes,' she said, not sure which storm he meant. Out of the corner of her eye she saw Clarissa suddenly turn and walk away from Nick, while he stared after her, fists clenched. After a minute he kicked his rake, then his shoulders slumped, and he picked it up and walked away towards the front of the building.

'What actually made you change your mind?' Laura asked, curious and grateful at the same time.

'My old boss, Stryker.'

'The "good cop"?'

'Yeah. I talked to him on the phone. He said some things . . . well, he made me see that my attitude wasn't getting me anywhere. Was probably making me worse.'

'*I* told you that.'

'Yeah, well – let's say he was more persuasive.'

'What did he do – threaten to break your arms?'

Gilliam managed a smile. 'As a matter of fact, that's exactly what he threatened to do. He said it would mean someone else would have to wipe my ass for me.' He grimaced. 'The prospect was not attractive.'

'But—'

'Look – he made me see that I was behaving childishly, okay? Can't we just leave it at that? Do I have to go into a song and dance, and grovel and apologize?'

'No, of course not.' She didn't want to push him back into his old truculence and it didn't really matter anyway. The great thing was he had changed and she had an ally – if a rather reluctant one – in her mission to find out who had killed Julie. 'Let's get you on to the bed. There are a few simple exercises we can do to see what your muscle tone is like.' She lowered the bed and helped him into it, then raised it again, helped him to turn over on to his stomach, then pulled his pyjama trousers down.

'Hey!' he said, startled.

'We'll start with some massage to relax any spasm,' she said briskly and began gently to knead his back, buttocks, calves and thighs.

'Hey,' he said in a different tone. 'This is okay.'

'Wait for it,' she said in a menacing voice and continued

working her fingers into the knots of muscle beneath the skin where she could feel both the tension and the lack of tone. No wonder he was convinced he couldn't walk – in their present condition his legs wouldn't have held up a small boy.

'Tell me about Julie,' he said suddenly. His eyes had been closed and she'd thought he was half asleep. 'I know about her dead – what was she like when she was alive? Was she happy here?'

Damn, Laura thought. He's quick. 'At first she was very happy.'

'And then?'

She hesitated. 'Then she wasn't. She was worried about something, but she never said exactly what.'

He sighed. 'They never do.'

'She did say she was frightened, in her last letter.'

'Yes – Gabriel included it with the other stuff he sent over,' Gilliam said. 'Interesting, if inconclusive.'

'Look, I don't want you to get the wrong idea . . .'

'No,' he agreed. 'You want me to get the right idea. For example, how come you came to work for your uncle now when you never wanted to before?'

'Because . . .'

'Because you felt like playing detective,' he said uncompromisingly. 'The Sherlock Holmes syndrome, a common illness, usually found in people who read a lot of murder mysteries and have an inflated idea of their own abilities. These people are often found dead, I might add. Are you nuts?'

'No,' she said evenly, digging her fingers in with far more force than was necessary. 'Just damned annoyed.'

'Ouch!' He was silent for a moment. 'Do you like your uncle?'

Wrong-footed, she blurted out the truth. 'He looks just like my father.'

He propped himself up on his elbows and twisted to look at her. 'What?'

'They were twins,' she explained, embarrassed. 'My dad

died a few years ago, from overwork, mostly. When I look at Uncle Roger I see my father and . . .'

'And that makes things *really* difficult,' he finished for her.

'Yes.'

'Especially since you don't like him,' he went on.

'I never said that!'

'You didn't have to.'

'It's not that I don't *like* him. I admire and respect him.'

'Do you trust him?'

She gave this consideration. 'I . . . think so.'

'What makes you hesitate?'

'The way he trusts other people,' she said abruptly. 'The way he trusts *her*.'

'Jesus . . . there's a bit of venom. Who's "her"?'

'Mrs Cunningham. His personal assistant.'

'What's wrong with . . . oh, wait a minute. Blonde, very brisk, very efficient, smile only goes up as far as her nose?'

'Yes.'

He nodded at the head of the bed. 'She "dropped by" a few days after I was brought in. She made me fill out forms. Frustrated schoolteacher.'

'I rather thought more frustrated prison guard,' Laura said. 'I can see her pacing the walkways, slapping her thigh with a riding crop.'

'Dear me.' Gilliam grinned over his shoulder. 'And that makes you suspicious of your uncle by association?' he pressed on.

'I don't know. I don't understand my feelings about my uncle at all,' she said sadly. 'Yesterday I wondered if it was something about patients dying unexpectedly . . . and now I wonder if it was something about drugs.'

'Drugs?'

'Apparently Nurse Janacek said something to David . . . Dr Butler . . . about drugs "going missing". I don't know what it's about. Maybe it was that.'

He grunted. 'Drugs always go missing in hospitals. They

expect it, allow for it, overlook it, absorb the costs. Just like staplers and envelopes go missing in ordinary offices.'

'Then why would Julie be worried about it?'

'Maybe she wasn't. What was that about patients dying unexpectedly? Don't much like the sound of that.'

'Oh, it was only Mrs McAllister . . . my uncle refused to do an autopsy even though David and Owen wanted it. He said the cause of death was perfectly clear and he didn't want to stir up a fuss.'

'He's the man in charge.'

'Indeed, he is,' Laura said slowly. 'But I think she was going to leave some money to the clinic in her will.'

He grunted in exasperation. 'And you think your dear uncle might be doing this wholesale, do you? Bumping off patients for their money? Wouldn't this look a little bad for the clinic, people coming in to get better suddenly popping off? Families would enquire, people would ask questions. It's kind of self-defeating, wouldn't you say?'

She had to admit it sounded far-fetched when he put it like that. 'No . . . I don't know,' she said wretchedly. 'I can't help wondering even though I don't *want* to wonder.' She took a deep breath. 'Mrs Strayhorn said Mrs McAllister was talking about leaving Dr Butler some money too.' She might as well get all the poison out, she thought.

He shrugged. 'And you think *he* killed her? Now *that* I could believe,' he said with some relish. 'That would be just fine and dandy. If he's mentioned in this will, he would have a nice little motive. But that would be too easy.' He certainly was not a fan of David Butler. He winced as she hit a particularly sore place. 'Your friend's letters were . . . unusual.'

'Yes, well . . . Julie was . . . unusual.'

He looked back over his shoulder and raised an enquiring eyebrow. He looked quite satanic when he did that. 'Oh?'

'Well, to start with, she was a busybody.'

'Nosy, you mean. Literally?'

'Well, I don't mean she was a gossip, it wasn't like that at all.'

Gilliam was getting impatient. 'What, then? What was she *like*?'

'Well – she was a great *listener.* She'd get you to talk about yourself, which is always flattering, I suppose. And she'd developed this habit of "pretending" when she was an Army brat. Her family kept moving around, and she kept having to make new friends in new schools and then lose them and start all over again. As she grew up she tried to control it, but it kept slipping out. For example, she read all the film magazines and would trot out the most amazing facts in this funny way of hers, and strangers would automatically think she'd practically grown up with Richard Gere and been chief bridesmaid at all of Cher's weddings. It was harmless and kind of pathetic, really. Once you got to know her you paid no attention, because aside from that one weakness she was a really nice girl. She didn't *need* to do that to be liked. The worst of it was, I think she convinced herself some of the time.'

'She doesn't sound like the kind of person your uncle would have hired for Mountview.'

'Oh, I was talking about the way she was in college,' Laura explained. 'By the time I met her again in the Omaha Hospital she had pretty much grown out of it. She was an excellent physio, technically. And her way of listening so attentively did wonders with patients, who'd usually bored the pants off everyone else with their symptoms. That was one good thing about Julie – she was *never* bored. Absolutely everything fascinated her.'

'So she was the kind of person who gave the impression she knew more than she was telling, is that it?'

'I suppose so,' Laura acknowledged.

'Very dangerous,' Gilliam said. 'Very, very dangerous.'

'I see what you mean – it might be, at that.'

'And might she have been the kind of girl who would use that knowledge, if she had it? Say, to make a bit of money for herself? Ouch!'

Laura's fingers had suddenly dug into his calf. 'Are you asking if she was a blackmailer?'

'Yes, I am.'

'The answer is no. Money never interested her. And she didn't like to make people unhappy, that wasn't her goal at all. She liked everything to be . . . nice.'

'How very *Good Housekeeping* of her,' Gilliam grumbled. 'Ouch! That hurts, damnit!'

'Does it? Marvellous. You complained much later than I thought you would.' She grinned down at him. 'There's hope for you yet.'

'Oh, go to hell,' Gilliam muttered. 'By the way – if you're going into town, there are some things I'd like you to take to the sheriff for me.'

'Oh?'

He gestured towards the bedside table. 'There. List of things he needs to look up for me. And I have a couple of questions too.'

Laura went into the sheriff's office intending only to hand over Gilliam's notes, but she had to ask the questions first. They seemed odd to her, but he had his reasons, all of which he had spelled out to her. She had to admit he seemed to be very good at it all, and he knew so much about murder and murderers that it was quite unnerving. 'He said to ask you what happened to her hair? Julie had a long pony-tail, but in the pictures her hair is cut short,' Laura told Sheriff Gabriel.

'What?' He stared at her. She repeated the question and he grabbed up one of the crime scene photographs. 'Damn! I should have asked, I should have *noticed* that,' the sheriff railed, hitting the desk with the flat of his hand. George Putnam and Tilly Moss were watching him with wide eyes.

'Why?' Tilly asked in a reasonable voice. 'You didn't know her, you didn't know what she looked like when she was alive. Anyway, women change their hair like they change their shoes. I have to admit it wouldn't have occurred to me to ask people how she *normally* wore her hair. I mean, it's not the kind of thing people mention without being asked – they don't say, "I'm shocked at her death and by the way how did her hair look?" It just wouldn't have come up. So many girls wear short hair, so many wear weird hairstyles these days. You didn't know the girl – how were you supposed to know about her *hair*, for crying out loud?'

'The Shadowman always—' George began.

'It's not the god-damn Shadowman,' Gabriel shouted. George took a step back and even Tilly looked astonished at the vehemence of his response.

'Forrester didn't say anything about it and he *saw* her,' Sheriff Gabriel went on, determinedly trying to ignore his deputy, who seemed eager to impart something vital.

'Yes, but her hair was wet from the rain and she was lying on her back. He would have just assumed it was underneath her, wouldn't he?' Laura pointed out. That's what Gilliam had said.

'I suppose so,' he conceded. 'But *your* man came up with it right away.'

'Which is the great advantage of having him there,' she pointed out. 'He's getting people to talk about her casually, remembering her in a relaxed way. And one of them happened to mention her bouncy pony-tail . . . it was as simple as that.'

'Jesus wept,' the sheriff said in exasperation.

'Can I say something?' George asked.

'No!' the sheriff snapped.

'Yes,' Tilly said. 'Tell him what you found, George.'

George glanced triumphantly at the sheriff, who was now apparently too annoyed with himself to care. 'You know I've been looking stuff up, Matt. Old murders and stuff. That girl killed in 1967 was named Patricia Cox. She was fifteen, a high-school sophomore from a good family. She was a cheerleader, very pretty, with long red hair. And when she was found in the woods she'd been hit on the head, her throat had been cut *and* her hair had been chopped off.'

'You mean she was scalped?' Laura asked, appalled.

'No – not technically. Her hair was just cut right off short,' George said. He gestured at the photograph of Julie. She tried not to look at it. 'Like that. She wore a pony-tail, too.' He put a file folder down on the desk in front of the sheriff.

Sheriff Gabriel stared at him. 'This is ridiculous,' he said.

'There's more,' George stated.

'Oh, God,' the sheriff moaned. Laura still didn't see why he was so upset.

'All the animals that were being killed back then? The ones who were stolen and strung up and their throats cut?'

'Yes?' The sheriff's voice was dull.

'Their tails were cut off too,' George said smugly. 'At least, most of them were. And I checked with Ted Perry – you remember, he found his dog dead last month? Well, his dog's tail was definitely cut off. I called up and asked him.'

'You mean there have been animals killed recently too?' Laura asked, then she remembered Terry's dog.

'A few,' Matt admitted reluctantly. 'As George said, there was a lot of it in the sixties, but for some reason it's started up again in the past few months. But nobody talks about it, because they think it's the curse of the Shadowman. They think being touched by it is somehow shameful. Perry himself didn't tell us about his dog, we only heard about this indirectly, from the local vet. There might have been more. God, there might have been hundreds!'

'Oh, settle down,' Tilly said impatiently. 'You *would* have heard about it if it was happening a lot. I'm afraid you've got a problem, Matt. It *does* sound like we've got a local psycho loose here.'

'I don't want to believe that,' the sheriff said flatly.

'Of course you don't,' Tilly agreed soothingly. 'Nobody does. But it would explain a lot, Matt.'

'It could also cause a panic if it got out that we were looking for a madman,' the sheriff said.

So that was what worried him. Laura spoke up. 'Tell me, deputy – you were looking through the records for the sixties, right?'

'Yeah,' George answered. He was obviously full of himself for having done 'research' like a real detective.

'Did you notice anything about arson?' she asked.

George stared at her, caught off-balance. 'Arson?' His voice was puzzled.

'Yes. Mr Gilliam said "random unexplained fires".'

'Oh. I didn't notice,' George admitted. 'I was just looking for homicides.' He frowned. 'What have fires got to do with it?'

'It was something Mr Gilliam said to me when we were talking about the case so I could relay his thoughts to you. I happened to mention this Shadowman thing and he got quite excited.'

'Yeah.' George nodded. 'Me, too.'

'Well, Mr Gilliam has had a lot of time to read, lately,' she explained. 'One of the books he read was about the work the FBI has been doing on what they call "personality profiling" – especially in relation to serial killers.'

'Oh, no,' the sheriff said in despair. 'Oh, no. Are you telling me I've got a *serial* killer here?'

'No,' Laura replied. 'At least, not exactly. I mean these two killings are thirty years apart, but they might be related. According to Mr Gilliam, psychopathic killers often demonstrate three characteristics in childhood – animal torture, fire-raising and bedwetting.'

George looked uncomfortable. 'We'd never hear about the bedwetting,' he said.

'No,' she agreed. 'But the arson could be checked. You have a local fire department, don't you?'

'Sure. Mostly volunteer, though.'

'But someone runs it officially, looks after equipment and records and so on?'

'Oh, yeah – Bud Nolan. He's got four permanent guys

and everybody else turns out when needed,' George said. 'They blow a siren. Or they used to. I think they have beepers, now.'

'And he's kept records?'

'I'm sure he has,' Sheriff Gabriel said. 'He's quite a traditionalist. Very big on history and all that. We've got a local history society in town and he's secretary or something of that. He's bound to have some kind of records at the fire station.'

'Then Mr Gilliam suggested that somebody takes a look at them,' Laura said. 'It might help build up a picture for you.'

The sheriff looked at her glumly. 'He thinks we have a serial killer in town?'

'I have no idea if he thinks that or not,' she said. 'But it's interesting that a pattern that happened thirty years ago may be happening again. As if whatever was at work in the child has now broken out in the man. Or woman – although he said it's usually a man. Or it could be someone who moved away and recently moved back. I'm pig in the middle, here. You really ought to talk to Tom Gilliam yourself. He's read the latest books. It's his idea, not mine.'

'Not every kid who wets the bed turns out to be a psycho,' George said in a worried voice. She wondered if he'd had the problem himself as a child.

'No, of course not. But according to Mr Gilliam, when you get all three of those things, plus – say – a dysfunctional family, deprivation, disfigurement, low IQ or a very high IQ, both of which can lead to social isolation, the pressure builds up.' She was feeling quite the detective, although she was only relaying this information, which was all new to her, to the sheriff and his staff.

'What about genetics?' the sheriff asked. 'Haven't I been reading in the newspapers lately that they've discovered some kind of gene for evil? Or, at least, for aggression? Something like that?'

'I don't know anything about it, myself,' Laura admitted

frankly. 'Mr Gilliam has had the chance – not that he wanted it – to read up on just about all the latest theories. He suggested you check out the pattern of the murder with somebody called Vicap?'

'It's not a some*body*, it's a some*thing*,' Sheriff Gabriel said. 'VICAP – Violent Criminals Apprehension Program – a way of recognizing serial criminals by comparing similar murders all over the country. Many of these guys roam. I've already sent off details of this murder because it seemed so random and unnecessarily brutal. Now I can update that with the haircutting thing. We didn't get a match before.'

'Maybe because this old murder wasn't in their database,' George pointed out.

Matt nodded. 'I'd better send that one off too.'

'Anyway, those are all the things he asked me to ask you,' Laura said. 'About the hair, about the fires and about the Shadowman.'

'Hah!' George said.

'Why was he so interested in the Shadowman?' the sheriff asked.

'He said it was possible that someone was using the legend as a cover-up. Copy-catting, he called it.'

'But that would mean someone with local knowledge.'

'Well, *I* know about the Shadowman and I'm not exactly local,' Laura pointed out. 'I've heard all about it from several people and I've only been here a little while.'

'So which does he think it is, a local psycho, a roving serial killer, or a copy-cat?' asked the sheriff.

She shrugged. 'I guess you really have to check out the background. If it's a psychopathic killer who's local it's possible he would have shown a pattern before now – maybe other attacks that were unsuccessful as murders but went down as odd incidents, plus the fires, and any other odd ritualistic things that might have happened between that old murder and this new one. A pattern will be there if you look for it. At least, Mr Gilliam thinks it will. If it's somebody who's just heard the story of the Shadowman and decided to make his murder *look* like the work of some spook, then I guess the pattern won't be there.'

'I'll go see Bud Nolan over at the firehouse,' George said eagerly. And he went out, looking like a gun dog on the scent.

Tilly spoke up. 'George did good, Matt. He picked up the similarities between the two murders. And that stuff about the animals. You have to give him that.'

'Oh, I do,' Matt agreed, as he reached for the folder George had left for him. 'And I'm grateful to you and Mr Gilliam,' he said to Laura. 'The trouble is – where do I start looking for a Shadowman? And what happens when the media get hold of it? This town could go crazy, Tilly. It's happened before. And we've got the Howl coming up, too.'

'What *is* the Howl?' Laura asked. 'The nurses keep talking about it.'

'It's our local version of Hallowe'en,' the sheriff explained. 'We have a carnival and people play practical jokes on one another. It's a way of letting off steam after the end of the tourist season. Sometimes it gets out of hand.' He turned to look at Tilly Moss. 'This kind of thing brings out the worst in people. Everybody gets scared. People start looking sideways at each other. Old feuds suddenly escalate and accusations are made. Innocent people get pushed around, things are misconstrued, acted upon without thought . . . And if the media get hold of it . . . I hate to think.'

'I'm sorry,' Laura said. He looked so upset.

He glanced at her. 'Not your fault, Miss Brandon.'

'But if Mr Gilliam is right . . .' she began.

'I don't think he is,' the sheriff said. 'But I have to look into the possibility, just the same. Give him my thanks. And thanks for his mobile number. Tell him I'll be in touch later on.'

She stood up, feeling suddenly superfluous. If this was going to be the answer – that some local psycho or a serial killer murdered Julie – then the clinic was free of blame. While she didn't very much like the idea of a madman running around maiming animals and setting fires and killing people, she felt a rush of relief. It had nothing to do with Uncle Roger. And nothing to do with her, either. Nothing at all.

Gilliam stared at the ceiling, exhausted by his efforts of the day. It had been too much too soon. But it had produced some interesting insights. As he had mixed with the other patients in the pursuit of his so-called investigation, it meant he'd got a lot of gratuitous information – such as details of other people's operations, their opinions on the stock market and the fact that Dr Jenks was a saint, Dr Forrester was charming and Dr Butler was 'dating' Ms Brandon.

Why the hell that last item should annoy him he didn't know, but he supposed it had something to do with male competition. He resented Butler – his looks, his charm, his intelligence.

His legs.

He found himself glancing over at Laura Brandon's apartment, the lights streakily visible through the rain that ran down his window. What he felt about Butler had nothing to do with what he was supposed to be doing, which was somehow spontaneously coming up with some brilliant solution to the death of Julie Zalinsky.

He now had *another* angle to consider, the kind of thing the sheriff had been looking for in the first place. And it had come from Laura herself.

According to her, the dead girl had been a 'busybody'. Which meant that in her way she'd led a very dangerous life.

And that could be the reason for its being a short one.

On the face of it, that was the first indication he'd got of a possible motive emanating from the clinic itself. God knew, there wasn't much forensic evidence, thanks to the storm – probably very like the one raging outside now – which had washed away any physical clues the killer might have left behind. He or she. *That* question was still open, too. It doesn't take brute strength to hit someone on the head from behind with a rock and to cut a throat once the victim was down.

Just implacable intent.

Or madness.

Laura had dropped by briefly to report that, yes, there *had* been a spate of small fires in the late sixties, right around the time another girl had been killed in the woods in more or less the same way as Julie Zalinsky. And there had been animal mutilations then, too. But they had stopped in 1974. There was nothing after that until about six years ago, just about the time the Mountview Clinic had opened its doors.

Since then there had been a few random fires and, apparently, some animal disappearances and/or mutilations, in particular the death of a dog a few weeks before Julie Zalinsky's murder. Head bashed in, throat cut and tail cut off. In both human killings, the old one thirty years before and Julie's, the victims had been brained with something heavy, had their throats cut and their pony-tails cut off.

It was consistent all right.

Very consistent.

Too consistent?

The catechism, according to Nellie Strayhorn, was as follows:

To begin at the top, Forrester was a silver-tongued devil. She seemed to admire rogues if they had style, dismiss good men if they had none. Still, it was a fair description, even if it left out the fact that Forrester was also a very able administrator and an innovative planner. Mountview might look from the outside like a little piece of the past, but behind the panelling there were some very sophisticated systems indeed. Which meant Forrester himself probably had a complicated and hidden mechanism too. Smooth on the outside, but what went on beneath the surface? Nothing showed. Except, perhaps, to that assistant of his, Milly Cunningham.

Nellie Strayhorn called her 'Iron-Panties'. To a man with

a discerning eye, and Gilliam thought he might still include himself in that category, Mrs Cunningham was intriguing. Her figure and facial bone structure were flawless, but she hid them behind severe clothes, glasses and manner. While Forrester might have been responsible for the guts of Mountview, it was his assistant who had supervised the décor. The woman had taste, but didn't care to show it except in her work. And, of course, in her devotion to Forrester. They had worked together for many years. Her husband, an incurable mental case according to Nellie, had apparently died in an asylum five years ago. She and Forrester had not married, although both were free.

Why not?

According to dear old Nellie, it was because Forrester had a roving eye and didn't want to be tied down. Had his roving eye fallen on Julie Zalinsky? There was no evidence of it, but apparently Forrester was an old hand at discretion. And the girl had lived alone in the staff quarters here at the clinic, while Milly Cunningham lived in town. Milly often stayed over, quite openly, but what about the nights she hadn't stayed?

Then there was Butler. Gilliam would dearly have loved to pin the murder on the boy wonder, but it looked unlikely. Grudgingly, he had to admit that the other patients' opinions seemed justified – Butler was an effective physician. He'd trained out west and then come east, contrary to the prevalent westward slide that seemed to be tipping most of America into California. Why had he done that? According to Forrester's records, which the sheriff had carefully noted, Butler's references were impeccable – he'd scored extraordinarily high marks in medical school, had served brilliant internships and residencies. He was an excellent example of what hard work and devotion could produce, and Gilliam couldn't deny it. Nor could he deny having an impulse to punch Butler in the mouth every time he saw him, but that had little to do with the case in hand. The only odd thing about Butler was why he would stick himself in a small clinic in the mid-west instead of pursuing a high-profile career. Laura had said it was because his ambition was to be a small-town family doctor and maybe that was true. Not everybody wanted to be a high-flyer. And sometimes those who wanted to be high-flyers came down very hard. He ought to know.

The nurses? There were a lot of them, but of them all he favoured Miss Hasker as a candidate. She was strong, she had a position to lose and she'd been alone during the relevant time. She had also, according to Nellie Strayhorn, been fond of Julie Zalinsky and had changed considerably since the girl's death. Had something gone wrong between them? Had Julie found out something about the older woman? Was it grief, or guilt?

Higgins the groundsman? Michaels the porter and odd-job man?

Both local men, but Michaels, being older and therefore a possible candidate for the earlier murder in 1967, was the more likely candidate. According to Gabriel's notes, he was a 'weasel', always ready to take advantage of a situation or an opportunity to promote a little ready cash. Did he have something to hide? Had he conceived a passion for Julie? Was he the person responsible for the earlier murder, arson and animal mutilations – or just a very unpleasant man?

Nick Higgins he had only glimpsed through the window, working on the flowerbeds and lawn. He could see he was a handsome man, too young to be responsible for the crimes of the past, but not too young to have heard about them while growing up. According to Gabriel's notes he had a juvenile record for assault, which could have been adolescent hijinks, or an indication of a deeper streak of violence. He was apparently a bright boy trapped by a family situation, a father who was an alcoholic and a mother who was an invalid, but he was hard-working and devoted to them both. He could have attended university on a scholarship, but was apparently content to save up in order to go to forestry school and to ensure that his parents could be properly supported while he was there.

A good boy, then. And good boys often snapped under the pressure of staying good boys. Certainly Higgins was a possibility.

He didn't know what to do.

In fact, he couldn't *do* anything.

Maybe, he thought bitterly, he should try taking up cocaine, like Sherlock Holmes, or raising orchids like Nero Wolfe. One thing was certain – he wasn't much good the way he was.

And sleep would not come.

# THIRTEEN

THE SIRENS WOKE LAURA.

At first, she merely turned her head on the pillow, so accustomed was she still to the mechanical street cries of city nights. But, as they grew closer and louder, something reminded me her she was no longer in the city. She opened her eyes.

Solomon's eager shape was on the bedroom window-sill, ears forward, whiskers akimbo and fur bristling – outlined by flashing red lights from beyond the hedge.

She squinted towards the alarm clock. Two a.m.? What on earth was an ambulance doing here? Mountview didn't take emergencies. Sleepy and bewildered, she threw back the covers and staggered over to the window, where all sleepiness immediately left her. It wasn't an ambulance.

It was a fire engine.

And another was coming up the drive.

She grabbed a pair of jeans and a sweat-shirt, pulling them on over her nightgown. Running down the stairs she collided with a shadowy figure that knocked her violently to the ground and ran on into the darkness.

'Hey!' she shouted. 'What's going on?'

But the runner didn't answer. Maybe it was Michaels, going to the shed to get some fire-fighting equipment or something. Although what would Michaels be doing there at night? Scrambling to her feet she ran on towards the clinic. Lights were on in all the windows, but none of them flickered with an ominous red. She pushed through the opening in the hedge and ran across the gravel and around to the wide-open front doors. There she nearly collided with another figure – this time a fireman. When he turned she recognized Mr Pugh, the town mortician. He looked considerably different in his hastily donned uniform, which was far more human and haphazard than his usual dark-suited austerity.

The reception area was full of people milling around and talking in loud voices. They called across the open space to one another, answering their own echoes in the confusion. Nurses and firemen rushed to and fro, shepherding patients or wheeling them to safety. It was not panic, but it was close to it.

There was a faint scent of smoke in the air, but no visible sign of it. Laura pitched in where she could, the main aim obviously being to get the patients out of the building as quickly and painlessly as possible. As the smell of smoke became stronger, some of them began to show fear, but still panic didn't break out. This was mostly because of Owen Jenks. White-faced and tight-lipped, as if in a barely controlled fury, he stood on top of the reception desk shouting directions in a loud, angry voice that penetrated to every corner. It was the kind of voice one obeyed now and questioned later, quite unlike his usual mild and diffident tones.

'Put that bed out on the drive, there are wooden ramps in the cupboard beside the elevator. Line the chairs up at the edge of the lawn. Laura, bring some more blankets from the linen store by the pool.' And so on.

If the firemen hadn't been there, it would all have been accomplished more easily, as the Mountview staff were very efficient and trained in evacuation techniques. But the firemen were so kind and helpful they got in everyone's way.

Eventually all the patients were safe. Everyone stood shivering, staring up at the beautiful façade of the clinic, as if waiting for a *son et lumière* show to begin. The rain had long since stopped and the wind had died down, but it was bitterly cold – the storm had been the forerunner of a decline in the weather. Winter was definitely here.

From inside could be heard shouts and noises, and – oddly – occasional laughter. Having satisfied themselves that everyone was out of the building, the volunteer firemen had completely disappeared, presumably to join their professional companions in fighting the invisible fire. Light spilled out of the open front doors and glowed behind every window. Faint tendrils of smoke could now be seen curling lazily across the reception hall, like blind snakes heavy with sleep.

'Kind of disappointing, isn't it?' said a voice at her elbow and she jumped. It was Tom Gilliam, who with some effort had propelled his wheelchair across the grass to her side.

'What?'

'Well, getting all dressed up like this and then – not even a flicker or a spark to be seen.'

The other patients were staying lined up in a semicircle; a few wheelchairs and odd chairs grabbed up for those who had been able to walk out. Everyone was clutching blankets around themselves. Some were beginning to talk in whispers, but everyone's eyes were fixed on the blank face of Mountview. Occasionally a fireman would be seen rushing across the reception hall, waving an axe or his arms, shouting incomprehensibly.

'I can't say I find it disappointing,' Laura said. 'And I'm sure Uncle Roger doesn't either. Insurance money couldn't replace this building, not ever.'

'Hm.' Gilliam seemed unconvinced. 'You know, in some ways this is like watching an old movie. Those are definitely the Keystone firemen.'

She couldn't suppress a giggle.

'Well, is it a fire or isn't it?' came Mr Cobbold's irritable voice out of the darkness. 'I'm freezing my god-damn ass off out here.'

A woman began to cry softly. Turning, Laura was amazed to see it was Mrs Strayhorn, looking ghastly. She went over and knelt beside her wheelchair, feeling the grass stiff and frosty under her knees. 'Don't worry – I'm sure we'll soon be back inside.'

'Don't pay me no mind,' the old woman said. 'Don't know what I'm snivelling about, anyway.' She tried to wipe the tears away with the back of her hand. 'Don't like being woken up and snatched about by people I don't even know, pushed out here like an old parcel to freeze to death.'

'Here,' came Gilliam's voice and a hand thrust a blanket past Laura. 'They gave me more than I need.'

Mrs Strayhorn was too cold and upset to argue. 'You're a good boy,' she snuffled, as Laura tucked the additional blanket around her.

'Shh,' Gilliam said. 'I don't want it to get around.'

'Sassy cuss,' Mrs Strayhorn said, but she was smiling a little, now.

'I wonder—' Gilliam started to say, but stopped as a figure in a dark-blue bathrobe appeared in the open doorway and raised its arms to cup a hand on either side of its mouth.

In the stillness of the night, Roger Forrester's voice rang thin and clear over the moat of gravel to the shadowed figures on the lawn. 'It's all over,' he said. 'Some rags and cleaning fluid had started to burn in a basement storage area, setting off the automatic alarms which were connected directly to the fire station in town. The firemen didn't even need hoses – they put it out with extinguishers. I'm sorry for keeping you waiting out here in the cold, but the firemen are making sure the fire hasn't spread behind the walls or under the floorboards. All we've lost is some cleaning equipment, which we can easily replace, and a few patient records, which unfortunately we can't. However, I shall charge the insurance company for a new operating theatre at least.'

There was a flurry of relieved laughter.

'I'm very sorry you've been so disturbed – we'll make it up to you somehow.'

'How about taking it off the bill?' came a suggestion from one of the beds.

Uncle Roger smiled, waved and disappeared back inside. A few moments later the fire chief turned up and told them they could all come back in. Laura helped the nurses get the patients back to their rooms and settled down, distributing hot drinks, extra blankets and heat packs to those who had been chilled. All the while she was soothing the patients her mind was with her uncle. Though he'd smiled and joked, she'd seen the set of his shoulders and, when at last she went down to his apartment, she found out why.

'Set deliberately,' he told her grimly.

'Again.' Sheriff Gabriel spoke laconically from the sofa. Apparently he'd arrived just after the firemen, and was sitting there with his hat in one hand and a cup of coffee in the other. Across from him, similarly equipped with coffee but without the hat, sat David Butler and Owen Jenks. She hadn't seen David during the evacuation and had assumed he was helping to fight the blaze, such as it had been. But he didn't look very smoke-stained.

'Again?' she said in amazement. 'You mean it's happened before?'

'Several times,' her uncle said wearily. 'I really thought it was over, though.'

'I don't understand,' she said, looking from one face to the other. From David's and Owen's expressions, neither did they.

'Before your uncle bought this place it was falling apart and had the reputation of being "haunted",' the sheriff explained. 'I knew the lights and noises people reported were really from the occasional bunch of teenagers on a scare-raid, or tramps dossing down – the signs were pretty clear. There was one tramp in particular who used it regularly every year around this time, passing through on his way south. When he found the construction crews here, he began to cause some trouble, hoping to scare them off. Fires, vandalizing, thieving – that kind of thing. Spite, mostly. I caught him and put the fear of God into him, and we didn't have any more trouble. At least, not that year. The next year he tried it all over again. The reconstruction was nearly complete by then and he set one really nasty little fire, then disappeared. After that, though – nothing. I figured he'd given up, accepted the situation. Apparently not.'

'It *has* been several years, Sheriff,' Roger said.

'True,' the sheriff conceded. 'But it's the same pattern and the same time of year. Maybe he's been in jail somewhere in between.'

'Oh – I never thought of that,' Roger admitted. 'I suppose that could be it.'

'Somebody knocked me down when I was coming over here,' Laura said. 'He ran off into the woods.'

The sheriff sat up. 'Did you get a look at him?'

'No – but he was outlined against the lights of the clinic,' she said. 'He was bulky – and he smelled funny.'

'Of what?'

She thought back. 'I can't really say.'

'Kerosene? Something like that?' Matt suggested.

'No. A foxy kind of smell, dirty, sweaty. Not very nice. And something else – some kind of herby smell, sort of bitter and sharp at the same time. I'm sorry, I can't really place it.'

'Are you going to look for him?' Roger asked.

The sheriff shook his head. 'He'll be long gone by now, seeing as his attempt at arson didn't exactly result in a spectacular blaze. We'll try and pick up his trail in the morning.' He finished his coffee and stood up. 'You all had best get some sleep while you can.'

After the sheriff had gone, Roger sank down on the sofa. 'My God,' he said. 'People could have died. And he tells me to get some sleep.'

'Well, he couldn't do much in the dark,' Owen said in a reasonable voice.

'The man's a fool.' Roger was angry. 'He's a hick, totally incompetent. Why they made him sheriff I'll never know.'

'Mr Gilliam seems to think he's good,' Laura put in thoughtfully.

'Then Mr Gilliam's a fool too,' Roger said in disgust. 'I

wish I'd never chosen this place, never come to this damn town. Never even had the idea that—'

'Now, Uncle Roger, calm down,' Laura soothed. She wasn't accustomed to seeing him anything other than neat, cool and controlled. Now his hair stuck up all over his head, his eyes were bleary and his hands were shaking. They were also filthy. 'You have a shower and go to bed. You'll feel a lot better in the morning.'

'Don't patronize me,' he snapped.

Owen leaped to her defence. 'She's not, she's talking good sense, which is more than you are, sir. The excitement's over and no real harm has been done. Isn't that the main thing?'

'I suppose so,' Roger grumbled, looking down at the carpet and the remnants of his slippers. He must have been playing fireman, Laura thought, for they were ragged and as filthy as his hands. 'But it must have upset the patients—'

'I'm just on my way up to make sure that isn't so,' David said, putting down his empty coffee cup and standing up. 'Now that the nurses have got them bedded down, Owen and I shall pass among them with soothing words and benign pats—'

'They're probably all back asleep by now,' Laura said. 'We could have used you half an hour ago.'

'Do I detect reproach?' he asked, amused.

'No.' She sighed. 'Just weariness. Where *were* you earlier, by the way? When we were trying to get them *out*?'

'Doing my nails.' He looked at her, puzzled. 'I was there, pushing and prodding with the rest of them. I saw *you*.'

'Oh.'

Roger stood up too. 'Good-night,' he said morosely. He was half-way to his bedroom when the office door burst open and Milly Cunningham came in, her hair unkempt and her eyes wide. 'My God, is everything all right? I just heard—'

'The whole place nearly went up in flames,' Roger said lugubriously. There had been a subtle but instantaneous change in him the minute Milly had appeared. Before, he'd seemed defeated. Now he had an audience – and a story to tell.

David, Owen and Laura went out.

'The sirens were an hour ago.' Laura's voice was thoughtful. 'I wonder what took her so long to get here?'

'Maybe she walked,' David suggested, not much interested.

'Maybe,' she said slowly. It did seem odd, though. Especially since Milly was supposedly so devoted to Uncle Roger.

Wasn't she?

The next morning was bitterly cold and grey, the sky low and heavy with probable snow. The air felt expectant and in a way resigned to what lay ahead.

A flexing of meteorological muscle.

One of the kitchen workers, shivering, came out with a large plastic bag of garbage for the incinerator. He scuttled across the paved area behind the annexe, in a hurry to return to the steamy kitchen where a hot cup of coffee awaited him. After thrusting the plastic bag into the malodorous chute he turned back. His eye caught and held on an object lying on the frost-rimed grass.

It was a woman's handbag.

He darted across and picked it up. After a quick search inside he carried it back to the kitchen. 'Hey, look at this,' he announced. 'It's Janacek's.' A leer twisted his mouth. 'I wonder what she'll give me as a reward?'

Nurse Janacek was due on duty at eight-thirty, but nine o'clock came and went, and she did not report. Then someone noticed that her car was still in the parking lot and the ground beneath it was dry. It had been there all night.

An hour later, the sheriff and his men found Clarissa Janacek in the woods. Her golden hair was sparkling with frosty dew and her beautiful blue eyes were wide open to the black tracery of branches overhead. In the cupped palms of her outflung hands two small puddles of rain had collected and were beginning to freeze, clear and bright.

# FOURTEEN

EVERYTHING CHANGED.

Suddenly the air seemed charged with electricity as people looked at one another and stared and wondered. One girl murdered was a shock. Two girls murdered in the same place and in the same way was a good deal more. Laura wondered what the sheriff was doing now.

Her uncle Roger was pacing up and down in front of his office fire when she came in answer to his summons. Milly Cunningham sat huddled in a corner of the sofa, looking uneasy without a notebook in her lap. She was watching Roger through half-lowered lashes, and her hands twisted and turned in her lap.

'Ah, Laura. They've had to send Nurse Goodfellow home, she went entirely to pieces when she heard. Will you go up and lend a hand until we can get an agency nurse over?'

'Of course. The patients must be pretty upset.'

'Upset?' Uncle Roger gave a sour laugh. 'They're loving it! Oh, they're all making the proper protestations of shock and horror, of course, but then that's easy when you're safely tucked up in bed and a maniac is loose outside.'

Laura felt a cold finger slide down her spine. 'Is that what the sheriff thinks?'

'What else is there to think? First Julie, now Clarissa, both dragged into the woods and murdered. My God – and to think I came here because I thought it would be peaceful!'

And to think I came here because I thought something

was wrong, Laura thought, as she left the room. It seemed she was right. She felt a shiver: someone walking over her grave.

Upstairs, she could see what her uncle meant. Those in rear-facing rooms almost all had company, for patients ambulatory enough to cross the hall had done so with alacrity, so as not to miss a single thing. If the owner of the lucky room was bedridden, the window-side visitors would relay each event as it happened: the arrival of Sheriff Gabriel and his men, the search, the finding of the body (inferred) and the arrival of the forensic experts from the State Police. Now they were waiting for the Big Event – the Removal of the Body.

Those patients bedridden in front-facing rooms had to be content with shouting out questions or waiting for the latest from the nurses or auxiliaries. There were rumours that Michaels was charging for information. She saw him at various times, either hanging around the police outside, or darting in and out of the immobilized patients' rooms, looking both furtive and gleeful. He seemed happier than she had ever seen him.

The patients' interest was ghoulish, it was morbid, but it was understandable.

There was no more malice in it than there was in Solomon's equally avid observation from the apartment windows. Ears forward and whiskers quivering at the sight of the red and blue lights atop the sheriff's car, she had left him happily overseeing the entire operation. His taut little shoulders seemed to say 'this reminds me of home'.

In the nursing office, Kay had her back turned firmly to the window as she sat smoking and drinking coffee.

'Uncle Roger said you could use some help up here,' Laura said as she came in.

Kay snorted. 'You must be joking. They're all as quiet as mice. I haven't even had to carry a bedpan in the past two hours, except for the six who can't get across the hall to watch the fun. It certainly beats television for keeping them occupied.' The hand holding her cigarette shook and the long ash fell off on to the desk blotter.

'I hear Goodfellow had to go home,' Laura commented, sitting down.

'Well, you know she worshipped Clarissa,' Kay said gruffly. 'She kept saying if only she'd gone home with her it wouldn't have happened. I told her if she had, there might have been two of them out there in the woods.'

'Why didn't she? Go home with her, I mean? They share a place in town, don't they?'

'She had a date who picked her up here last night and dropped her off here this morning.'

'Oh.' Laura flushed slightly. 'I didn't realize she had anyone like that.'

'Like what?'

'Well . . . serious. To be honest, I thought perhaps she and Clarissa were . . . you know. *Very* close.'

Kay met the veiled suggestion with aplomb. 'Oh, no. It was men all the way with both of them. And I don't think either of them had to be serious to make a night of it,' Kay observed caustically. She started to reach for her coffee cup but knocked it over as one of the buzzers on the panel went, startling her. 'Oh, damn! What next?' she cried, standing up and snatching some files out of the path of the spreading liquid.

Laura was staring at the panel. 'I didn't know anyone was in Mrs McAllister's room.'

'There isn't, officially – but it's a good viewpoint. Hand me some of those paper towels, will you?'

Laura did and left her to clear up the mess. She went down the hall, fully expecting to discover the ghost of Mrs McAllister – but finding, instead, Tom Gilliam in his wheelchair, staring out of the window like all the rest. The set of his shoulders was exactly like Solomon's. When he turned, she was almost disappointed to discover his moustache was not quivering like Solomon's as well.

'Have you seen Sheriff Gabriel?' he demanded, when he saw who it was.

'No. Should I have?'

'Damn.'

'Sorry. Did you want to confess or what?'

'Nobody will tell me anything. Who was killed?'

'Nurse Janacek.'

'Ah. The beautiful blonde. How? The same way as Julie Zalinsky?'

'I don't know.'

'Damn,' he said again, under his breath. 'How about wheeling me out there?'

'Absolutely not. We're two nurses short and I've got to help out.'

'*Two*?'

'One of the other nurses was a friend of Clarissa's. She was so upset they had to send her home.'

'Which one was that?'

'Nurse Goodfellow.'

'Goodfellow. Small, dark, very soft voice?'

'That's right.'

'The Queen of Spain and the monkey.' He nodded.

'What?'

'Oh, you see that sometimes. Beautiful girl with a homely friend. The Queen of Spain used to walk around with a monkey so she'd look more beautiful by comparison.' He leaned forward. 'That must be Sheriff Gabriel now. Go tell him to come up here.'

'I will not. For one thing I'm not a messenger girl and for another he has far too much to do to just—'

She stopped as he leaned forward and impatiently pushed up the window, causing his wheelchair to roll back in reaction. With a muttered curse he pulled himself forward again and shouted, 'Hey! Sheriff! Up here!'

'That's quite enough,' Laura said furiously and slammed the window shut. Through the glass she saw Matt Gabriel turn and look up at the clinic, then shrug and turn away. She glared down at Gilliam, who glared back. 'The last thing we need is to have your case complicated by pneumonia.'

'Oh, shut up,' he said sulkily. 'Look, he's bound to be inside questioning everybody sooner or later. Now I can talk to him face to face. Tell him to come up here first.'

'I will not.'

He regarded her speculatively for a moment, then grinned. 'Sure you will. You want me to get better, don't you?'

'What's that got to do with it?'

'Everything. There's a fresh murder to work on. I must say, you go to extreme lengths to motivate your patients.'

Infuriated, as usual, she glared at him, then marched towards the door. Half-way out, she turned. 'That moustache is pathetic,' she announced. 'You should shave it off. My cat has better whiskers than you do.'

She could hear him laughing all the way down the hall.

Later that afternoon, when she entered the medical library, where Matt Gabriel had been conducting interviews, she could see that he was weary. She sat down gingerly in the seat he indicated. It had grown dark outside and the table lamps that softly lit the room were reflected in the black mirrors of the many-paned windows. There, too, she saw herself; pale-faced, glimmering, fragmented.

'This is a routine interview, Miss Brandon,' the sheriff said in a dull voice. 'We're taping it because Seth, my deputy, can't take shorthand and neither can I. Do you have any objection to that?'

'No.'

'Good. As you know, this is a murder investigation. The fact that I've called you in here doesn't mean I suspect you in any way. I'm just trying to set up a timetable for last night so as to pin-point, if possible, Miss Janacek's movements prior to her death. And to see if anyone noticed anything unusual. Did you?'

'You mean *aside* from somebody setting the place on fire?'

He sighed. 'Let's start with an outline of your afternoon and evening. Yesterday afternoon and evening.' He leaned back in the leather chair, which creaked a little under his weight. Then he reached for and lit a pipe, still watching her through the smoke of his slow exhalation.

She cleared her throat. 'Well – I had treatments all afternoon. Mr Schultz from two until three, Mr Pollard from three until three-thirty – he's new, it was just an assessment.'

'Yes. Go on.'

'Then I had a break. I went down to the staff dining-room for a coffee and a Danish pastry. They're very good here.'

'I know. I had some. Then what?'

'Well, then I had to go up to Mr Gilliam's room.'

'For a visit?'

'Oh, no. I had hoped to start him on pool work, but I had to put it off until today.'

'Why was that?'

She flushed. 'Well, first of all there was no rush about it. And – I had a date, I had to get into town before the shops shut to get some things and I had to see you.'

'What things?'

'Food, mainly. I'd asked Dr Butler to come across for dinner last night and I didn't have anything in the house.'

'So you put Gilliam off. What did he think about that?'

'He didn't mind. We talked for a bit and I gave him some exercises to start his muscles remembering.'

'Remembering?' he asked, then waved his hand as she opened her mouth to explain. 'Never mind, you talked, he did his knee-bends or whatever like a good boy – and then you went into town?'

'Yes, you know I did. I came to see you.' She glanced over at the deputy who was watching her with a blank face. The tape machine turned slowly, silently.

'And did you see Miss Janacek any time during the afternoon, either before you left or after you returned?'

'I saw her in the morning,' she said carefully.

'But not in the afternoon?' His eyes narrowed. 'Well?'

'I'm . . . not sure.'

'What do you mean?'

'Well . . . when I was talking with Mr Gilliam I thought I saw her outside for a moment. But she was some distance away and it was—'

'What time was this?'

'It must have been just before four. The storm had begun to blow up. That's why I'm not sure because the light outside had a funny sort of yellowish tinge . . . you know how it gets before . . . and she . . . whoever it was . . . had a dark cloak with a hood. A nurse's cape – some of the girls have started wearing them again.'

'So it could have been any nurse?'

'Any *blonde* nurse,' she corrected him. 'Some of her hair blew out from under the hood.'

'I see.' The sheriff made a note on the pad in front of him, despite the slow reeling of the tape with which he could, if necessary, check every word. 'And what was this nurse doing?'

She swallowed. 'Talking to Higgins.'

The sheriff looked up. 'Nick Higgins the groundsman?'

She nodded.

'That's all? Just talking?'

'Yes. Well. Yes.'

'Or were they arguing, maybe?'

'I don't know. The wind – I couldn't see—'

'You mean you couldn't hear.'

'No, I meant I couldn't *see*,' she repeated. 'Their faces. I couldn't see their expressions. They *were* shouting, you could tell that by the way they were standing. You sort of thrust your head forward when you're shouting, you know.'

'Do you?'

'Well, yes. It has to do with the diaphragm and—' She stopped. 'Anyway, you do. And they were. But since I couldn't see their faces, I didn't know whether they were shouting angrily, or laughing, or just . . . shouting. Into the wind. I mean, either way, the wind was . . . they'd have *had* to shout.' She trailed off lamely under his amused expression.

'I see. And that's the last time you saw her?'

'If it was Clarissa, yes.'

'Talking to Higgins.'

'Yes.' She felt nervous, suddenly. What if she was getting Nick into trouble? Frankly, she didn't care who killed Clarissa, unless it turned out to be the one who killed Julie.

'And did Dr Butler come over to dinner last night?'

'Yes, he did.'

'And what time did he arrive?'

'I don't know, exactly. It was some time between seven-thirty and eight. I'd noticed Dr Jenks's car drive up about seven and it was a bit after that when David finally appeared. They had to hand over duty, you see.'

'Hand over?'

'That's right. They take turns doing night duty, not that it's very difficult. There are very rarely any problems that the nurses can't handle. It's really just a matter of sleeping arrangements. The one who's "on" sleeps over at the clinic itself, the other one sleeps at their flat. There's nobody in the clinic who could be classed as a worry at the moment, except maybe Mr Cobbold and Mrs Armstrong. But there has to be a doctor on duty all the time, for the record. My uncle hasn't really been an active medical practitioner for some years, now. He's qualified, of course,' she put in hurriedly, in case Gabriel misunderstood. 'It's just that most of our cases are convalescent. Even so, David had to talk with Owen, let him know of any problems or difficulties that might arise. Anyway, they could have beeped David if they particularly needed him to do emergency surgery or something. But, of course, they didn't.'

'Didn't what?'

'Beep him. There was no need.'

'All right. Let me see if I've got this straight. You came back from town about . . . ?'

'About a quarter to six.'

'Okay. And you did what?'

'Started the first part of the meal cooking, had a shower, dressed and got the rest of the meal ready. It was a little dried out, actually, because when I saw Owen's car come back I thought David would only be a few minutes.'

'But it was nearly an hour?'

'Yes. I guess Owen had to settle himself first, then David had to shower . . . that kind of stuff.'

'What kind of stuff?'

She was sightly exasperated. 'You know – all the little things that seem to happen when you're trying to hurry.'

'Oh, *that* kind of stuff. Lose one sock under the bed, catch your pocket on the doorknob . . .'

'That's it.'

'And during the time you were getting the dinner ready you heard or saw nothing unusual outside?'

'No. It was dark by then and the wind—'

Matt sighed heavily. 'I know. That's what everyone says.'

'Well, that's the way it was.'

'Uh-huh. So you were alone from five-forty-five until some time after seven and you didn't hear or see anything unusual. Is that it?'

'That's it.'

The sheriff thought this over. 'And Butler left you – when?'

She flushed. 'About one-thirty, perhaps a little later.'

'Which means Butler was with you continuously between, say, eight o'clock and one-thirty, right?'

She stared at him. 'You don't . . .'

He raised an eyebrow. 'Don't what?'

'S . . . s . . . suspect David Butler?' she stammered.

'It's my job to suspect everybody, Miss Brandon,' Gabriel said casually. 'Even you. She could have been killed by a woman or a man.'

'But I thought . . . wasn't she raped? I'm sure somebody said she was raped.'

'Who said?'

'I don't know. Someone. The patients have been talking about it all afternoon. The rumours have—'

'I can imagine.' Gabriel looked at her levelly. 'Clarissa Janacek was hit over the head repeatedly with a rock or other blunt object, Miss Brandon. She wasn't raped. She wasn't robbed.'

She met his eyes. 'Was her throat cut?'

His answer dropped like a stone into the warm silence of the room. 'Yes.'

She felt the hairs rise all up her back and along her arms and shivered involuntarily. 'So it *is* the same as Julie.'

He ignored that. 'That's all, Miss Brandon, thank you. Your account of the evening tallies with Dr Butler's. Like you, he was pretty much alone between six and seven – your uncle only saw him just before seven, Dr Jenks just after. If there's anything else, we'll let you know.'

'But . . .'

'That's all.'

She stood up uncertainly and took a step away from her chair, then stopped. 'Mr Gilliam said he'd like to talk to you.'

He glanced down at what looked like a list of patients and room numbers. 'I'll get around to Mr Gilliam in due course. Nurse Hasker said they'd be through dinner by six-thirty.'

'They?'

'The patients whose rooms face that side of the woods. Just routine, of course.'

'It's all routine, isn't it?' she flared. 'Two girls are horribly murdered and it's still just routine for you. You and Tom Gilliam, you're two of a kind, cold as stones. As gravestones.'

Matt Gabriel nodded. 'Very literary. The fact is, we're more like garbage collectors, aren't we, Seth? If they don't stick to their routine, the garbage piles up and begins to stink. Our sort sets up what you might call a moral stink, but it's still garbage. Difference is, our kind of garbage might get up and walk away. We've got to collect evidence and it has to be done correctly in order for it to stand up in court. That means sticking to routine and not getting carried away by your emotions.'

'If you'd collected it a little more quickly, Clarissa Janacek might still be alive,' she pointed out.

'You don't know that.'

'Neither do you.' She felt a sudden irritation at his cool manner. 'That's why I feel sorry for you.'

It was after nine o'clock before Gabriel managed to drop in and introduce himself to Tom Gilliam, whom he discovered watching the news.

'You made the state round-up,' Gilliam commented, when Gabriel had dragged over a chair and settled himself beside the bed. 'If you're going to make any more television appearances you ought to get those bags under your eyes seen to.'

'Minute I get a chance,' Matt promised. He regarded Gilliam with interest. Jack Stryker had said he was smart and intuitive, but he looked neither at the moment – only like a man who had been in bed too long.

'Well?' Gilliam prompted impatiently, when Gabriel didn't seem to have anything to say.

'Same story, same method as Zalinsky. Same botched job on the throat cutting.'

'What are you going to do?'

Gabriel had bent over to tie a shoelace. 'Don't know. Kind of depends on whether you've got anything new to tell me or not.'

Gilliam shrugged. 'Plenty of gossip, very few facts. I think the porter, Michaels, is on the take here and there. Petty thieving, too.'

'That's not new.'

'I didn't figure it was. I also don't figure why Forrester keeps him on, if that's the case.'

Gabriel nodded. 'Another mystery, but one I can't bother with now. It does look as if we have a psycho on our hands.'

'I don't agree,' Gilliam said.

'Nobody asked you to agree.'

'Funny – I thought I was supposed to be—'

'That was before,' Gabriel said tersely. 'This second killing changes things. The only thing you can do for me in here now is to find out if Forrester is hiding any nutcases under the beds.'

'He doesn't take serious psychiatric—'

'I know what he *says*, damnit!' Matt interrupted. 'What else would he say? But just because somebody has a pickled liver or a pair of lungs like old lace doesn't mean they couldn't be crazy on the side, does it?'

'You sound a little desperate, Sheriff,' Gilliam said mildly.

'Maybe because I am a little desperate. Some loony bastard goes around murdering nurses in my town—'

'Julie Zalinsky wasn't a nurse.'

'Jesus wept, she wore a god-damned white uniform, didn't she? What more does one of these psychos need?' He got up and strode to the window, glaring down at the parking lot. As he did, Laura Brandon appeared and walked across it towards her apartment, her white uniform glimmering in the half-light beneath the shadow of the coat she'd slung over her shoulders. 'Look at that, for God's sake – two women dead and she walks out the door by herself, bold as brass, just asking for it.'

'Who?' Gilliam was unable to see the ground from the bed.

'Miss Brandon, the little dimwit. He could see her a mile off in that uniform.'

'You think that's important?'

'It's *a* common denominator,' Gabriel said, watching Laura until she was safely through the hedge, up the stairs and into her apartment. One by one her lights came on and he turned back into the room to face Gilliam. 'Both wore them, didn't they?'

'Yes, but—'

'Don't you think I'd like to believe it *isn't* a nut?' Matt demanded. 'Do you realize what's going to happen around here now? Hysteria, witch-hunts – the media will whip things up into a frenzy in order to sell it – and me the only one to yell at for action. What do I go on if it's a nut? They're the worst, you know they are, the hardest to pin down. They're sly, they're clever. Could be the vicar, could be anybody respectable on the outside, but underneath . . . God, how I wish it wasn't a psycho.'

'But you're sure it is?'

Gabriel turned the chair he'd been sitting in earlier and straddled it, leaning against the back. 'You want to know why? Let me give you a little history.' He proceeded to outline the history of Mountview, starting with the story of the original 'Shadowman'. 'Last of all, we've got Arthur Spradling.'

'Who?'

Matt explained about the tramp who had used the derelict building and had reacted destructively when renovation had intruded upon his annual occupancy.

'And you think this tramp is responsible for the murders?'

Gabriel looked bleak. 'I don't know. But most of those guys are alcoholics or mental cases, right? What started as spite could have turned into a full-scale obsession by now. Maybe when he came back this time he went over the top. He was pretty unstable when I hauled him in a few years back. And he knew about the Shadowman thing too. Talked about seeing him in the woods, about him wanting revenge. We got him put away for six months for the arson, then he disappeared.'

'The fire last night . . .'

'Uh-huh. Kind of a strong coincidence, wouldn't you say?'

'Have you—'

'Done all I can, issued a description, contacted the FBI to see if they have him on record? Yes, done all that stuff. If he's around we'll find him.'

'Okay, he seems a possibility,' Gilliam conceded. 'But

what if he's not responsible, what if he didn't exist? What would you have then?'

Matt sighed and took out his notebook. 'Damn all, same as last time.'

'When was the girl killed?'

Matt managed a wry smile. 'Okay, okay – ME's rough guess is between five and eight last night.'

Gilliam looked gratified. 'How convenient for somebody. One murder committed while shifts are changing is one thing, but two seems a little too much of a coincidence, wouldn't you say?'

'You don't like Arthur Spradling for it, do you?' Matt asked.

'I can't discount him any more than you can.'

'But you like somebody inside for it a little better?'

'I do.'

'But you have no candidates?'

'Not yet. Give me a bit more time.'

'I can't stop you.'

'You don't have to listen to what I say.'

'I'd be a fool to ignore anything or anybody at this point,' Matt admitted.

'Then humour me and tell me what you've got so far.'

'Okay. Have to get a handle on it myself.' Matt assessed the notes that had seemed so coherent and tidy when he'd written them, but appeared to have undergone a sea change since and turned themselves into a muddled series of scrawls.

'Let's see. Nobody has an alibi and everybody has an alibi, like last time. "About" such and such a time, nothing tighter than that. Between five and seven-thirty nearly everybody in the place was on their own *some time.* Forrester's car comes back at six-fifteen, but he doesn't actually make contact with anyone else until seven. Mrs Cunningham alone in the office, waiting for him to come back. Shirley – Miss Hasker – in *her* office, going over the day reports – she came in at five-thirty. Other nurses in and out, here and there, so on. Butler alone from six-fifteen until seven-ten, in his room getting cleaned up for his big date with Miss Brandon, who is ditto in *her* place doing the same. Never saw such a clean bunch of people in my life.'

'I know,' Gilliam muttered. 'I get washed so often I squeak when I turn over.'

'Yeah.' Matt was deep in his notebook. 'Michaels went off duty at five-thirty, stops at bar, gets home about eight, have to check that out.' He jotted a few more squiggles in the margin. 'Higgins ditto, only *he* leaves about six-thirty because of this big branch coming down near the kitchen, but not cleanly, so he had to cut it free. Nuts about trees, that kid. Said it would tear the rest of the tree apart thrashing around in the wind.' He looked up. 'Miss Brandon says she saw him talking to Clarissa Janacek yesterday afternoon.'

Gilliam nodded. 'I saw them too – at the far side of the parking lot, by the hedge.'

'She wasn't sure it was the Janacek girl.'

'I am.'

'Were they arguing?'

'I don't know. They could have been. I didn't really pay all that much attention to them. Sorry.'

'Shame. Still, the thing is, *he* didn't mention it when I interviewed him, which was before I talked to Miss Brandon.'

'Maybe he was afraid to. According to the latest gossip, Janacek went out with Nick a few times, just to make Martin Hambden jealous.'

Gabriel lowered his notebook, staring. 'You're kidding.'

'Did you ever see Clarissa Janacek when she was alive?'

'Sure. Interviewed her when the Zalinsky girl was killed. And I've seen her around town.'

'Does it seem *so* unlikely that a man like Hambden, lonely widower about to retire, might not take an interest in a beautiful young girl if she encouraged him? And she *did* encourage him, I'm told.'

'Well, I guess not, at that.'

Gilliam sighed. 'The trouble is, she encouraged a lot of

men. According to the gossip, that is. Patients, visitors, whoever took her fancy. I'm not saying she followed through on any of it – just that she was a congenital flirt.'

'You're not going to tell me I have to look for two murderers, are you? One for each girl?'

'There are such things as copy-cat murders.'

'I know,' Matt conceded. It didn't make him happy to say it.

'But I don't think that's it. I think the two murders are connected and I think they were done by the same person. I just don't *see* the connection yet.'

'Of course, you've only been on the case a few days,' Matt said sarcastically. 'No doubt it will come to you.' He closed his notebook. 'What it comes down to is motive. And we haven't got one for either of them. Which is why I will be looking for a psycho – he won't *need* a motive. Not a logical one, anyway.'

'Did any of the patients hear anything?'

'None of them heard a damned thing – except the wind. The fall is a great time to kill people – plenty of weather to hide behind. I don't see any of the patients as suspects.' Matt seemed to take a sudden interest in the knees of his trousers. 'One of them worried me a little, though.'

'Mrs Panotis?'

Matt's eyes came up, wide and startled. 'Now how the hell did you know that?'

Gilliam smiled. 'They didn't teach it to us at the Police Academy, but it's there. I don't know if it's a smell, or a gesture, or a tone of voice, but some people raise the hairs on the back of your neck.'

Matt nodded. 'She kept smiling.' He shifted on his chair. 'But she's hardly strong enough to lift a spoon, much less kill a woman bigger and healthier than she is. And she's so . . . young.'

'You were going to say innocent.'

'Yes, I was. You think so, anyway, until you look into her eyes. Her face is young, her eyes are old – ancient with passion, vengeful. She *could* kill, if she could stand up.'

'She can. When she wants to,' Gilliam said. 'I saw her standing up the other day, as a matter of fact. She was standing in the door of her room, watching her husband.'

'And what was he doing?'

'He was talking to Clarissa Janacek. They seemed pretty cosy. Mrs Panotis looked capable of murder right then.'

'Oh, hell,' Matt said in disgust. 'How many *more* suspects have you got up your pyjama sleeve?'

'Dozens.' Gilliam grinned.

# FIFTEEN

NICK HIGGINS SLOUCHED IN THE chair across from Matt Gabriel, looking totally miserable. George had brought him from home, where he had been in bed suffering from flu. He looked very unwell. 'I don't care who saw me, I didn't kill Clarissa,' he growled. 'Yeah, we had a little argument, but it didn't amount to anything. Nothing at all.'

'I'm told you were shouting at one another,' Matt said quietly.

'Sure. It was windy, we were beside that damn hedge – it was like standing next to a waterfall or something, all the leaves rustling. It's a good, solid hedge.'

'But a noisy one?'

Higgins managed a weak grin. 'Yeah.'

'And what was your "little argument" about?'

'She broke our date.'

'You've been dating her?'

'Sometimes she had nothing better to do,' Nick said wearily. 'But that night she said she did.'

'Did she say what it was?'

'Nope. That was what made me lose it – she was always doing that, making a date until something better came along. I was like some kind of handy back-up, in case she got bored, or wanted somebody else to pay for her drinks.'

'Why did you ask her out if she was like that?'

'You ever see her?'

'Yes, but—'

'To her a date with me meant bed – who'd be dumb enough to pass that by? She was . . . enthusiastic. Almost professional, you might say.' His voice took a turn for the worse. 'She was a beautiful bitch, but you don't say no to opportunities like that, do you?'

'Are you saying she slept around?'

'I'm saying she slept with me when she felt like it and I was lucky to get it. I don't know what she did with anybody else,' Nick growled. 'I knew my place. But that day she just pissed me off, you know? A person gets tired of being put down all the time. "Can't make it tonight," she says. I asks her why. She says, "Business." I say what kind of business. She says, "It's better you don't know."'

'What do you think she meant by that?'

'Beats hell out of me. She was all kind of smirky and full of herself, though. Like she had some big secret or something.'

'Was that usual for her?'

Nick considered this. 'No, not really.'

'Where did you go on your dates?' Matt asked. He couldn't remember seeing Nick and the lovely Clarissa anywhere in town.

'Oh, out to that place on one eighty-three – the Stick-to-your-Ribs? She loved to line-dance and she loved those ribs.'

'And then?'

'And then what?'

'Where would you go after that? Home?'

He actually blushed. 'To her place – she rents a house with another nurse. I live with my folks, I couldn't take her back there.'

'I see. And how long had this been going on?'

'You mean how long have I been taking her out?'

'Yes.'

Nick shrugged. 'About a year, off and on. Mostly off.'

'When she said "business", what did you think she really meant?'

Nick looked confused. 'I don't know what you mean.'

'Did you think she was going out with another man?'

'No . . . no, it didn't seem like that, to tell you the

truth. From what she said, it meant some kind of money for her. I figured she was going after another job, or something. Maybe moving on . . . I guess that kind of made me angry too.'

'How angry were you, Nick?' Matt asked gently.

Nick's head came up. 'Not angry enough to kill her. That would have been real dumb, wouldn't it? She never said she wasn't ever going out with me again, she just said she couldn't come that night . . .' He struggled with it. 'She had this way of laughing at you the madder you got, which made it worse. Otherwise it wouldn't have amounted to a hill of beans.'

'Do you date any of the other nurses, Nick?'

'Sometimes. But they're just dates, if you know what I mean. And not very often. I've got responsibilities, I can't get out all that much.'

'Yes, I know about how you look after your parents.'

'They looked after me when I was little, it's only fair,' Nick said defensively.

'But it's a burden.' Matt was sympathetic.

'Some things you just get on with. Some things there's just no other way and that's that. No sense in getting upset about it, only makes things worse. And they can't help it, can they?'

'No, I suppose not,' Matt said. 'Are you sure Clarissa didn't say anything, anything at all about what she was going to do instead of going out with you?'

'No. The more I asked, the more she laughed. She was real pleased with herself about something, like I said. And to tell you the truth, I was kind of worried about her. I mean, she said I shouldn't know and so I wondered if it was something . . . something . . . bad.'

'Bad? What do you mean by that?'

Nick shrugged. 'I don't know. I'm all kind of mixed up, I got a fever, my head feels like somebody hit me with a sledgehammer. And she's gone, which don't make it any better. But she seemed kind of . . .' He paused.

'Kind of what?'

'Like a naughty kid,' Nick finally said. 'Like a kid who was going to rob the cookie jar.'

When Laura went in to work she met Shirley Hasker going off duty and was astonished at the change in her. Shirley looked as if she'd shrunk inside her body and was staring out of its eyes, trapped. 'Shirley, are you all right?'

'I'm fine.' Her voice was hoarse.

'But . . . should you drive?'

'I never drive. My brother is coming for me, he's probably waiting out there now.' She pulled away from Laura's tentative touch on her arm.

Laura found Kay in the nursing office, slapping down files and tidying the desk as if it were a naughty child. 'Is Shirley ill?' she asked her.

'Not medically speaking,' Kay said.

'Are *you* all right?'

'Right as rain – except for a tendency to climb the wall barefoot every time I hear a noise,' Kay answered. 'I nearly had a heart attack this morning because I thought somebody was chasing me across the parking lot.' She laughed hollowly. 'In fact, somebody *was* chasing me – Marilyn McNeilage, as scared as I was. Something tells me we're going to have a lot of very fast-moving nurses around here until they catch this guy.'

'I know what you mean,' Laura said. 'I think I set a new record for the 400-yard dash last night, going home. I had the terrible feeling somebody was watching me the whole way.'

'And guess who has to go back over to nights next week?' Kay went on. 'Yours truly. Shirley and I alternate, which is just as well, as we don't get along together much. I'm going to get Chris to drive me over and pick me up in the morning the way Mitch always does for Shirley. There's no way I'm going to wander around the parking lot in the dark, that's for sure.' She looked at Laura questioningly. 'Are you sure you ought to go on staying in that apartment over there on your own?'

'I'm not on my own, I have a cat.'

'My God, a lot of help a cat's going to be. Why don't you get yourself a big canary, too – then it can peck the Shadowman to death.'

'You think it's the Shadowman?'

'No, not really. Of course not.' Kay spoke quickly. Too quickly.

'That's just a superstition,' Laura said. 'Surely you don't believe in it?'

Kay looked uneasy. 'Common sense says no. But when you get out there in the dark, and the branches on the trees rub together and the wind rustles the leaves in the hedge . . . you get spooked.'

'Well, Michaels is putting two extra bolts on my door and locks on the windows. Not that he wanted to, because he's terrified of Solomon, but Uncle Roger made him. They're installing lights in the parking lot. And David promised to walk me home every night after this.'

'You said you ran home last night.'

'Yes – well – David was busy and I was in a hurry to get home so—'

'So you took a chance,' Kay interrupted. 'Like Clarissa probably took a chance. And Julie.' She shivered. 'Chris wants me to quit my job up here.'

'Oh, no – you mustn't.'

'Damn right I mustn't – not if we want to keep up the payments on the house,' Kay said with brisk practicality. 'But I sure wish Matt Gabriel would get off his ass before somebody *else* gets killed.'

'Go slowly,' Matt instructed his deputies. 'Look for anything – signs of a campfire, discarded cans or bottles, whatever. I know after the first murder we did a sweep of the immediate crime scene, but this time I want you to go *all* the way in. I want to cover the entire woods.'

'We can't corner him,' George Putnam objected. 'There just aren't enough of us.'

'I know that. We'll cover what we can and if we come up

with anything I'll put in a call to the State Police barracks. Spradling can hide from us, but he can't hide his traces. Once we know he's in there we can do the thing right, drive him into the net.'

'What if he's moved on?' Seth asked.

'He didn't move on after the first killing,' Matt pointed out.

'What makes you so sure he's in there?'

'The physiotherapist at the clinic said someone ran into her during the alarm over the fire, someone who smelled dirty and strange. It might just be someone living rough in the woods, but we have to start someplace.'

His men had spent yesterday going over the crime scene inch by inch, but nothing had been found. As before, the storm had blown and washed away any clues that might have been found by the victim's body. It occurred to Matt that storms were a common factor between the two murders – the killer could have been stimulated by it. Animals and children often became restless in the wind – why not someone who was mentally unbalanced? Alternatively, he could have been taking advantage of the noise to cover his activities. Waiting for storms to blow up before he did what he wanted or had to do, knowing that evidence that might lead to him would be blown and washed away. That implied considerable intelligence and a cold-blooded patience that was quite horrifying.

Alternatively, the storms could have been coincidental.

The blows to Clarissa's skull had not been as frenzied or as extensive as those to Julie Zalinsky's, although they certainly would have rendered her unconscious. The killer had used Clarissa's own silk scarf to strangle her, a detail he hadn't released to the press. Then – and only then – had the strange attempts at throat cutting been made, as if by an awkward and reluctant hand, more ritualistic than lethal.

And there had been no cutting off of hair either, for Clarissa had worn her curls short and close to the head. Her handbag had been found by one of the kitchen staff, apparently intact – although they had no way of knowing if anything like papers or a letter had been removed. Her wallet was still there, with money in it.

That bothered Matt. It seemed to him somebody like Arthur Spradling, a tramp who lived from hand to mouth, would certainly not have missed an opportunity to take money – yet with both killings there had been money left behind.

Of course, ghosts have no need for money.

He scowled at himself as he moved through the woods, keeping his eyes on the ground, looking for anything that might indicate someone's presence. He hadn't been able to stop Emily Gibbons this time. The story in the paper would have a bad effect on the townspeople. Hell, it was having a bad effect on *him.* Even if you knew the Shadowman tale wasn't and *couldn't* be true, the woods seemed spookier and more menacing than they had been before. He hated admitting it, but he felt nervous and instinctively wary in among the trees and undergrowth. Things whispered and rustled and snapped around him, there were shadows and sudden moments of brightness, and screeches and whistles, and odd thunks and tappings. He wasn't a woodsman or camper, never had been, so the surroundings were unfamiliar and therefore somehow threatening. Someone could spring out from behind a bush or drop from a tree overhead and he would be caught by surprise, off balance and slow to defend himself. If he'd ever been a soldier it might have been easier, but he had still been in high school when the war in Vietnam had begun, in college when it had ended, eligible but never called. He often felt he would have been a better police officer if he'd been trained as a soldier. Teaching college was dangerous in its own way, but any knife in the back you were apt to suffer there would have come from a jealous colleague rather than an enemy assassin. He worked out fairly regularly, he was fit enough – just not experienced in the ways that would have been useful now.

He stopped suddenly, his eyes fixed on the thick, broken end of a low branch sticking out of some kind of bush.

Caught on it was a narrow ribbon of dirty grey fabric, thick wool by the look of it, ragged and stained. He felt in his pocket for one of the plastic evidence bags they were all carrying and carefully shook the piece of cloth into it. Then he held the bag open and sniffed.

It smelled odd all right.

But not unfamiliar.

George Putnam was pissed off.

Two girls dead. One not bad-looking, the other an absolute knock-out. Somebody was being very wasteful of local resources.

He trudged on.

This whole investigation had been cocked up from the beginning, in his opinion. He had all the respect in the world for Matt Gabriel, but it seemed to him that his pigheaded refusal to acknowledge the possibility of the Shadowman's existence had held things up considerably. Once again, Matt had turned to Jack Stryker for advice, instead of going ahead under his own steam. And he'd made contact with this bozo patient in the hospital to dig up gossip and information he didn't need.

George didn't really believe in the Shadowman.

He didn't really believe that some two-hundred-year-old monster lived in the woods, reappearing every once in a while to kill women. But he didn't disbelieve it, either.

You only had to watch *The X-Files* to know there were a lot of things going on that people couldn't explain. You had to have an open mind, and Matt's mind was closed to everything except logic and facts. He had no imagination, that was his trouble.

George had plenty of imagination.

In his mind's eye he could see the scene: the wind howling overhead, the beautiful nurse grabbed and dragged into the woods, her screams unheard above the noise of the storm. He could see her thrown to the ground at the feet of a huge, shadowy form, see its arms upraised with the crushing rock, see the rock brought down on the defenceless head of the pleading, cowering girl. And then the monstrous shape hunched over the outstretched figure, the twisting of the scarf, the slashing of the throat. Perhaps grunting as he worked, perhaps laughing, perhaps even whispering things, strange things, as the blood flowed.

It was pretty terrible and had kept him awake for a lot of the previous night. Even Tilly had noticed the dark circles under his eyes this morning. He'd tried not to think about it, but it kept coming back. And here in the woods, now – it seemed more real and more possible than ever.

Even though he kept telling himself to settle down.

He walked on determinedly and kicked it before he saw it.

Whatever it was, it flashed, before disappearing into heavy undergrowth. 'What the hell was that?' George asked a passing squirrel, then hunkered down and peered under the twisted branches. Parting the growth, he kneeled and leaned forward until he spotted it against the trunk of a small, struggling tree. He expected to see a tin can, or a piece of jewellery stolen by a jay and dropped, or an Indian knife, possibly still showing signs of its murderous ritual use.

What he saw was a scalpel.

And it was very clean.

Charley Hart shambled through the woods, taking note of trees, bushes, wildflowers, small animals and insects. He was at home in the woods, camped out often, hunted small game and in general looked upon the great outdoors in much the way he looked upon his small indoors – that is to say, home ground.

Not that he knew *these* woods. Nobody he knew ever came in here. They said it was because it was private land and they didn't want to get prosecuted for trespass. But that wasn't the reason. It was because they were superstitious. Because of the Shadowman. So these woods were pretty virgin territory, left to run wild, because the renovation of the clinic only extended to the edge of the lawns. Beyond that lay who knew what? There was about a half-mile of trees between the clinic and the river, with a path leading through it, but the woods behind the clinic ran for over a mile north and east. Because they were unmanaged there were knots and tangles of underbrush, deadfalls, thickets, all kinds of things that could help hide a man. It was old forest, overgrown, dark and secretive.

He reckoned a man could live out here during the warmer months, augmenting his needs with a few purchased necessities – such as beer, for example – and be fairly comfortable, providing he could protect himself against the rain. Even in the best of seasons rain will come, after all. He'd done it himself, for short periods, and made a good job of it. Of course, he always knew he could leave and go home, that he had, in fact, a home to go to, and that knowledge had sustained him, making it a matter of choice rather than necessity. It would be different for someone like Arthur Spradling. It would be all the time, with no alternative. So no wonder he had looked upon the derelict remains of Mountview as his castle in the wilderness and had come to see it year after year as his rightful place.

Charley could understand his being upset upon finding it taken over and made off limits, turned into someone else's castle. He didn't condone the things Spradling had done then, but he knew where the man had been coming from, metaphorically speaking.

Nobody knew where Spradling *actually* came from, or indeed where he disappeared to when he left. That he would appear in spring had been accepted, if not necessarily welcomed, and that he would disappear at the end of summer was also accepted, with some relief. People in Blackwater Bay were easygoing when it came to tramps like Spradling, as long as they didn't steal much or throw up on church property. When he'd set that last fire years back and Matt had thrown him in jail, it had seemed to put a scare into him. Nobody was particularly surprised that he didn't return the following spring. Or indeed, in the springs after that. Nobody particularly noticed – in the same way they had hardly noticed when he *was* there. That was the kind of man Spradling had been. Not invisible, exactly, but kind of translucent.

That Spradling might have set the fire at Mountview the other night Charley could accept, although there had been none of the usual sightings of Spradling during the summer. What he found difficult to believe was that Spradling had moved up to murder. He remembered the man, bitter and snarling, but more from fear and isolation than from actual malice. Easier, almost, to accept that it was something to do with the Shadowman.

For all the practicality of his nature, Charley gave some respect to the legend. Of course he didn't *really* believe it, no sensible man would, yet there had been times in other woods, at night, when a screech owl screamed, or the wind moved stealthily through the undergrowth, when Charley had been scared, been moved to run away, sweating and panicked, until reason reasserted itself and he would slow to a walk, and stop, ashamed of himself for being 'spooked'.

So when he came upon the display in the small clearing he was wary but unsurprised, in a way. Prepared for the worst, he found merely the inexplicable: the undergrowth cleared, a ring drawn in the dirt, a circle of feathers, a circle of small stones, a circle of leaves and, in the centre, a white nurse's cap.

Seth Anderson wished he had been left in the office to get on with some paperwork. He was nineteen and his only qualifications for the job of newest deputy were some ROTC training in high school, a reluctance to follow his father into the dry goods business and an insatiable appetite for paperback thrillers. He read them all the time, when he wasn't writing out reports on the various high excitements of Blackwater Bay, such as stolen boats and broken windows. This murder business had caught him on the wrong foot, however, and he'd been marching out of step ever since, well behind the sheriff and the other deputies. Reality was not what he had signed on to deal with, but he was trying his best. He was gaining on it, slowly.

He'd never seen Arthur Spradling and had no idea what he was looking for out here. He was certain that if he came upon Spradling each of them would be as scared as the other and they would both probably run a mile. The thought of drawing his weapon and making a stand, demanding the other man's surrender, was making him feel sick to his stomach. He didn't think he could do it. He knew that at the last moment he would fail, and fail badly, and never be able to admit it to anyone.

Then one of the other deputies would find Spradling and the tramp would laugh and tell them about the chicken-hearted kid who wasn't man enough for the job.

And Matt would fire him.

The other deputies were all fine, strong, brave men. He felt that in his bones. Especially George Putnam, the chief deputy. Seth thought George was wonderful. So did George, of course, but Seth was prepared to overlook that, because George had been a deputy for so long and read *Modern Lawman* and knew all about things like DNA testing and fingerprints and stuff like that. So much to learn, Seth thought despairingly, as he pushed some branches aside and moved with difficulty through the thick undergrowth. Birds sang overhead and there was a squirrel chattering somewhere. It was nice here in the woods, he thought. If he was really lucky, he wouldn't find anything.

He was not lucky.

# SIXTEEN

LAURA HAD HAD A BUSY morning.

The patients who had spent hours watching the sheriff and his men the day before were now feeling the effects of so much unaccustomed activity – sore legs from standing at the windows, sore arms from leaning on canes and walkers, sore necks from craning to see everything and miss nothing.

Now she had to hang Mr Bledsoe.

Michaels, having delivered the morose Mr Bledsoe (and having rendered him even more morose by making the same puerile jokes about hanging that he made every time), stepped into her office and delivered a bombshell as well. 'They've arrested your boyfriend.'

She looked up, startled, and it took a moment for Michaels's words and smug expression to sink in. 'My boyfriend?'

'Yeah. Mountview's answer to Dr Kildare – Babyface Butler. Guess they caught up with him at last, hey?' Michaels was full of the news – it practically dribbled down his chin.

'You're not serious.'

'How much you wanna bet? Sheriff came and tapped his shoulder just after lunch. No fuss, no trouble – just led him away.' Michaels pondered with some satisfaction the picture he was creating for her. He decided it needed embellishing. ''Course, they don't have the death penalty in this state any more,' he said in a regretful tone. 'Otherwise he'd be for the hot seat. Wonder if they'd sell tickets?'

'Stop it!' she practically shouted and, out of the corner of her eye, saw Mr Bledsoe turning in his wheelchair out in the treatment room, focusing baleful eyes on them through the glass. She pushed the door closed and glared at Michaels, who was hugging himself with quiet delight. He hadn't had this much effect on a female in years. 'Now tell me the truth!' she demanded.

He opened his eyes wide. 'I *have* told you the truth,' he said reproachfully. 'Matt Gabriel took Dr Butler into town this afternoon. I saw it myself, I was as near to him as I am to you. And Butler didn't argue – he just went.'

'Who else knows about this?'

'Everybody. I wanted you to be the last to know,' Michaels said archly.

'You ran a risk there, didn't you?' Her voice was nasty. 'Somebody else might have beaten you to it – now, wouldn't *that* have been a disappointment for you?' She wanted to hit him, or to string him up instead of Mr Bledsoe – and without a safety harness.

'I'd have survived.' Michaels was unperturbed. 'Can't say as much for Babyface Butler, though. Matt Gabriel can be *tough.*' As she started for the door, he called out. 'Hey! Don't forget your patient. Duty first, remember.'

She went through into the treatment room. 'Sorry to keep you waiting, Mr Bledsoe,' she said sweetly. 'How is the neck today?'

Bledsoe turned away and grunted, hunching lower in his wheelchair like a turtle into an aluminium shell.

'Right,' she continued briskly. 'I have everything ready for you. Let's get started.' With gritted teeth she strapped Mr Bledsoe into the vertical traction 'noose' and adjusted it to relieve the compression in his neck. 'There, now – comfortable?'

Mr Bledsoe grunted, his jaws clamped shut by the canvas bands. They didn't really make any difference – all he ever did was grunt, anyway.

'I'll be right back,' she said. His eyes swivelled sideways in some alarm as she went towards the door. 'Don't worry – won't be a minute.'

She left him dangling there and darted down the hall.

Without knocking, she burst into Gilliam's room and demanded to know what the hell was going on.

'In what context?' Gilliam asked mildly, putting down the newspaper in which he was doing the crossword.

'The sheriff has arrested David!' she said shrilly. Her throat was constricted by both fear and outrage.

'Who said?'

'Michaels.'

'Ah, the brayboy of the western world.' Gilliam nodded.

'Now, listen—'

Gilliam raised an eyebrow. 'I'm listening.'

'I mean – *do* something.'

'What do you suggest? That I run right down there?' he asked sarcastically.

'No. Phone him.'

'I already have,' Gilliam said, in what was meant to be a repressive tone. 'He is merely questioning Butler, he has made no formal arrest.' He picked up his newspaper. 'As yet.'

'But . . . but . . . why *David*?'

Patiently Gilliam put down his newspaper again, placed the pencil on top of it and removed his glasses. 'Apparently, in going through Nurse Janacek's personal effects with Miss Goodfellow, he found some things he felt Dr Butler should explain.'

'*What* things?' Laura was only just managing to keep control of herself.

'He didn't say.' He started to replace his glasses.

'Call him up and ask him,' she ordered.

'I expect he's too busy to come to the phone just now,' Gilliam said. 'What's a five-letter word for—'

'Bastard.'

He regarded her owlishly over the top of his glasses. 'Too long.'

'I'm going down there, right now,' Laura said, infuriated by his blasé attitude.

'What are you afraid of?' Gilliam asked quietly.

'What?' She faltered, half-way to the door.

'Anyone would think you didn't trust Butler.'

'But I . . . of course I trust him!'

'Do you think he killed Clarissa Janacek?'

'No. *No*!'

'Well then, relax,' Gilliam suggested. 'You go haring down there full of hellfire and outrage, and the sheriff might think you were protesting a little *too* much, don't you think? Oh, I forgot – you don't think, do you? You just react.' He began to erase something in the crossword, as she came slowly back to the bedside.

'Are you serious?' she asked in a small voice.

'Matt Gabriel strikes me as a good law officer,' Gilliam said, filling in another answer. 'He is conducting a murder investigation and, in doing so, will be questioning a lot of people, from here and from elsewhere. People who knew Clarissa in the past, friends, former employers . . .'

'David used to go out with her . . . before I came,' Laura said slowly.

'Then it probably has to do with that,' Gilliam told her. 'What's more, I don't think Butler himself would be any too pleased to have you running around trying to protect him like some kind of mother hen, would he?'

'I *wasn't*,' she protested.

Gilliam eyed her. 'You were about to,' he said. 'Anyone would think you were in love with the guy.'

'I . . . I like him very much.'

'Not sure, hey?'

'Of course I'm sure. Anyway, it's none of your business.'

'Well, then, what are you doing in here?' he asked her in a reasonable tone.

'I don't know,' she said bleakly. 'I had the stupid idea you'd know what to do.'

'I do. Nothing.'

'Nothing at all?'

'Nothing at all. No doubt Butler will be back in time to tuck you in tonight – or whatever. He'll tell you all about it, say a few nasty things about Gabriel, then life will go on as before. You'll see.'

She stared at him in horror. 'Oh, my God!'

'What's wrong?'

'Mr Bledsoe . . . I left him hanging . . .'

She waited until dusk, but David did not reappear. She'd spent the entire afternoon torn between wanting to phone or rush down to the town to rescue him and acknowledging that Gilliam's advice had been sound. It wasn't that she didn't trust David, but she supposed she could see how it might *seem* that way. After all, he hadn't been arrested, not actually *arrested*, had he?

Nobody seemed to know.

But to assume so meant that she allowed for the possibility that he might be guilty. And she would never admit that. She tried to think of an excuse to ring the sheriff's office – but any emergency at the clinic would have been dealt with by her uncle or Owen Jenks, who had been called back from the Hatchville Clinic.

Her uncle Roger said not to worry, he'd been down to talk to the sheriff himself, at lunch-time, and *he* wasn't in jail, was he? Milly just looked at her pityingly. Harlan Weaver took one glance and recommended a tranquillizer.

'No, I'm fine,' Laura protested. 'Just a little . . .'

'Strung out?' Dr Weaver smiled. 'Taking a tranquillizer is not an admission of failure, Laura. It's a simple crutch. You give crutches to your patients who have broken bones, don't you? With a view to them getting rid of the crutches as soon as they can?'

'Yes,' she admitted.

'Well, then – think of a tranquillizer as a simple crutch to be used in an emergency – not to be adopted for life.' He went to a cupboard in his office and produced a small black-and-green capsule. 'Just the one, with water. And stop worrying about David and everyone else in the world. You take too much on yourself – it's not good for a professional. You have to develop a tougher shell. Believe me, you won't survive if you don't.'

She took the capsule, ready to do anything, and looked

at him over the top of the water glass. 'Do you have a thick shell, Dr Weaver?'

He smiled ruefully. 'Not as thick as I'd like, not even after all this time.'

'And do you take tranquillizers?'

He regarded her thoughtfully. 'No,' he said evenly. 'It's tempting, but no. I have an obsessive nature and could become addicted. We psychiatrists have to be analysed before we can practise ourselves, you know. It weeds out a lot of the problems before they start. I know my weaknesses. I practise yoga instead. Do a lot of standing on my head.' The image seemed to amuse him.

'A lot of doctors are tempted by drugs, aren't they?'

He sighed. 'I'm afraid so. Mostly by uppers rather than downers, though. In order to keep going, in order to counter the terrible physical and emotional fatigue most of them feel. And then of course they need sleeping pills to get their rest . . . and so it starts. You'd think doctors would have a healthy respect for drugs, but often it's just the opposite. They think they know all about them – and they don't. Why, do you think any of our doctors are on drugs?'

'No. Oh, no. It's just that I know it's a problem in some hospitals.'

Dr Weaver smiled. 'As if doctors didn't have enough problems just doing their job, right?'

'Yes. It's just that . . .'

'What?'

'Well . . . David did say something the other day about drugs going missing here at Mountview. He seemed worried about it.'

Dr Weaver looked uncomfortable. 'Well, so he should be. Did he say what kind of drugs?'

She shook her head. 'No . . . he didn't say much at all. Just that he was worried.'

'Drugs are "borrowed" all the time in hospitals,' Dr Weaver said.

'Yes, I know. But he seemed to think this was more serious.'

'Well, that's interesting. I'll have a word with him about it when he comes back.' Weaver frowned. 'If we do have a secret addict on the staff we ought to find out who it is before they damage themselves or one of the patients.' He smiled down at her. 'Thanks for mentioning it. I'll have a word with Roger, too.'

'Okay. And thanks for the little crutch,' she said.

'Any time. But not every time.' He patted her on the shoulder. 'Just for today, remember.'

The tranquillizer helped her through the rest of the afternoon. The patients were rebellious, questioning everything, threatening to leave, bursting into tears. Owen had a particularly rough time.

She ran into him in the hall and he looked extremely harassed. 'I don't know what's got into them all,' he said plaintively. 'They're behaving like children.'

'I think it's just reaction. They're beginning to feel unsafe, wondering who to trust, aware of their own frailties.'

'Yeah – just as I'm beginning to be aware of mine,' he said, brushing the recalcitrant lock of dark hair back from his forehead. It continually flopped forward and Laura often had to stop herself from pushing it back for him. As tall as he was, and as competent, Owen had a boyish appeal that brought out the mother in her. She knew some of the nurses had crushes on him – and the rest had crushes on David Butler. It was pathetic, but understandable. The patients being chronic or convalescent meant that there wasn't much drama in Mountview. Or hadn't been, until the murders. Now everybody had *too* much drama. And obviously Owen, too.

'I'm much happier in my clinic,' he said slowly. 'At least there I'm presented with things I can deal with practically – and make a difference. David is better at handling people than I am. He'd have them all soothed down in no time. I just seem to be making things worse.'

'Don't feel badly. I don't think David could be doing any better than you are. The nurses are all saying the same thing – it's getting like a kindergarten in here.'

He sighed. 'Well, I'd better get on with handing out teddy bears, then.'

By evening, Laura's personal teddy bear, the tranquillizer, had begun to wear off, but Dr Weaver had gone home.

Finally, and uneasily, she decided to go back to her apartment. There was dinner to eat, Solomon to feed, which would give her something to do other than just sit staring at the phone or looking out of the window watching the parking lot to see if David had returned.

Of course, it was now dark.

The wind tugged at her as she came out. The new outside lights were on, so there was only the distance between the hedge and the stairway up to her apartment to reconnoitre – the only place where it would be really dark.

She crunched across the gravel, glancing towards the highway for a sight of David's car turning up the drive, but the occasional headlights kept to the road, moving quickly past. The wind was fitful – now a gust, now a vacuum, and the sky was still faintly blue-green with the last light of day, darkened here and there by small black scudding clouds. The lights of the bridge twinkled in the distance and could have been fallen stars caught there. When she got to the hedge she hesitated. The gap looked so black, so – like a mouth. She took a deep breath and darted through. She was a few feet beyond the rustling hedge when her foot caught on something and she fell flat on her face, knocking the wind out of her lungs, although she managed to keep hold of her flashlight.

The beam lay along the grass like a path, starting at her clenched fist and ending—

—on a pair of filthy boots.

Gasping already from the impact of her fall, she sucked in the cold air and struggled to rise.

The boots started towards her.

She took a deep breath, preparing to scream or run back into the clinic, as the beam of light travelled up the boots to an indescribably dirty and frayed bottom edge of a great cloak. It was made of some kind of thick fabric and hung in folds, but the material was obscured by painted symbols, bits of feathers, small pieces of junk jewellery, stones, shells and ribbons. It was filthy, but through the dirt she could see colours and patterns.

She couldn't bring the flashlight beam up any higher. She *couldn't.* She didn't *want* to see who – or what – was inside that cloak. She felt frozen in place.

Suddenly, the boots were next to her. Above her, someone moaned and spoke in a strange language. Then there was an odd noise, and something warm and wet touched her hair. Was the guy urinating on her? How disgusting!

'Cut that out!' she shouted and rolled sideways, terrified, beating about her with flailing hands.

'Unnnhhhhh!' the figure shouted and jumped back. She had scared *him*!

It moved away. Fast.

Her heart was pounding so hard she couldn't have screamed again if she'd wanted to. She pointed the flashlight wildly at the sound of running feet and caught only a confused image of a figure fleeing towards the woods, a ragged figure, the wind catching at the cloak and spreading it out like wings. Above the cloak there was a tangle of long grey hair with feathers sticking out above it, like fingers pointing to the sky. The figure ran awkwardly, stumbling in the long grass, and finally reached the woods.

She tried to keep the light on it, like a long accusing finger, not easy the way she was shaking. Just before it disappeared between the trunks of the trees it turned. The power of the flashlight was not great at that distance, but it was sufficient for her to see the blur of pinkish tan that was a face and the terrible black shadows of the huge eye sockets that made it resemble a skull with a dark band lying across the forehead.

Then it was gone.

Rage rapidly unfroze her. 'Come back here, you son-of-a-bitch,' she shouted, scrambling furiously up from all fours and starting after him. Nobody peed on her and got away with it! Besides, if she had scared him he couldn't be very dangerous, could he?

She ran into the woods after him.

Aside from the beam of her flashlight it was very dark in there. The trees grew closely together, and the underbrush was thick and clinging. She fell twice, before she came to her senses and halted. She couldn't hear him running. Had he stopped? Was he coming back for her? An owl screeched and she suddenly realized that she was alone in the woods where Julie and Clarissa had been murdered.

And it was a really stupid place to be.

She turned back and finally located the glow of the clinic lights, shining beyond the thick woods like the illumination of a giant ship passing silently by. She stumbled towards them, fear accelerating her until she was free of the trees and running across the grass, the gravel and up the stairs to her apartment.

'Dear God.' She jabbed at the lock with her key several times, before successfully inserting it, and somehow got inside. She leaned against the panels, panting, while Solomon (who had been the cause of her falling down in the first place) came through the cat flap and commenced purring and butting his head against her shins.

She brushed at her hair and nearly screamed again when her hand encountered something alien, wet and horrible. She ran to the mirror.

It was blood. Fresh blood.

It matted her hair and was starting to run down over her forehead, red, sticky, ghastly. Bile rose in her throat and she ran for the bathroom, sobbing.

Twenty minutes later her little sitting-room was full of men – including David.

He arrived with the sheriff and George Putnam. Once they'd ascertained she was unharmed, they'd left to search the woods in the direction she indicated. Beyond David's shoulder she could see the beams of their flashlights darting between the tree trunks and disappearing into the woods. David nudged the door shut with his foot.

'Oh, David – I was so scared.'

'It's all right now, Laura, just settle down,' David said in his best patient-soothing voice.

She sniffed luxuriously. She'd been fine, dry-eyed and controlled, but the minute she'd seen David's concerned and slightly bewildered face, she'd broken down like any foolish woman. She hated herself for it, but it was nice to be held so tightly. Her hair was still wet from the shower she'd frantically given herself and she felt chilly after scrubbing her flesh so hard. Her skin crawled at the thought that there might still be blood on her somewhere.

'You should have come across earlier, while it was still light,' David scolded her. 'Or waited for me.'

'Oh, pooh,' she said, much braver now that he was here. 'It wasn't so very dark yet – and how did I know when you'd be back?' She blinked up at him. 'Aren't you arrested?'

He stared down at her. 'Arrested? What for?'

'They said they'd arrested you.'

'Who said?'

'Well . . . Michaels said, for one . . . and . . .' She paused. Nobody else had actually said 'arrested'.

David made an exasperated noise. 'Yes, I suppose Michaels would be the one to say something like that. I went into town to talk to the sheriff about Clarissa.'

'But . . . he came to get you.'

'Sure. I had a flat tyre this morning and Higgins is off sick, Michaels would never do it for me and I hadn't had a chance to fix it myself. The sheriff was just finishing his search of the woods and gave me a lift in.'

'Oh.'

He pulled away slightly and looked down at her in puzzlement. 'Did you really think he'd arrested me?'

'No . . . well . . . he could have been stupid enough . . .'

'He's not a stupid man, Laura.'

'No . . . but . . .'

Heavy footsteps again sounded on the outside stairway,

but slower this time. David let go of her and opened the door for the sheriff and a very irritated George Putnam.

'Did you find him?' she asked eagerly.

'Nope. Just a dead squirrel by the edge of the trees,' Matt said, holding up a plastic bag with a pathetic little body in it. 'I guess this was where the blood you talked about came from. It was still warm. Looked like maybe a cat had got at it, or someone had cut its throat open.'

She remembered the odd noise just before the blood had started to drip on to her head. 'Is its tail gone?' she asked.

He looked uncomfortable and thrust the plastic bag into the pocket of his jacket. 'Yes,' he admitted. 'Kind of – bitten off.'

'And so you think my *cat* did it?' she asked, amazed.

'Well—'

'Weren't there any footprints besides mine?' The ground was still moist from the storm, surely those big boots had left footprints.

'Nothing.' He looked at her and began to unbutton his coat. After a minute Deputy Putnam did the same. The sheriff sat down on the easy chair and Deputy Putnam, after a look around the room, settled for the rocking chair, perching gingerly on its forward edge. Solomon eyed him for a moment from the hearthrug, then jumped up on to his lap and began to knead his thighs, staring all the time into his wary face.

'Maybe you'd better tell me just what happened,' Matt suggested.

Slowly, jerkily, Laura related what had occurred earlier. As with nightmares, it didn't seem much in the telling, but the memory of it made her voice unreliable. She could have sworn there was still blood in her hair, she was sure she could feel it running down over her scalp.

'You didn't actually see his face, then,' Matt concluded, jabbing his ballpoint pen into the pad as he wrote.

'No. That is – he turned just before he went into the trees, but he was too far away by then. I could only see dark shadows where his eyes were.'

'Beard, moustache – anything like that?'

'No. Just that long grey hair flying everywhere. I suppose it could even have been a woman, but it didn't run like a woman. He was very awkward, or old . . . it looked as if it hurt him to run.'

'And he poured blood on your head?'

'Yes. And he spoke in a kind of moaning voice, some kind of words I didn't recognize. And then he ran away. That's all.'

'I see.' He glanced at David, who was approaching with a tray of coffee mugs. 'And you didn't recognize anything about him?'

'I'm afraid not.'

'Here one minute, gone the next,' Matt went on.

'Well, yes – that's right.' She looked at him, puzzled.

He seemed to be thinking things over as he accepted a mug of coffee and stirred it with the top of his pen. David gave another to Deputy Putnam, who was now rendered immobile by Solomon lying in a circle on his lap and had to be careful not to spill anything or rock too violently. He drank his coffee with his elbows high. David settled down beside her on the sofa.

'Dr Butler says you were supposed to wait for him to walk you back here, after dark.'

'Yes, but David wasn't here, was he?' she pointed out. 'He was with you.'

'That's right.' Matt nodded. 'Dr Butler was with me.'

She stared at him, still puzzled by his odd manner, then it slowly began to dawn that he didn't believe what she'd told him about the strange figure. 'He could have killed me.'

'But he didn't.'

'Would you have been happier if he had?' she demanded in a nettled voice.

Matt raised his eyebrows. 'Now that's a foolish thing to say, isn't it?'

'Well, I get the strangest feeling you don't think I saw the Shadowman.'

'Is that who you think it was?'

'Well, for goodness sake, he was wearing feathers in his hair, his cloak was all covered with . . . with things . . . bits of colour and . . . who else could it have been? Most people don't go around pouring blood on other people, do they? Or is life really that different in Blackwater Bay?'

'Not really,' Matt said. 'Fact is, Miss Brandon, we've never had a consistent description of the Shadowman – or whoever is pretending to be the Shadowman this time around. This could just have been some tramp you frightened, the one we've been looking for, maybe the one who set that fire the other night.' He looked at her wet head, her shivering body inside the terry-cloth robe. 'Sure wish you hadn't washed your hair,' he said.

'Sorry,' she said sarcastically. 'I didn't like the way the blood clashed with my outfit.' Didn't he realize how horrible it had been, how disgusted she'd felt? 'Anyway,' she continued, 'I already thought of that.' She felt in the pocket of her robe and produced a little plastic bag of her own. In it was a tissue with some of the blood on it. 'I saved this for you.'

He accepted it in some surprise.

'I'm not a total dunce,' she said to him with asperity. 'I know you need all kinds of evidence. This could have been the person who killed Clarissa and Julie. It seems to me you're pretty casual for somebody who has a couple of murders in his lap and is called out because a strange man is seen running around in the very area where those murders were committed. Shouldn't you have men searching the woods, shouldn't you put up road blocks or—'

'Road blocks are to stop cars, Miss Brandon, not ghosts.'

'You really don't believe me, do you?'

'I didn't say that.'

'No, you don't have to actually say it, but it's true, isn't it? You're just sitting there doing nothing because you don't believe me.' She leaned forward. '*Why* don't you believe me? I'm not in the habit of lying or making things up.' She held out her arms. 'See? No cuts . . . that *is* some of the blood that was in my hair.'

Matt glanced at David briefly. 'Everybody's a little het up, what with the killings and all. This man you say you saw—'

'You mean this man I *did* see—'

'Whatever. He did you no real harm.'

'He scared me half to death.'

'And vice versa, from what you say. You chased him—'

'Only until I realized that was a stupid thing to do. You just don't want to believe me, do you?' she said slowly.

He sighed. 'I don't want to have people out here running around in the dark with their shotguns out, looking for some phantom and blowing each other's brains out by mistake, no. And I don't want even more reporters than we already have crawling all over the place and turning the town into a forty-three-ring circus, no. Everybody is scared, it's only natural. And it's only natural to be scared for other people too.' He glanced at David again, then stood up. 'It's not that I don't believe you, ma'am. It's just that I haven't got the manpower to search those woods again safely or properly in the dark. We'll have another try in the morning.'

'But—'

'The main thing is you aren't hurt.' He glanced round and saw his deputy, who looked at him rather desperately across the mound of fur in his lap. With a grunt of amusement the sheriff went over, plucked up Solomon and dropped him on the hearthrug. 'Come on, George, I want to go up to the clinic for a minute.'

At the door, Matt paused. 'You'll keep this other thing to yourself, Butler?'

'Yes, of course.' David nodded.

When the two men had left, David drew her close. 'You little idiot,' he murmured. 'You didn't have to do that, you know.'

'Do what?'

'Say you saw someone running around the woods and put stuff on your head, just to divert suspicion from me. I don't know whether to be flattered that you care, or insulted that you thought I needed . . .'

'David.' She pulled back and looked at him. 'I *did* see someone, just as I said. And he did do what I said.'

'The Shadowman?' He smiled at her fondly, running a finger along her jaw and pushing back her wet hair. He glanced at his hand, but apparently saw nothing out of the ordinary. So the blood was gone, after all.

'Maybe.' She was getting angry again and pushed his hand away. 'I wanted a shower and a shampoo. I wanted to wash the Shadowman right out of my hair.' Even as she spoke she recognized the lyric and felt herself blush.

'Oh, Laura, come on. There *is* no such thing.'

'David – I saw him.'

He gazed into her eyes for a long time. 'You're serious,' he finally said.

'Yes, yes, *yes*!'

'But . . . that's impossible.' He seemed confused.

'Is it?' She sat up a little straighter. 'There's a long history of nasty things happening in this town that had to be done by someone. I'm not saying it was a phantom or a monster who did those things – but some of them might have been done by the person I saw tonight. There really might be some sick, unhappy man living wild out there . . .'

'No. I'm sorry, but no. I can't believe that any more than the sheriff can. This isn't some unmapped wilderness. People have lived around here for centuries and they must know these woods. No man could live undetected in them for more than a day or two. The sheriff searched this morning, didn't he? He would have told us if he'd found any signs of someone living out there.'

'I . . . saw . . . him.' She spaced the words out for emphasis. Why wouldn't he believe her? Why didn't the sheriff believe her? Her frustration was overtaken by another thought. 'What was that "other thing" he wanted you to keep to yourself, by the way?'

'If I told you I wouldn't be keeping it to myself, would I?' David said lightly.

'Oh, David – what was it?'

'Well, let's just say it might be a clue to the reason Clarissa was killed. You remember I told you she said something to me about drugs the other morning?'

'I don't . . .'

'In the linen closet,' he reminded her.

'Oh, yes . . .' She flushed slightly. 'I remember now.'

'Well, she wasn't very clear – Clarissa never was if it meant she could keep people guessing – but it sounded like someone has been stealing certain drugs from the clinic.'

'Good heavens. Does Uncle Roger know?'

'No, obviously not. And neither does the sheriff, for certain. That's why he doesn't want me to say anything yet. And *you're* not to say anything either, not even to your uncle. The sheriff will do that, if he finds out anything to confirm it. I've told him all I know – the rest is up to him.'

'It seems to me far too much is up to him,' she muttered. 'No matter what anyone tells him, he just goes on his own sweet way in his own sweet time.'

'Now – just because he didn't believe your story about the Shadowman . . .' David began.

'But he was there,' she said in desperation. 'He really was.'

'Okay, okay,' David soothed. 'But try to forget it, now. Put it out of your mind.'

He really believed she could.

Matt was surprised to find Gilliam in a wheelchair and not in bed. The room was dimly lit and the chair was drawn up by the window that overlooked the car-park.

'You took your time about getting up here,' Gilliam commented, turning the chair to face his visitor.

'How'd you know I was here?'

'I saw the reflection of the red flasher on the ceiling – the rest was simple deduction. I *am* a detective you know. Or was.'

'You and Ironside,' Matt said and immediately regretted it.

Gilliam scowled. 'What were you doing in the woods?'

'Miss Brandon claims she saw the Shadowman. Rang me up, hysterical, said to come and catch him. So I came.'

'Was she hurt? Is she all right?'

'She's fine. She says he put blood on her head and then ran away.'

'Blood?'

Matt held up a plastic bag. 'Possibly from this little guy. He was fresh killed and left behind.'

'Anything else?'

'She says he spoke some words over her.'

'And that was all?'

'That's the whole thing.' Matt shrugged and sat down in the visitor's chair. 'What do you know about drugs?' he asked.

'What kind of drugs? What the hell has that got to do with—'

'Prescription stuff. Is there much money in that these days?'

'There's always money in drugs. Listen, am I to gather that you didn't find this Shadowman character?'

'You don't see me leading him around on a string, do you?' Matt snapped. 'She might have made the whole thing up, scared I was arresting her precious Dr Butler.'

'And were you?'

'Nope.'

'Does she really strike you as that type of woman?'

'No. But then I'm not very good on women's motives,' Matt admitted. 'By the time we got here she'd washed her hair and there was no blood in it that I could see. But she had the presence of mind to keep some blood on a tissue for me. Bright girl.'

'And that makes you *suspect* her?'

'Not really.' Matt hunched forward, his elbows on his knees. 'How much do you know about a guy named Panotis?'

Gilliam made the connection easily. 'His wife is a patient here.'

'Uh-huh. And Stryker tells me he's known to the

Grantham drug squad, but nobody has ever pinned him down. What quantity of drugs do you figure goes through a place like this in a week?'

'Not enough to interest someone like Panotis, that's for sure,' Gilliam said firmly. 'Anyway, the big money is in heroin, Ecstasy, cocaine, crack – they're the volume business. There are only about forty patients here. Most of them are on pain-killers, maybe some morphine post-operatively, but not much. And probably barbiturates or anti-depressants. But it can't amount to anything.'

'What about psychotropic drugs?'

'LSD, Ecstasy, that kind of thing?'

'Yeah.'

Gilliam shrugged. 'No idea. I guess Dr Weaver would be the one to ask about those. Can't imagine why he'd have them, though.'

'Any addicts being treated here?'

'What did Forrester say?'

'Forrester says a lot of things. What do *you* say?'

'I say no. Not at the moment, anyway. Not since I came or since Mrs Strayhorn came. Any that might have been here before that I wouldn't know about, but I think it's not their policy. Too complicated. They'll dry out rich alcoholics now and again, probably, and I know there are several mildly crazy "nervous breakdown" patients here.'

'Yeah, I know about those.'

'I'd also guess a few of the patients sniff coke when they're at home, but not here.'

'Just a nice, clean establishment?'

'You think otherwise?'

'According to what Miss Janacek told Butler, somebody is stealing certain drugs here. As you say, not on a big enough basis to interest somebody like Panotis, but steady. That's the thing, Tom. It's steady – a nice little income supplement for someone connected with an addict, for instance. Or who might be an addict themselves.'

'Any candidates?'

'That's what I want from you.'

'You think this is the motive for the Janacek murder?'
'I think, maybe.'
'And for the Zalinsky killing?'
'That I can't connect,' Matt admitted. 'According to Butler a physiotherapist doesn't have direct access to drugs or drug orders.'
'You talked to Butler about this?'
'He's my source for what the Janacek girl claimed. She told him about it shortly before she was killed.'
'She was a bitch, Matt.'
'I know that. I know there were a lot of people who didn't like her. But this is the only thing I've found that might make somebody *kill* her. The Zalinsky thing—'
'Julie Zalinsky was an odd kind of busybody,' Gilliam said and relayed what Laura had told him. 'She could have found out about the drugs somehow.'
Matt leaned back, gratified. 'Now that was worth the trip out here.'
'Glad to be of help,' Gilliam said wryly.
'Still, I'd like to know how drugs are handled here.'
'Surely Butler told you that.'
'He told me how they're *supposed* to be handled. I want to find out what's really going on. I want you to find the hole the stuff is slipping through. Can you do it?'
Gilliam shrugged. 'Look, you know and I know that nurses and paramedics help themselves to samples and stuff all the time—'
'This might be more than that.'
'Could be. Might be. What's the real story on this, Matt? You asked me to find out about the people here to help you figure out who killed Julie Zalinsky. I did my best. Then the Janacek girl gets killed, and you decide it's some psychopath after all and take me *off* the job, so to speak. Someone pours blood on Laura Brandon's head but you don't believe her because she washed it out and only has some on a tissue to show you. Wouldn't *you* wash it out if somebody did that to you?'
'I suppose so,' Matt conceded.

'Now you've come up with this drug angle, which seems pretty tenuous to me. You're very jumpy, Matt.'

Matt sighed and looked out into the night. 'All I want is an answer. All I want is no more killings and somebody in jail for the two we've had, that's what I want. What's wrong with that?'

'Nothing.'

'A good law officer has to look into every option, right? Every possibility, every angle.' He looked belligerent and a little angry. 'Right?'

Gilliam smiled a very small smile. 'Right. So now you're discounting the psychopath and the Shadowman for good?'

'No, not exactly.' Matt now looked uncomfortable.

'You don't want it to be that, do you?' Gilliam said slowly. 'But you're still worried about it. . . . What did you find in the woods this morning, Matt?'

'A few things . . . a bit of cloth, a scalpel—'

'A *scalpel*?'

'Yeah – a nice, clean, shiny one.'

'Was it used to cut throats?'

'Who can say? It was clean, no prints, no blood, no anything. Scalpels are pretty common around a hospital – somebody could have taken an old one into the woods to cut wildflowers, for all I know.'

'Interesting. Anything else?'

Matt sighed. 'Charley found some kind of display set out, with a nurse's cap in the middle of it. Seemed a little too neat and convenient to me, somehow. Like a stage set. Nothing else around it, no fire traces, no blood, nothing. But Seth . . . my youngest deputy . . . he stumbled into something all right. Literally. Kind of a hell-hole, I guess you'd call it. A pit full of bones.'

'My God.'

'Oh, no human remains. Animals. Dogs, cats, small mammals. Old dry stuff on the bottom – but on the top – fresher stuff. Rotting. He went right into it, up to his belt buckle. Had to send him home. He was . . . upset.'

'And so are you.'

Matt's hands clenched into fists. 'I don't want this. I don't *want* all this superstitious crap. The media – Jesus, Tom, do you know what the papers and television people are making of this already? It's a witch-hunt, they're going wild with it, they always do. They've already started to try it on, stories here and there, getting local people to talk about the Shadowman. When they find out about the stuff we found this morning . . .'

'And yet you still don't believe that Miss Brandon saw something tonight?' Gilliam asked.

'I suppose she must have,' Matt conceded. 'Her description was so detailed . . . so . . . particular, that I guess I have to believe her. But I didn't let her think so. At least I hope I didn't. I really can't picture her killing a squirrel just to distract me from arresting her boyfriend. But I don't want to be stampeded. She's a very insistent woman – and she wants to know who killed her friend.'

'Well, who would this mysterious person be?' Gilliam asked. 'If it wasn't really this Shadowman character?'

Matt leaned forward. 'Someone in the chain of drugs using a disguise to hide behind. To scare people from looking too closely,' he said. 'Someone who was making contact with his supplier here at the clinic. Could be anyone, a nurse, a paramedic, a technician, a cook, Higgins, Michaels . . . even Forrester himself.'

'You're getting desperate, Matt,' Gilliam warned. 'If you really think you should examine all possibilities then you can't go on ignoring evidence that's right under your nose, just because you don't *want* it to be there. I mean, that display you mentioned and that bone pit thing . . . there's definitely something weird going on out there.'

Matt stood up abruptly. 'Or someone wants us to think so. I have to attend a town meeting and I'm already late. Just see if you can get me a line on this drug business. Leave the Shadowman to me.'

# SEVENTEEN

MOUNTVIEW WAS NOT A HAPPY place.

The very air seemed infected, both with staphylococcus germs and with suspicion and fear. The nurses were stretched to the limit.

Laura had been late coming across because she'd spent a long time walking over the ground between her place and the edge of the woods, trying to find some evidence of the apparition she'd seen.

There was none.

Incredible as it seemed, she could find nothing, no mark, no imprint, nothing of any kind to prove that what she'd seen had been solid and real. Of course, the ground had been frozen last night and the grass was fairly thick, but even so, on the bare stretches near the trees she'd thought there would be *something*.

But no.

As the day wore on her preoccupation occasioned a few reproachful reminders from patients she either left under heat lamps too long or pummelled and manipulated a little too enthusiastically. They were all on edge and many had begun to have second thoughts about remaining at the clinic. Tempers were short. She began to think about asking Dr Weaver for another tranquillizer, but reasoned that she would probably have to stand in line.

The one thing that kept returning to amaze her, aside from the fear that had arisen from being startled and being touched, was the fact that the Shadowman himself – or whatever it had been – had left her feeling so curious and so sad. She thought it had to do with the way he'd run away. If it was he who was responsible for all the things attributed to him he was definitely dangerous. Yet he himself had seemed frightened. He had run so awkwardly, so . . . she paused, her hands still on Mr Dorrington's shoulders. The Shadowman had run as if his feet hurt. She knew that kind of movement – she certainly ought to in her profession. As if every step burned.

'What's the matter?' asked Mr Dorrington, peering up at her over his shoulder.

She resumed his massage. 'Nothing. I was just thinking.'

Depite her lack of terror of the Shadowman, whatever he might be, she had definitely resolved not to go wandering around the grounds after dark again, if she could help it. That meant using her lunch-hour for something more constructive than consuming calories.

Therefore, at just before one o'clock, she got into her car and headed for town. At the foot of the drive she slowed, or tried to, but only after a steady pumping of the brakes did she succeed in stopping. Well, now there was something else wrong with the damn car. She'd already had to have the carburettor and the fuel pump replaced, and two new tyres put on. And the battery had been dead the other day. It was all mounting up. At least she could afford repairs now.

She turned on to the highway and put on the radio, hoping for some music. All she got was the local news, including some meant-to-be-funny references to the Shadowman. They weren't very funny, not to someone who'd encountered him so recently.

The road ran straight down to the bridge at the foot of the hill and it wasn't until she was a third of the way down that she realized the earlier episode of the reluctant brakes had been more than just a symptom of trouble to come. The trouble was here. The brakes were gone.

She hadn't been going fast and had merely touched them to slow the car slightly. The touch had produced no firm response. She jammed the pedal to the floor.

Still nothing.

And the car was picking up speed.

Now, keep calm, she told herself, trying not to scream. You have two options. You can jump out. Or you can keep going and hope for the best. The side of the road, blurring now, didn't look all that great a prospect and letting the car go on without a driver meant that it might cause a terrible accident. She took a firmer grip on the wheel and, thanking the gods for having a stick shift, pushed in the clutch in order to drop down into third. The car's engine, protesting, finally accepted the lower gear with a lurch. Two more gears to go and still the car was picking up speed. She tried again, this time attempting to get straight into first.

The car jerked like a hooked trout, the gearbox screamed a protest and the stick was thrown back into neutral. Gritting her teeth, she went through the sequence again, this time holding the gear-stick in place despite the horrendous sounds coming from beneath the hood. Bucking and howling, the car finally dropped into second. She was afraid to try for first at the speed she was still travelling. The car didn't seem to like what was happening any more than she did.

They bottomed out at the foot of the hill and shot between the steel supports of the bridge. She was still holding on grimly to the steering wheel and a car coming in the other direction blared its horn at her, presumably because of her speed. At the far end of the bridge the road forked, the right fork going into Main Street, the left towards the high school.

She turned left, with a squeal of tyres. The gas station also lay along this road. The high-school parking lot loomed up ahead on the left. Her speed was steadily coming down now, but she was still travelling too fast to consider trying to stop the car by running into something. She turned into the entrance of the lot, whirled along the semicircular drive and out the other end. There was a slight rise in the drive and that slowed her even more. She came back on to the highway, fortunately free of traffic at that instant, and skidded into a turn towards the gas station a few hundred yards ahead. She had some control of the car, now. She turned in and gently bumped to a stop directly in front of the pumps. Shaking, she turned off the ignition, put her head down on the steering wheel and burst into tears.

There was a knocking on the window beside her and she looked up. The cheerful face of the station owner beamed down at her. 'Shall I fill her up?' he asked hopefully.

An hour later she was back on the road into town, shaken but unbowed. Jake Miller, his grin wiped away by what she'd had to tell him, had put the car up on the rack for inspection. Hardly surprising the brakes hadn't worked, he said after a minute. There was a hole in the brake line where it ran along under the door and all the fluid had leaked out. Damn stupid place to put a plastic brake line, he said. Typical of these foreign cars. She should have bought American.

'When brakes go they can go fast,' he told her. 'You should check your brake fluid reservoir as regular as you check your oil.'

She didn't tell him she hardly ever remembered to do *that* and she didn't even know where the brake fluid reservoir was, much less what it looked like or what to put in it.

'I can replace the line,' he said. 'But I think you'd better think about a new gearbox. What you done ain't what we call "recommended practice".'

She didn't recommend it herself, she told him. 'I've been thinking about getting a new car anyway.'

He nodded. 'I'd do it before winter really sets in,' he advised. 'No sense asking for trouble if you can avoid it. This ole thing's about wore down to the rivets and that's a fact. I can get you a good deal on something reliable. Don't you go to that old robber Molt.'

Well, she thought, I can afford it now. Her pay in Omaha had been barely adequate for city living, but her salary from Uncle Roger was quite the opposite and she had no rent to cover either. Living in the country she'd need a more reliable car, the distances were greater, the elements more daunting than those encountered on city streets. To say nothing of the hills.

She paid him for the repair and agreed to let him find her a good, reliable second-hand car. He said it would only take him a few days and he'd call her up at the clinic when one came in. She drove off with an ominous grinding from under the hood.

She had a difficult time trying to find a place to park, which seemed odd, seeing that it was out of season. Then she spotted the sheriff standing in front of his building, surrounded by a bunch of strangers in city shoes, and understood. The media had arrived.

Matt Gabriel looked like granite from the neck up as he tried to push through the throng that followed him like gadflies to his car. They bent down to shout through the windows as he drove away. Their quick eyes darted around the street in search of new sources to tap. She parked on a side-street, grabbed her books from the back seat and walked resolutely to the library, glad her coat covered her uniform. It would have been like waving a flag at the reporters.

She put her books down on the empty desk and looked around. No Mitch Hasker. She decided she might as well stock up on reading matter if she was going to be confined to barracks in the evenings. She glanced at the clock on the wall – not much time. If she was going to do all her errands during daylight hours she should really be visiting the supermarket or the laundromat – but she wanted to talk to Mitch Hasker.

She found him in a back room, where a great many windows looked out on to a long, narrow strip of garden. He was deep in conversation with a middle-aged couple wearing coats and galoshes. The man was nondescript, the woman's wispy brown hair was covered with a battered brown felt hat held on firmly with a rather garish scarf.

Mitch looked up at the sound of her footsteps, made his excuses to the couple and came over. 'I didn't expect you until Saturday,' he said.

'Saturday?'

He smirked slightly. 'I find people usually have a favourite day for coming in,' he explained. 'You've come in twice on a Saturday and I'd more or less put you down for then.'

'I didn't realize you ran an appointments system.'

His face tightened. 'Well, hardly.'

She saw he couldn't take a joke. 'I only meant you must keep a vast mental file on people to remember each of us individually. I have a difficult time keeping my patients and their treatments straight without my trusty written schedule.' She realized she was babbling. 'Anyway, it's nice to be remembered.'

He accepted the tribute and bestowed a small smile in return. 'I have a long memory,' he said. 'My mind is naturally precise and, of course, I've trained it. I almost never have to refer to the computer when people want a particular book.'

'That's wonderful.' You old fraud, she thought, I'll pour it on and you can soak it up. 'You're the ideal person to help me, then. I want to find out anything and everything about the Shadowman.'

His face went blank. 'Whatever for?'

'Because he paid me a visit last night and I want to know more about him.'

'Paid you a visit?' Hasker seemed horrified. 'You mean, you actually *saw* him?'

'Indeed, I did.' She was surprised at the effect of her announcement. 'And I'll know him next time I see him, too. I expect to become firm friends with the silly old fool.'

Hasker stepped back a pace and gazed at her with a kind of awed fascination mixed with reproach. 'You can't be serious,' he finally said.

'Why not?'

'Why, this is a figure of fear and mystery, a legend, a myth out of the . . .'

'He's real, he's dirty, he smells and he's pathetic,' she said firmly.

'Pathetic?' Hasker almost squealed, then glanced at the couple who were watching them, leaning forward to hear better, their spindly bundled-up bodies at exactly the same angle, like two birds on a branch. 'Come in here.' Mitch took her by the arm and bustled her along to his office. 'Now then,' he said, settling her down in a chair and glaring at her like an angry schoolmaster. 'Tell me.'

'There's nothing to tell.' She was rather breathless from her forced march. 'One minute he was there, the next he was running off, nearly falling over himself to get away from me. He was scared of me, so why should I be scared of him?'

'I'm certainly surprised to hear that you found him a laughable sight.'

'Not laughable,' she corrected him. 'Sad. Poor old man.'

Hasker leaned back in his antique captain's chair and regarded her with dismay. He picked up a pipe and began to fiddle with it. Her father had smoked a pipe, but from the look of Hasker's it was merely a prop. It could have been new, of course, but when he continued to fondle it without reaching for either tobacco or matches she was sure. Just part of the scholarly image, like the small and elegantly furnished office, and the gold chain across his middle from which dangled a Phi Beta Kappa key, prominently and dead centre. There was a smell of aftershave, of leather bindings, of brandy, even – but not of tobacco.

'This "poor old man", as you call him, has been responsible for some dreadful things over the years,' Hasker said.

'I doubt that.'

'I wouldn't, if I were you. Remember, I've lived here all my life, you haven't. The Shadowman has always been here. Always. He represents a tradition that goes back to colonial times. And an older tradition that goes back to the caves.'

'What tradition?'

'Evil mischief,' Hasker said with some satisfaction. 'Retribution, vengeance, spite, come-uppance – call it what you will. You're inviting it by your attitude, you know. The Greeks called it "hubris" – the conviction that one knows better than the gods.'

'I'd hardly call the Shadowman a god,' she said drily. 'And nobody is seeing my "attitude", as you call it, but you.'

'Don't be too sure, my dear.'

She looked around melodramatically. 'You mean the walls have ears?' She didn't know why Hasker brought out the irreverent side of her nature, but he did. Perhaps it was his pompous manner, or his smug air of knowing all and telling little. She simply couldn't resist it. She'd meant to ask him seriously about the Shadowman, but it was proving difficult. 'Look,' she said, trying to get herself in hand, 'I did see someone out at the clinic and I don't *think* it was a spirit, or a ghost, or even a tradition.'

'What do you think it was, then?'

'I don't know,' she admitted. 'Probably just some tramp. But I thought I'd try to find out more about it.'

'About the Shadowman?'

'Yes.'

'What would you like to know?'

'Aren't there any books on it?'

'Only the one I'm writing myself.'

'Oh. Nothing at all?'

'Nothing at all.'

'Then, can you tell me?'

'I'll try.'

Hasker leaned back, tapping the stem of his pipe on his chest as he pursed his lips together, preparing to lecture to this interested young woman who obviously needed to be taught some respect. 'You may have heard the Shadowman also referred to as the Shaman. A Shaman is actually a sorcerer or witch-doctor or – in Indian lore – a medicine man. Or, perhaps, "sham-man", meaning a spirit pretending to be a man, taking the form of a man but not a man. Either way, we find reference to it in the diaries of the earliest settlers in America, who didn't always have an easy peace with the local tribes as they cleared land. The Indians were masters of guerrilla warfare, of course.'

'Of course,' Laura murmured.

'They would strike from the shadows, from the dark shadows of the woods, which of course were much larger and more dense in those days. I don't think any of us can imagine what it was like then, the absolute enclosure of the small farms and settlements by the great tracts of forests that stretched unbroken for hundreds of miles in every direction, familiar ground to the Indians, but totally unknown to the white men. It's no wonder they were filled with awe and fear.' Hasker put down his pipe. 'Anyway, there *was* real danger then, in straying away from the camps and enclaves. Hence the cautionary phrase folks around here still use to keep their kids in line – "Beware the Shadowman".'

'But what I saw wasn't an Indian.'

'No, I'm sure it wasn't. Let me see – it was a man with long white hair, wearing a uniform of some kind, is that right?'

'Well, the long hair, yes, but he had some kind of cape or cloak over whatever was underneath. It was all decorated with ribbons and painted symbols and bits of feathers.'

Hasker nodded. 'Yes, that's been reported too. You see, our local legend grew up around an early settler who was captured by the Indians in retaliation for one of their tribe being hanged. They tortured him to the point of madness, then turned him loose to wander in the forest, apparently as a warning to newcomers. You must remember, the Indians were frightened too. Everything was being taken from them, inexorably, by people they didn't understand. Everything was being destroyed, all that they had, all that they'd known, inch by inch, foot by foot, yard by yard.'

'You're trying hard to be fair, but what they did to that man was a terrible thing.'

'Indeed it was. So was the British habit of rewarding good Indians with nice bright red blankets. Blankets, I might add, that were straight off the beds of dead smallpox victims.'

'No!' Laura was shocked, but she believed him.

'I'm afraid so, my dear.' He shook his head. 'They were terrible times.'

'And this tortured man is supposed to be the Shadowman? That's who I'm supposed to have seen?'

'It sounds like it.'

'But he was no ghost. He was *real.* I could see his boots, they were cracked and muddy. I could – *smell* him.'

Hasker's face wrinkled with distaste. 'Smell him?'

'Yes. Age and dirt and bitter sweat.'

'Was there a sensation of sudden cold?'

'It was cold anyway.'

'Spiritual phenomena are often quite complete,' Hasker said. 'Including smells,' he added. 'It's well documented.'

'And this is the "thing" that's supposed to have gone around setting places on fire, killing pets – maybe killing nurses?' she asked.

Hasker drew himself up. 'Never people,' he said firmly. 'I told you before, evil mischief, no more. Retribution, punishment.'

'For what?'

He shrugged, as if suddenly uninterested. 'Who can say?'

'Presumably, those people who'd offended it.'

'But they never say,' Hasker pointed out. 'They accept their punishment.'

'If I hadn't seen it myself, I'd say it's a bunch of nonsense,' she said.

Hasker smiled. 'But you did see him. I envy you.'

'*Envy* me?'

'Oh, yes, indeed. You see, I've researched him and written about him, talked to people like yourself who claim to have seen him, but I've never seen him myself. Very few people have. Your uncle's clinic is built on the spot he used to appear most often. He was supposed to be the father of the man who built the original Mountview – Jeremy Hasker.'

'Hasker?'

'Why yes – I'm sorry, I thought you knew. But of course, you wouldn't. That's the source of my interest – the Shadowman is a direct ancestor of Shirley's and mine.'

'Good Lord.'

'Yes. I've always been a bit ashamed when he strikes. It's rather like having an embarrassing relative who turns up at parties uninvited and behaves badly.'

She wondered, suddenly, if he was laughing at her. 'Don't let the reporters hear that,' she said. 'They'll go bananas.'

'Reporters?'

'Yes. I saw them trying to corner the sheriff earlier. I guess it must be a slow news time or something – there's a bunch of them haunting Main Street right now.'

Her choice of words drew a chuckle from him. 'As if the Shadowman wasn't enough haunting to put up with,' he said.

'Yes, well – so far the murders have only made the local and city papers. They're bad enough. If it gets on to the national networks or some of those horrible freesheets – Uncle Roger will go berserk.' She stood up.

'Poor man,' Hasker murmured. 'It must be particularly upsetting for him, seeing as he was so *fond* of both girls.'

She stopped and stood very still. Mitch Hasker's voice had been quiet, almost a whisper to himself. 'What do you mean?'

His eyes were pale grey and watered slightly in the bright overhead light as he looked up at her. 'Why nothing in particular. Just what I said. Should it have meant something?' He put down his pipe on his desk blotter. 'Shirley tells me that your uncle has a very strong feeling for his staff, most commendable in my opinion. Family affection is beyond price, whether by blood or adoption, as it were.' He smiled suddenly. 'And it's so much easier to feel like that when people are personally attractive, don't you agree?'

He didn't really seem to expect an answer, as it wasn't a question but an oblique statement about Uncle Roger that left everything to the imagination and was intended to do so. 'I appreciate your telling me about the Shadowman,' she said without smiling. 'I have to get back to the clinic, now.'

'Of course,' he said, graciousness itself, a kind host speeding a guest on her way. He stood up and with a courtly gesture, pushing wide the already partly open door to his office. As they emerged she saw the couple Hasker had been talking to earlier, standing one on each side of the doorway, pretending to peruse the shelves. She had no doubt they'd listened to every word and could probably, *would* probably, relay them far and wide.

'Now, if you have any more questions about your "visitor", please don't hesitate to come in again,' Hasker said.

'I'll give him your regards,' she promised. 'I'm sure he'd like to know his descendants are doing so well.' Nettled by his remark about her uncle, she was pleased to see Mitch Hasker's cheek-bones grow pink as he caught her meaning. The Haskers were once the wealthy owners of Mountview. Now a Hasker was just the local librarian in a small town, despite his scholarly pretensions. His lips tightened and he went back into his office, like a badger into its sett. She knew it had been a petty shot, but didn't regret it.

Once outside, she went striding towards her car and nearly collided with the hunched figure of Martin Hambden, who was walking down the street apparently in a daze. Recognizing her, he smiled, but it was a weary effort.

'I didn't know you were back already,' Laura said in surprise. As far as she'd known he was attending a medical conference in Switzerland.

'Oh, yes – I came back early. Picked up some kind of bug over there, I think. Or perhaps I just can't handle jet lag any more. Thought some fresh air might help.' The smile didn't reach his eyes.

'Are you sure you should be out of bed?' she asked worriedly, for over the weeks she'd been at Mountview she'd grown to like this extremely gifted man. He might frighten others with his short temper and plain speaking, but he didn't scare her a bit. The respect and affection were mutual, although based on very few encounters.

'I don't know,' he admitted with a sigh. 'I had hoped to come up to the clinic to see if I could be of any help to Roger. He must be deeply distressed by this latest tragedy.'

'Oh, I don't know if I'd say he was *distressed*,' she said slowly, wondering why Hambden should think he would be. 'He's certainly outraged and harassed, and afraid the media will make a big . . . thing . . . about it.'

Hambden nodded. 'It's a terrible process they use to

make the death of a beautiful and vulnerable girl into a cheap sensation. It's sickening.'

Clarissa? Vulnerable? 'It certainly is,' she agreed. 'But, of course, they'll connect it with the other murder.'

'Other murder?'

'Julie Zalinsky's murder.'

'Oh, yes. Of course.'

She stared at him. How could he have forgotten Julie's murder? He'd worked with her, probably more closely than anyone else at the clinic. He really didn't look well. 'They're saying it's the Shadowman.'

Hambden snorted, a sudden clear light of derision in his eyes sharpening them momentarily. 'What rubbish. The killing was obviously done by a sexual psychopath, which is dreadful enough. We hardly need to add to the lurid sensationalists by dragging in local legends, do we?'

'I saw him, last night.'

'Who?' His attention was wandering again and his eyes seemed to fix on the small group of reporters who were now settled, like a flock of magpies, on the steps of the sheriff's office. Smoke from their cigars and cigarettes rose above their heads to mix with the vapours of their breathing as they exchanged theories and tried to find ways to warm up their stories.

'The Shadowman.'

'Oh? How is he?'

'What?'

'Gilliam. How is he?' It was a perfunctory question, his wandering attention mutating Shadowman to Gilliam. She decided to let it go.

'He's improving. I'm starting him in the pool this afternoon.'

'Well, well – I thought you were the right girl for the job.' Hambden nodded, coming back to focus on her with some surprise. 'I must come along and see.'

'Whenever you're well enough. He's doing just fine,' she reassured him. 'Of course, he has a long way to go.'

'Yes . . . yes.'

She could see he was shivering with the cold and weariness. 'I don't think fresh air is the right thing for you, Doctor. If you don't mind a layperson's diagnosis – I think you should be home in bed.'

He sighed again. 'I suppose so. It's difficult to accept weakness.'

'Why not let me drive you home?'

He started to protest, but gave in. She helped him fold his long legs into the little car, then followed his directions down the side-streets until they pulled up in the drive of a beautiful white clapboard house caught like a snowflake in a stand of green pines. No autumn colours here – just the white house with the shutters echoing the dark green-black of the trees and the accent of deep-red curtains in all the downstairs windows.

'What a beautiful house!' she exclaimed.

Hambden looked at it dully. 'Beautiful, yes. Also big and very empty. Only full at Christmas time. The rest of the year my housekeeper Mrs Davis and I rattle around like two dried peas in a gourd.'

'You're usually only here at weekends, aren't you?'

'If that.' His expression was glum as he looked at the house. 'Soon it will be all the time. Retiring, you know.' He extended his hands in front of him and stared at the gloves as if he could see through them. In a way, she supposed, he could. His hands would be more familiar to him than most people's. 'Not good enough any more. Have to use good tools if you want to do a job right. Going all to hell with arthritis, now. Proper judgement on me, don't you think?'

'But you can still teach,' she protested. 'With all your experience, David says—'

He glanced sideways at her. 'David? Young Butler, you mean? He could have been a good cutter himself, but he's too pigheaded. Won't be told, you know. Good enough, but if he could be taught, no knowing what he might do. Shame.'

She had never seen David in that light and was startled. 'What do you mean?'

Hambden shrugged. 'A good surgeon needs ego, of course. He certainly has that. Also needs a little humility. He *hasn't* got that, yet. Maybe it will come. Leaving it late, though. Shouldn't have holed up at Mountview – should have stayed out where it was cold and tough. Been much better for him.' He turned in his seat and regarded her with a faint, momentary interest. 'Been better for you, too. You want a brave man, my dear, not a smug one.' He reached for the handle of the passenger door. 'Well, perhaps you'll be the brave one. It might make the difference to have a woman like you behind him. Made a difference for me, come to think of it.' He pushed open the door, but made no move to get out, as if he were reluctant to commit himself to the house. As if it were an admission of defeat to leave the car and the bright, crisp day and the attentive girl, and walk into lonely darkness. But he was not well. 'Silent in there, now. Mrs Davis drops a spoon in the kitchen, occasionally. That's all.' He glanced at her. 'Thank God for electric blankets,' he said suddenly and levered himself out on to the drive. Bending down, he gave her a brief twinkle of a smile. 'Thanks for the ride, my dear. Give my best to your uncle, tell him I'll be along . . . when I can.'

'I will. You take care of yourself,' she admonished him as she started up the engine.

He slammed the door with a wave through the window and she thought she heard him say 'Nobody else will', but she wasn't sure. She wasn't sure, either, whether he was genuinely coming down with the flu, or was just an old, tired man. Either way, he shouldn't have been out in the cold, and she felt a wash of relief when he'd safely negotiated the steps and closed the big front door behind him.

She'd tell Uncle Roger that he wasn't well and he'd come down to visit Hambden, she was sure of it. Hambden wasn't a man to suffer being fussed over, but Uncle Roger was good at getting around people. He'd make sure his friend was all right.

As she drove back through the centre of town she was surprised to realize she had been thinking of Hambden as an old man. He'd never seemed that to her before. Flinty, odd, abrupt, eccentric, unpredictable, yes. But they were all descriptive of an active man. Hambden had become a hollow man overnight.

A shadow man, in fact.

As she passed the group of reporters in front of the sheriff's office, she saw they were now gathered around a figure and were throwing questions eagerly at him, writing notes as he pontificated. Pressing her lips together, she rammed down the accelerator and nearly missed her turning.

Obviously unable to resist a chance to show off his 'expertise', Mitch Hasker was lighting a few fires.

She wondered who would be first at the stake.

# EIGHTEEN

'DO YOU THINK YOU COULD possibly manage to forgo the cigar while treatment is actually in progress?' Laura asked through gritted teeth.

Gilliam, his elbows propped on the gutter under the lip of the hydrotherapy pool, removed the long thin cigar he'd been puffing and regarded it with affection. 'It gives me confidence.'

'Well, it gives me a headache,' she grumbled. She took it from him and deposited it on the tiles beside the pool. 'Now, then – I want you to turn over on your stomach and float, holding on to the edge of the pool. When you feel comfortable, I want you to start to kick very, very gently.'

'Kick who?'

'Yourself. Come on – over you go.'

With a grimace, Gilliam complied and, after a moment of getting his balance, began trying to kick as instructed, slowly and unevenly. After a moment or two his legs started to sink and his arm muscles tautened as he struggled to keep himself afloat. She moved closer and placed one hand under his stomach while, with the other, she lifted the recalcitrant legs up again towards the surface. The shift of his belly muscles under her palm revealed that at one time he must have been extremely fit.

'That's good – just keep up a nice, steady rhythm,' she murmured over the gurgle of the water. 'Let the water take your weight – relax – that's good.'

Through the big windows sunlight suddenly appeared. Clouds had been gathering and the bright light was all the more beautiful because of its unexpectedness. The pool room, panelled and raftered in pine, took on a golden glow and brightness glinted on the water's surface. It was lovely, but she had to squint to see Gilliam's leg movements. They were slight and spasmodic, but there was definitely an improvement. When she glanced at his face she could see perspiration travelling down the hollow above his cheekbone and his lips were white as he compressed them in concentration.

It hurt. She knew it hurt, but he was working hard at last and his legs were actually moving. After all the resistance and sulks and reluctant compliance, he was finally making a real effort. Suddenly he let out his breath in a gasp and sagged against the side of the pool.

'That was terrific!' she said enthusiastically.

He nodded, ducked his face in the water for a moment, then lifted it, dripping, and grinned. 'How about that?' he said, genuinely pleased with himself and obviously suprised. No smart remarks, no caustic observations, no sarcasm. He looked ten years younger.

Her heart contracted, then leaped like a bird. He was beginning to believe it could happen. His delight was as complete and guileless as a child's.

The brightness in the pool room faded as the sun was again covered by clouds.

'Now, turn over on to your back and we'll work on the quadriceps,' she directed. Her voice came out a little husky.

'Can I have my cigar back?'

'No.'

'Jeez, what a grouch,' he muttered and leaned back on his elbows.

'Don't force it – easy does it,' she said. For some reason he was tensing up again.

When he spoke she realized why. 'You know, there's no reason to assume a man committed these murders. A woman could have done it. *You* could have done it,' he announced.

She stared at him, taking a moment to catch up with his train of thought. 'I wasn't here when Julie was killed,' she pointed out.

'You could have been. You could have flown in from Omaha, rented a car at the airport, driven over here and killed her, then gone back to Omaha.'

'Why?'

'You wanted her job.'

'I see. Of course, I couldn't have known *you'd* be part of that job, or I might have had second thoughts,' she said wryly.

'I'm just pointing out that this little town and this clinic are not exactly a closed community. Everybody assumes the killer is here, or from here. He or she needn't be. It's narrow thinking. Lots of things out there reach into here.'

'Mm. You can rest for a minute.' She removed her hands from the small of his back and his legs drifted down towards the bottom of the water. He took a tighter grip on the side of the pool with his elbows and glanced longingly at his cigar. She had to hide a grin when he realized it was now in a puddle and quietly disintegrating. The water swirled between their bodies, warm, silky, soft.

'You know this Shadowman they talk about?' she said diffidently.

'Yes.'

'I saw him last night.'

'I know. The sheriff told me.'

'He thought I'd made it up so he wouldn't arrest David.'

'And did you?'

She shook her head. 'No. He *was* there and he scared the hell out of me.'

'Language,' Gilliam chided.

'I wish I hadn't said anything, now,' she went on, and told him about visiting the library and later seeing Mitch Hasker talking to the reporters.

'Nothing people like better than a monster story,' Gilliam said.

'I can see the sheriff's point about my making up a lie,

but for a minute or two last night I thought he believed me. Even if he didn't, you'd think he'd be a little interested in the *possibility* that I might be telling the truth, and that this person I saw might be the one who killed both Julie and Clarissa.'

'Maybe he's more interested than you think. Hear that?'

She lifted her head. 'What?'

It came again.

'Dogs,' Gilliam said.

The dogs weren't any more successful in finding the Shadowman than the sheriff's men had been earlier. They apparently spent a couple of hours following up fascinating scents, but to no conclusion.

When she got home she expected to find Solomon at the window, watching the dogs from a position of safety, but he wasn't there. She made a cursory search of the apartment, for he had been sleeping in some of the oddest places while becoming acclimatized to his new domain. But he wasn't under the bed, or in the closet, or on top of the water heater, or behind the refrigerator. She went to the door and opened it, hoping to see that he'd noted her return, but only saw Matt Gabriel and his men getting ready to leave.

She shrugged and went into the kitchen to prepare her dinner. She was a little worried, but decided Solomon would be back when his stomach reminded him it was mealtime. Maybe he was hiding somewhere until the dogs were gone.

His mealtime came and went, but Solomon did not return. Uneasy now, she went to the door and called him. There was no answering chirrup from below, no furry bundle running up the steps mewing apologies or demanding instant sustenance. There was nothing outside but the stillness, the shadows, the bitter cold, and the windows of the clinic glowing what seemed miles away on the other side of the hedges and the parking lot. She could see Tom Gilliam's corner window was dark and glanced at her watch. Perhaps he'd braved the common room after dinner. Or maybe, tired from his first session in the pool, he'd gone to sleep early.

She closed the door, shivering, and built a fire. When he did come back, Solomon would appreciate a warm welcome and he'd come to adore having a real fireplace. In the evenings he could usually be found in front of it, paws tucked neatly under his chest, blinking lazily into the flames.

Every ten minutes or so she'd go to the door and call him, but without result. Her mind turned to the dogs – perhaps they had frightened him and driven him so far into the woods that he wasn't able to find his way back. There were foxes and badgers out there. Solomon was a good street fighter, he had a ragged left ear to prove it, but she wondered whether he could hold his own against a wild animal.

She turned on the television for company and went into the kitchen to wash the day's dishes. She was just drying up when she heard her uncle's name coming from the television set. The national news had given way to local items and the announcer was outlining the story of the two murders in Blackwater Bay, site of 'the exclusive Mountview Clinic'.

'This normally peaceful resort town is tonight in a state of panic as rumours circulate about the existence of what has heretofore been merely a legendary figure – the Shadowman. Two young nurses have been murdered – and people are locking their doors at night in case the Shadowman comes *their* way.'

'Oh, my God,' she breathed, sinking down on the sofa in dismay, with a wet plate in one hand and a towel in the other. So Mitch Hasker *had* been blabbing to the bored reporters – and it was probably her fault for going to him and asking about the Shadowman. If she hadn't mentioned the reporters he might have kept his mouth shut. She should have realized he would want to put Blackwater Bay's legend 'on the map' and show off his own 'expertise'. Sure enough, there he was on camera, being interviewed by an eager little girl reporter with big blue eyes.

'As president of our local Historical Society, I am naturally aware of the legend of the Shadowman and how it came about. There are moments in our history of which no one should be proud, and when folklore and superstition are mixed in with a few fractured facts, this is the result. The Shadowman is a vengeful figure, a mischief maker, a malevolent spirit. Our own bogeyman, as it were. But never has it been recorded . . .'

'Two women have been murdered,' the girl reporter interrupted.

'True. And terrible. But the Shadowman has never killed humans,' Mitch intoned. 'He is simply—'

'Perhaps he's been watching too many violent movies,' said the girl wryly and turned to the camera before Hasker could answer. 'In the dark streets and gardens of this small town, you can smell the fear,' she continued. Her melodramatic commentary continued over film of the town, the clinic (a moody shot making it look very sinister) and the woods. Some enterprising cameraman had managed to catch a glimpse of Roger Forrester going into the sheriff's office. He was described as 'the wealthy owner-director of the Mountview Clinic, where the two beautiful girls were employed', making it sound like some thinly disguised centre for debauchery.

Laura didn't know whether to laugh or cry. Then, as if on cue, she heard a shrill scream from outside. A cat, certainly, not a human. Solomon? She dropped the dish and hurried to the door, opening it wide. At first she heard nothing but the fitful wind, then it came again.

'Oh, no – he's fighting with something . . .' she gasped, and was down the steps and running across the frozen curds of snow that crusted the lawn before she knew what she was doing. 'Solomon . . . Solomon!'

As if he'd answer.

Crouched somewhere, ears back and growling deep in his throat, she knew he wouldn't be listening to anything except the beating of his own heart and the first sound or sign of a move from his adversary. She'd seen cats fighting often enough, and knew they heard and saw nothing else. She floundered and slipped over the treacherously uneven surface that had thawed and then re-frozen into ridges and pits invisible in the darkness, marked only faintly by crescents of dirty snow.

The cry came again, slightly to her left, from the trees behind the stables. She veered towards it, squinting in the darkness, trying to see the shape of cats or at least one cat against the snow which still lay quite thickly at the edge of the treeline.

But when she did see a shape her heart seemed to contract into a painful fist that hammered against her ribs. Not cats – but a big, heavy figure wearing a long flapping cape, darker than the dark trees, its back to her as it struggled with something. As she ran she saw it stretch its arms up towards a branch overhead. And in its hands, twisting and snarling with outrage, the figure of Solomon, his back legs tied cruelly together with string.

The Shadowman – for it was definitely the wild-haired creature she'd seen the night before – hung the cat upside-down from the branch and produced a knife that glinted in the faint light from the distant clinic windows.

'No! No!' she screamed and launched herself at the figure, rage obliterating her fear and caution. She leaped and clung to its back, its very real and solid back, and began to kick and scratch and pound wherever she could, screaming curses all the while.

The figure roared and shook itself like a bear, and a fetid, choking smell of sweat, bitter and inhuman, filled her nostrils. There was another smell there, too, but she was too wild with fury to classify it just then. Clinging as a cat would, sinking her fingernails in like claws, biting, kicking, scratching and screaming, she fought. She could hear the sounds she was making, but it was as if they were coming from far away instead of from her own throat.

The big dark thing she held on to continued to roar

wordlessly, then deliberately backed into a tree, again, again, trying to rid itself of her as an animal would attempt to dislodge a gadfly. Her head struck the hard rough bark and she felt her fingers loosening their hold, felt herself falling . . . falling . . . falling . . .

. . . into darkness.

# NINETEEN

SHE AWOKE TO DARKNESS AND cold, and something warm dripping on to her face. Shivering, she realized she could only have been unconscious for a short time. Turning her head slightly she could see the beams of flashlights bobbing and jerking as they came closer. Dizzy, she looked up. High above her, hanging from a branch, was the limp figure of Solomon, twisting and turning on the lashings that bound his legs. In the distance she could hear church bells ringing down in the town and she realized at the same time that the warm wetness dripping on to her was Solomon's blood.

She struggled to get up, to free him from that cruel torment, but the darkness came again and she fell into it, sobbing . . .

'No – let me up! I have to get him down!'

Strong arms pressed her down and her uncle's face swam into view overhead, obliterating the glaring light that hung above her.

'Laura! Listen to me!' Her uncle's voice was sharp, but not unkind. 'He's all right. Your cat is all right.' He spoke to someone behind him. 'My God, you'd think it was a child.'

'He was bleeding all over me,' she muttered stubbornly.

'Yes, I know. But he's a tough little brute. He'll survive,' Forrester said, apparently thankful to get a coherent statement out of her at last, even if it didn't make much sense. 'I'm more worried about you.'

'I'm a tough little brute too,' she said, sitting up and looking around. 'Where is he?'

'We've called the police. They'll catch him.'

'No, no!' she interrupted irritably. 'Where's Solomon?'

'Right here,' Owen's voice said and he came across to the treatment table where she was lying. He was holding a large instrument tray and on it, cushioned carefully all around with sterile towels, lay Solomon, a white collar of gauze and adhesive under his chin. He looked so small and defeated that she began to cry.

Solomon half opened one lime-green eye and attempted a miaow, but there was no sound.

'He had a nasty gash and lost of lot of blood, but with care he'll be fine,' Owen said gently. His own face was as white as the bandage he'd put on Solomon.

'Neatest piece of embroidery I ever saw,' came a caustic voice from the corner of the room. Looking around, Laura saw Tom Gilliam in a wheelchair. 'If they ever throw him out of the AMA he'll make a fine vet.'

'Mr Gilliam heard you screaming and called out the militia,' her uncle explained. 'If he hadn't . . .'

'You were both lucky,' Owen said, putting Solomon down next to her. She stroked Solomon's damp side gently and felt a faint answering vibration under her fingers. I'm okay, he was telling her. I'm just resting my eyes.

There were hurried, heavy footsteps in the hall and Matt Gabriel appeared in the doorway, his eyes darting around the room quickly and settling on her. 'Did you see his face?' he asked without preamble.

'Now, wait a minute, Sheriff,' Roger Forrester protested. 'My niece has had quite a shock as well as a severe blow on the head—'

'I only saw him from the back,' Laura said, responding to the urgency in Matt's voice almost automatically. 'He was big – and he smelled.' She glanced down at herself, the grimy mud-streaked sweater and skirt. 'I can still smell it.'

'You didn't see his face? His hands? Anything that might help us?' Matt persisted.

She shook her head and glanced across at Gilliam. He looked pale too, but it was the whiteness of anger, not shock. He was in his pyjamas and they were buttoned up wrongly under his robe. She had an almost uncontrollable impulse to get down from the table, walk over to him and do them up properly. But her head ached abominably, she felt sick to her stomach, and she wanted nothing more than to take her cat and go home, thank you. The expression on Gilliam's face stopped her.

'What did he smell like?' he asked.

She thought about it. 'Sweat,' she said. 'Sick sweat, bitter, rancid. Dirt. And . . .' She paused, thinking back.

'And what?' Gilliam asked. They were all looking at her.

'I don't know,' she said helplessly. 'Something . . .'

'Mothballs?' Matt asked.

'Why . . . yes,' she said, surprised. Of course – it had been so familiar and yet so out of place.

He didn't explain. 'Anything else? *Think!*'

'He was tall and broad. He was wearing gloves – knitted gloves, very dirty . . . and rubber boots.'

'We got that much from the footmarks in the mud and snow,' Matt said. 'And he had to be big to reach that branch. We *know* that.'

'She's doing the best she can,' Gilliam said quietly. 'She was more concerned about the cat than the man. Or herself, for that matter.'

'You must have been mad to run out there like that, Laura.' Forrester's voice was despairing. 'Two girls have been murdered and you run out into the dark just for a cat . . .'

'Not *a* cat,' Gilliam said. '*That* cat.'

She stared at him. So he understood. How strange. She wouldn't have expected *him* to see that Solomon had been the one living thing she'd had to cling to through the agony of her father's sudden death and her divorce. Solomon was the only creature she loved that hadn't gone away or turned on her.

'Then there are actually tracks?' Owen asked the sheriff.

'Yes, there are tracks of a kind, broken branches, skid marks. We followed them,' Matt muttered, his leather-gloved hands clenching and unclenching by his sides. 'They circle around the clinic and end up at the highway about half a mile up.'

'Hah!' There was a look of triumph in Gilliam's eyes.

'I don't understand,' Forrester said. 'What does that mean, exactly?'

'It means—' Matt began.

Gilliam's voice cut in. 'It means your so-called Shadowman probably drives a car. Did you get any tyre prints?'

'All frozen slush there,' Matt said. 'Sharp as razors and hard as rock.'

'Maybe he ran down the highway a bit and ducked back into the woods further along,' Forrester suggested.

'Maybe,' Matt agreed.

'Well, then – you can catch him, can't you? Bring those dogs back? Get a search party together?'

'I don't like being stampeded.' Matt scowled. 'The State Police have been on my back, those damned reporters are swarming like wasps down in town, people are stopping me on the street—'

'Poor Matt,' Gilliam said softly.

Matt turned on him. 'Damnit, don't *you* start! I have enough troubles without some city cop pouring pity all over me. If you've got an answer to this mess let's hear it. Otherwise, button up.' He whirled on his heel and walked out.

'That was entirely uncalled for,' Roger Forrester said angrily, his protective instincts widening to include his patient as well as his niece. 'The man's incompetent . . .'

'He's not incompetent, he's just pissed off,' Gilliam stated. 'I would be, too.'

David had come into the room, and listened to the exchange between Gilliam and the sheriff. 'I just don't understand,' he said raggedly, staring out of the treatment room window at the bobbing lights in the woods. 'I thought this Shadowman character was just a joke—' He stopped, cleared his throat and turned with a puzzled expression on his face. 'It just doesn't make any *sense*.'

'Why not?' Gilliam wanted to know.

David shrugged. 'From what I understood, stories about him have been circulating for *centuries*. You aren't going to tell me this is some kind of *X-Files* type Sasquatch thing that's lived in a cave for hundreds of years . . .'

'And drives a car,' Owen put in.

'There's no question of that,' Roger Forrester said. 'It's obviously a tramp of some kind. We had trouble with one when we first came here. They're pretty wily, they get to know the ins and outs of an area. Or it could be a psychopath . . .'

'Guesses we can provide any time,' Gilliam said. 'Sense takes a little longer. And, if you don't mind my saying so, Doctors, your patients look in need of a little attention . . .'

Their voices seemed further and further away as Laura slipped into something like sleep and something more, heard her uncle curse under his breath as he grabbed the tray with Solomon on it with one hand and her with the other. They'd been so caught up in their guessing game, they'd practically forgotten she was there. Nobody had been looking at her.

Except Gilliam.

Matt stood under the trees, looking up at the branch where the cat had hung. A length of rope was still knotted there, but ended abruptly where someone had cut the animal free. It was ordinary clothes-line, available in quantity from any hardware or discount store. And, if the girl was right and the 'Shadowman' had been wearing gloves, there would be no usable prints.

George came up, puffing a little. 'I've packed the thing in a plastic dry-cleaning bag and told the others not to say anything,' he said. 'Weird.'

'Very.' They had found the cloak of the Shadowman, discarded under a bush. The fastenings at the throat had been torn, perhaps in the struggle with the girl. It was the first piece of solid evidence they had and Matt was not going to announce it until the State Police labs had gone over it thoroughly. It was made of a thick grey flannel material, possibly an old blanket. And it had been covered with badges – everything from the Boy Scouts to old election buttons – plus bits of ribbon and feathers and other oddments. It had been colourful and filthy, reeking of dirt, sweat and mothballs – as if it had never been washed, but had been carefully preserved.

'What can they find out?' George asked curiously.

'An amazing amount, with luck,' Matt replied. 'For a start, they will be able to get a blood type from the sweat – and maybe find a bit of skin that would give them a DNA sequence. They might be able to trace the material, although it looked pretty old to me, and as for all those bits and pieces sewn on – they came from somewhere, George. They were bought, stolen or collected by someone. This is the best bit of luck we've had – but it won't do us any good if it gets out. Not yet, anyway. We've got to keep it out of the papers.'

'So say we get the guy's blood type or DNA – that doesn't give us the guy without anything to match up with, does it?'

'No,' Matt agreed, still looking up at the dangling rope end. 'But it will give us a benchmark if we arrest anyone. If all else fails, we can do a mass DNA testing of every man in the town.'

'Oh, my God,' George said, correctly envisioning the work that would involve.

'Meanwhile, we can ask if anybody noticed a car parked on the highway beyond the clinic earlier tonight. Put *that* in the paper, on the news. Might get something.'

'Long shot.'

'Very. They all are at the moment.'

'What about these prints?' George pointed down to the marks in the mud.

'Take a cast if you can find one that's not been trampled on by the brave rescuers,' Matt answered wryly.

'Okay.' George looked at him narrowly. 'You all right?'

'No,' Matt said levelly.

'What's wrong?'

'Everything. Everything about this is wrong. Why did he attack the cat? Why *didn't* he attack the girl?'

'She made a lot of noise, apparently.'

Matt shook his head. 'He still had time to kill her – or at least injure her. But instead he ran away, left her lying there. Why kill the other two girls and not this one? Why attack the damn cat at all?'

George looked at him. 'I don't know, Matt.'

'No. Neither do I. But it doesn't add up.'

'Look, the guy's crazy. Why should it make sense?' George asked reasonably. 'Maybe he just didn't feel like killing her. Maybe attacking the cat was enough for him. Maybe she hurt him.'

'That's a point,' Matt conceded. 'We'd better start looking for guys with scratches.'

'Looking where?'

'In town, of course.'

'Why just town? He could be driving around right now, waiting to come here and sneak back into his room. Maybe he has a place he kept his Shadowman outfit, maybe he kept it in the trunk of his car, just parked in the lot with all the rest of the cars. There must be more than forty or fifty of them there during the day, what with staff and visitors and patients who drive themselves over. Maybe we should get a search warrant and look into all the trunks.'

Matt looked at him for a moment, considering, then shook his head. 'We'd probably have to get a separate warrant for each car and we haven't got reasonable cause. Even then, the person might have kept it in a plastic bag – I would have, the way it smelled – so there might be no corresponding traces. But it's not a bad thought, George. The answer *could* still be here at the clinic.'

'Well, there you go,' George said, pleased.

'But neither of the resident psychiatric patients seems likely. And others who have been here long enough aren't strong enough – or motivated enough, as far as we've been able to find out.'

'So, it's probably one of the staff,' George persisted. 'Maybe we should look at them all again. And Dr Weaver has patients that come in and out during the day, too, remember?'

'So he does, George, so he does. But all he'll tell us are their names.'

'Maybe *he* did it,' George said with gloomy suspicion. 'I said right along he's crazier than his patients.'

'Just because you don't like psychiatrists—'

'I just don't like *him*. He gave a lecture once at the high school and said that guys who work out are repressed gays.' George was proud of his physique and worked out regularly at Mayor Merrill Attwater's gym.

'I'm sure he didn't say that,' Matt assured him. 'Or if he did he meant a certain *kind* of homosexual . . . those California Muscle Beach types.'

'I don't care,' said George sulking. 'It was a dumb thing to say. *And* his wife killed herself, remember.'

'She was suffering from depression, George,' Matt said.

'And why was she depressed we ask ourselves?'

'Because their baby died. Two months old.'

'Oh. Well, I still say you should look at old Weaver again. He's big, he's in and out of the clinic and he's nuts.'

'He's not nuts, George.'

'Then why does he go out walking around town at night?' George asked meaningfully.

'Does he?'

'Sure. Charley and Duff have both caught him at it.'

'Caught him at what?'

'Walking around town in the middle of the night.'

'Did they ask him what he was doing?'

'Well, of course.' George was impatient. 'He said he couldn't sleep and was going for a walk to get tired.'

'Nothing crazy about that.'

'He was wearing his dead wife's fur coat, last time,'

George said triumphantly. 'Over his pyjamas. Is that crazy enough for you?'

Laura was put under observation and the next morning Roger Forrester took Solomon to the local vet, who pronounced Owen's needlework excellent. Aside from some bad bruising of the back legs where he'd been tied and suspended, Laura's old boy was in good shape, although weak from blood loss. It was fortunate, the vet said, that he was such a big, strong cat. The stitches in the neck could come out in a week. She recommended a high-protein diet, plenty of rest and administered some precautionary injections against infection.

Solomon bit her.

'I've left him there for a few days, until you're feeling better,' Uncle Roger told Laura when he reported back.

'I'm better *now,*' she grumbled. 'But David won't let me get dressed.'

'Good,' her uncle said. 'That bang on the head doesn't appear to have done you any harm, but twenty-four hours of rest and quiet are essential. For goodness sake, Laura, you *know* the procedure in head injuries where the patient has been unconscious.'

'I feel useless, lying here.'

'Well, you look beautiful, so lie back and enjoy it,' David said, as he came in. 'This is your doctor speaking, so pay attention.' He lifted a corner of the bandage and made a show of assessing the damage. 'Only a *little* bit of brain leaked out,' he assured her.

'I'm not a child,' she muttered. Really, he was being ridiculous.

'Then stop behaving like one,' David shot back. 'I have enough trouble from my *real* patients, thank you.'

She obeyed his damned orders for an hour, then got up, put on the robe they'd brought over for her and went across the hall to Gilliam's room. He was on his mobile telephone and she hesitated in the doorway, but he beckoned her in.

'That's right, Phil, the whole structure if you can.' He

listened for a minute, nodding. 'I realize that, but don't tell me you haven't got some contacts on the Street who are willing to . . .' He paused again. 'Yes, of course use the name if it will help you. Offer some business out of my own portfolio if it will open any doors, I don't give a damn. But I need to know.'

Laura sat down in the visitor's chair by the bed. Gilliam looked harassed, excited, edgy and impatient.

'Good. Fine. Now the other side of it . . . you're giving to Doyle? Can he . . . ? Well, if you say so. Sign whatever he needs. And pay the kid at the university whatever *he* needs too. Thanks a lot. And fast as possible, right?' He looked as if he wanted to break off, now, but whoever was at the other end kept talking. 'I'm fine. No, really – making progress. No, I don't think so. Maybe. Phil – I don't give much of a damn what the family think, frankly. And you can tell them so if they ask, but believe me, they won't ask. Very funny. Right. Phil, I have to go now – thanks a lot. 'Bye.' He cut off the phone quickly, although sounds were still coming from the receiver. Then he turned and glanced out of the window. 'I suppose you know the circus has come to town?'

It took her a minute to realize he was speaking to her, she'd been so intrigued by the play of emotions across his somewhat battered features. Up until now he'd been more or less the Great Stone Face. She stood up and went over to the window.

Along the highway a row of cars was parked and faces within were pressed against the glass of the windows like so many pink balloons. A county bus, passing slowly, was similarly adorned. The clinic drive was blocked by the sheriff's car and in the parking lot, visible from Gilliam's other window, stood two or three other official-looking vehicles, with men in uniform milling around talking, smoking and kicking at the gravel.

'I hear it's even worse in town,' Gilliam commented.

'It looks as if we're under siege, or something,' she said.

'Or something,' Gilliam agreed.

Her eyes met his, then she looked away quickly. 'It sounds corny when I say it out loud, but I wanted to thank you for saving my life. And Solomon's.'

'You're right – it sounds corny. All I did was raise the alarm. Your big-hero boyfriend Butler did all the running and carrying, and Jenks did the hemstitching.'

She glanced out at the men in the parking lot. 'They haven't found him yet?'

'The so-called Shadowman? Nope. Nor have there been any reports of a hairy monster driving a car anywhere in the vicinity.'

'Oh, look – you can't go *on* saying there isn't something out there . . .'

'Sure I can,' Gilliam said calmly. 'I can say it until I'm blue in the face, as a matter of fact. I admit something or someone attacked your cat last night—'

'Attacked me, too.'

He shook his head. 'Oh, no – he attacked your cat. *You* attacked *him*. You jumped on him. And what happened?'

'He . . .' She stopped.

'He got rid of you as fast as he could and ran like hell,' Gilliam pointed out. 'If I had you on my back – and lately I have – I'd probably do the same. Except, of course, I can't run.' He simply said it, without sarcasm, without self-pity, and went on from there. 'Whether he wants it or not, I feel sorry for Matt Gabriel. Thanks to that Hasker guy and your uncle, the whole thing has got out of hand.'

'My *uncle*?' She was nonplussed. 'The last thing he wants is this kind of publicity around the clinic—'

Gilliam was shaking his head again. 'Sorry. Given the ugly fact that he's going to get publicity of some kind, your uncle would infinitely prefer a monster hunt in the woods to an in-depth investigation of his precious Mountview Clinic, I assure you.'

'Why on earth do you say that?'

'I am, for lack of a better phrase, a trained observer. Whether by natural talent or experience, I've learned to look a bit beyond what people say. Would you accept that?'

'I suppose so.' She didn't like it, but—

'Last night, and again this morning, your uncle has been doing and saying things to fan the excitement of the search for this Shadowman character. He was caught by reporters and I heard him interviewed on the radio. There was nothing like a rush past and "no comment" – oh, no. Dr Roger Forrester was only too happy to expound on the patterns of psychopathic symptoms among the social outcasts of this world. And to deplore the lack of success by the local police in catching this monster. And to suggest he was considering offering a reward for the capture of the Shadowman, in memory of his beloved nurses. And so on. He said he found it hard to sleep nights. *That*, I believed.'

'Are you implying that there's something wrong with my uncle?' she demanded angrily.

'No, I'm *inferring* it from the evidence. Aside from the two murders, there's the possibility of a dandy little drugs racket going on. There are also people here who pay their bills with what we in the law-enforcement business quaintly refer to as ill-gotten gains.'

'Even crooks get sick.'

'Too true. The oftener the better, I say. The fact remains, a pretty high percentage of them seem to get sick and come here. Now, that may be coincidence . . .'

'Perhaps they recommend it to one another at the Annual Crooks Convention,' she suggested sweetly.

'Look, I'm sorry.' Gilliam's apology didn't exactly ring true. 'I have a suspicious nature. When someone starts jumping up and down and screaming "look over *here*", my inclination is to look over *there*, instead. If your uncle had kept his mouth shut, fair enough. But he hasn't.'

'I can't help what my uncle does. He's probably upset and confused—'

'Poor old man,' Gilliam said sarcastically.

She had to admit that description seemed to have little to do with Uncle Roger as she'd seen him this morning. He'd been firm, decisive and bright-eyed. Too bright-eyed?

After a long silence she spoke again. 'What do you mean by a "drugs racket"?'

'Well, perhaps that's putting it a bit strongly,' Gilliam conceded graciously. 'Someone is ripping off the clinic drug supplies on a regular basis, that's all. Didn't you know about that?'

'Oh, *that*. David did mention it.'

'You don't seem surprised.'

'Well, of course not. When you said drugs "racket" I thought you meant some kind of . . . big ring or something. Hospitals are *always* getting ripped off on drugs – that's nothing new. No matter how carefully you lock them up, people get them.'

'This isn't a big hospital. It's a little clinic.'

'How big does it have to be?' she wanted to know. 'And anyway, what kind of drugs are you talking about?'

'Addiction isn't limited to heroin,' Gilliam said. 'People can get addicted to aspirin, even. And if an aspirin addict couldn't buy what he needed over the counter he'd pay plenty to someone who could get it for him. That's what stinks about people like—' He paused and took a deep breath.

'Like who?'

He shrugged. 'It doesn't matter.'

'Like my uncle? Is that what you're saying?'

Gilliam looked at her in surprise. 'Did I say that?'

'Not in so many words, but—'

He sighed. 'If and when I have an accusation to make, I'll make it in so many words. If *you* think your uncle is capable of selling drugs for profit I'd say you've got a problem.'

'I *don't* believe that,' she said defensively.

'But you're beginning to wonder?'

'I . . . I just don't know him very well, that's all. He and my father were twins, but—'

Gilliam raised his eyebrows. 'So you said. Identical or fraternal?'

'Identical.'

'What was your father like?'

'Absolutely honest in every way,' she said flatly. 'In fact, that was usually the problem.'

'Oh?'

'Well, he expected everyone to be as honest as he was. Very few were. He was hopeless at business, the con-men could see him coming a mile away. He trusted everyone. Anyone. If he hadn't been such a genius he would have died broke. As it was . . .' She stopped, frowning, her hands fisted in her robe pockets.

'He died rich?' Gilliam finished for her. 'Then how come you're working for a living?'

'*You* worked for a living and you're rich.'

'Ah. Scruples.' He made them sound like warts.

'If you like. Anyway, Uncle Roger isn't anything like Dad, except that he's honest. I'm sure he is. But he also knows that other people aren't honest and so he's done very well in business.'

'Apparently.'

'What's that supposed to mean?'

'I'll let you know when I know. If you're interested.'

'Of course I'm interested.'

'Good. Don't call me, I'll call you.' It was a dismissal.

Defeated by his evasiveness, she went back to her room and was grateful to slip back into bed. Suddenly she felt very tired and her head was throbbing under the bandage that sloped rather rakishly above one eye. In the mirror that morning she'd noticed that the skin around her eye was turning dark – she'd have a nice shiner by nightfall. She lay between the cool sheets and stared at the ceiling, so perfectly painted there wasn't even an interesting crack to focus on. In the end she closed her eyes and slept, a light, fitful sleep in which half-remembered impressions resurrected themselves in painful detail. She ran again, screamed again, and raged again at both the cruelty done to Solomon and her inability to help him. She awoke with a jerk and stared around.

Waking or sleeping, the memory was a nightmare.

* * *

Roger Forrester put down the phone and stared sightlessly at a tiny piece of mud that lay on the carpet a few inches from the door.

'Well?' Milly finally asked. 'Do we get it?'

'We don't.'

'What?' Her voice rose a little towards a shriek, but she managed to control it.

'At least, not in time, anyway. It's blowing up into a real lawyer's delight, what with the estranged husband weighing in with his objections. Says that I used "undue influence" . . .'

'That's ridiculous,' Milly said. 'You didn't.'

'Of course I didn't,' he agreed, staring down at his hands. 'Not really. I told her about the work we hoped to do one day, but that was all.'

'How long will it take, all this arguing?'

'Months . . . years, probably. It's a big estate.'

'We haven't *got* months,' Milly said in exasperation.

'I know that,' Roger agreed. 'We haven't even got many weeks, now. I'll have to talk to Laura about using her trust. There's no other way.'

'But . . .'

'There's no other way,' Roger said firmly. 'It's family money. And it would just be a loan, anyway. We'll pay it back long before she might need it. I'm damned if I'm going to let Armstrong and his cronies win by default. I want Mountview to remain a medical facility, not be turned into some luxury spa. That's what I told him this morning – if this had been a spa, his wife would have been dead by now. As it is, she's getting the best medical care available. He seems to think we let her develop a staph infection for some bizarre reasons of our own. I'm telling you, the man's dangerous. There's no way we can let him take over Mountview. Never.'

Milly turned away, her eyes bright with anger. Of course, there was another way. There was always another way. It was just a matter of careful planning, that's all. And she was good at that.

She'd always been good at that.

* * *

Laura pushed away her dinner tray. Her head was throbbing and there was a tightness in her chest that wouldn't go, no matter how deeply she tried to breathe. She'd started coughing, too. All in all, she felt mean, rotten and inclined to kick someone one minute; then abject, small and miserable the next.

She got out of bed and put on her robe and slippers. In her experience, the only way to get out of a mood like this was to concentrate on someone other than yourself. She headed for the day-room, ready to play the patient for a change.

In the day-room, now an evening room with curtains drawn against the cold darkness and a glow of light and warmth within, she found Mrs Strayhorn holding court. She was still not her old self and seemed oddly incomplete without the soft whine of Mrs McAllister to underline her pronouncements, but she seemed genuinely delighted to see Laura. 'Come over here and tell me all about it,' she urged, gesturing towards the couch beside her wheelchair. Laura sank down and coughed deeply. 'My, my,' Mrs Strayhorn said sympathetically. 'You *do* sound poorly.'

Laura attempted a smile. 'I *feel* poorly . . . but it's only a cold coming on. Nothing to do with last night.'

'They said you were lying on the ground. You must have got a chill,' Mrs Strayhorn diagnosed.

'I wasn't there very long,' Laura pointed out. 'Still, I suppose it could be that.'

'Mr Strayhorn was just the same. Didn't take more than him going out in his slippers to get the paper off the lawn and the next thing you knew he'd be sniffling and coughing, just like you are. Never mind, you're young and healthy, no thanks to that monster who attacked you. Was it awful?'

'Fairly awful,' Laura conceded.

'And do they reckon it was the same one who killed those two nurses?' Mrs Strayhorn leaned forward eagerly to hear her reply.

'They don't know.'

The old lady sat back with disappointment. 'Well, there can't be two of them running around, now, can there?'

'It seems unlikely.'

'Well, then.' She tucked in her blanket energetically. 'Been weeks since he killed the first one, then the second only a few days ago, now you. He's speeding up, ain't he?'

'I suppose so.' Laura was beginning to think coming down here was a mistake. She felt woozy and miserable. She began to cough again and Mrs Strayhorn looked at her with concern.

'Don't much like the sound of that,' she said.

'You ought to hear it from inside.' Laura smiled. 'You'd like it even less.' Was she starting a fever, or was it just that the lounge was kept very warm?

'I'm beginning to think this place isn't so healthy after all,' Mrs Strayhorn said. 'First of all we got some kinda monster going around killing nurses and all, then we got people like Myra dying, then there's this damn bug that people are catching like flies and now, would you believe it, we've got a thief going around here too?'

Laura stared at her. Did she mean the drugs thing? How could she know about that? 'A thief?'

'Yep. Well – maybe he's not a thief, 'cause he didn't steal anything. Or she didn't. But somebody sure was poking around in my things, because they were all messed up. Made me madder 'n a wet hen, I can tell you.'

'When did this happen?'

'Not sure. Not certain sure, anyway. But I think it must have been that night of the fire we had – the one that burned down that very valuable store-room.' She cackled at that.

'I think it was one of the firemen, myself,' put in a voice and they turned to see Mr Cobbold hunching past on his way to the television set.

'Now, don't you go putting on any nonsense,' Mrs

Strayhorn directed him. 'We're all waiting for the big movie to start.'

'I only want to see the news,' Mr Cobbold said.

'Was something taken from your room, Mr Cobbold?' Laura asked.

'No – but it was messed up.'

'Oh.' She leaned back. 'I expect they had to move things around a little, to make sure . . . to get to the windows and so on.' It sounded a little feeble to her.

To them, too. 'Don't have to mess drawers around to fight a fire, do they?' Mrs Strayhorn demanded, one eye on the television set as Mr Cobbold tuned it in. 'We want Channel 9 at eight o'clock, remember,' she said in a loud voice.

'All right, all right,' Mr Cobbold muttered and painfully settled himself on the forward edge of a chair, his plaid flannel back showing a line of obstinacy. Laura had a feeling there was going to be an argument in a little while and she really didn't feel up to it.

'Anyway,' Mrs Strayhorn said, turning back to Laura. 'You haven't told me about last night yet.'

'There's nothing to tell, really. It's all a kind of blur in my mind. That happens, sometimes, with a head injury.'

'My land,' Mrs Strayhorn said. 'You might have been killed, just like those other two. I didn't like either of them much, but I like you all right. Don't think I would have liked losing you. Especially not right after . . . Myra and all.'

'Thank you.'

'Seems funny it should be *those* two,' Mrs Strayhorn mused. Raising her voice she said, 'Nearly eight o'clock, Mr Cobbold.'

'I know that, I know that,' came the acid reply. Mr Cobbold kept his eyes on the screen, but raised his hand to show his watch. 'Micky has his big hand on the eleven and his little hand on the eight.'

'Hmph,' Mrs Strayhorn said sourly.

'What do you mean by "those two"?' Laura asked curiously. 'They weren't friends, surely?'

'Hah! Not a bit, no siree. Just the opposite, I'd say. The

only time they got together was in Myra's room, and then it was mostly an accident. It was supposed to be me, but I was having my hair done at the time and . . . eight o'clock, Mr Cobbold,' she interrupted herself.

He turned round and glared at her. 'Now I missed the basketball scores, thanks to you bellowing.' Standing up as much as he could, for he seemed in a perpetual hunch to protect his delicate stomach, he reached out and switched off the television set. 'You want it on so much, you can tune it yourself. I'll watch in my room.'

'We're having popcorn later,' Mrs Strayhorn called out cheerfully as he stomped off.

'He can't eat popcorn,' Laura murmured.

'I know it,' Mrs Strayhorn said smugly. 'Any more than he can speak politely to a lady, the crabby old bastard.'

'He's in a good deal of pain.' Laura wondered why she was defending Cobbold, who *was* unpleasant.

'So am I,' Mrs Strayhorn said. 'So are most of us, one way or another. No call to forget your manners, is it? If he feels so bad he can stay in his own room, can't he? Why come out and bother us?'

'I'll turn it back on for you,' Laura volunteered and went over to retrieve the remote from where Mr Cobbold had left it. She turned on the set, then returned with the remote control and handed it to Mrs Strayhorn.

'Thank you, dear.' Mrs Strayhorn switched to the channel she wanted.

Laura smiled, then had a fit of coughing. She liked Mrs Strayhorn very much. 'Why were they in her room?'

'Who?' Mrs Strayhorn's eyes were on the television and her attention was slowly focusing on it.

'Miss Zalinsky and Miss Janacek – you said they . . .'

'Oh, that.' Mrs Strayhorn chuckled. 'Nothing to it, really. They were witnessing one of Myra's wills, that's all. She was always changing her will, was Myra. Regular demon for it. Made her feel powerful, I guess.' She blinked rapidly, keeping her eyes on the screen. 'Must have been her last one. Wonder what was in it this time?'

'Didn't she tell you?'

'Nope. Hinted at it, of course. Always was hinting at it, gonna do this, gonna do that, so on. That's how she was.' She smiled reminiscently. 'Always a game with her. She had no idea of money or business. Her lawyers handled it all, paid her bills and everything. Foolish, if you ask me. I guess they were honest enough, but then people are always honest until they turn crooked – and you never know when that's going to happen, do you? They keep smiling, but underneath . . .' She looked up. 'Well, speak of the devil.'

Laura followed her glance. Roger Forrester and Milly Cunningham were coming into the lounge. He glanced around, smiling at everyone, then came across as he spotted Laura. 'Ah, here you are. Good evening, Mrs Strayhorn, how are you this evening?'

'I'm just ducky, but my body is falling apart,' Mrs Strayhorn said cheerfuly. 'How are you?'

'Fine, thank you.' He smiled at her but his eyes went to Laura. 'Laura, my dear, if you don't mind my saying so, you look as if you should be back in bed.'

'That's what I told her,' Mrs Strayhorn said with some satisfaction. 'Caught a chill, like as not. Nasty cough, looks peaky. You can see for yourself.'

Laura stood up. 'I think I will go back to bed.'

Her uncle nodded. 'That's a good girl. Another night's rest is what you need. There was nothing to worry about on the X-ray, but still . . .'

'Thank you, Uncle Roger.' She started to cough again.

'You go on, my dear. Milly and I must get away if we're going to make the city in time. I wanted to have a talk with you, but I think it had better wait until morning, feeling the way you do.'

'It's only a cold, really. I get them all the time.'

'Not when you're under my care, you don't.' He beamed. 'Off you go, now.'

'Bully,' Laura heard Mrs Strayhorn mutter as she walked towards the door.

'She really doesn't look well, Roger,' Milly Cunningham

murmured. 'It could be she's picked up this staph thing. Maybe you ought to give her something.'

'Yes, I'll speak to Shirley on the way out. Now then, who have we here this evening?'

Laura was brushing her teeth when, through the closed bathroom door, she heard someone come into the room. 'Who is it?' she called.

'Shirley Hasker. I've brought you some medication your uncle wants you to take before you go to sleep. I'll leave them on the table.'

'Thank you,' Laura said. 'What is it?'

But there was no answer. She went out into the room and looked at the small paper medication cup. Inside were two innocuous white tablets. They could have been anything. She sat on the edge of the bed and tipped them into her hand. As she poured out a glass of water, however, something made her pause. It was silly, of course, but best to check just in case.

She picked up the phone and dialled the nursing office. One of the Bobbsey twins answered. Feeling a little embarrassed, she cleared her throat before speaking. 'Miss Hasker just brought down some tablets my uncle prescribed for me.'

'Yes?' Merry's (or Cherry's) voice was bright with sunshine.

'What are they?'

'Just a minute, I'll check the chart.' There was a pause and then Cherry (or Merry) returned. '"Penicillin, 500 mg. three times a day" it says. I guess it's for that cough. Why?'

'Oh, nothing. I just wondered. Thank you.'

'Okay. Sleep well.' More sunshine.

Laura hung up the phone and stared at the tablets, so small and nameless. They could have been aspirin, or even saccharine. But they weren't. They were poison.

She was hyper-allergic to penicillin.

And her uncle Roger knew it.

# TWENTY

'I'M SURE IT WAS A mistake,' David said slowly, looking at the two tablets in the little paper cup. 'He must have forgotten.'

Laura made a fist under the blankets. My God, how these doctors stuck together! Why couldn't one of them admit just once that a fellow physician could be a boob and a bungler?

'After all,' David went on, 'I would have prescribed the same thing myself.'

'Yes, but you would have asked me first if I were allergic to it, wouldn't you? It would be automatic.'

'Automatic for me, yes, but you must remember your uncle doesn't do real clinical work any more and hasn't for a long time. At best, he does what could only be called an overseer's job here. Jenks and I do all the hands-on work. It was twenty years ago, Laura. He could have forgotten. Anyway, you didn't take them, so that's all right. And your chest doesn't seem to have got any worse, so . . .'

'David, I could have *died*,' she pointed out.

'Well, possibly, but you didn't,' he emphasized.

'Just like Mrs McAllister,' she said, staring out of the window at Nick, working in the garden below.

'What?' David asked sharply.

She took her eyes from the husky, red-jacketed figure. 'I said just like Mrs McAllister. I'm not just allergic, David, I'm hyper-allergic. The penicillin I had when I was nine put me into anaphylactic shock. I wheezed and choked and strangled myself half to death, just like an acute asthmatic.

It was awful, terrifying. And I know Uncle Roger was told, because I remember my father asking him if we should sue the doctor who'd prescribed the drug for me. I remember hearing him on the telephone in the hall outside my room. He was very angry, he wanted to tear our doctor limb from limb.'

'Who, Roger?'

'No, my father. Uncle Roger was in Boston at the time.'

'Oh.' David walked into the bathroom, tipped the two tablets into the toilet and flushed them away.

'You don't suppose he did it deliberately, do you?' she asked quietly.

David took so long to turn round she wasn't certain, at first, that he'd heard her. 'You don't mean that,' he finally said.

Her chin came up. 'Why not? What about the railing on the steps outside my flat? You said yourself I could have broken my neck.'

'That was just a figure of speech and you know it. You wouldn't have fallen more than ten feet at the most.'

'And what about the brakes on my car going like that?'

'It's an old car, Laura. These things happen.'

'David . . . I'm serious. Uncle Roger would get all my money if I died before the trust came to me.'

'And does he strike you as so desperate for money he'd kill his beloved niece to get it? Especially when all he has to do is ask you for it, like he did before?'

'What do you mean?' She was puzzled.

'Well, you bailed him out when Mountview got into money troubles a few years back, didn't you? Anyway, he's not in difficulties now, so I don't see what you're getting at. After all, he's very fond of . . .'

'How did you know about that?'

'About what? The loan?' She nodded and David shrugged. 'He told me himself.' He looked into her face. 'Uh-oh, I've put my foot in it, haven't I? He *told* me you were funny about that trust fund, that you never wanted it mentioned. Sorry.'

'What else did he tell you about me, David? Did he tell you about my rotten marriage, perhaps? About the time I tried to kill myself? Lots of fun details like that?' She was rigid with anger.

'Hey – settle down,' David said, surprised at the ferocity of her reaction. He sat on the edge of the bed, took her tight fist and began to unfold the fingers one by one, rubbing them gently. 'Why all the fuss? Of course he'd talk about you. He's proud of you, for all your stubborn ways. Maybe because of them. He didn't tell me anything about your marriage except that it was unhappy, certainly not about any suicide attempt. Was it a serious try, or . . .'

'A cry for help?' Her mouth twisted wryly. 'The latter, I suppose. I'm too nosy to kill myself, really – I always have to see what happens next, no matter how awful it might be. But I did take an overdose, thinking my dear husband would be back soon. Except he wasn't. He stopped off for a quick one and I don't mean in a bar. If he'd got home on time it would been an attempt to get his attention. As it was, I nearly got buried instead.'

'You seem to make a habit of "nearly" dying. Must be tougher than you look, hey?' David smiled into her eyes encouragingly.

She looked away. 'I'm not proud of having done that, it was stupid and childish. I wasn't really . . . in control of myself at the time.'

'But you are now?'

'Oh, yes. *Definitely.*'

'Then why are you shaking?'

'You must have fallen asleep during that particular psychology lecture. It's not fear that makes me shake, it's rage.'

'About what?'

'Oh . . . female impotence, I guess.' She tried to laugh, to distract herself from her true feelings, which were fighting to emerge in some kind of screaming fit. 'I mean, here we all are, getting bumped off right and left by some big hairy monster who kills cats . . . or tries to . . . and people . . .

everybody pretends it isn't making any difference to us in here, but it is. Every day that goes by . . . we're just waiting to see who'll be next.'

'Now you're getting morbid.'

She felt the tears gathering in her eyes and choking her voice. 'And . . . Uncle Roger . . . nearly poisons me . . . the niece he *supposedly* loves . . .'

'Ah – is that it . . . you feel betrayed.'

She sniffed and looked into his eyes. 'I'm just being silly, aren't I? I'm just tired and I'm over-reacting.'

'I'm afraid so,' he said gently, stroking her hand. 'You need someone to look after you, you know. I'm not being a male chauvinist, I just happen to think you're a very vulnerable person. You hide it well, but . . .'

Laura *was* tired. She'd slept only fitfully all night, waking up repeatedly, her mind racing, questioning, wondering. The thought of having someone like David to turn to, David to lean on, David to hide behind, was very appealing. Not her usual style at all. He was right – not about her vulnerability, but about her over-reacting. And yet—

'When Uncle Roger told you about the money . . .'

'What money?'

She'd startled him, he'd been about to say something else. 'That I gave him – when he was in trouble.'

'What about it?'

'Did he tell you how much it was?'

'Of course not. That's hardly any of my business, is it? He only mentioned it in passing, to illustrate the way you used to refuse to . . . well, almost refused to admit the money even existed. He's really very fond of you, Laura.' He reached forward and tilted her face up to his. 'And so am I.' He kissed her gently. 'I just wish I didn't have to leave right now.'

'Leave?' she whispered.

He pulled back slightly. 'The medical conference, remember?'

'Oh, no . . . is that *this* week?'

'I'm afraid so. I'm leaving in a few minutes to drive to the airport.'

'Can't you . . . send your regrets?' She wanted him around, she wanted him there. She had been very cautious about her feelings towards David Butler, knowing his reputation, knowing his easy charm was as automatic as breathing. But he did appear to be interested in her. He did *seem* to mean what he said. And while she didn't take it seriously – she didn't dare – she had found herself wondering if he felt something more for her than simple physical attraction. If, indeed, he was capable of feeling any more than that. She had met David's type before. Good heavens – she had married one of them. They cut through hospital staff like cruising barracuda, a bite here, a bite there, breaking vulnerable hearts, hardening others, never meaning to hurt, but hurting and wounding none the less. Owen Jenks was just the opposite. When he gave his heart – and he seemed to have given it to Clarissa – he gave it completely. And probably got kicked in the teeth for it. Certainly he had been strangely quiet since Clarissa's death. Brooding, almost. Laura was worried about him. Perhaps she cared more for him than she did for David, come to think of it. Was that possible? He'd never shown any sign of interest in her, other than that of a friendly colleague. She shook herself – she was being silly. It was because she'd been hit on the head. Because she was feeling vulnerable. Because she was . . . frightened.

David was speaking to her. 'I'm giving a paper, remember? I showed you, in the programme.'

'Oh, yes, of course.' Vaguely she remembered him showing her the list of speakers and his own name among them, with a kind of shy pride.

'Believe me, if I'd known last year that you were about to come into my life I'd never have signed up for it. But I had a lot of time on my hands and—'

'Hah, don't give me that. I've heard how you romanced every female in sight,' she said, teasing him. He scowled and she realized it was a wrong approach. 'You're just trying to make me feel sorry for you, sitting alone with your medical books, wistfully staring into the fire.'

The scowl lightened to a smile. 'Is it working?'

'Only a little.'

'Anyway, I'll be back next Sunday night. Surely you're not going to pine away in a week?'

'I'm not the pining away type. I may be here when you get back . . . and then again . . . I may not,' she offered archly.

He stood up and looked her straight in the eye. 'You'll be here,' he said firmly. His beeper began to chirp in his pocket. 'Damn.' He reached for it and read the message. 'I've made sure the locum who's filling in for me is totally repellent in every way, so stay away from him. Owen is – Owen. He's not very happy at the moment, so try to cheer him up, will you? I'll see you Sunday night. Wait up for me, because I'll bring you a present from Chicago.'

'Do you think I'm that mercenary?'

'Every woman is mercenary when it comes to presents,' he stated blandly.

She started to argue the point, but he went out with a wave and a grin, leaving her with her mouth open. She closed it with a snap and stared at the bump of her toes under the blankets. Thoughts and feelings were whirling round and round in her head, like a spiral of gnats in a shadowy barn, visible one minute, gone the next. David did seem to be getting serious about her. Was she glad? Did she want to give up her freedom? What freedom? What about the penicillin? The stair rail? The brakes? Who or what was the Shadowman? Had he killed the two girls? Was it Uncle Roger? Was she over-reacting? And the biggest gnat of all—

*What* loan?

After about ten minutes of this Laura got up, put on her robe and slippers, and marched downstairs to her uncle's office. Roger and Milly were both there, he dictating, she taking it down in quick, efficient shorthand as he paced back and forth. They both stopped in mid-sentence as Laura came in without knocking.

'I'm allergic to penicillin,' she announced, hands on hips.

'Yes, I know you are,' Roger said. 'Come and sit down, you look dreadful, my dear. Milly, get Laura some coffee.'

He came across and made Laura sit on the sofa in front of the fire. 'You shouldn't be up, you know.'

'I'm fine,' she said crossly, trying to ignore her still-whirling head.

'Now, what's all this about penicillin?' he asked, then his face went pale. 'You haven't taken any, have you?'

'Uncle Roger, you *prescribed* penicillin for me last night,' she said carefully.

'I did no such thing,' he said. 'That is . . .' He looked embarrassed. 'I *did* tell Shirley penicillin, but when I was half-way downstairs I remembered your allergy and sent Milly back to change it to erythromicin.' He turned to Mrs Cunningham, who was bringing a cup of coffee across from the percolator on the sideboard. 'You told Shirley, didn't you, Milly?'

Mrs Cunningham handed Laura the cup and saucer, keeping her eyes on its brimming rim in case it tipped. 'She wasn't there, so I wrote out a note and left it in the centre of her blotter. There was nothing else on the blotter, she couldn't have missed it.'

'But . . . they said it was penicillin when I called,' Laura protested.

'You called?' her uncle asked sharply.

'Yes. I wondered . . . I wanted to make sure . . .'

'Very wise,' Milly murmured.

'So I didn't take them.' Laura swallowed. 'I thought . . . you'd probably forgotten.'

'I nearly did,' her uncle admitted slowly. 'I'm sorry.' He gave a half-laugh. 'You must have thought—'

'No,' she said quickly. Too quickly.

Her Uncle Roger's face showed a rapid succession of emotions, from embarrassment to concern to affront.

She rushed on, unable to stop herself, now. 'And David said you told him about my giving you some money from the trust fund a few years ago,' she blurted out. 'Why did you tell him that?'

'I don't remember telling him that,' Roger said. 'When did he say I told him?'

'Before I came.'

'Oh,' Roger said. 'I remember talking to him about you when you'd finally decided to come . . . that would have been just after Julie's death. I really can't remember any details.'

'Can you remember any details about this so-called loan? Because I can't.'

He stared at her as if she were mad. 'But we spoke on the phone about it, you signed the papers, it was all quite straightforward, my dear. About six months after Richard died . . .'

The time when her marriage was breaking up. The time when she was living in a turmoil of shattered emotions and a total inability to think straight for more than four minutes at a time. A bit like now, in fact. 'Tell me again . . .' she whispered.

'I'll do better than that,' he said, putting an arm around her shoulders. 'Milly – get me the file, will you?' He hugged Laura briefly. 'I haven't spoken about it because I know how you feel about the money, but I was, and am, extremely grateful to you. As a matter of fact, I've been meaning to speak to you about this, because . . . ah, here we are.'

Silently, Milly Cunningham held out a file. Laura noticed her hand shook slightly, before Roger took the heavy grey cardboard folder from her. Milly thrust the hand behind her and sat down on the opposite sofa. 'Now, let me see.' Roger sorted through the papers until he found what he wanted. 'The relevant letters, a copy of the transfer papers with your initials, all here.' He handed the papers to Laura and she stared at them, turning them over slowly, as if hypnotized by the sight of her own words and name.

'A hundred thousand dollars,' she whispered.

'That's right.' Roger nodded. 'Invested in Mountview shares which I hope, one day, will more than pay you back.

That's one of the reasons I so much wanted you to work here – Mountview is a family project, a family asset.'

'I don't remember any of this,' Laura whispered. How could anyone forget that huge sum? 'I don't remember it at *all* . . .' she wailed, looking up at his concerned face.

'But, Laura . . .' He seemed nonplussed. 'There it is.'

'I must be losing my mind,' she said in a strangled voice. 'All Daddy's money—'

'Hardly all,' Uncle Roger said drily. 'Accumulating royalties and dividends have already replaced this in the fund, and more. It's really time you stopped hiding your head in the sand and took charge of your financial affairs, Laura. In eighteen months the trust reverts to you completely, you know. Your father was pretty certain you'd be well away from Mike's influence by the time you were thirty . . .'

Laura blinked at him. 'Is that why he set it up like that?'

'More or less. He *wanted* you to be comfortable on the income, which has been steadily accruing as you wish to have nothing to do with it. But he was afraid of you inheriting the capital sum outright. Mike would have found some way of getting his hands on it. What he did *not* foresee was your refusal to touch any of it and live a miserable life with lots of pride and not much else. We've done well for you, Laura. You're a very rich woman. Isn't she, Milly?'

'Very rich,' Milly said quietly.

'I'm sorry if you don't remember giving permission for the transfer, dear. I'm afraid the money has long since been spent—'

'Oh, that's fine . . . of course . . . I didn't mean I wanted it back or anything,' Laura stammered, her mind spinning again. 'It's just that I didn't remember . . .'

'Milly, call up and get someone down here,' her uncle said suddenly, his voice cutting through the haze in her head like a scalpel. 'Laura isn't well.'

'I'm all right,' Laura protested. 'It just upsets me to talk about the money, that's all. I guess you're right, it's time I did look at it more sensibly. Dad would have expected me to.'

'I can't tell you how glad I am to hear you say that,' Roger said with every evidence of relief and delight.

'But not now,' Milly intervened. 'When you're better . . . when you feel really capable. You don't feel very capable at the moment, do you, dear?'

'No, not really,' Laura admitted.

'But soon,' Roger persisted. 'Because there are some . . .'

'Roger, can't you see she's practically ready to faint?' Milly put in, standing up. 'Fine doctor *you* are.'

'I do feel a little . . . odd,' Laura said. 'I'll go back up to my room now.'

'Good girl. We'll talk later.' Roger glanced at Milly. Laura smiled noncommittally and went out, closing the door gently behind her. But not before she heard her uncle say, 'Oh, dear, what a shame.'

Once out of sight of her uncle's office doors, Laura straightened up, strode up the stairs and down the hall and walked in on Tom Gilliam, buoyed up by the rising anger she felt.

He was in the process of transferring himself from the bed to his wheelchair and glared at her. 'Well?' he demanded. 'Are you just going to stand there?'

She came over and inserted him into the chair. 'What have you found out about Mountview?' she demanded.

'What do you mean?'

'On the phone, you were asking someone to investigate my uncle, weren't you?'

'Well, it's not—'

'I'm glad you did. I want to know what you found out.'

'Are you sure?'

'Very sure.'

He sighed. 'Your uncle borrowed heavily to finance the annexe to this place. It extended the facilities, but it didn't increase the income very much – and with costs escalating the way they have been in the past twelve months he's now in a bind. The word is the notes are coming due and he hasn't got the capital to pay them off. Nor has he got the muscle to get them extended. Everybody's in trouble, nobody's doing anybody any favours.'

'How long does he have?'

'About three weeks.'

'And then?'

'And then the money men take over. I understand the main interested party is a local named Jack Armstrong. His wife is in here, I think.'

'Yes, she's very ill.'

'Well, at best he'll bring in new management, at worst he'll force Forrester to sell out his participation and probably quite a bit of the land as well. He's a property developer, you see, and . . .'

'And how much does Uncle Roger need?'

'A million and a quarter to pay off completely. Of course, if he can come up with half he might talk them into an extension.'

'I see.' Laura sat down, and forced herself to think clearly and coldly about the situation. Gilliam watched her. Finally, she began to speak in a voice that sounded very odd to her, as if it were coming from a stranger. 'If I die before I'm thirty, which is in about eighteen months' time, Uncle Roger gets my father's money. When I reach thirty the money comes to me absolutely, to do with as I please. Are you with me so far?'

'Yes.'

'Uncle Roger knows that I hate that money. I've always felt that he wanted me to invest it in Mountview and that's one of the reasons I put off coming here for so long. I didn't want to start worrying about it or caring about it. I wanted the money to end up as far away from me as possible, but the trustees wouldn't let me give it away, so it has just gone on getting bigger and bigger. And I hate it. Do you understand?'

'Not really, but then we Gilliams have always been quite practical about money. It doesn't have a personality, it doesn't have a name, it just goes from here to there and gets bigger or smaller. We don't love it or hate it. My brothers use it. I ignore it. You hate it.'

'It's like a great monster following me around, breathing foulness over my shoulder. It killed my father. Now, I think it may be killing me.'

'Oh?'

Carefully, she told him about the stair railing and the brakes. She told him about the penicillin. Then she told him about the loan she hadn't made. 'I swear to you, I may be a fool, but I am *not* capable of forgetting a transaction like that.' She was leaning forward, her fingers pressing into her knees. 'Do you see what I'm getting at?'

'Yes.' Gilliam's voice was careful too.

'David thinks I'm crazy. Do you?'

'No, I don't. On the other hand, rails do give way, brakes do fail and your uncle did try to change the prescription.'

'He *says* he changed it. And Milly would back him up in anything. *Anything.* She could swear she wrote that note and that it got "lost". Blown off the desk or something. An unfortunate accident, nobody to blame and so on.'

'I thought you liked your uncle.'

'So did I,' Laura said miserably. 'But the way he brought out that file, as if it had been ready for me all along, and just smiled at me. He stole the money. He took advantage of my emotional state at the time, because he knew he could always say I just didn't remember. I couldn't prove otherwise.'

'Was it your signature?'

'It looked very much like it.'

'Ah.' He waited.

'There's something else,' she said in a small voice.

'I thought there might be.'

She looked up, irritated. 'You're very good at your job, aren't you?'

'I was. But don't blame me if you're feeling bad about all the things you're telling me.'

'Is that how it seems?'

'You're very angry at someone.'

'I hate *lies*,' she burst out. 'And I hate liars.'

'Hm – just what your friend Julie said. What's the something else, then?'

'It's not about me.'

He sighed. 'All right.'

'You've said all along that you were looking for something that would connect Julie Zalinsky with Clarissa Janacek.'

'Yes.'

'I found out something last night that might be it.' She took a deep breath and let it out in a despairing sigh. 'They were both witnesses to Mrs McAllister's last will.'

'Yes, I know that.'

Her eyes widened. 'You do?'

'That's not the interesting part. The interesting part is the contents of that will, as opposed to the contents of the one immediately prior to it.'

'What do you mean?'

'In her previous will, made in September, Myra McAllister left a million dollars to Mountview. In her subsequent will she left Mountview five hundred thousand and the same to David Butler. Her lawyer drew up the second will according to her instructions and sent it up for her to sign, but he never got it back. Unless he does, the former will is the one going to probate. Her estranged husband is contesting that, saying your uncle used undue influence.'

'She left money to *David*?'

'She intended to, yes.'

'But that's wonderful!'

'If you like money,' Gilliam said drily. 'You don't. I presume he does. The difficulty, as I said, is that the revised will can't be found. Her lawyer has to assume it wasn't signed.'

'So David won't get anything?'

'Apparently not.'

'Does Mrs Strayhorn know where the second will is?'

'I asked her this morning. She doesn't. And the two people who witnessed the signature are dead. Conveniently dead.'

Laura stared at him in horror. 'But the Shadowman killed *them*.'

Gilliam looked at her with pity. 'If you really believe that, why did you come here and tell me about the two things together – your worries about your uncle and Mrs McAllister's will?'

Laura began to cry.

# TWENTY-ONE

THE DAYS WENT BY. LIFE became a waking nightmare. Laura felt as though she were being slowly claimed by a progressive paralysis. It started with a numbness in her brain and made everything seem grey, slow and claustrophobic.

Her uncle simply moved her, lock, stock and underwear, into the nurses' quarters at the top of the clinic. There was no one else staying there; all the nurses on the staff were commuters at the moment and she had the rather bleak accommodation to herself. Solomon could join her there, because there were two doors between it and the clinic itself, so he could effectively be sealed off and hygiene could be maintained.

There was a brief warm spell, then a slight fall of snow, which left the grounds looking as if they'd been strewn with dirty laundry. Nick had been away again with flu and the untended drive was a mass of muddy ruts. When he returned, paler and thinner, he set about trying to remedy the mess, only to have it resubmerged under a sleety coating of ice that came suddenly and glazed everything overnight.

Laura gazed at Solomon, newly returned from the vet's and royally ensconced in a blanket nest at the bottom of her bed. 'You should be glad you're a high-class invalid in weather like this, old buddy,' she told him, looking out the window and shivering at the vista of ice, mud and scummy snowdrifts that lay far below the attic windows. 'All you have to do is teeter over to your litter tray and teeter back. You don't even have to get your paws wet. You might even get to like it.'

He yawned. His expression said he doubted it. His was a life dedicated to adventure. A little set-back like having his throat cut was nothing. He was only resting to please her. He had a few irons in the fire, a few offers, some possibles.

Laura sighed.

Three more days before David returned.

Laura had spent more and more time with Tom Gilliam with David away. Bad times, strained times, because she knew he was trying to think of a way to prove her uncle guilty of murder. All the talk in the newspapers and on the radio and local television was about the Shadowman, where he'd strike next, who would be the next victim and what was taking the sheriff so long to find him.

Despite it all, Roger Forrester seemed just the same. He went his usual elegant way about the clinic, and was as charming and delightful as ever. If there were tighter lines around his eyes and mouth, Laura was probably the only one to notice them.

'I'm afraid it's a matter of proof, Laura,' Gilliam had told her on one of the few occasions they'd spoken of it. She had brought him down to the pool for hydrotherapy the previous morning and they had been alone in the water. Normally they went through his exercises keeping everything on a 'professional' level. But the pool made things more intimate. It was difficult to be distant when you were both in bathing suits. He was improving amazingly now, as if he could only release the tension by punishing his body for its inability to support him in his quest for evidence. The hard work was doing wonders for his body, but nothing for his peace of mind. 'Matt Gabriel is caught up in the media hysteria about the Shadowman and he's trapped by it. A cop can't work in that kind of atmosphere, especially in a small town. They swarm after him, he can't move freely or talk to anyone without their swooping down for their sound bites or their snapshots. We're both stuck in our own little hells.'

'But what do you *need*?'

'Just what he needs – solid evidence. A lot more than hearsay, a lot more than implications. On the face of it your uncle had good reason to kill those two girls, especially if he had found and destroyed the second will. But if he hasn't found and destroyed it, killing them was pointless because it could show up at any time.'

Laura had let herself float in the water, staring up at the ceiling of the pool room, while Gilliam swam down the pool and back again. Using the wheelchair had strengthened his arms considerably, so that his uncooperative legs didn't impede his progress too much. Even they were beginning to come under his control and she knew he now believed he would be able to walk again some time. Probably with a limp, but no more. One day he'd stand up and walk out of her life. Another triumph for medical science. She hoped it wouldn't be too soon. She certainly hoped it wouldn't be before . . .

'Do you think you'll ever be able to prove anything against him?' she'd asked as he swam up beside her and grabbed for the edge of the pool, breathing hard.

'Do you want me to?'

'I want it to be over.'

'And you'll marry your David and settle down to be a nice little doctor's wife in a nice little town, and I'll limp my way back to the city and a desk job, and one day it will seem as if it never happened?'

'It will never seem like that,' she said in a low voice. 'If my uncle really *is* a murderer . . .'

'I thought you were so sure?' Gilliam's voice was soft, barely audible above the plash and tinkle of the water in the trough that edged the pool, its echo a mere whisper in the vault of warm, humid air above them.

'I admit it's an explanation that fits everything, but I find it so hard to . . . accept.' She let the water swirl around her fingers and trailed her hand back and forth through it. 'I've told him I'm willing to put the trust money into Mountview. That should keep me alive, anyway.'

He'd winced at the bitter edge in her voice. 'Laura, I'm sorry—'

'So am I.' She forced her legs down and stood up, swaying in the water as she faced him with a tight smile. 'What can't be cured must be endured . . . but I wish to *hell* you or your friend Matt Gabriel could put me out of my misery. I don't know how much longer I can go on pretending I'm still my uncle's loving niece. Now that Milly's away on her little annual Christmas shopping jaunt he seems to want to spend all his evenings with me . . . talking about my father.' Her voice broke. 'And he looks just like him . . .'

'Oh, Laura . . .' He had pulled her body against his own, the water trickling down between them as she gave way to her sobs. He stroked her hair gently. 'Why don't you just leave? You don't have to explain, you don't have to pretend . . . just go and be done with it . . .'

'I couldn't do that . . . the patients . . .'

'Will survive. Even me. Just about.'

She shook her head and pulled away, suddenly conscious of their proximity. 'No. I'm sorry I cried all over you. I'll be fine, now. It's just with David away . . .'

'With David away you don't mind who you cry over? Even cripples will do?' He'd meant to make it funny. It wasn't.

She moved back further and looked into his face. Roughly he pulled her back to him and kissed her, hard. Then he thrust her away and swam towards the hoist in the corner.

'Time I was hauled back into the boat,' he'd said. 'I'm beginning to feel like a barracuda.'

Now, thinking back and remembering the tension and confusion of that moment, she blushed. She was usually sensitive to the feelings of her patients, but she'd been remiss in the case of Tom Gilliam. Attraction of patients to carers was very common and she just hadn't seen it. Her blindness was probably a product of the strange atmosphere of Mountview and her own distracted emotions.

She didn't pity Gilliam, far from it. If the truth were told, he frightened her a little. He was, or had been, a big strong man before his accident. Now that strength was returning, but was still pent up, glowering, waiting for full release. Instead of his former abject self-pity his predicament had become one of impatience as he became convinced that he *would* walk again. Realizing that made all the slow, painstaking work of rehabilitation even more frustrating. He seemed dangerous. And, in a way she didn't understand, but should have – exciting. She had to put him out of her mind.

'I've put the little table over by the window,' she told Solomon, who still hadn't got down from the bed, although he'd sat up with paws folded to watch her every move as she dressed for the day's work. 'If you want to look out and see what you're missing, feel free. Your breakfast is by the fridge.'

He gazed at her with liquid eyes, seeming to absorb every word. She knew he was just waiting for her to get out the way so he could have the place to himself. God knew what he would get into, even in his 'weakened' convalescent state.

The day before he'd pulled down the curtains.

Laura had decided the night before that it was time she visited the free clinic in Hatchville. Anything to get away from the tense atmosphere of Mountview itself. She left herself a couple of hours free around lunch-time and picked her way gingerly across the icy parking lot to her 'new' car, in fact, a compact a couple of years old, bright yellow. She had taken delivery of the little sedan a few days before and was very pleased with it, although it had just been sitting in the parking lot ever since.

The engine turned over easily, but when she tried to back out the wheels spun in little pockets of icy mud.

Nick appeared by her window and she rolled it down. 'Put it in reverse and I'll rock it out for you,' he instructed and went round to the front of the car, forcing himself in between the front bumper and the thick hedge. He grinned encouragingly at her and nodded.

She revved the car in reverse, while he pushed rhythmically until it rolled free on to firmer gravel. He really was very strong, she realized, and had been pushing so hard he nearly fell as the car suddenly lurched out from under his hands. She smiled at him as he straightened up. 'Sorry,' she called. 'It just sort of leaped off. I'm not used to it yet.'

'That's okay.' He smiled, rubbing his wrist above his gloves and pulling down the sleeves of his red plaid jacket.

'You've cut yourself,' she said, concerned as she saw blood trickling out from under his glove.

He glanced down, raised his wrist to his mouth like a child and sucked it. 'Just knocked a scab off,' he said. 'No problem.' He shoved the offending hand into the pocket of his jacket.

'Nick, are you sure you should be working out in the cold so soon after having the flu?' she asked, still concerned. Despite his show of strength in shoving the car out of the rut, he seemed pale and distracted.

'Best thing for it,' he said. 'Got to show them bugs who's boss. I hate hanging around inside, anyway. Can't stand being closed up, not even when I'm sick. Some like it, not me. Have to be *out*.'

'Yes, but if you're ill . . .'

'I'm not. I feel fine,' he said, with just a trace of irritation. Obviously he felt his virility was being questioned.

She sought for soothing words. 'You men are all alike,' she said lamely, but it seemed to be the right response. He grinned at her, anyway.

He watched her car go down the drive and absently took his hand from his pocket to suck again at the back of it, where the long scratches were still oozing blood. Things always seemed to take longer to heal in the cold weather. This was the second time those cuts had opened up.

* * *

George picked up the phone, leaning back in his chair. He was sitting with his feet up on the desk, but soon dropped them. 'Matt!' he called. 'It's the State Police lab.'

In his office, Matt picked up the phone. 'This is Sheriff Gabriel.' He listened for a while, the hope on his face slowly fading. 'So let me get this down right,' he said, picking up a pen and drawing a pad towards him. 'The blood type was O-positive, a match for about fifty per cent of the population. Male. Height somewhere between five-ten and six foot, because you think the bottom of the thing is worn where it dragged on the ground, yeah, got that. What about all the badges?' He listened again. 'Yeah – I can see it will take a long time. And any hope on the DNA? Weeks? Why on earth . . . oh, I see. I didn't know that. Well, would you send us photos of the "decorations" so we can get started on tracing them? Thanks. And I'll wait to hear about the rest. Right. Thanks again.'

He hung up the phone and stared at it. They had found skin particles around the neck of the cape, but it would take some time to isolate the DNA apparently – it was not an overnight process. Once they had that, all Matt would have to do was test every man in Blackwater Bay and the surrounding area. Assuming they agreed to be tested. Not everyone would agree and not everyone who didn't agree would necessarily be guilty – but they might warrant further investigation. It would be a massive undertaking that would take further weeks of hard slog – and then might not produce results if the guy wasn't local. Suppose he drove over from Hatchville or one of the other towns in the vicinity? He sighed. That way lay madness.

That left the badges and paraphernalia sewn on to the cloak itself. Another hard slog, time-consuming, wearying. And a lot to ask of his small staff. Of course, it might be time, now, to call in the State Police investigators. They were certainly giving out some heavy hints and there had been a few phone calls from the capital.

But how would it look? Like the sheriff was incompetent, that's how. And the election was only a few weeks away. It was selfish, it was risky, it was probably irresponsible – but he wanted to hold on to the investigation for as long as he was sheriff, in case the coming election changed things. If Molt or – God forbid – Armstrong took over his job, then it would be their failure, not his.

He was not proud of himself for this.

He thought he already knew the truth about the Shadowman.

But there was no proof.

Not yet.

And instincts weren't evidence.

Instincts didn't win court cases.

Or elections.

And they didn't stop a killer from striking again, either.

# TWENTY-TWO

AS THIS WAS LAURA'S FIRST time in Hatchville it took her quite a while to find the clinic. Although the neighbourhood was poor, the clinic itself was freshly painted. It was a converted store-front. A small sign welcomed patients and promised free, confidential treatment, hours from nine to twelve and from two until four-thirty. The door was locked. She knocked and after a minute Owen appeared, holding half a sandwich in one hand.

When he saw who it was he opened the door and swung it wide. 'Welcome!' he said, swallowing the bite of sandwich he had been busily chewing. 'You never said anything about coming over.'

'Well, it was an impulse,' Laura admitted. 'Everything was getting kind of . . . tense back at Mountview. I wanted a change of scene.'

'We're certainly that,' Owen said, waving around at the empty reception area that held many unmatching chairs, a box of broken toys and a stack of magazines so tattered it was a wonder they held together at all.

'You keep a long lunch-hour,' she observed as he re-locked the door behind her.

'Not really. We lock the doors at the appointed time, but there are always people in here still waiting, so we often don't get much more than half an hour to grab lunch before it's time to open up again. Same thing at the other end of the day – the last straggler is often still here at six. I try to see everyone I can.'

He took her across the waiting-room and through a door

into a narrow corridor that led to the back of the building. On either side of the hallway were doors – one on the left and two on the right. He went through the left-hand one, which proved to be an office of sorts. There were three dilapidated filing cabinets against the far wall and a battered desk with the balance of Owen's lunch sat in the middle of the room. There was also a large cupboard partly open, which Owen slammed shut as he went past. 'Tuna sandwich?' he offered.

'Thanks, no – I ate before I drove over,' she said.

'Then, what can I do for you?' Owen asked.

'I just was curious, I guess. About what the clinic was like, what you do here and so on. In the back of my mind was the possibility that I might come over occasionally if there was any call for a physio's services.'

'Have you consulted your uncle about that?' Owen asked.

'Why no – should I have?'

Owen grimaced. 'We have a pretty tight budget here, the minimum, really. I had hoped he would live up to his promises when we opened the clinic, but he keeps us to the bottom line. I don't think a physio would figure in the plan, much as I would love to have your help.'

'Oh,' she said, rather nonplussed. 'You mean he limits your resources?'

'Yes. I can see his point of view, Mountview is the money-cow and this was a concession in order to get what he wanted. Even so, I had hoped his support would be better.' He sighed and looked worried. 'Listen, I'm not complaining, really. I don't want you to think—'

'You don't want me to tell my uncle off.' She smiled.

'Well—'

'Because it would rebound on you? I understand. I'll do it if you think it would help, but only if you give me permission. Your budget is between you and him.'

'Actually, it's more between me and Mrs Cunningham,' Owen said, balling up the wax paper his sandwiches had been wrapped in and tossing it into a waste basket by the desk. 'He leaves it to her to approve or disapprove my requests.'

'That can't be right.' She scowled. 'He's the head of Mountview, not Milly.'

'Well, I suppose he has to delegate *some* things and we're hardly top priority,' Owen said reasonably. 'Come on, I'll show you round before the afternoon rush starts.'

The 'tour' didn't take very long – the exam rooms were as bare as his office had been and the tiny 'lab' at the rear was more like a high-school set-up than a medical facility.

'How many people do you see a day?' she asked.

He shrugged. 'I lose count. Imogen could tell you.'

'Imogen?'

'She is – or was – a retired RN, worked in the Hatchville Hospital's ER and she really knows her stuff. Half the time she diagnoses before I even get to a patient and most of the time she's absolutely spot-on.'

'I know what you mean – an experienced RN usually can teach young doctors more than they ever learned at medical school.'

'I couldn't run this place without her.'

'What do you do for supplies?'

'I requisition through Mrs Cunningham – and don't think that isn't a fight to the death every month,' Owen said with a scowl. 'I can't do much here without even the basics, but she questions every bandage, every syringe, every bottle of—'

The door to the reception area opened and what had to be Imogen stood there. 'Hi,' she said. 'I'm back. The supermarket was unbelievable. Who's this?'

'This is Laura Brandon – she's the physio over at Mountview. She wanted to see how we do things over here.'

'Very badly and very slowly.' Imogen smiled, coming forward to shake Laura's hand. Her grip was firm and friendly. 'Hi. Are you going to work here too?'

'I wish,' Owen said.

'I'd love to give you a few hours a week,' Laura said. 'But apparently I have to clear it with my uncle first.'

'With the ogress, you mean,' Imogen contradicted, with a scowl that comically echoed Owen's. 'She's never been here, not once, but you'd think it was her own precious bank account she was emptying just to give us a bit of local anaesthetic.'

So Milly Cunningham's personality percolated even over here to Hatchville, Laura reflected. She knew a facility like this could bleed money from every orifice, but if maintaining it was part of the deal for Mountview, the least they could do would be to do it properly. Or if not properly, then with grace.

'Do you prescribe much?' she asked.

Owen glanced sideways at her. 'You're asking if I help addicts who try it on to get free drugs? No, I don't. I refer them for a rehab programme if they're willing, otherwise they're out on their ear. They're not hard to recognize. I prescribe all the time – but whether these people can afford to buy the stuff is another thing altogether. I give out what I can, but . . .'

'I know,' Laura said sympathetically. 'It's never enough and everybody is a deserving case.'

'Well,' Imogen said. 'Not *everybody*. If someone comes in bleeding then they get priority, but those cases usually go to the ER at the hospital downtown. What we get are the runny noses, sick babies, malnutrition, measles, mumps, nits, scabies, ringworm, food poisoning – all the really good stuff.'

'We get some freeloaders and malingerers,' Owen added. 'But, mostly, it's as you say – you want to help the world and you can only bandage a corner of it. It breaks my heart. If only city planners would realize how much they could *save* with a decent preventative medical programme—'

'Uh-oh, don't let him get started.' Imogen chuckled. 'It's nearly two o'clock and we don't have time for the Jenks Lecture on Public Health. Nice to meet you, Laura.' She went back into the reception area, shrugging out of her coat resolutely as she prepared for The Onslaught.

They returned to Owen's office. Laura glanced at the

cupboard he had so carefully closed when she'd first walked in. 'You seem to have plenty of drugs,' she said casually.

He flushed and opened his mouth to speak.

'Never mind. I won't tell my uncle. Or Milly.'

'Thanks,' Owen said. 'It's just that . . .'

'I understand. Really, I do. I used to work in an outfit a lot like this one. I would have done the same thing if I could have.'

'What the hell are you doing, working in a place like Mountview, then?' he demanded. 'I do it to keep this place open. But you . . .'

She took a long breath and let it out. 'I came because Uncle Roger kept asking me, because I was fed up where I was and because . . .' She paused.

'Because?' he prompted.

'Because Julie Zalinsky was a friend of mine.'

'Oh.' He seemed taken aback. 'I didn't know that.'

'Did you like her?' Laura asked. She hadn't really had a chance to talk to Owen about Julie, or anything else seriously, come to that. He was still pretty much a mystery to her, as he spent so much time here at the free clinic.

'Julie? Sure, I liked her a lot,' Owen said. 'She worked hard – harder than she needed to. I respected that.'

Laura looked at him – underfed and overstretched, dedicated, even fanatical in his way. Yes, he would appreciate a hard worker. Killing someone like Julie would have seemed to him to be a criminal waste. On the other hand, if he *was* stealing drugs and supplies from Mountview and Julie had found out about it . . . how far would he go to protect his precious free clinic?

'Well, since you respect hard work I guess I'd better get back to my patients.' Laura smiled. 'Thanks for showing me around.'

'My pleasure. And if you *can* talk your uncle into lending us your services for a few hours a week that would be great.'

'I'll try,' she promised. 'Really, I will.'

When she went back through the door into the reception area she was stunned to see that although the doors of the clinic could only have been open for a few minutes, every chair had silently filled, with people standing around the walls as well, all waiting to be seen. Young, old, poor and poorly, mothers with haunted eyes, children with pale faces, men with despair in every line of their dejected bodies. Oh, yes, Owen was needed here. And about a dozen like him.

She climbed the long, long stairs to her temporary quarters with resignation. She still got headaches and the free clinic had depressed her.

There was no Solomon to greet her. When she went into the little kitchen she saw his food had been eaten. In the bathroom there was a scatter of gravel around his litter tray. In the communal sitting-room there were more loose threads hanging from the end of the elderly sofa which he had adopted as a scratching post and the table in front of the window had been knocked over.

But no cat.

She called him several times, without success. She felt no pang of fear this time because the door at the foot of the stairs had been firmly shut. There was no way he could have got out.

Unless someone had come in.

'Solomon?' she called again, standing perplexed in the centre of the little sitting-room. This time she was rewarded by the sound of a very faint miaow. Frowning, she turned round and round, trying to locate its source. It came again, seemingly from the landing at the top of the stairs. She went out and looked around.

The wallpaper on the left-hand wall seemed to be askew.

When she went closer she realized that in fact there was a door there, papered over neatly and concealed by the pattern of roses and leaves someone had chosen to 'brighten up' the rather dismal area. Now that she was closer she could see a small white china knob, and that at the lower corner of the door the paper was clawed and shredded. Obviously, Solomon had worked long and devotedly to get the door open. Feeling a little like Alice in Wonderland, she bent down and pulled the rather small door open completely, revealing a dark gap from which flowed a current of icy, musty air.

Of course. This must be the entrance to the attics over the east wing. She turned slightly and looked over at the wall on the far side of the landing, finally locating a duplicate white handle to a door that presumably led to the attics over the west wing.

'Solomon! Come out of there this instant!' she commanded. Her voice echoed back, indicating a vast expanse beyond the door. Looking up she saw tiny chips of light like stars overhead and realized that what was left of the late afternoon sun was shining through dozens of gaps between the old shingles. She got tired of bending and sank to her knees in front of the opening, wrapping her arms around herself and shivering.

'Solomon,' she wheedled. 'Come on – I've got you some salmon for dinner.' Her voice whispered back at her. He knew the word salmon; it usually brought him running. There was another faint miaow, but it was no closer. She pushed her head and shoulders through the opening, squinting to see if she could spot him in the darkness – a black cat in a dark attic? – fat chance. She noticed a small round switch just inside the door, fastened to one of the rough joists that framed the opening. Not hoping for much, she flicked it and immediately the entire space beyond the door sprang into view.

Whoever had put up the lights, probably Michaels, had made sure there were plenty of them. A line overhead marched away along the roof ridge and there were more bare bulbs spaced along the rafters at the sides, every few feet or so. The connecting wires drooped like garlands in between each fixture, some with a mossy covering of dust.

The attic was not completely floored, but boards had been laid along the centre of the space. Obviously, as objects had been relegated to the attic, new areas of board had been put down to support them. Mostly she could see boxes and crates. Some wore thick coats of dust, others were obviously more recent additions to the store. Here and there they glinted, where small drifts of snow had come in between the shingles. The area between the joists was thickly filled with insulating material so none of the warmth of the floor below came up here. She rubbed her arms to get some warmth in them.

'Solomon! Come here!' she called again, not relishing the prospect of picking her way through the obstacle course in the search for one recalcitrant cat. On the other hand, he might be trapped. He didn't ordinarily hold out against her for this long.

'You do realize,' she grunted, edging her way through the low, wide doorway and standing up on the other side, 'that I could fall right between the joists and end up in some patient's bed, don't you?' There was another miaow.

'Oh, all right . . . I'm coming.'

Twice she nearly came a cropper. The first time her foot slipped she judged she was just about over Mr Cobbold's room. He would have been fairly astonished to see her legs come through the ceiling over his head, to say the least. The second time she lost her balance she grabbed the corner of a crate and nearly pulled it over. From the label she saw that the patient files from 1992 had almost descended into the sluice room and grimaced. Plaster and mess aside, sorting out the files would have been a nightmare.

'Solomon?' she called again when she was about half-way down the length of the attic. A miaow seemed to come from virtually beneath her feet. She glanced to the left and saw, beyond the first cardboard box, a stack that had been overturned. The loosely fastened lid of the top box had spilled books, papers and clothing into the space between the joists. She edged her way over and tipped her head to one side to read the label.

'Zalinsky – personal effects.' So Milly Cunningham hadn't got rid of them after all. And there had been no one to claim them. From the darkness beneath the box she heard another faint miaow, along with a scuffling noise. So that's where he was.

'All right, monster – hang on,' she muttered, and righting the box she knelt down gingerly and began tossing the contents back in any old way in order to free and rescue the Intrepid Explorer. As she heaved up the last folds of a thick blue blanket she shrieked. A tiny grey shape shot past her, followed by a snarling Solomon. The rumpled but obviously unbowed mouse and the cat disappeared between the boxes on the other side of the gangway as she clutched for support and nearly overturned the whole mess again.

'Damn you, Solomon Brandon!' she cursed and got up to go after him. She saw his black rump sticking out from between a couple of boxes and grabbed. There was a monumental struggle as he held on to a joist with all claws extended and she pulled steadily. When he lost his hold on the joist he grabbed for the nearest box and then another, slowly but surely being eased out of that dark night into the light of accusation. Eventually she had him, whiskers cobwebbed, coat dust-streaked and the wild manic light of the hunter blazing in his eyes. Slowly they refocused and he gave her a reproachful glare.

So that was what had kept him scrabbling so steadily at that door all afternoon – the sound and scent of mouse.

'Bad cat. Bad cat!'

He looked at her, sneezed and looked away, craning his neck towards the place where the mouse had been. Securing his writhing, yearning body between her elbow and hip, she started back.

She closed the little door firmly and dropped Solomon unceremoniously. He shook himself, gave one last look at the attic door and trotted towards the little kitchen. She might not understand the emotional requirements of a hunter, but she did know how to handle a can-opener. Solomon, like all his kind, was pragmatic by nature.

After she'd fed him, she shut him in the kitchen and went

back into the attic. Stepping carefully, she returned to the box of Julie's effects and carried it back to her room.

She assumed one of the nurses, probably Shirley Hasker, had packed Julie's things – she couldn't imagine Milly Cunningham deigning to perform such a mundane task. *Somewhere* in here might be a clue as to why Julie was killed.

And if it was there, she meant to find it.

# TWENTY-THREE

IT WAS EMBARRASSING.

It was pathetic.

It nearly broke her heart.

Julie's life was in that box. And Julie was gone.

For a woman who moved from place to place as often as she had, Julie had retained an amazing amount of 'junk' and rather than just throwing it all out, Shirley or whoever had packed the things up had carefully preserved everything (or so it seemed) for the relative who had never arrived to claim it. Old photos, ticket stubs and programmes from shows Julie had seen, souvenirs from various parties, medical effluvia – notices, conference programmes, business cards, several very elderly nursing magazines, newspaper clippings of medical interest or showbusiness gossip, all kinds of things. And lots and lots of letters, including Laura's own to Julie.

She assumed that Sheriff Gabriel had gone through Julie's things after the murder – it would have been standard procedure. Would he have read all the letters? Presumably. But, not knowing Julie, he might not have noticed something that she might. It made her uneasy, but the need to find the answer to the question of who had killed Julie outweighed any embarrassment she felt about reading someone else's mail. Her own letters she could ignore. But there were still many others – Julie had apparently filled her lonely hours by writing to old friends all over the place – there were even a few letters from someone in Nome, Alaska. Some were from mutual friends with whom she herself had long since lost touch.

The thought made her so lonely that she decided to call David instead of waiting for him to call her. She rang the hotel and asked for him. There was a long pause and then the switchboard operator returned. 'I'm afraid he doesn't answer. Would you care to leave a message?'

'Yes, please. Would you tell him Laura Brandon called and would like him to call back, no matter how late it is? He'll have the number.'

'I'll be certain he gets the message,' the operator assured her.

In a fever of impatience, Laura put on the television set and sat down to wait. He could be anywhere, of course. She glanced at the clock on the mantel. Dinner would be over, but there were probably . . .

The phone rang and she grabbed it up. 'David?'

'Hi,' he said. 'Are you missing me like crazy?'

'Where were you? I called you a minute ago but there was no answer.'

'Oh – I was in the shower, I didn't hear it ring.'

'Well, it must be telepathy, then. I was thinking about you.'

She explained about Solomon and the attic, and the letters, papers and souvenirs. 'She had a lot of friends, I must say. There was even one who knew you.'

'Oh, really? Who?'

'Somebody named Valerie? She was with you at St Anselm's in Denver, apparently. Or was it when you were a resident at Memorial? I forget. Anyway, she seemed to have had quite a crush on you.'

'Really? I can't say I remember the name.'

'Well, of course, there have been so many thousands of women who were in love with you.' Laura didn't sound very convincing to herself.

'Thousands? It must have been millions, at least.' David chuckled. 'Any more?'

'None I can remember,' she said carelessly. She could hardly read him the woman's burblings about him, could she? And it was obvious from the way this woman had answered Julie that Julie herself had been infatuated with David, too. Just like all the others at Mountview. Including Laura herself. How nice to be a member of such a big club, she thought wryly. It gave sisterhood a whole new meaning. Or demeaning.

'I don't think you should be reading someone's mail,' David said. 'Especially if they're dead.'

'Oh, but that's what makes it all right.' Laura was surprised at his rather stuffy attitude. 'It can hardly hurt her now, can it? And it might help. Or it might have helped – I haven't found anything at all, as it happens. She had a lot of friends, or, at least, a lot of correspondents, but they were all just sort of . . . general. None of them seemed to be particularly close or intimate.' Not even me, she thought to herself. 'Anyway, I don't see why you're so disapproving.'

'Not disapproving, exactly. I don't know – it seems sort of ghoulish.'

'Oh, all right then,' she said rather stiffly. 'I'm sorry.'

'Oh, don't be like that,' David chided. 'Read the damn stuff if you want. Knowing what she was like, I'd think her friends were as boring as she was.'

'Well, thanks very much,' Laura said.

'Oh, I didn't mean you. But—'

'I know, I know. Listen, did Robert Redford really visit some patient called Rollo here?'

'Good God, is that what she said?'

'Well, I don't know what she *said*, exactly, but according to what her friends wrote back, this place has been a regular stopoff for the stars of stage, screen and television.'

David snorted. 'Typical. We have had a few "names", but nobody like Robert Redford. Probably she saw some blond guy with a square jaw and drew her own conclusions. It would have been like her.' Laura couldn't have argued with that. It had been Julie's abiding weakness to see what wasn't there – or to wish it there out of boredom.

When David didn't say anything more, she changed the subject. 'Did they like your paper?' She knew he had been scheduled to read it the previous night and so hadn't been able to call her as usual.

'They were suitably impressed,' he said with mock modesty. 'Nobody's offered me the Nobel Prize yet, unfortunately.'

'Just shows how blind they can be. I miss you.'

She could almost hear him smile. 'About time you admitted it.'

'What are you doing now?'

'Well, I just had a shower, and I'm about to go downstairs and have some drinks with some old friends from Med school.'

'I can hear music and women's voices. Are you sure you're not at a party?'

'No, I am not. I am sitting in my room, virtuously alone. That's the television you hear – some old film. Do I detect jealousy?'

'No, not really. It's just not very nice here.'

'What do you mean?'

'Oh, it's cold and miserable. It's started to snow again and everybody jumps at the least noise from the woods. It seems hard to believe that Thanksgiving and Christmas are only a short time away. Nobody's exactly in the holiday spirit that I can see.'

'Poor love, you sound really down.' David was sympathetic. 'I'm amazed Gabriel hasn't made an arrest yet.'

'Tom says he hasn't enough hard evidence.'

'You mean Gilliam? Calling him "Tom" now, are you?'

'Why not?'

'Sounds a bit . . . cosy.'

'Not with a porcupine like him.' She forced back the memory of Tom Gilliam's mouth on hers and the way she had momentarily responded despite herself. 'I wish you'd come home before Sunday,' she said wistfully.

'I can't – I've agreed to sit in on a round-table discussion Saturday evening. It's quite an honour to be asked.'

'Was it because of your paper?'

'I guess so. I never thought it would go that well.' He

seemed surprised at his own success. How typical, she thought. Doesn't he realize how good he is, how far he could go? He's too modest, too unambitious. Imagine wanting to be a small-town GP when he could go so far in a city like Chicago or New York.

'At least you know it's not because of your smile,' she teased him. 'Doctors aren't impressed by other doctors' bedside manners. You're *good*, David.'

'I can also tap-dance. Want to hear my bird calls?'

'No, I do not want to hear your bird calls.' She laughed.

'I'll be back on Sunday. Until then, stay away from Gilliam and watch out for the Shadowman. I don't want him to get you before I do.'

'I hope not.'

After more foolishness they hung up.

Feeling even more lonely now, she turned on the television set and channel-hopped, catching the tail-end of the old movie she'd heard in the background while she was talking to David. At least she was pretty sure it was the same one – *The Bad and the Beautiful*. Who could forget that gorgeous theme music?

The letters had been a let-down because she had been so certain Julie would have said what had been worrying her to someone. But she hadn't – or if she had, it was buried in a way Laura couldn't fathom. Solomon, released from the kitchen as she had passed by with her 'treasure', came over and sat on the sofa beside her, curling up in the crook of her knees. She stroked him gently and he began to purr. The shaved area of his neck looked so vulnerable and the marks from the stitches, now removed, showed bright pink. Owen said he had been lucky, no major vessels had been severed and that was why he had survived. It seemed the Shadowman was not only cruel, he was inept – fortunately.

Remembering that terrible night made her very aware of her isolation up here in the attics – she felt even more alone than she had in her little flat over the old stables. This surprised her. After her ex-husband had left she had become accustomed to being alone (with Solomon, of course) and hadn't been aware of being lonely. Now she felt it. Was this why Julie had become depressed too? Reading those letters made her realize – as Julie must have done – that she was just one of a long line of women attracted to David Butler. And, no doubt, had as little chance of . . . of . . . what? Marrying him? Is that what she wanted? He was certainly not a good bet for marriage. Laura had little doubt that his flirtations would not be stopped by a few words of legal attachment. He might protest devotion, but he did it automatically, knowing it was required, knowing it was desired, wanting to please, wanting to be liked, wanting to be wanted. And didn't that make him a bit pathetic?

That startled her. David? Pathetic? And yet, in a way, that was part of his appeal. Despite his abilities as a doctor, his looks came across as the beautiful little boy lost. And he played on it. Owen, on the other hand, was strong and purposeful. Not handsome, but still attractive because he was so very alive. And Owen did not flirt – he was too serious for such things. But Owen had been taking medical supplies from Mountview surreptitiously, driven no doubt by his mission to the poor at the free clinic, but thievery none the less. Didn't that indicate some kind of obsession? And didn't obsessives sometimes strike down anything that stood in their way? What if Julie and Clarissa had found out it was Owen who was stealing drugs – would he have killed them to keep it quiet? It seemed unlikely and yet obsessions drove people to do odd things, sometimes terrible things, because they thought they were right and therefore justified. Dr Weaver had even admitted to being obsessive – although he hadn't specified his particular object or subject of desire. Could Dr Weaver have been under those smelly clothes? He was big, he was strong – and for all his pleasantness to everyone he was a very private man. Did he have something to hide?

Laura had been unconscious after the Shadowman had fled. How quickly had the others found her? Who had come out first? David? Owen? Her uncle? Had one of them had time to shed the disguise and return as a concerned party to her rescue? And where had Michaels been at the time? She longed to talk to Tom Gilliam, but it was late, too late to get dressed again and go downstairs. Maybe tomorrow.

'I'm getting stir crazy,' she announced and got up to look out of the small window that overlooked the rear of the grounds. Cupping her hands on either side of her face, she peered out into the darkness, but could see nothing. It was still strange to her to see how absolute the darkness was in the countryside. To her left there was a slight glow in the sky over the town of Blackwater beyond the woods and the river, and in the far distance another bowl of pale light stood out over Hatchville. But in between lay the woods, utter darkness and fear.

Was he out there now – the Shadowman? Was he watching the clinic from behind the trees? Could he see her up here, a tiny figure in a tiny window, outlined against the light, mercifully out of his reach?

She *was* afraid, now. The panicky bravado that had sent her running out into the windy darkness to rescue Solomon was gone. The very thought of going outside in the dark made her tremble, and she abruptly left the window to return to the sofa and Solomon – warm, solid and affectionate.

She wished she were brave. She wished she could do the clever thing she had come here to do, boldly go where no physiotherapist had gone before, find out the truth. But some parts of the truth that seemed to be staring her in the face were unpleasant and too close to home. If only Julie had been more specific in her letters. If only she had said something to give a clue.

Or had someone got to these things before the sheriff did? Extracted the dangerous bits? Destroyed what might in turn have destroyed him or her if it had been found?

She stirred through the bits of paper again, trying to

put them in order, to relate one to another, or to see if something obvious was missing, but could get nothing from them. There was a picture of David in a little home-made cardboard frame – something Julie had done herself. And there were other pictures of him, taken without his knowledge, it appeared – walking with a patient in the garden, talking to Mrs McAllister, talking to Owen. Had Julie stalked him? It looked like it. But there was no camera among Julie's effects. What had happened to it? There were other pictures taken at Mountview: Owen, her uncle, several of the nurses and so on. These were loose in an envelope. But no camera. Odd.

She looked through a pack of older photographs that were held together with a thick elastic band. Mostly they were of people Julie had presumably worked with – doctors and nurses – a few even looked as if Julie had saved them from high school. There were the classic young faces with execrable hairstyles and silly dedications written on the back of some of the smaller photos. Others were of groups of young people on picnics, at parties – many of them obviously drunk and very merry.

There were programmes from theatres, conferences, hospital staff 'events' like dances and so on, all carefully preserved for posterity. There was even a souvenir from the little party they had thrown in Omaha when Julie had left the hospital there – she recognized the tiny figure she herself had made for the top of the cake. Julie had loved parties. She was in some of the pictures, but had apparently taken others herself. (Where was that camera?)

Laura stared at one picture disconsolately. Julie, in a pussycat costume, raising a glass of wine to someone, looking carefree and happy.

'I'm sorry,' she whispered. 'I can't do it. I can't find out who it was. Or why. I've tried. I'm afraid, just as you were, and I don't know why. Maybe you didn't know why either. Maybe your fears were just as uncomfortable as mine. We're all thinking about you – me, the sheriff, Tom

Gilliam – but nobody is getting anywhere. God, I wish you could tell me.'

But Julie smiled back silently from the photograph, lifting her glass, revealing nothing.

# TWENTY-FOUR

CARRYING HER DAILY REPORTS, LAURA edged rather quietly into her uncle's office, hoping not to be noticed. He was on the phone and it was obvious who was on the other end of the line.

'Of course, if you feel you need another day or two, I can muddle through here. Enjoy yourself.'

Laura knew that Milly Cunningham had gone on her annual Christmas shopping expedition to New York, apparently a ritual excuse to see old friends and new plays. She watched her uncle's face as he spoke, and wondered how anyone as handsome and distinguished as he could do anything evil.

Roger Forrester was laughing, his fine grey eyes crinkling at the corners. 'I can imagine it. Listen, I've got Laura here in my office at the moment. How would it be if I got her to sign those papers now? Well, surely . . . it's just a matter of a few . . .' He paused and winked at Laura. 'Yes, I do know where they are, actually. And I know where you keep that precious little key, too. You talk as if I were totally incapable of dealing with anything on my own. Makes me seem a bit feeble, don't you think?'

Laura suppressed her instant resentment at being rushed. It made sense to get the thing over with. She wouldn't have to think about it ever again after that. And it wasn't as if she were wasting the money. Forrester's creditors had agreed to accept the trust fund as surety for the time being, that's all. And she would be very slow about doing anything further, since it would have to be undone as soon as Sheriff Gabriel . . .

'Nevertheless, Milly, I'd like to get the ball rolling now. You know how things can get fouled up over the Christmas season. No . . . no, leave it with me. Yes, I do mean it. You enjoy yourself. See you on Saturday. Goodbye.' He hung up rather quickly and gave Laura a shamefaced look. 'She seems to think I'm an imbecile.'

'Most women have that secret conviction about their bosses or their husbands,' Laura said, softening it with a wry smile that did not come easily. 'It's the way we justify our existence. Sometimes we're even right.'

'Thank you *very* much,' Roger said, but his eyes twinkled. She had to admit he was giving a consummate performance as the fond and loving uncle. 'I assume this display of irony is the result of your pining for young Butler? You sound far less steely when he's around, I've noticed.'

'Um. What are these papers, exactly?'

'The approval we require, as set down in the rules of the trust, for any transaction involving the fund. As before.'

Laura started to protest there hadn't been any 'before', but closed her mouth tight. It would only confuse matters, now. Roger started to stand up, but the phone rang. 'Damn. The forms are in the black filing cabinet next door, the one where all my private papers are kept,' he said, reaching for the phone. 'She keeps the key in a blue enamel box in the upper right-hand drawer of her desk.' He picked up the receiver but kept his hand over the mouthpiece. 'Do you mind getting them?'

'Of course not,' Laura said.

As she went out she heard him say 'Roger Forrester', sounding so polished and mellow that she wanted to throw something at him.

She went through into the administration office and smiled at Beth, who was handling the phones and routine paperwork alone while Milly was away. 'I have to get something for my uncle.' Beth nodded, returning her smile shyly.

Laura moved over to Milly's desk, located the blue box, then went to the black filing cabinet in the corner. The key was on a ring with several others, including what looked like one to the door of the office itself. She unlocked the cabinet and began opening the drawers. There were three of them, all unlabelled. Within, the contents were equally mysterious, half the file folders having simply coloured tabs or coded markings that obviously meant everything to Milly and nothing at all to anyone else. Laura soon saw that not everything in the cabinet was to do with her uncle. The clinic's personnel files were in there, too, and a few patient files, presumably awaiting special additions of some kind.

It wasn't until she reached the second drawer that she found what she was looking for: the files that related to the Richard Forrester Trust Fund. There were several folders, some with financial statements, others with carbons of letters, faxes and memorandums. The whole collection dated back to her father's death, over three years ago now. She sorted through it rapidly until she found a separate smaller folder with what appeared to be the correct forms and extracted them.

She slammed the cabinet drawer shut and closed her eyes momentarily at the sudden rush of dizziness which was a result of straightening up too fast and having been faced with copies of her father's will and all the reminders of his life and death.

'Laura . . .'

Her uncle stood in the doorway. Beth, gazing at him adoringly, blushed. 'That was Milly,' he said. 'She seemed most upset at my having . . .' His mouth twitched in a half-smile. 'At my having the *temerity* to try and run my own affairs. We'd best leave signing the papers until she gets back.'

'I'd rather sign them now.'

He sighed. 'You don't know what you're letting me in for.'

They went through into his office and settled themselves on either side of his desk. He leafed through the file, nodding. 'It all seems to be in order, she's made it quite straightforward. God knows what she's fussing about.' He shuffled more papers. 'That's funny.'

'What?'

'Well, I don't see any provision for an audit yet. They'll require a complete list of securities and so on . . .'

'Yes, I'd like one too,' Laura said.

'Would you? Good girl. You really must start taking an interest. In that case, we *had* better delay signing these until the whole process is complete. Milly said she'd be back tomorrow, after all.'

'I thought she was staying until Sunday.'

Roger nodded, still shuffling papers with an air of perplexity. 'Yes, that's what she called to say she was doing, but apparently she's changed her mind again.' He looked up and smiled. 'Afraid I'll get into mischief, I suppose.'

'Then she shouldn't have gone away in the first place,' Laura said firmly.

Laura picked up her tray and looked around for an empty place. The staff dining-room was small and at the lunch-hour it was at its busiest. The place was buzzing with the latest news – she heard it on every side as she edged between the tables.

Nick Higgins had been taken in for questioning.

Having only just heard, she couldn't think what it meant. It wasn't an arrest, of course. When she'd taken all Julie's things down to Tom Gilliam he had told her that unless a formal charge was made Nick would be released over the weekend. Without hard evidence, Gabriel would have to let him go.

'But what made him take him in in the first place?' she had asked.

Gilliam had smiled wryly as he'd started picking through the box of Julie's letters and other things. 'If you want my opinion, I'd say it was desperation,' he'd said. 'With the local elections coming up he has to appear to be doing *something*. Nick knows the people here and he knows people in town. He could be a lot of help to Matt. It's a matter of questioning him away from the clinic – it sometimes helps.'

Laura hadn't been convinced.

Now, surrounded by conjecture on every side, she felt resentment rising. Snatches of converstion here and there made it clear that most of them were happy to be convinced that Nick Higgins had 'done it'.

'Always was sneaky . . . hell-raiser when he was a kid . . . great one for the ladies . . . couldn't take no for an answer . . . comes from bad stock . . . drunk of a father and a mother . . . arrested before . . . has a juvenile record . . . Forrester should have known better than to hire him . . . never liked him . . . sly . . .'

She saw Shirley Hasker, alone at a table in the corner. She put her tray down firmly and pulled out the chair opposite. Shirley, after glancing up to see who'd had the nerve to join her, nodded and went back to her meal. A paperback book was flattened out beside her plate and she kept her eyes on it as she chewed stolidly.

'Just listen to them,' Laura muttered, unfolding her napkin. 'They've got Nick tried and convicted already. It makes me sick.'

Shirley turned a page, glanced at her, then went back to her reading.

'I mean . . . he'll probably be let go . . . there's no evidence . . . the sheriff will *have* to let him go,' Laura continued.

'Why should he? Nick Higgins killed those girls and that's an end to it,' Shirley said in a flat voice. 'Let him get what's coming to him, it's no more than he deserves.'

'So you think he's guilty, too?'

'Of course. Always thought so.'

Laura stared at her. 'Did you tell the sheriff that?'

'Of course. It was obvious enough.'

'My God,' Laura breathed. 'I hope they get a change of venue if it comes to a trial. He'll never get justice here.' She attacked her salad. 'Mr Gilliam says—'

'I suggest you and your precious Mr Gilliam leave local matters to local people,' Shirley said brusquely. 'We know what we're doing.'

'And are we supposed to believe that Nick is the Shadowman, too?' Laura demanded.

Shirley shrugged. 'Must be.'

'Well, I *saw* the Shadowman and it wasn't Nick Higgins.' Laura was busy buttering a roll and didn't see Shirley's hands tighten on her knife and fork as she stared. 'If he's a ghost he's a pretty solid one. And it certainly wasn't Nick who attacked my cat, either. Since I find it hard to believe that there are *two* crazy men running around . . .'

'Shut up!' Shirley hissed. She stood up, her face white and her lips drawn back from her teeth. It was an amazing transformation and not a pretty one. Laura was stunned.

'There's no such thing as the Shadowman. It's a myth, a lie. It's stupid people like you who keep him alive with your silly chatter and big eyes . . .' Shirley's voice wasn't raised. If anything, it was lower than normal, but there was a quality of venom in it that was ummistakable whether you could make out the words she spoke or not. Laura gaped at her, as did several people at nearby tables, but she quickly recovered.

'What I saw wasn't a ghost. What attacked my cat wasn't a ghost. It was a vicious and sick person who should have been put away years ago. It *wasn't* Nick Higgins. But it might have been the person who killed the two girls – if it was, he's still out there. I wonder who he'll attack next? He's getting worse all the time. And if he kills again while the sheriff is holding Nick, that will prove that Nick is innocent, won't it? Then what will you say?'

'You bitch,' Shirley said. 'You little know-it-all bitch. I wish he'd killed *you* when he had the chance.' She seemed to notice, suddenly, that other people were listening and watching. The lines of strain and tension that had been etched into her face over the past months went deeper still, and she drew her breath in sharply as she realized what she had said – and what they had heard. She turned and, with pale-faced and massive dignity, looking neither left nor right, walked out of the dining-room.

Slowly the faces that had watched Shirley's departure turned back towards Laura. Conjecture was on many of them. Would Roger Forrester's niece run crying to his office and demand Hasker's instant dismissal? They were faintly disappointed when Laura simply went on eating her salad with, perhaps, a little more concentration than was necessary. Gradually the chatter of the other lunchers re-attained its former decibel level. She forced herself to finish every morsel on her plate, though it was like eating straw. She hated scenes. She'd had her fill of them with her ex-husband. She pretended to be aggressive with Tom Gilliam, but it was done to help him. And it was hard work. Anger and emotions that blew up over nothing – those she couldn't handle. Shirley's assault had caught her off-guard. She was shaken by it and even more by her own spirited reaction to it. She hadn't known she had that much anger left over from the attack on Solomon. People could hurt her all they liked – but not a defenceless animal.

Her support of Nick rose out of the same deep roots. He, too, was vulnerable. She didn't care what the juvenile record said, or how big and strong he appeared. He, too, was a dumb animal in his way. Because he was kind. Because he was good. Because he took trouble when he didn't have to. She'd seen him, often, walking patients around the flower garden, talking to the most impossible of them with patience and gentleness, doing small favours, remembering things other people were too busy or self-centred to bother with. He'd gone all the way into Hatchville, once, to match some knitting wool for Mrs McAllister. Michaels, on the other hand, was vicious, small-minded, and quite capable of cruelty for its own sake and his gratification. Why hadn't the sheriff taken *him* in?

She sighed and stood up, brushing the crumbs from the front of her uniform. As she started to put her chair back under the table, she saw that Shirley had left the paperback book she'd been reading beside her plate. She reached over and picked it up, glancing at the cover expecting it to be some romance or mystery. It wasn't. The title leaped out at her.

*The Psychopathology of Drug Dependence.*

'I didn't have anything to do with it,' Nick said sullenly. 'I don't know why you're picking on me, all of a sudden.'

Matt felt a surge of guilt, but fought it back. He had a legitimate reason for interviewing Nick again – for interviewing anybody again – he was simply exercising his authority as sheriff of the county faced with an intractable problem.

But he didn't like it.

'You had a fight with Clarissa Janacek,' he said mildly.

Nick glared at him. 'I already told you all about that.'

'Did you have a fight with Julie Zalinsky?'

'No. *No!*'

'Calm down, Nick. I have to ask these questions.'

'Sure, sure. But I don't notice you asking them of anyone else.' He crossed his arms and stared down at the table in the interview room. Although new, like all the other equipment in the sheriff's department it was already showing signs of wear and tear – rings from coffee cups, graffiti created by prisoners left alone for too long, odd stains.

Matt leaned forward. 'Where did you get those scratches on the backs of your hands, Nick?'

Nick buried his hands under his crossed arms. 'Just from bushes.'

Matt reached over and pulled one hand free, with difficulty. 'Those are a lot deeper than anything caused by a rose thorn,' he said pointedly. 'They look like something made by an animal – or a woman – fighting for life?'

'Don't be ridiculous,' Nick snapped, pulling his hand back and thrusting both below the level of the tabletop.

'Well?'

Nick muttered something.

'I didn't quite catch that,' Matt said patiently.

Nick's head came up. 'I said my mother did it.' His voice was loud. 'She was . . . not very well.'

'You mean she was drunk?' Matt asked, not unkindly.

Nick sighed. 'Yeah, she was drunk. She's all knotted up with arthritis, she drinks to forget the pain, then she gets scared and stops, so when the DTs come she hits out at everything. I got in the way, that's all. Trying to calm her down before she hurt herself.'

'Does this happen a lot?'

'It happens sometimes.'

'Doesn't your father do something about it?'

Nick just looked at him. 'He's different,' he said glumly. 'He don't react the same.'

And Matt remembered Joe Higgins, sitting in the back of one of the poorest of the local bars, nursing a beer, looking like the end of the world had just been announced and he had been too far away to hear all the details.

'He gets depressed,' Matt said sympathetically.

'So would you if you couldn't work.'

'Nick, you work all around the grounds of the clinic. You've seen us searching after each of these murders. You know we've found a few things. Why haven't you?'

Nick didn't answer.

'Have you found anything? Anything odd, out of place?'

Nick shrugged.

'Any sign of the Shadowman?' Matt asked.

Nick glared at him. 'Load of crap,' he snapped.

'Is it?'

'There's animals in the woods, animals that make noises,' Nick said. 'People aren't used to the sound of natural things any more. And there are tramps, sometimes, coming through.'

'Do you see them?'

'Yeah, I see them. They know I see them. But they don't cause any trouble. Mostly they come through in the summer – hoping for a hand-out at the kitchen. We get a lot of waste food there. Sometimes we pass it on. I've found bits of old fires, empty tin cans, bottles, that kind of thing. Too late, now. Too cold. They're all down south by now.'

'We found evidence of someone who is in the woods even now,' Matt told him. 'Someone who kills animals.'

'Hunters.'

'No – not like that. This person tortures the animals, then kills them and throws their bones into a big pit. And he's been doing it for some time. Do you do that, Nick?'

'Hell, no!' Nick showed every evidence of outrage. 'I love animals, all animals. Who is doing that?'

'We don't know. But we're beginning to wonder if it isn't the same person who killed these girls. Maybe they saw him at it, maybe they recognized him and he couldn't afford to have them talk about it or tell anyone.'

'Sicko,' Nick said uncompromisingly. 'Some kind of sicko, you mean.'

'I think someone very sick, yes,' Matt agreed. 'Maybe someone who occasionally gets drunk . . . loses control . . .'

'No,' Nick said.

'You have to face the possibility, Nick.'

'No – not them. Not my folks.' Nick looked horrified. 'That's what you're saying, isn't it? Jesus wept, Matt, there are plenty of drunks in Blackwater – why them?'

'Because you work up there. Because there's a *connection.*'

'You're wrong. You *know* you're wrong.'

Matt sighed. Yes, he knew he was wrong. Nick's parents were ill, dysfunctional, alcoholic, sad. Nick was the glue that held the little family together. He looked after them, protected them, shopped, cooked and cleaned for them. But who knows what might happen in an alcohol-sodden brain? What deterioration might have taken place over the years? What repressed angers, resentments and frustrations might in some strange way have rebounded on the boy who did so much for them? It was a pathetic and worrisome situation, but he didn't really think what he was suggesting was possible. Nevertheless, he had to consider it. He had to consider everything.

'Tell me about Michaels,' he said.

Nick snorted. 'What's to tell? He's an ornery, sneaking, cunning son-of-a-bitch.'

'Why does Forrester keep him on?'

'Because Forrester owes him. The little bastard told me all about it. A long time ago Michaels's wife died in a hospital Forrester was working in somewheres in the east. Maine or Boston or somewheres. There was an investigation. Forrester was cleared of negligence, but apparently he felt guilty about it because he gave Michaels a job when Michaels showed up at the clinic a few years ago. And Michaels does the job. Whatever else he's like, he works hard.'

'Did he put up the railing on the stairs leading to the apartment Miss Brandon occupies? The one Julie Zalinsky used to have?'

'Yeah. He did all that conversion work. He knows his stuff, wiring, plumbing, all that. He gets good money from Forrester, but he earns it.'

'Even so, nobody likes him.'

'I don't think he wants anybody to like him. I think he just hates the world and doesn't give a damn who knows it. He likes to sort of step on people when they're down, it gives him some kind of satisfaction to have even a little power over them.'

'Does he have any power over you?'

'Why do you ask?'

'Well, it seems to me you must work with him a lot, one way and another—'

'We stay out of each others' way.'

'Did he have any power over Julie Zalinsky? Over Clarissa Janacek?'

'I think he had a crush on Julie. He hung around her a lot. Clarissa he hated with a vengeance – she told him what she thought of him in no uncertain terms. A couple of the orderlies place bets with him from time to time, for themselves, for the patients. And he can get stuff. I expect you know about that.'

'I know Forrester has had to tell him off from time to time about bringing liquor and other things to the patients.'

'Yeah.'

'But he doesn't fire him.'

'Michaels always says he won't do it again. He whines, he crawls around Forrester. Then he takes it out on someone else. That's why they don't like him much.'

'I see. Could he have been "taking it out" on Miss Zalinsky and Miss Janacek, perhaps?'

'You'd have to ask him that. I can't read his mind. Wouldn't want to if I could. Must be like a cesspit in there. I don't know why you haven't dragged him in here instead of me.'

Because he's too obvious, Matt thought to himself. Because it would be so easy if it were Michaels. And I don't think it is. Even so, I know where to find him, don't I? 'I will,' he told Nick. 'I will. Meanwhile, tell me about the orderlies up at the clinic.'

# TWENTY-FIVE

WHEN DAVID CALLED THAT NIGHT Laura told him about Nick Higgins being taken in for questioning. His reaction was the same as those she'd overheard in the dining-room and she began to wonder if she was wrong, after all. 'But he's too *nice*, David,' she protested.

'You mean "he was always such a good boy"?' David asked sarcastically. 'That's what mothers and neighbours say when some damned rapist or killer is put away. "He never caused any trouble at all" and so on.'

'He's not been put away,' Laura said. 'Sheriff Gabriel hasn't even made a formal charge – or hadn't, the last time Mr Gilliam called him.' She was careful to say 'Mr Gilliam'.

'So he's still interested, is he?'

'Yes, of course he is. I don't think he believes Nick did it, either.'

'Why?'

'I don't know. He doesn't say much, but I know he's still working on his own theories,' she said. And added silently, he's also working on the possibility that it was my own uncle who's guilty. Which reminded her of something. 'David, you know that thing about the drugs Clarissa was telling you?'

'Yes.'

'Well, I think I might have solved it.'

'Oh?'

'Yes. It's Owen. He's taking things for the clinic because Uncle Roger – or Milly Cunningham – won't give him enough money.'

'What kind of things?'

'Oh, antibiotics, pain-killers, stuff like that.'

'Have you told your uncle?'

'No! I wouldn't do that. I had a look at the clinic.'

'Pretty lousy, isn't it?'

'It doesn't have to be. Uncle Roger could afford to supply it a lot better than he must be doing if Owen has to steal things to keep it going. I'm on Owen's side, frankly.'

'Party to a felony, that makes you.'

'Oh, David . . .' She twisted the phone cord round her hand, unwound it, twisted it again.

'Oh, don't worry. I won't tell either. I wondered why we had so much there, but he does all the ordering, not me, so I didn't question it. Owen is just so obsessive, I think he'd do anything to keep that damn clinic going. Even commit murder.'

'You don't mean that!'

He chuckled. 'No, I don't mean that. Not really. But his zeal and enthusiasm can be a bit tiring at times. You don't have to listen to it – I do. Whenever we're in the apartment together he just won't shut up about it. Makes me want to commit murder myself.'

'Stop saying that word so lightly,' Laura snapped.

'Sorry. I just feel a little removed from Mountview at the moment. It all seems a bit overheated from this distance.'

'Because you're dealing with such *important* things?' she asked, with not a little sarcasm.

'Well, yes.' His voice was serious. 'We had a talk on the Ebola virus today. And on the new multiple drug resistant strains of tuberculosis. And the lack of results in AIDS research. Makes the little dramas of our precious Mountview Clinic seem rather . . . unimportant. I don't think if I gave a paper on "The Discomforts of the Ill Rich" I would be received with much applause.'

'And applause is important to you?' She was beginning to get irritated.

'No,' he replied calmly. 'But practising good medicine is important to me. Sheriff Gabriel will find out the truth about the murders in the end and life will go on. By this time next year it will all be forgotten. No big deal, Laura. It has nothing to do with us.'

She didn't say anything. The phone cord had left a red mark round her wrist.

He sighed. 'What are you going to do with yourself this evening?' he asked finally.

'Well, I'm having dinner with Robert deNiro, then I'm going clubbing with Al Pacino, then I thought I'd drop in on—'

'Good-night,' David said in a resigned voice. 'I'll call you tomorrow.'

'Byee!' she said with specious gaiety.

What was she going to do with herself tonight? She glanced at the clock on the mantel.

Wouldn't he like to know?

It seemed to her she should have obtained a few illicit Dexedrines for herself from the drug cupboard, to keep awake. But she managed without them, and just after midnight she crept down the stairs and into the clinic itself. It was surprisingly easy to avoid night staff, for they tended to congregate at the nursing stations drinking coffee until it was time for rounds, or someone summoned them by buzzer. The long, carpeted halls were low-lit and peculiarly expectant. It was not totally silent, for in the distance she could hear someone's television muttering with a late-night movie, probably left on when the patient fell asleep. There were odd clinks and hums from the machinery of a working hospital, oddly out of place in the luxurious surroundings of Mountview. There always seemed to be something going 'clink' in a hospital, she thought to herself. Always the sound of water running, and the occasional murmur of voices, indistinct and somehow threatening.

Accustomed as she was to the eerie atmosphere of a hospital at night, alive but not alive, filled with the whisper of patients sleeping and people on watch, she found herself unnerved, scurrying around the balcony and slipping down the curving stairway, not wanting to be seen and questioned, although she could always say she was going down to talk to her uncle, she supposed. She had every right to be there – and yet she knew what she was about to do was wrong. That changed everything.

Milly's keys were still in her pocket, where she'd casually dropped them that afternoon, and she intended to put them to good use. It wasn't as if she were prying, exactly. She had a right to know about her own affairs and their mismanagement, if any. She should have been interested in it long ago.

She unlocked the door behind the counter in Reception as quietly as she could and slipped through into the inner office. Taking the flashlight from her pocket, she went to the corner of the room and the black filing cabinet. If Milly was coming back tomorrow instead of Saturday, this would be her only chance to examine the records they'd thought were so safely locked away. Obviously, Uncle Roger left such details to Milly – more fool, he.

Working quickly – for she couldn't risk lingering there to read them – she extracted the folders she wanted and put them into a plastic shopping bag she'd brought along for the purpose. Then, out of sheer nosiness, she pulled out some of the personnel files.

As she was about to close the drawer her eye caught sight of a file marked 'McAllister' and she slipped that out for good measure. She couldn't have said consciously why she was taking the extra files – there was only a vague feeling in the back of her mind that there might be some connection between them. She'd glance through them and put them back with the rest in the morning.

She closed the drawer quietly and bearing her swag lightly, slipped back to the quiet and seclusion of her eyrie, high above the clinic.

Two hours later, gritty-eyed and nauseated by all the coffee she'd consumed, she leaned back in her chair and stared at the scatter of paper on the table. It was all there. Milly kept meticulous, if secret, records.

There had been a steady extraction from the trust fund since it had been established six years before. Laura had found carbon copies of letters she'd supposedly been sent – oh, they'd gone to great trouble to make it look good – concerning the transfer of capital funds from solid commodities to Mountview shares. And there were cheques, too, drawn on the account where the trust income steadily accrued, ignored and disowned by herself. She'd never signed them. She'd never even seen them. They were made out to 'Cash' and added up to a considerable sum.

She sighed. How easy it had been to put the facts down on paper, then file them away, unseen. To make up lies and give wrong impressions – only to be able to say 'but it's all in the records' if challenged. How easy to make records tell lies, too. Who asks? Who challenges? She certainly never did. Her hatred of the money was deep-seated and grew from her sense of her father having been stolen from her by his work.

Once they'd realized how she felt, they had taken quick advantage of it. And, they had probably reasoned, why not? They had had to take what they could while they could, for upon coming of age she might well have given it all away to charity. If Julie hadn't been murdered she would never have come here, never have questioned anything about the trust.

In a world filled to overflowing with printed information computers ticked away, taking account of facts as presented and accepting them as truth because they were not programmed to question, only to list. Lists were everywhere, on everything, but nobody put them side by side.

Nobody bothered.

Nobody had time.

And everybody was faced with the great dilemma of modern civilization – if you ask questions of Them, They can ask questions about you.

Lie low.

Say nuthin'.

They had thought she would never ask.

Well, they had been wrong.

She gathered the files together and put them back in the shopping bag. She had no taste for looking further. Beth would come into the office just before nine. She had to get there long before that, to photocopy what she needed from the files so she could show them to Tom Gilliam and have them back in place before Milly returned. What she'd do with the copies she didn't yet know. She'd think about that later. Bed and a few hours of restless sleep before an early alarm rang would give her the time she needed.

It wasn't the coffee that made her feel sick. It was herself. The trusting fool she had been.

As nervous in the dawn light as she had been in the dark, Laura set about her task furtively, glancing often at the clock on the wall and her own wrist-watch, checking one against the other, expecting lies even there. She finished everything with time to spare and, folding the photocopies into a compact packet, slipped them into the capacious pocket of her heavy cardigan. Fortunately the photocopier was quiet-running, but even so, with the width of his office between it and his bedroom, she'd had no fear of waking her uncle. Long accustomed to hospital noises of all kinds, he'd sleep until summoned by bells.

Not so Milly.

'What are you doing?'

Laura nearly leaped out of her skin. She'd finished replacing the files and, with a knee-wobbling sense of relief, had just been about to replace Milly's keys in the desk drawer. Now Milly herself stood in the doorway, the circular hall awash with morning sunlight behind her.

'I was returning your keys. When I put on my uniform this morning I found them still in my pocket,' Laura said with a coolness that surprised her.

'How did you get them in the first place?'

'Uncle Roger told me to get some things from the file yesterday. He was talking on the phone to you.'

'I see.' Milly came in, letting the door swing shut behind

her. She looked immaculately groomed as always, a small mink hat set back on her blonde hair, a mink coat open over a neatly tailored black dress with touches of white at throat and cuffs. 'Did you sign the papers, then? I asked Roger to have you wait – the file wasn't complete yet.'

'So he discovered. No, I didn't sign them. I believe he still has them.'

'I see,' said Milly again. Laura hoped she didn't see too much. For example, the light was still glowing on the photocopier. She moved to stand in front of it and as Milly turned away to hang up her coat Laura reached behind and flipped off the switch. Milly took off her hat and put it on the desk, watching her. 'You're up early.'

'I live here now, remember? I like an early start.'

'Ah, of course.'

Laura headed for the door. 'I've decided to take more of an interest in the trust from now on.'

'Oh?' Milly closed her open desk drawer firmly. 'It's rather complicated, you know, if you don't understand finance.'

'I can always ask questions, can't I?'

Milly measured her with cool eyes, assessing. What questions? her eyes seemed to say. Dangerous questions? 'I suppose you can – if you can understand the answers.'

'I'm not a fool,' Laura snapped, irritated despite her determination to stay calm.

'You've often acted like one,' Milly murmured.

'And you've been quick to take advantage, haven't you?' Laura flared, forgetting her good intentions to wait, to be careful.

Milly's neck stiffened at that and her eyes narrowed. 'What do you mean?' she asked guardedly.

Before Laura could answer, the door to her uncle's quarters opened and he was there, beaming at them both. 'I *thought* I heard voices. Welcome back, Milly. Were you successful?'

'I think so, Roger,' Milly said coolly, stripping off her

gloves. 'He's agreed to let the lawyers discuss a settlement, anyway.'

'Wonderful!' Roger beamed, coming over to kiss her on the cheek. Milly accepted his tribute as her due. Roger turned. 'I'm afraid I told you a little white lie, Laura. Milly didn't go to New York.'

'Oh?'

'No. You may suspect otherwise, but I don't really want to use your trust if I don't have to. That's why I asked Milly to go to Simon McAllister and see if we couldn't come to some agreement out of court about Mrs McAllister's will. There's no sense in paying half the estate over in legal costs, no matter who wins. Apparently, as usual, my beautiful genius carried it off. You're quite brilliant, Milly, my dear.'

'No need to exaggerate, Roger,' Milly said mildly. 'It isn't settled yet. He's a very awkward man. He seems to relish the idea of a fight.'

'But you'll get round him. She gets round everyone,' Roger said, as if praising a clever child to a sceptical stranger. 'Have you had breakfast yet?' he asked them.

'I ate before I left Grantham,' Milly said. 'But I'll have some coffee with you.'

'Laura?' He turned to her, smiling.

'I'm meeting someone in the dining-room,' she improvised hurriedly.

'Oh.' He seemed genuinely disappointed. He turned and went back into his sitting-room-cum-office, from whence came the smell of coffee and bacon. Laura stared at Milly, who was looking at herself in the mirror, flicking invisible dust from her shoulders.

'Coffee's poured,' came Roger's voice from the other room.

'Coming!' Milly called, then glanced at Laura in the mirror. 'Was there anything else?'

'Not really,' Laura said. 'Not yet.' She managed to get out of the room without looking back.

* * *

Milly watched Laura cross the reception hall and go through the door to the staff canteen, then turned and went into Roger Forrester's office. Her eyes met his and she frowned slightly. 'Laura's been behaving rather oddly, darling, don't you think?' she asked, concern vibrating in her voice. 'I think she's overworking. She hasn't really recovered from that attack . . . her nerves . . . she's very very depressed. I do worry, you know.'

Matt emerged from the shower, rubbing his hair dry with a rather battered old towel. Max, the station cat who shared his quarters over the office, was sitting in his favourite chair, appearing to watch breakfast television. He yawned. Not much on, apparently, for cats.

It was while he was shaving that Matt caught sight of a familiar face on the screen. He switched off the shaver and went closer. 'Oh, my God,' he breathed.

Mitch Hasker, tweeds, leather patches, bald patch, pipe and all, was being interrogated about the Shadowman by a not very bright but very pretty blonde girl. 'It sounds really spooky.'

'Not at all, not at all,' Hasker said benignly. 'I think it's rather wonderful that these myths continue down through the generations, just proving their natural power. Of course, there may be a perfectly rational explanation, but people are superstitious. I think they *like* to frighten themselves.'

'Then there isn't really a Shadowman?' The girl looked disappointed.

'Come on, Mitch, say it ain't so.' Matt startled both himself and the cat because it came out more loudly and desperately than he had expected.

'Oh, there's *something* out there all right,' Mitch said rather grandly.

'Shit!' Matt said. 'Damn you, Hasker. She gave you the perfect opportunity to shut it down . . .'

'There's a strand of legend and belief we call folklore that is wound around the whole of history, rather like ivy winds itself around a tree,' Hasker intoned.

'And kills it,' Matt said in disgust.

'These legends are powerful because they relate to people's real fears and hopes,' Hasker continued. 'There may indeed be a lost soul who wanders at night, wearing his history on his sleeve as it were, carrying on his eternal quest for revenge and justice.'

'But who—' the girl asked, glancing at the studio clock.

'Oh, not an ordinary living person, but a spiritual entity embodied in a human soul, drifting and wandering, seeking retribution—'

'Retribution for what?' the girl wanted to know.

'Why, for pain and suffering, of course,' Hasker answered, as if it were perfectly obvious. 'The old story of the poor man driven mad by the tortures of the Indians may have a true parallel in people of today who are subject to social tortures and pressures, and who are ostracized by their peers—'

'Who was this poor man?' the girl enquired.

'Why his name was Jeremiah Hasker, as it happens. We in the Blackwater Bay Historical Society have many papers referring to him and his tormented destiny. In 1817 he purchased a huge tract of land from the local Indians – for a pittance it must be admitted – and on it he built a grand house he called Mountview. In 1826 he met—'

'Is *he* the Shadowman?' the girl interrupted, again casting rather desperate eyes towards someone who was just out of camera range.

'I have no idea,' Mitch admitted, toying with his pipe, drawing the stem alongside his jaw. 'Some say it's his spirit that haunts the woods of Mountview, others think it's that of the Indian who was so wrongly accused of the murder of Hasker's daughter.'

'There's been another murder?' the girl squeaked, suddenly hoping to have scooped the press.

'No, no, of course not. This was in 1845. His daughter—'

'Oh,' said the girl glumly. 'In 1845.'

'I certainly *hope* there won't be any more murders,'

Hasker said with a jolly laugh. 'Our rather inept sheriff has enough trouble dealing with the ones we already have, to say nothing of the day-to-day problems of theft, vandalism, delinquency and drunkenness.'

'Gee, thanks, Mitch,' Matt growled. 'That's certain to gain me a few votes.'

Maddeningly, Mitch was rolling on. 'Ours is a lively area, you see. We never know what is going to happen next. Why there's been a regular *upsurge* in troubles over the past two or three years. We have a long and violent history. I myself am writing a book about Blackwater Bay's notable—'

'And I'm sure we all look forward to reading that,' the girl interrupted. 'But for now we'll have to leave this fascinating subject for some important messages. We'll be right back with tips on how to deal with treatment-damaged hair.'

Matt sat down on the end of the bed. 'The great horse's ass,' he muttered. 'The boring, droning, stupid *clod*!'

The cat looked at him, curious as to the cause of the sudden agitation of his friend and master. As far as he could see, nothing had happened. They were alone in the room.

'He could have dismissed it,' Matt went on in despair. 'He could have calmed everyone down. Instead . . .'

He stood up. He didn't know how many people watched that particular morning programme – he, for one, would never tune in to it again – but those who did would no doubt be on the phone to their friends, talking about it. And about the 'poor sheriff' who was having trouble dealing with the murders he already had.

He wondered if adding Hasker to the list of murder victims could be discreetly accomplished before nightfall.

# TWENTY-SIX

'WHAT SHOULD I DO?'

Gilliam, on his back in the gym, looked up at Laura as he handed back the photocopies. 'What do you want to do?'

'I want to murder them,' she said through gritted teeth.

'I didn't hear that.' Gilliam spoke quietly, resuming his slow efforts against the weights.

'You asked me what I wanted to do, not what I was going to do. I was only being honest.'

'A rarity around here, if you ask me,' Gilliam observed. 'Well, you can do the obvious – hire a lawyer and bring suit against your uncle and his accomplice. Or you could go straight for the jugular and report it to Matt Gabriel as a crime – he'd be forced to investigate and the resulting furore would bring the clinic and your uncle to their collective knees.'

'I don't know,' Laura whispered miserably, feeling like twelve kinds of wimp. 'It's all such a mess and it's really my fault for not taking responsibility for my own affairs. How can I sue someone for my own negligence?'

'Then report it as a crime.'

'I don't want to destroy them – just . . . just . . .'

'Just what?'

'Let them know I know, I suppose. Face them down, make them pay back what they've taken.'

'How tall are you?' Gilliam asked. 'Five foot four, five-five? Highly strung, too. I'd go for a lawyer and let him do the arguing for you. Stand well back, that's my advice. In the end it's your word against theirs, and it will involve a lot of expert testimony concerning forgery and what have you. They will talk about your mental state after your divorce and so on. It won't be fun, whatever you do.'

'I know,' she said. 'Anyway, Sheriff Gabriel is too busy arresting people like Nick Higgins to want to pay any attention to my problems.'

Gilliam grunted. 'As far as I can see, Matt Gabriel has taken the one man who *isn't* guilty of something in for questioning. You know, I'm getting damned sick and tired of this place, all of a sudden.'

'You don't have to stay,' Laura pointed out.

'Don't I?'

She looked away. She was finding it more and more difficult to be with him, to maintain her professional distance. She didn't want him to want her or to like her or anything like that. But he was such a difficult man, so hard to hide from, to pretend with and to turn to, even now. It all seemed to mean so little to him. He'd seen so much crime – nothing appeared to shock or disturb him, or even frighten him, apparently. He was getting stronger, getting his confidence back. Soon he'd be able to walk.

Away.

'I wish David were here,' she said morosely.

'What's the matter? Doesn't your brain function on its own?'

'Of course it does. I just meant it would be easier to face Uncle Roger with all this if David were here to back me up.'

The weights rose and fell. 'The crooks we put in jail are amateurs compared with the guys sitting behind the desks in Wall Street. Gilliam Enterprises are absolute pirates – a real bunch of cutthroats. Your uncle is a minnow alongside them.'

'Is that why you didn't join the family firm?'

'Nope.' He grunted with effort, pushing against the weights. 'I would have jumped right in if I'd thought I could have got away with it. But I knew after a month or two that I couldn't. I kept wanting to call up the opposition and explain things. Something in me was apparently convinced that if they *knew* they were being stabbed in the back it would make it some kind of fair. My brothers are real Machiavellian types – clean-cut, clear-eyed and totally amoral. I'm a throw-back.'

'Me, too. I think we're a dying breed.'

'Is it any wonder?' Gilliam's laugh was ironic. 'We keep getting in the way with our moralizing. We're anachronistic, we're counter-productive, we're old hat, and – worst of all – we're *boring*.'

'David's even worse.' Laura smiled reluctantly. 'He was upset when I told him I was going through Julie's belongings.'

The weights fell with a thump. 'You told him about finding them?'

'Sure. Why not?'

'No reason,' he grumbled and began working the weights again. 'I just sort of thought it was between the two of us.'

'Secrets?'

He glanced at her pityingly. 'You still think it's some kind of game, don't you?'

'No, but—'

'Did you tell him you'd given them to me?'

'No, but—'

'Good. Don't.'

'All right,' she said crossly. 'But since there's nothing there to see, I don't understand—'

'Humour me. I'm a difficult patient, remember?'

'How can I forget?' she asked him. 'It's true.' He turned his head away and began working the weights even harder. After a minute she shook her head and walked away, leaving him to work out his jealousy – because that's what it was. He hated David being any part of her life and certainly resented him knowing anything about their mutual 'investigation'.

'They've let that gardener go,' Mrs Strayhorn announced, as one of the Bartlett sisters wheeled her through the door.

'Good,' Laura said. 'He's no killer.'

'It doesn't mean he isn't a killer, it just means the sheriff is a jackass,' Mrs Strayhorn said flatly.

'He is not,' came a voice from the door. Martin Hambden shambled in. Laura was glad to see more colour in his face than there had been the other day, but as there was still snow clinging to his fur hat it could have been attributed to his walking in the wind. 'He's a good man in a bad situation.'

'You old fool,' Mrs Strayhorn said affectionately. 'Where have you been hiding?'

'I have been in a decline,' Hambden stated ponderously, unbuttoning his thick red plaid hunter's jacket. 'I have been sighing in my bower upon the cruelties and vicissitudes of life. On love sought and love lost. I finally came to the conclusion that I had nearly made a fool of myself. I also got bored and decided it was time I came over and stirred up some trouble here. My housekeeper was threatening to resign if I didn't get out of the house so she could vacuum in peace. How are you, Nellie?'

'Fair to middling. This girl's good, Martin.'

'So I hear.' He turned and called through to the gym, 'And how are you this morning, Mr Gilliam?'

'He's in a snit,' Mrs Strayhorn confided, not very *sotto voce.* 'He's been rattling those weights and muttering to himself ever since I came in here.'

'Oh?' Hambden lifted an eyebrow and rubbed his hands together as he came towards the treatment table. He raised his voice slightly and directed it at Gilliam, who indeed was clattering the weights and talking to himself. 'I can't think of anything that would do him more good.' He turned to Mrs Strayhorn. 'Now, let's have a look at those knees.'

'He used to try to get his hands on my knees for other reasons,' Mrs Strayhorn confided with relish.

'I see,' Laura said, amused.

'Nellie and I go way back, don't we, girl?' Hambden's hands moved lightly and knowledgeably over Mrs Strayhorn's swollen joints. 'Laura, there's real improvement here. Much less crystallization.'

'She works me hard,' Mrs Strayhorn said, but it was more in the nature of praise than complaint.

'You'll do, Nellie. Keep taking the pills.'

'Hmph, the brush-off again.'

He scowled at her. 'Nellie, your trouble is here to stay. I can replace those knees, but surgery at your age isn't to be gone into lightly and you know there could be dangerous complications. I'd like to see you a lot thinner and a great deal stronger before I start cutting.'

'Oh, I know that. I'm just so sick of pills. Can't you get me some pink ones for variety? Or stripes? One little white pill after another – it gets me down. They all look alike. Myra used to say the same thing. "All the pills they give me look alike, Nellie," she'd say. "All little white pills – I can't tell one from another. I could be taking arsenic for all I know." That's what Myra would say.'

Laura stared at the old woman, her mind spinning. All little white pills look alike. Penicillin and aspirin and saccharine. All little white pills look alike.

'Tell you what,' Hambden was saying. 'I'll ask the pharmacist to make up some especially for you, a different colour for each day of the week. How's that?'

'You can't do that, can you?'

'I can do anything I want to.' Hambden smiled. 'They're all scared of me around here. I made sure of it. Saves an awful lot of time.'

'That's what Dr Butler always says.'

'What?'

'He says – "I can do anything I want to",' Mrs Strayhorn said. 'And *then* he says, "So can you, Mrs Strayhorn, if you're willing to give up enough else in order to do it." Young devil.'

'You're full of quotes today, aren't you?' Hambden laughed. 'He's right, of course. Achievement always involves sacrifice of some kind. You have to make choices.'

'I'm too old to make choices.' Mrs Strayhorn glanced at Laura. 'Now, what's the matter with *you*?'

Laura blinked and shook her head. 'Nothing. I was just thinking.'

'She's in love,' Mrs Strayhorn confided to Hambden. 'You'll have to forgive her.'

'I'd forgive anything for love,' Hambden said in a surprisingly gentle voice. Then he grinned at Mrs Strayhorn. 'And you can quote me.'

'Have you found anything, Sherlock?' Laura asked, coming into Gilliam's room where he was again going through Julie's things.

'Aha, Watson! You're here at last!' Gilliam leaned forward in his wheelchair.

'Very funny,' she retorted. 'I told you I looked through it several times and I couldn't find anything at all that would tell you why she was murdered.'

'You're a friend, I'm a detective,' Gilliam said smugly. 'If it's here, I'll find it.'

'Sure – *if* it's there,' she agreed. She sat down on the edge of his bed and watched him pick up the pack of letters. 'Those are all *replies* to her letters – you sort of have to reason backwards as to what she said to them.'

'Oh, gee, I never would have guessed that.' Sarcasm dripped. He leaned over and looked into the box. He drew something out. 'Oh, and a dear little picture of our favourite Dr Kildare clone.'

'Yes.' She hesitated. 'You know, I think that's from David's personnel file. There was no picture attached to it, but there is to most of the others. I wonder how she got it?'

'You got into the files, didn't you?'

'Yes, but I had Milly's keys.'

'Well, maybe Julie did too. Maybe she got something out of the files that you missed.'

'Well, if she did, she didn't put it back. And as far as I could see she never wrote to anyone about it. Of course, I found out Shirley Hasker is the one who gathered all that stuff together after Julie died. She could have taken things out, thrown things away.'

'Have you asked her?'

Laura shivered slightly. 'Shirley doesn't like me very much. No, I haven't asked her or talked to her about Julie at all. According to my uncle they were very close and Shirley seems very upset about Julie's death.'

'And Clarissa's death?'

'Not . . . so much,' she admitted reluctantly.

'Maybe I'll have a word with Nurse Hasker,' Gilliam said abstractedly, as he began reading the notebooks where she'd found only Julie's patient comments. Laura seemed to have been dismissed.

Harlan Weaver was closing his office door when she came up to him. He had a thick bundle of files under one arm and some of them began to slip as he manoeuvred the key in the lock. She reached out and caught them before they scattered over the hallway.

'Ooops!' She laughed. 'Your patients are dropping like flies, Dr Weaver.'

'Thanks.' He smiled vaguely. He appeared preoccupied.

'Is everything all right?' she asked him.

'What?' He seemed to come to himself. 'Oh, yes. Everything's fine, really. How are you?'

'Bearing up.' She hesitated. 'Do you . . . do you ever see staff members?' she finally asked.

'Occasionally,' he said. They began to walk down the hall side by side towards the rotunda. 'Why? Do you feel the need for therapy?'

'Sometimes,' she admitted. 'But I wasn't wondering about myself. I just was thinking, with these two deaths and the stress of caring for patients who are often difficult, the staff must need some psychological support sometimes.'

'They do, they do,' Weaver agreed. 'Without naming names, I can say that I know a lot about some members of the staff – more than they know themselves.'

'And are any of them murderers?' Laura blurted out.

He stopped and stared at her. 'Do you honestly think I would keep quiet if they were?' he asked.

'Doctor – patient privilege—' she began.

'If I had a patient I thought was a murderer I wouldn't hesitate to call in the authorities,' Weaver said flatly. 'I would, of course, encourage the patient to turn himself in, but if, in the end, he or she wouldn't . . . well . . . I would have no alternative. I am not a priest. I have a responsibility to my patients – but I also have one to the community, Laura.'

'Yes, I can see that,' she conceded.

'I mean, how could I live with myself if that person killed again?' Weaver continued, protesting, she thought, a little too much. 'I couldn't. It would be unthinkable.'

'Yes,' she agreed, startled by Weaver's vehemence. Was he feeling guilty, she wondered? Did he know something he wasn't telling? Or was he just guessing? 'Are you seeing Shirley Hasker?'

'Why do you ask that?' His tone was guarded.

'I don't know.' They'd reached the balcony surrounding the rotunda and stopped at the head of the long, sweeping stairway. 'She seems very agitated lately. Very edgy and short-tempered. People have told me she didn't used to be like that. At first I thought it was just me, but . . .' She told him about Shirley's flare-up in the cafeteria and the book she had been reading.

'That's very interesting,' Weaver said, when she'd finished. 'Of course, everyone on the staff has been affected by the murders. Nobody is really themselves at the moment. Stress affects different people differently. Shirley may just be grieving for Julie – as you say, they were fairly friendly.'

Laura sighed. 'I suppose so.' She took a breath and plunged. 'Are you counselling Milly Cunningham? Or Uncle Roger?'

'I really couldn't tell you that, Laura,' he said gently.

'No, of course not.' She ran agitated hands through her already disarranged hair. She didn't seem to be able to get any answers to any questions, no matter whom she asked, no matter where she looked. 'I'm sorry I asked.'

He looked down at her and frowned slightly. 'You seem a little tense yourself. Do you want a prescription for some of those tranquillizers you had the other day?'

'No, no – I'm fine, thanks,' she assured him. 'Just – trying to figure things out, I guess.'

'Well, if you ever want to talk, you only have to ask.'

'Thank you,' she said. 'I'll remember that.'

With a smile he turned and started down the stairs. From the floor below, Laura heard a door close. It was done very quietly, but the sound echoed softly and clearly through the rotunda.

# TWENTY-SEVEN

ON SATURDAY MORNING LAURA TOOK her books back to the library and collected another armful – anything to keep her mind occupied with something other than the situation, the murders, the air of tension and fretfulness at the clinic. She was amused to see Mitch Hasker had gathered a coterie of admirers following his television appearance and was holding forth happily on 'his book' and the history of Blackwater Bay.

Then she managed to see a young lawyer named Dominic Pritchard who looked at the photocopies she'd made of the trust file and listened to what she had to say with patience and good humour. She still didn't know what she wanted him to do, but talking it over with a neutral mind seemed a very good place to start. She had Tom Gilliam to thank for that suggestion, anyway.

She did her other bits of shopping and slowly drove back to the clinic. She wished she could take more pleasure in her new little car, but she felt a distinct lack of enthusiasm about everything at the moment.

She paused half-way up the drive, as she had on that first morning, and gazed at the clinic. Even architectural appearances can be deceiving, she thought. Probably most of the patients don't realize what goes on here behind the scenes – the petty squabbles, the gossip, the emotional tensions, the feuds and the frictions. They know two murders have been committed somewhere out there in the woods, but it doesn't touch them, not really. Whatever else the staff might be, they are all too professional to allow the patients one moment of unease or worry.

Being a patient at Mountview was lovely.

Working there had proved to be something else.

Especially for Julie and Clarissa.

And now, for her.

She continued up the drive and parked in the lot, near the building. Clutching her coat closed against the freezing cold, she ran in through the front door and gave another wry look at the beautiful rotunda reception area. Lovely paintings, lovely flowers, lovely carvings, lovely old polished wood floor.

Lies, all lies, she thought.

The girl sitting behind the reception desk looked up at her. 'Good-morning, Mrs Brandon.'

'Good-morning, Beth. Is my uncle around? Or Mrs Cunningham?'

'Oh, no, I'm sorry. They left for the airport about half an hour ago.'

'The *airport*?'

'Yes. Apparently Mrs Cunningham was catching a plane to New York again. Dr Forrester drove her. He should be back in a couple of hours. Shall I leave him a note? I go off at noon.'

'No, no . . . it's okay. I'll catch up with him later,' Laura said. So Milly was off on her 'travels' again. Was it really New York this time or back to Grantham to persuade the recalcitrant widower to come to a settlement over Mrs McAllister's will?

'Mrs Cunningham just came back from New York, didn't she?'

Beth nodded. 'Yes – it was odd, wasn't it? She was only here for a few hours and then off she goes again. Not that I'm sorry – it's a lot quieter without her.'

Laura smiled and leaned on the reception desk as she unbuttoned her coat. 'What did Mrs Cunningham do while she was here?'

Beth shrugged. 'I don't know – we had some check-outs

and some check-ins this morning, so I was kept pretty busy. She was fussing around in the office as usual. Why?'

'Oh, just curious – wondering why she would come back and then leave again so fast.'

'Yeah, but she's like that. Never explains anything, makes snap decisions without telling anyone, and then expects us to know all about it and carry out the work.'

'She's difficult to work for.'

'Yes – but your uncle pays so well and if you know what she's like, well . . . you can handle her.' Beth smiled placidly. So, Laura thought, Beth was *not* quite the tender little flower she appeared to be after all. Working for Milly either would have destroyed her or toughened her – apparently it had been the latter.

'I just want to come through and check something,' Laura said, lifting the hatch and going into the office. She went to Milly's desk and looked in the little enamel box. The keys were gone.

So Milly wasn't taking any chances. She tried not to feel smug. Too late, Milly, she thought. The photocopier and I know it all.

Gilliam had re-packed the box of Julie's things, except for the notebooks, for when Laura knocked and came into his room he was going through them and making notes in a notebook of his own.

'Don't tell me you've found something,' she said, annoyed.

'No. At least, I expect it's nothing. I've got Matt Gabriel chasing down a few things.' He glared at her mockingly. 'Heaven bless the cellular phone.'

'What things?' she demanded. 'What on earth did you find that I didn't? There wasn't anything there, nothing at all.'

Gilliam shrugged. 'You don't have an analytical mind.'

'What's that supposed to mean?'

'You read on the surface only. You have to look behind things, look at things laterally. My boss discovered that looking at photographs of a crime scene in reverse shows up things that we never noticed the first time around. So now the scene of crime people have to print all the shots two ways.'

'What kind of thing are you talking about?' She was annoyed that he might have found something she'd missed. Who did he think he was, anyway – Sherlock Holmes?

'Okay. Did you know your uncle was suspected of embezzlement once before? In Boston?'

'You're joking. There wasn't anything about that in there.'

'Oh, yes, there was – a little piece in the back pages of one of the old medical journals. He resigned and nothing more was done about it.'

'Good heavens,' Laura said. 'I never—'

'Then there was an article about that drug scandal in the Denver hospital – that had some interesting facts and details.'

'That's the one in that movie Mrs McAllister was watching the night she died,' Laura said slowly.

'Right. And what about Doppleman?' Gilliam challenged her.

'Who?'

'Doppleman. Julie goes on about him here, at the back of this notebook.' He tapped the cover of the relevant document. Laura had looked through it but noticed nothing odd. 'About how she's worried about him. About how shocked she was at the news. How he was going to be destroyed by it and there was no telling how he would react when it came out.'

'What news?'

'I have no idea. Test results? Cancer? Would she know anything about cancer?'

'Bone cancer, perhaps. She might have noticed something and reported it to Hambden or whoever was treating this Doppleman. The name sounds familiar – I think I might have seen it in the inactive section of my files. Anything else?'

'A few things. All this stuff about Butler—'

'Oh.' She flushed a little. 'I think it's pretty clear she had a crush on David and wrote to her friends about it. I was sort of prepared before I met him. She was kind of – gushy, sometimes.'

'Some of her correspondents seemed to know him.'

'Yes – he's cut quite a swath through nursing staffs wherever he's worked, I gather.'

'So I notice. Physiotherapists, too.'

'He's very charming—' she said defensively.

'Oh, very,' Gilliam agreed tonelessly.

'He can't help it if women fall all over him. Being attractive and a doctor is a recipe for disaster, you know. Patients get crushes, nurses get crushes . . . and people don't really believe they know anything, either. You know – handsome men and beautiful women are supposed to be stupid.'

'Or gay.'

She laughed. 'I don't think there's any question of that.'

'Oh?' Gilliam looked at her with a raised eyebrow. 'Is that testimony?'

'That's none of your business,' she snapped.

'I'm very aware of that,' Gilliam murmured. He flipped a few more pages in his notebook. 'Now there *was* one woman who didn't think much of Butler. Called him a "smug little bore", I believe. Sour grapes?'

'Probably,' Laura said slowly. She had missed that and it rankled.

'He's moved around a lot,' Gilliam said. 'And he sure attends lots of conferences – your friend Julie seems to have collected details on quite a few. Seems odd that he'd find time to do that and work full-time.'

'I don't know about other places he worked, but his duties here aren't exactly overwhelming,' Laura pointed out. 'He told me he had a lot of free time to use the medical library downstairs and work up papers on various subjects. Being published in the journals gets you noticed, builds a reputation. He has a lively mind. Why are you picking on him all of a sudden? Is it a crime to be good-looking and clever at the same time?' He's jealous, she thought. How sad.

'Would he have treated this Doppleman? Or would it have been Jenks?' Gilliam asked, ignoring her question and flipping back some pages in his notebook. 'The dates are pretty close to when Julie was killed, as it happens, so they both would have been here.'

'I'm sure he must have. I'll ask him,' she said. 'And you can ask Owen yourself when he does his rounds tonight.'

'I thought Butler wasn't coming back until the beginning of next week.'

'Late tomorrow, actually,' she said. 'But he phones me nearly every night.'

'Does he now? How devoted of him. I assume he knows you're a future heiress, then?'

'That's a rotten thing to say!' she flared. 'I don't know who it insults more, David or me.'

'I'm just a cad at heart,' Gilliam admitted with absolutely no sign of remorse. 'Always think the worst of people. Industrial injury caused by being a cop.'

'It obviously affected your manners, as well. I don't know why I bother with you.'

'Because you are a noble creature bent on helping the poor and helpless, of course,' Gilliam said. 'Am I going to have a swim today, or a massage, or are you going to put me on one of those God-awful machines?'

'I can think of a number of machines I'd like to put you on, but as a matter of fact, I don't feel like it today. You can rest.'

He folded his arms and glared at her. 'How unprofessional of you. And just when I was doing so well, too. Quitter.'

'I'm not a quitter, I just don't trust myself to touch you at the moment. It might lead to violence.'

'Dear me . . . I do get under your skin, don't I?' He actually smirked at her, risking all.

She turned away, clenching her fists. 'I'm just on edge,

that's all. Milly Cunningham came back this morning and nearly caught me putting those files back. Now she's gone off again. I have a terrible feeling she took those trust records with her, plus the keys. Uncle Roger is driving her to the airport.'

'What's the matter – afraid they're going to abscond?'

'No!' She took a breath. 'No, of course not. They don't have any idea I know anything about what they've been doing.'

'Then why else would she take the files?'

'I don't *know* she took them,' Laura admitted. 'But without the keys I can't check up, can I?'

'You have the photocopies.'

'She doesn't know that.' She picked up a book, put it down, picked up another, put it down. 'Do you think she knows that?'

'I have no idea. You're on your own with that one.'

'I saw a lawyer when I was in town,' she said slowly.

'Good. It's a start.'

She felt sulky. 'I don't know why you found so many things in there that I didn't.' She poked at the contents of the box and noticed that while Julie's handmade frame was there, the picture of David was gone. It must have fallen out, she thought, and turned over a few bits of clothing to see if it had slipped down. 'After all, I *knew* Julie.'

'And that, my dear Watson, is your problem. I never met her, she is a complete stranger to me, I bring no emotional baggage with me, I have no preconceived notions about her.'

'Oh.'

'Maybe you didn't *want* to find anything. Not anything bad about people you know and like.' His meaning was clear.

'And maybe you did,' she said pointedly.

He gazed up at her, his green eyes as hard as jade. 'You can believe what you like. Two women are dead. That's a fact. The person who killed them is still here, somewhere. Nothing will stop him or her killing again if they are threatened – they have nothing to lose, now. I'd be very careful if I were you.'

'Is that a threat?'

'No. Consider it a warning. From an interested party.'

They stared at one another for a long moment, then she turned and left the room.

The rest of the day passed in a blur. Caught in limbo, she performed her tasks by rote, treating patients, eating meals, looking out of the window, staring at her hands.

She knew her uncle had returned from taking Milly to the airport – or wherever she had gone – but she didn't want to see him or talk to him. Only when she had spoken again to the lawyer would she feel able to proceed. And Gilliam was no use. He was obviously trying to frame David in some way, hating him because he was handsome and whole. And because she liked him.

Loved him? No – she was not that foolish. At least, she didn't think so. Her feelings there were very confused, as well. She felt as though she were treading water in a deep pool, with no stable point to cling to. In the late afternoon she went back upstairs to the nurses' quarters Solomon and she still occupied, and took a nap. Only in sleep could she find peace.

But there were dreams.

She awoke to the sound of the telephone. Groggy, half sick with the sudden return to awareness, she groped for the receiver.

It was David. 'Hi!' he said cheerfully. 'How are things back at the ranch?'

'Um – fine, I guess.' She glanced at the bedside clock. After six! She was surprised Solomon hadn't woken her, demanding his supper.

'You sound funny,' David said.

'I just woke up,' she explained. 'I was having a nap.'

'Oh – sorry.'

'No, no – I never wanted to sleep this late. How did the seminar go?'

'The what?'

'The seminar they wanted you to—'

'Oh. Fine. Great, in fact. I made some good contacts. You might be right, you know. Maybe I should aim higher than being a small-town GP. There are opportunities out here just begging to be taken up. I met this guy from Chicago who works in AIDS research, he's looking for a partner and another from New York who is looking into programmed cell death . . .' He rattled on, while she tried to clear her eyes and head.

'I told you,' she finally managed to say. 'I told you, didn't I?'

'You did, indeed.' He was clearly charged up and full of enthusiasm at the vista of new prospects before him.

She rubbed the back of her neck. 'David – do you remember a patient named Doppleman?'

There was a moment's silence. 'Who?'

'Doppleman. It might have been a bone cancer case – some time earlier this autumn. Just before Julie . . . died.'

'I don't think so. Doppleman? It doesn't ring a bell. Why?'

'Oh, Julie was going on about him in her notebooks.'

'Notebooks? You never said there were any notebooks.'

'Oh, mostly patient notes, ideas for treatment, that kind of thing. She seemed to be very worried about this man.'

'Hm. Maybe it was while I was away. You'd better ask Owen. If it was bones it would have been Hambden.'

'Okay, I will. I'd better check the files first.'

'Whatever. Anything else of interest back there? Has the sheriff still got Nick Higgins in the cooler?'

'No, he let Nick go, then he pulled in Michaels for questioning.'

David laughed. 'I bet that was an interesting session.'

'Yes. I feel sorry for the sheriff, actually.'

'Well, don't. It's his job, not yours.'

'I suppose so. Oh – there was another thing I wanted to ask you. Did they bury Mrs McAllister or cremate her?'

'*What*?'

'I said did they—'

'No, no, I heard you. I have no idea. Why do you ask?'

'Well, I've been thinking about what she said.'

'What did she say?'

'She said to Mrs Strayhorn that all little white pills look alike. What if Uncle Roger gave her something that brought on her heart attack? The way he gave me penicillin – or tried to?'

'That's a terrible thing to think, Laura.' He sounded deeply shocked. 'Surely you can't think Roger Forrester would do anything like that?'

'Well – he does stand to inherit from her estate. And he does need money for the clinic,' she said miserably.

'But even so—'

'You wanted an autopsy, didn't you? And Owen did?'

'Yes.'

'And Uncle Roger wouldn't let you ask for one?'

'Yes, but he had reasons, Laura. Good reasons. Why are you suddenly thinking all these terrible things about your uncle?'

'Oh – I have my reasons, too. When are you coming back?'

'I'm catching a late-afternoon plane tomorrow.'

'So you should be back in time for dinner?'

'Yes. And I think we should go out to celebrate so I can tell you all about what I've been doing here.'

'Good. Great – that will be something to look forward to,' she said, glad of anything that would remove her from the clinic and any possible contact with her uncle, even for a few hours. 'Meanwhile, I'll follow up on this Doppleman person. Mr Gilliam seems to think he's important.'

'*Gilliam* does?'

'Yes – he's been looking through Julie's things. He's so damn smug, he thinks he's the Great Detective,' she fumed, suddenly remembering Gilliam's face. 'If he weren't in that wheelchair, I swear I'd smack him one sometimes.'

David laughed. 'Obviously you need a soothing hand. See you tomorrow. 'Bye.'

And he was gone.

She got up, washed her face, fed Solomon and made herself a simple meal rather than go downstairs to the cafeteria. She just wanted to stay there, read a book, watch television, be apart from everything. And she nearly was – until the phone rang again.

'Hi,' said Gilliam. 'Have you found the Doppleman file yet?'

'No,' she answered.

'Have you *looked* for the Doppleman file yet?'

'No. I've been asleep.'

'I see. Nice for some.'

'Look, leave me alone, will you? I'll look for the file tomorrow.' She slammed down the phone.

After a moment, it rang again. And it was Gilliam. 'Hi. I've missed you.'

'What is it *now*?'

'Temper, temper. I just think that you ought to find it for me. I asked Jenks if he knew the name and he professed total ignorance.'

'So did David.'

She heard a sharp intake of breath at the other end of the line. 'So it *does* mean something after all. You simply *have* to—'

'All right, all right, all *right*!' she shouted. 'I'll go and do it now. I'll bring it up to you if I find it. *Then* will you go to sleep like a good little patient and leave me the hell alone?'

'Dear me,' Gilliam tutted. 'Such language. I thought you were a lady.'

'I thought I was too.' Again, she slammed down the phone. Why did he have the power to agitate her so? He was easily the most aggravating man she had ever met. She got up from the comfortable nest she had made on the old sofa, disturbing Solomon who had been curled up beside her. 'I'm going out,' she told him. 'I may be some time.'

He blinked.

That should have told her he was planning something.

* * *

Laura sat in her office, too shocked to move, the Doppleman file open before her on the desk.

It could have been the old case notes for any patient. It looked like all the others, buried at the back of the drawer, between Dawson and Dwyer.

But it wasn't.

Little Julie Zalinsky, the two-in-one wonder. Privately she was silly, dreamy, hopeless. But when she went through the gate in her mind that led to work she became professional, efficient, reliable. Her methods were sound, her functioning sensible and orderly. The file proved that.

When faced with the dilemma that might have led to her death, half private and half professional, her years of training had won. She had been careful and thorough. She had made certain the facts were verified and the truth, however appalling, was carefully notated and set out.

Here, appropriately enough, in the dead files of old, discharged patients. Where it had been all along.

But her private sense of melodrama had made her take one small, important precaution. As if she were keeping it a secret even from herself. She had mislabelled the file that held copies of all the proof that might be needed. The proof she felt, in all conscience, she had to collect before proceeding. And so, instead of the name that should have been on it she had labelled it 'Doppleman'.

It looked like all the others.

But it wasn't.

Laura heard a step behind her. She turned.

Gilliam was fuming in his room. It had been almost an hour, now, and Laura had not appeared, nor had she called. He had rung her room, then her office, with no result. Frustrated, he finally phoned the sheriff, hoping for *some* result, *some* information he could use. 'Matt? I'm glad you're still there.'

'Who is this?' Matt demanded, roused from a particularly complicated chart he was constructing.

'It's Gilliam. I'm going crazy up here. Did you get that stuff I sent down this morning?'

'Yes, I did.'

'And did you follow it up?'

'Yes. Very interesting. Just about the last thing I expected.'

Gilliam grunted. 'No surprise to me. Was I right?'

'I think so. There are a few more things to come through, but it looks pretty convincing. I've just been going over these dates, trying to make sense of them. If you're right, he might certainly kill to cover up what he's been doing.'

'That's what I'm afraid of,' Gilliam said.

'Maybe I ought to come up there. It's snowing like hell, but I want to talk this through with you anyway, before I take any action. Just to tie the whole thing up once and for all.'

'Yes. Okay. I'll be in my room.' After Matt rang off, Gilliam stared out of the window, the phone still in his hand. What price your legs now, stupid? he asked himself. Why don't you run down and see that file for yourself? Why don't you just leap to your feet like Action Man and take charge? Bitterly, he scowled at his reflection in the glass.

# TWENTY-EIGHT

GILLIAM *KNEW* SHE WASN'T ANSWERING because she was mad at him. She'd found the damn file and was just letting him stew while she looked at it first, determined to outdo him in detection. Aggravating woman.

Sheriff Gabriel was taking for ever to appear. Gilliam looked out of the window. The sheriff was right, it was snowing hard. Already, a deep rim of snow had built up on the window-ledge. The snow that had been falling gently all day had suddenly become a blizzard.

Driven by frustration and a nagging sense of something wrong, he manoeuvred himself into his wheelchair. If she wasn't coming to him, he would damn well go to her. He overbalanced in the doorway and lost time righting the chair and settling himself in it again. He could have cried it enraged him so and he forgot that just a few weeks ago he couldn't – or wouldn't – even rise from his bed without help. Even so, whatever he could do now wasn't enough.

He went out into the hall and down it. It was very quiet, now, visiting hours over and the night shift happily in place, chirping away in the nursing office over coffee and patient status reports. He wheeled past the open door, but no one looked up.

Pushing through the double doors that opened on to the balcony that circled the rotunda, he rolled to the door he knew led up to the nurses' quarters. But when he opened it, all he saw was a flight of stairs rising up steeply. Impossible. He'd have to get someone to go up there. He looked down over the balcony railing into the dark space below: dark, save for a few dim night-lights and a sword of light from the open door of Roger Forrester's office. There was no one behind the reception desk.

He turned back to the narrow stairway and called up in a hoarse whisper, 'Laura! Laura!' A feeling of relief swept over him as he heard a sound from above. It was all right, she was up there, she'd heard him. But then, after a moment, a cat appeared at the top of the stairs, looking down at him curiously. It was the biggest cat Gilliam had ever seen. It gazed at him with lively interest, then sat down to await further orders.

Gilliam pushed the door closed and looked around. He started back towards the double doors to get help from someone in the nursing office, when out of the corner of his eye he saw a light shining at the end of the small passage that connected the main building with the annexe: not just one of the night-lights, but a brighter glow – Laura's office.

Was she there?

He rolled his chair through the open door towards the light at the far end.

Behind him, Solomon pushed open the door at the bottom of the stairs and looked around. Hearing a noise in the passage to his left he padded softly down it, ears pricked, whiskers akimbo.

He liked to be where the action was.

Gilliam paused at the double fire doors that blocked the actual entrance to the pool end of the annexe. The light streamed through the glass windows above his head, too high to look through. From beyond them he heard a noise, as if a chair had fallen over in Laura's office overlooking the pool. Then footsteps. He backed his chair off a little, expecting someone to come through, but no one did. After a moment, he rolled forward again and nudged the double doors slightly apart. As he did so, those at the far end of the hall that led to the service stairs whooshed softly to and fro. He caught a glimpse of someone beyond them, turning to go down the steps. Someone who was carrying something.

Someone wearing a red plaid hunter's jacket.

He rolled.

He went through the double doors so fast and hard that they swung back and forth for some time. Time enough for a cat to slip through and come slowly and silently along behind the wheelchair, trotting lightly, moving steadily.

So as not to miss anything.

Gilliam went through on to the balcony that overlooked the pool area. Below him, in the shadows, moved a darker shadow. In the faint light reflecting up from the water he could see the figure moving along the edge of the pool, hunched and awkward, carrying a long, limp shape, with hair that dangled down and waved softly as if she, the burden, were nodding acquiescence to her fate.

'That's far enough!' Gilliam shouted into the darkness. The light from the doors behind him gleamed in a halo all around him, which brightened slightly as the door moved open for a moment, then shut again. He felt a soft presence near the floor, a shadow beside him, and was momentarily distracted. He looked down again. 'I know what you're planning and it's no good. It won't work this time.'

Below him, in the darkness, the footsteps stopped. He saw the figure bend and deposit its burden on the tiles beside the pool, and come slowly back along the edge and peer upwards. The new intent was clear. Kill the cripple, *then* kill the girl.

Gilliam waited until the shadow was below him, then spoke again. 'I'm coming down. I've got my gun. I've phoned the sheriff and he's on his way. There's absolutely no point in trying anything – we know it all.'

He rolled the chair on to the elevator platform and pressed the button. The small electric motor whined into life and he began to descend. In his lap he held part of the armrest he'd just detached, hoping that in the dark the glint of its metal would pass for a gun. All he needed was a little time, a brief advantage. He'd lie, he'd cheat, he'd do anything for that time. He sure as hell couldn't kick his opponent in the knee, could he? So he was doing the best he could.

The little elevator whined to a halt and the dark, bulky shadow of his enemy loomed above him. They were far away from the main clinic here, far from the night staff and the patients, far from saving, far from hope.

'Suicide, I think,' said the voice in the dark. 'While in a fit of depression over your situation.' The voice was calm and slow, but the movement was not. It was quick, malevolent and knowledgeable. The wheelchair, pivoted on the one weak spot in its construction, teetered on the edge of the pool and fell in, carrying Gilliam with it.

The splash was very loud.

Solomon, on his way over to see why Laura was sleeping by the pool like that, leaped sideways at the sudden cascade of water that showered on him and crashed into a pair of legs, one of which kicked out at him. He spat and struck out with a retaliatory claw. There was a loud cry above him and another splash. Water everywhere. He scuttled over to a dry spot beside Laura and began to wash frantically. He *hated* to get wet.

Gilliam, moving free of the heavy wheelchair which sank away from him to the bottom, was trying to reach the safety of the pool's edge when the big dark shape of his assailant dropped over him with an outraged yell and sank beneath the surface. A moment later the surface broke and the shadow came with it, solid and menacing.

Choking, Gilliam couldn't resist an explanation. He'd always felt he needed to explain before he destroyed. 'Now your legs don't count any more than mine,' he said and lunged.

Laura came to slowly, her head throbbing like a buzzsaw. The last thing she remembered was sitting in her office looking at the Doppleman file, then – nothing. She awoke to darkness and noise and splashing and shouting. The words made no sense, echoed in the dark vault over the pool, bounced off the surfaces of window and pine panelling. She tried to sit up and something nudged her in the face. Panic momentarily took her by the throat until she realized it was Solomon, butting her on the chin and purring deeply.

She was by the pool, she'd known that instantly by the smell of the chlorine and the damp warmth that surrounded her. Water was flying everywhere. It seemed as if some kind of monster was struggling in the pool, a dark two-headed hydra that cursed and waved tentacles and thrashed and sank and rose to sink again, gurgling and choking. With her head spinning from the second hard blow she'd sustained in a week, it took her a minute to register that it was two men fighting savagely in the pool.

Fighting to the death.

She staggered over to the wall below her office and hit the alarm automatically, the bells that would summon help should there be some sudden difficulty in the pool. She couldn't hear them from there, but she knew they were ringing in the nursing station and in the main office.

Then she hit the pool light switches and blinked as they flashed on. Both men were under the water as the illumination flooded over them and, as they rose and broke the surface, she saw in astonishment who they were.

And shouted 'No!'

Gilliam made one last, wild effort. His arms, strengthened by propelling the wheelchair and swimming to sustain the drag of two useless legs, tightened around his opponent's chest and he squeezed. Slowly, slowly, he forced the face under the water. The wild eyes stared up at him through the film, the mouth bubbling incomprehensibly.

Gilliam heard Laura's shout and it shocked him. Wanting only to destroy, he relented. He loosened his hold, allowed the figure to float upwards, then drove one hard, angry fist into its face.

He let go of it and reached for the edge of the pool. Having secured his hold, he dragged the figure over and propped it up, wedging one limp arm into the overflow trough to support it.

Feet were pounding down the corridor towards them and he looked up at Laura. Winded, it took him a few seconds to get the words out. 'There's your killer,' he said.

Solomon, stepping carefully between the puddles, came over and looked down in fascination at the face that floated, hair waving gently around it, just below him in the pool. Then he began to wash. He didn't know what all the fuss was about, or why Laura was crying.

It was only that nice Dr Butler.

# TWENTY-NINE

'HE WAS NEVER *IN* CHICAGO,' Gilliam said through chattering teeth, as Kay Pink slipped another hot-water bottle under the blankets. She herself was dressed in a rather odd assortment of borrowed clothing, for it was she – along with Roger Forrester – who had jumped into the pool to help Gilliam.

Kay told Laura later that it was only after they had finished that she'd remembered she couldn't swim.

The sheriff had arrived just as they were dragging Butler out of the water. Whether he could get back into town with his prisoner was another question – the snowstorm had turned into a blizzard and Mountview was temporarily cut off.

The clinic itself was warm, dry and comfortable, thanks to Roger Forrester's planning for just such eventualities, but it gave the situation an unreal quality – rather like a shipwreck.

Forrester, too, was dressed haphazardly. Laura thought his unruly hair and collar, half in and half out of his hastily donned pullover, made him look younger, nicer and exactly like her father. His befuddled expression helped. Like his brother, he found human reality difficult to cope with on a rush basis. Like his brother, given time, he'd take it in. Maybe they all would. For the moment they were only listening.

'He never went to the conference, never intended to present a paper,' Gilliam went on.

'But I saw the paper,' Laura protested. 'I saw his name listed in the programme.'

'Uh-huh. And it was a very good speech,' Matt said. 'Given very well by Dr David Butler, who is short, bald, near-sighted and furious at finding out that someone had been using his name under false pretences.'

'I don't understand,' Roger Forrester said, not for the first time.

'The man you know as David Butler is *not* David Butler,' Sheriff Gabriel explained. 'His real name is David Bremmer. He once worked in the same hospital as David Butler, interning while Butler was a resident. The hospital was the St Charles in Denver.'

'Oh,' said Forrester.

'Does that mean anything to you, Uncle Roger?' Laura asked.

'Yes . . . I'm afraid it does.'

She saw that Tom was barely holding on to his consciousness, but he seemed determined to explain all before lapsing into the exhausted sleep he so clearly needed. His voice was rough and growly, like a grumpy bear's, but he went on.

'There was a scandal brewing at that hospital while Mrs McAllister was there. She was in a pretty bad state at the time, apparently, but both Bremmer and Butler were on the staff and had contact with her. Butler is a no-nonsense type, but Bremmer . . . well . . .'

'We know what he's like,' Kay said with asperity.

'Yeah, well – she thought he was wonderful. She left the hospital before the scandal broke and went into a nursing home. While she was recovering she heard the reports and stories, and naturally assumed in her own dreamy way that the beautiful young doctor who had been so kind to her was the innocent Butler and the wicked drug-dealing culprit was Bremmer, that nasty little resident who'd told her to stop thinking so much about herself. That was how she wanted to see it and that was how she saw it.'

'But . . . we have Butler's references . . .' Forrester protested. 'Everything checked out.'

'Sure,' Gilliam agreed. He had nearly stopped shivering.

'All the background checking was done by mail and computer, right? He simply gave you Butler's name, educational history and Social Security number – which he picked up while he was at the St Charles – and the computers and secretaries did the rest. It was a routine background query and they made a routine reply. Bremmer had taken the State Boards here under his new false name and passed, of course, because he *was* a doctor. The real Butler had left the St Charles by this time and was practising in New Mexico. Bremmer–Butler kept up with his professional progress by reading the medical journals and through old contacts. The Department of Social Security might have picked up the fact that two incomes were coming in under the same number, but they apparently haven't yet and why would anyone ask? Again – all in the computer, nothing in anybody's brain.'

'Why did he pick up Butler's background details in the first place?' Laura wanted to know.

'He knew what was going to happen,' the sheriff said. 'He knew the drug-selling thing he was involved in was going to get exposed. He'd used the information to try and frame the real Butler, as a matter of fact. But it was a sloppy attempt and didn't work. He got much more careful later on. The hospital didn't bring criminal charges, but Bremmer lost his licence to practise and was thrown out of the AMA. He knew if he wanted to continue as a doctor he would need a new identity.'

'But he was a good doctor,' Roger murmured. 'A *really* good doctor.'

'Yes, he was,' Gilliam agreed. 'That's what makes it doubly nasty – that he should have wasted his ability so dreadfully. But he wanted money at the time and he turned to selling drugs on the side to get it. What's worse, he felt he *deserved* money. He's a classic example of psychopathic egocentrism.'

'My, aren't we the intellectual in our blue pyjamas and blue lips,' commented Kay Pink. Gilliam grinned at her.

'Well, that doesn't explain about the murders,' Laura said. 'Are you *sure* that David—'

'Stubborn, isn't she?' Gilliam asked Forrester.

Roger smiled. 'Like her father. Go on – let's hear it all. I still can't believe it.'

'You got distracted by the business about the wills, Laura,' Gilliam said, not looking at Forrester. 'David knew nothing about the second will, leaving him all the money he could want. If he had known about it he'd have been careful *not* to kill the two witnesses to its signing. By the time he found out about it, it was too late. He'd killed Julie and Clarissa and anyway – he had you on the hook.'

'He thought he did,' she said. Was it true? She would never know, now, whether she would finally have succumbed to David's charm or not.

'He had taken the job at Mountview because it was the perfect hideaway. Even if someone came along who knew the *real* David Butler, he could claim the two names were a coincidence. After all, it is a pretty ordinary name.'

'There are about fifty David Butlers in the AMA records,' Sheriff Gabriel explained. 'But only one who was at the St Charles Hospital at the same time as Bremmer.'

'Yes,' Gilliam said. 'Bremmer had taken the job here with an eye to good money and safety, but that eye brightened when he learned that you were eventually coming into a fortune, Laura. The beloved only niece of Dr Roger Forrester and a good bet to inherit the whole caboodle, money, clinic – everything. A great prospect for the future – with himself as eventual head of Mountview with an income to match.'

'But Laura was never going to come here. He knew nothing about her,' Roger protested. 'It was only *after* Julie's murder that I finally persuaded her to join me here.'

'Yes, I know,' Gilliam said wearily. 'Julie Zalinsky was the first.'

The sheriff opened his mouth as if to protest, then closed it again.

'If it had just been the will, Julie should have been the second or third. That's how I finally saw the thing the right way around. She wasn't killed because she was a witness to a will. That would have been irrelevant as long as Mrs McAllister was alive. No, Julie was killed because she found out that "Butler" was really Bremmer. It hit her hard. She was in love with Butler and he'd played her along, as he did most women. She was on the premises, she was . . . convenient.'

'So they did have an affair,' Laura murmured, her voice thick with self-disgust and pain.

'I think so.' Gilliam's voice was very soft. 'But she made a mistake, a very small and pathetic mistake. She wanted a picture of David to send to her friends so she could brag about him. He wouldn't let her take one, for obvious reasons – you notice all the snapshots she did have were taken of him unawares – so she stole one. The one he couldn't avoid having taken – the one on his personnel records downstairs. She often helped out in the office, I understand—'

So that's why it was missing from David's file, Laura thought.

'And she wrote to her friends, enclosing copies. One friend lived in Denver and worked at the St Charles. She wrote back telling Julie that Butler wasn't Butler at all, but Bremmer, and that he wasn't supposed to be practising, either. After that, given Julie's penchant for orderliness in her work, it was just a matter of gathering the information together. Bremmer had got into the habit of following Butler's progress and when it appeared that Butler was attending any kind of medical conference Bremmer used that to take time off if he could. Julie noticed that a few dates didn't match. She made phone calls.'

'So did I, once Tom had tipped me off,' Matt Gabriel said. 'It wasn't difficult, once I knew where to look and what questions to ask.'

'Unfortunately, Julie made the mistake of confronting Bremmer and telling him that she intended to expose him. She had written everything down and was taking it to the sheriff, she told him. I think she might have been offering him a chance to get away. He didn't give her the same chance. I'm guessing here, but this is how I think it went. He was doing an operation that afternoon and saw her leaving the clinic carrying an envelope. He slipped out, saying he needed to use the toilet, killed her, then came back to clean up. The blood-stains on his surgical scrubs, if anyone had analysed them, would have been of two types – the patient's on whom they had just operated and Julie's. But of course, nobody analysed them. Why should they? You expect to see blood-stains on surgical scrubs, don't you?'

'Oh, God,' Roger whispered.

'He didn't know about the will at that point,' Gilliam went on doggedly. 'No problems for him in that direction at that time. He'd heard about the Shadowman myth in town – he'd been here long enough to pick that up – so he tried to make Julie's murder look like the Shadowman's work.'

'But *he* didn't cut her hair,' Matt said.

They all looked at him. 'What?' Gilliam asked.

'Nothing,' Matt replied. 'Go on.'

'He cut her throat messily – no one would accuse a doctor of not knowing where the jugular vein was – and then he thought it was over. He thought he was safe. Until the night Mrs McAllister saw the movie about the scandal at the St Charles Hospital. She was excited about it, she was looking forward to it, she *knew* the doctors involved, she said. And so she did, although her memories were vague.'

'She once said David would look good in a moustache,' Laura blurted out.

'Ah,' Gilliam said. 'That would have done it. The minute he heard that, Bremmer knew it was only a matter of time before her memory cleared and he knew he had to kill her. Even if she didn't put it together that night, she soon would.'

'But he was with me that night.' Laura blushed.

'For every single minute?' Matt asked.

'Oh . . . well . . . the railing on the stairs had given way and he went out to the shed to see if he could get something to put it back in place. But he was only gone a little while. Maybe ten minutes . . .'

'That would be enough,' Gilliam said. 'He was a fast mover, he'd proved that before when he killed Julie. He'd worked every step out far ahead, so all he had to do at the crucial time was go on and do it, if he could. And he was lucky, if you like. He did it.'

'Did what?' Roger wanted to know. 'Myra McAllister died of heart failure following an acute asthmatic attack. The signs were quite unmistakable.'

'He gave her penicillin,' Laura whispered, horrified. 'Like you almost gave me by mistake.' She couldn't look at him and concentrated on her hands.

'But—' Roger stuttered.

'She was allergic to penicillin, according to Mrs Strayhorn and your own records,' Gilliam said. 'Butler had cut down on her sleeping pills that night, knowing she would be restless. So when he appeared by her bed and said he would give her another sleeping pill – so kind, so understanding – she took it without a murmur.'

'"All little white pills look alike,"' Laura whispered. 'He said he couldn't get into the shed – that was why he took so long.'

'He never even tried. It took only a minute to run across the parking lot, up the rear service stairs and along to Mrs McAllister's room. Anyone who can walk could time it easily,' Gilliam said.

'Did he cut my brakes, too?' Laura asked, ready by now to believe anything.

'No. Nobody cut your brakes, Laura,' Gilliam answered. 'They just went – it was an old car and you didn't look after it properly. You see, it's a funny thing about connections. People make them all the time, so do statisticians. But things that might seem related often have absolutely nothing to do with one another. Like Mrs McAllister's will, for instance. Completely irrelevant.'

'What's all this about brakes,' Roger Forrester wanted to know, looking at Laura with concern.

'Nothing,' she said miserably. She almost wished she *had* crashed that day. The wish passed as quickly as it had come. No, she didn't wish that. But it was agony standing here listening to this. Even though Tom Gilliam was trying to be kind. Surprisingly kind. She looked up and met his eyes, a kind of agony in them, too. He hated hurting her, she could see that. But he hated a man like David Bremmer even more.

And David had tried to hurt her.

David had tried to kill her.

'I was so sure he was in Chicago,' she said.

'Remember that film you told me about – the one you heard in the background when you were talking to him – the one you watched yourself later on because it made you feel "close" to him?' There was an edge of sarcasm in Gilliam's voice. 'That film wasn't networked – it was only shown locally. That meant he was in the vicinity. It was the first thing that didn't check out about him, the thing that started me looking for others that might not check out. And when you gave me Julie's things . . . well . . .'

'What I don't get is why he was wearing Nick Higgins's old jacket,' Kay said, picking up Gilliam's arm and taking his pulse almost automatically. It was something to do.

'He was setting him up,' Matt Gabriel explained.

'Yes, that's why he was so interested in knowing whether the sheriff had let Nick go or not,' Gilliam agreed, snatching his arm back from Kay. 'I'm fine,' he snapped.

'The hell you are,' Kay said. 'You should shut up and go to sleep.'

'No . . . I want to hear all of this,' Roger contradicted. 'He's all right, he's tough.'

'What's going on here?' came a voice from the door and they turned to see Owen Jenks looking blearily at them.

'Join the party.' Kay had given up all pretence at looking after her patient. 'The more the merrier.'

'David was in a unique position to fake some very necessary evidence. In fact, he'd been doing it right along. As soon as it was convenient after killing Julie Zalinsky, he spattered some blood of her type on Higgins's red plaid jacket. When it was damp Higgins wouldn't have noticed it because it was red and when it dried it was brown – just more dirt as far as he was concerned. He only used it for work, after all – left it hanging in the shed when he went home. When he killed Clarissa, David did the same thing.'

Owen gaped at him. 'David killed Clarissa?' he gasped.

'I'm afraid so,' Gilliam said.

'But why? *Why*?' Owen was clearly distressed. He didn't know that David was sedated and handcuffed in Forrester's office downstairs, watched over by two nurses and an orderly. He didn't know why everyone was standing around a clearly exhausted Gilliam's bed, hanging on his every word. He certainly didn't know why the sheriff was there, and why Roger Forrester and Laura looked so distressed. The only normal-looking person in the room was Nurse Pink and she didn't look particularly like her usual jolly self either.

'I was woken by bells ringing,' Owen said dazedly. 'I thought it was another fire. But I couldn't seem to find anyone who knew what was going on. What *is* going on?' His face was comical and in any other circumstances his confusion would have made them all laugh. As it was, he leaned against the window-sill and tried to make sense of it all as Gilliam went on with his explanation.

'Clarissa was in the patients' lounge when that documentary drama about the St Charles Hospital was on. She saw David's concern and it puzzled and intrigued her. I would guess that she had her eye on David most of the time. And I would further guess – but it's only a guess – that she saw him go into Mrs McAllister's room later that night. It's the only explanation I can come up with. She probably tried to blackmail him into something . . . maybe we'll never know, unless he tells us. There's a lot he could tell us – I'm really only guessing on that one, too,' Gilliam admitted.

'But Clarissa was killed by the Shadowman.' Owen was still trying to catch up.

'There is no Shadowman,' Matt said firmly. 'This man Bremmer used the myth to cover his tracks, that's all. He was going to pin the whole thing on Higgins. He knew Clarissa and Higgins had been friendly—'

'They were?' Owen asked.

'Yes. And they had fights from time to time,' Gilliam said. 'So Higgins was a natural for the crimes. If Bremmer could—'

'Who's Bremmer?' Owen interrupted. He was obviously feeling weak.

'Bremmer is David Butler and David Butler is Bremmer,' Roger Forrester supplied patiently. 'I think.'

'I see.' Owen didn't see at all.

'If Bremmer–Butler could make it look as if *Higgins* was crazy, that he had murdered those girls and that he was the Shadowman, then the whole thing would be over. He would never be suspected of killing Mrs McAllister, because everybody thought she died a natural death. And if he killed someone else this week – when he was supposed to be in Chicago – then he could do the blood on the jacket thing again.'

'What about DNA?' enquired Matt. 'We might have checked the DNA.'

'Are you sure?' Gilliam asked. 'If Bremmer had put drugs in Nick's coffee, for instance, and made him appear unstable, and you had found matching blood types on his jacket . . . would the prosecution have spent further money on DNA testing?'

'No, but the defence might have demanded it.' Matt was thinking of Dominic Pritchard. Dom rarely let anything get past him and he would have sprung to Higgins's defence simply because he always fell for the underdog in a fight.

'You taking Nick in for questioning threw Bremmer's plans off a little – he'd figured on doing it on Wednesday or Thursday – but as it was he had to wait until you let Nick go. And by that time there was someone else he *had* to kill – not just to make the case against Higgins complete, but—'

'But me,' Laura said miserably. 'Because I had the Doppleman file. Because I told him about it and he realized what it meant even before I did.'

'That's it,' agreed Gilliam and closed his eyes with a sigh.

'The man's a monster,' Roger breathed. 'I can't *believe*

that someone who was so good at healing others could have been so sick and evil himself.'

Thinking of Milly Cunningham, Laura said nothing. She was convinced in her heart, now, that her uncle had known nothing of the money embezzled from her trust. It had been all Milly's doing, Milly's alone. He had left everything to her and she had taken advantage of it. Perhaps she had been taking advantage of his love and trust for years. Had *she* been the culprit in that old embezzlement scandal? Had he taken the blame for her? It was possible. He was more like his brother than Laura had thought. Trusting, believing the best of everyone, wondering at his good luck when no doubt Milly had engineered much of it. She wondered if Milly had *really* gone back and told Nurse Hasker about changing the penicillin – for if Laura had died, Roger Forrester would have inherited the trust and all would have been well for Mountview. Why, she wondered? Why hadn't Milly done it for herself instead of for him? Perhaps she had. Perhaps those cheques for 'Cash' on the trust fund had paid for things like her designer clothes and mink coat.

Was everyone at Mountview a kind of Shadowman?

David, Milly, even Uncle Roger in his way – all of them something other than what they seemed. Gilliam, too – pretending to be a kind of monster when really he was as scared and vulnerable and thoroughly . . .

Tom Gilliam, eyes closed, was making a funny sound. It seemed almost as if he were laughing to himself, lying there. Nurse Pink leaned over him, concerned by the change in his breathing. She put her ear close to his lips, frowning. Then her face cleared and her mouth began to twitch. She looked up at them.

'He says . . . he says the butler did it.'

# THIRTY

AS LAURA HAD PREDICTED, TOM Gilliam suffered a bad cold from his immersion, but nothing worse. In the morning after his exposure, when the snow had been cleared from the highway, Matt Gabriel had taken Butler away and was making a full investigation of all the killings. Everything was settling down at Mountview.

Except Gilliam.

He came into Laura's office three days later on crutches. She stood up in alarm as he swung, pale-faced but determined, through the door.

'My God, you aren't ready for those yet!' she said, coming across and practically pushing him into the nearest chair.

'Leave me alone. I'm not going back in that god-damn chair,' he said petulantly, when she tried to take the crutches away.

'Where did you get them?' she demanded.

'Michaels sold them to me for fifty bucks.' He grinned.

'The little weasel . . . you could have fallen . . .'

'But I didn't,' Gilliam said firmly, his breath returning. 'And I'm not going to, either. You'll just have to teach me to use them, that's all.'

'I'll do no such thing.' Laura was outraged. 'Not until you're properly prepared.'

'What's the matter, don't you want me to get better?'

'Of course I do.'

'Well, then – stop holding me back.'

'Holding you *back*?'

'Yes. I could be back on the force by now if it weren't

for the fact that you can't bear to let me go. I'm your prize patient, admit it.'

'You're a prize looney,' she said in disgust, getting back to her desk. There, on her blotter, was Martin Hambden's latest evaluation of Gilliam's condition. He'd never be a working cop again. Oh, he'd walk, eventually – but with a heavy limp that would render him useless for active duty. She'd felt terrible when Martin had told her. So had he. They both knew how much being a detective meant to Gilliam – they both felt they had failed.

'Okay – now the way I see it is this,' Gilliam said. 'I'll need a lot of coaching on these things. Seems to me I'll need your exclusive attention from now on.' He heaved himself up on to the crutches again and lurched towards the desk, sitting down on the edge of it with a thump of triumph and pain that brought tears to his eyes, momentarily – and to hers. She looked away so he wouldn't see. He was so . . . stubborn. And quite wonderful. David Butler – or Bremmer – had been beautiful – and a monster. Gilliam was battered and broken – and perfect. How could she have been so blind and foolish all along? It wasn't David's sweet words that had made her feel alive again. It had been Gilliam's teasing and arguing, the fights and the struggles, the challenge of his complex personality and the pain she felt at the vulnerability which he strove so hard to conceal.

'Do you think I'll look good in a grey snap-brim and a cigar?' he asked.

'What?'

'Isn't that what private detectives are supposed to wear?' Or, I suppose I could be the more elegant type – like Nick Charles or Philo Vance. I could grow a small moustache. Get a dog like Asta . . .'

'You know?' she said softly.

'About never getting my gold badge back?' he asked lightly. 'Dr Hambden laid it on the line last night. He's one tough bastard and he didn't leave me much room for pretending he could be making a mistake.'

'I'm sorry.'

'Never mind,' Gilliam told her. 'I accepted it about four o'clock this morning so you'll have to, as well. It's only a limp, you know – everything *else* will work all right.'

'It always did,' she pointed out.

'So – how about coming to work for me?'

'Of course not,' she said. 'You don't need a full-time physio, but Mountview does. Anyway, you're not ready to leave here yet.'

'You're a very difficult woman.' Gilliam dropped the crutches with a clatter that made her jump, then reached over and jerked her to her feet with one hand, bracing himself on the desk with the other. He pulled her to him and looked deep into her eyes. 'You really want to go on working here?'

'Y . . . ye . . . yes,' she faltered, attempting to avoid the look in his eyes, trying not to believe it.

He kissed her, quite thoroughly, then pulled away and looked around her office – the adjacent gym filled with gleaming chromium equipment, the treatment tables littered with elastic bands and bandages, heat lamps, wax baths and all the other esoteric items of her profession.

'Damn poor place for a honeymoon, if you ask me,' he said.

Roger Forrester sat in his office, staring at the letter from Mrs McAllister's lawyers. Her estranged husband had seen reason concerning the cost of a long legal battle, they said, in tones of apparent surprise. The will giving Mountview a million dollars would now go through probate and, barring any further complications, he'd have the money early in the new year.

So Mountview was safe. He also had Laura's money, if he wanted it. He was rolling in capital – he could go on as he had done, proud of what he had achieved and possibly achieve even more.

If only it weren't for the other letter on his blotter – the one from Milly Cunningham. He didn't understand any of it, he'd have to look through the files, to ask Laura. It was all so confusing and it couldn't possibly be true. She'd forged Laura's signature on the letters of consent for the old loan. She'd also been taking money from Laura's trust over the past three years. Where had it gone? And no reason given. The letter said just 'forgive me and goodbye'. Would he ever know? Would they ever find her? He thought probably not – someone as clever as Milly had been at covering her actions could just as easily cover her tracks. He didn't know whether to be glad or sorry about that.

He was a success and it was like ashes in the wind.

Milly was gone.

He didn't know what he'd do without her.

It was very cold in the garden, but they didn't notice it. They went round and round the frozen flowerbeds, their boots making footprints over footprints.

'He'll have to be hospitalized, Shirley,' Harlan Weaver said gently.

'But, please—'

'Shirley, we can't cover up for him any longer,' Matt Gabriel said. 'We have a killer in custody and that will help stop all the fuss about the Shadowman. But if Mitch goes on as he has been doing or gets worse—'

'He *will* get worse,' Weaver said. 'It's inevitable.'

'When did it start?' Matt asked.

She shrugged. 'When he was in his teens. There was that girl killed . . . Patty Cox?'

'Yes. Did he kill her?' Matt asked.

She stared at him, shocked. 'No! He didn't. But . . .'

They waited.

'But he saw it done,' she finally said. 'He'd been roaming in the woods at night since he was ten, but doing no one any harm. He was all caught up with the family history and everything. It seemed romantic to him, I guess. And then . . . one night . . . he came back shaking and crying. He came to me – he never went to our parents with his troubles. He'd seen Chad Turkle with the Cox girl. Chad was her stepbrother, you know.'

'Yes, I remember Chad,' Matt said.

'Well . . . Chad killed her because she wouldn't let him . . . you know. And Mitch . . . watched. He was terrified of Chad.'

'A lot of people were.' Matt grimaced. 'Me too.'

She nodded, sniffing. 'I told Mitch he should tell your dad what he'd seen, but he was too scared. Then Chad got killed in that car smash and there didn't seem much point.' She shrugged. 'But after that, Mitch was different. Secretive. Angry. He . . . did things, nasty things. Maybe he'd been doing them before, I don't know, but now he didn't care if I knew or not.'

'Torturing animals? Setting fires?'

She nodded miserably. 'Daddy beat him, but he didn't stop. He got better later, when Daddy died, but then, when he went away to college, he got stressed and it started up again. They . . . found him one night, cutting up . . . a rabbit . . . while it was still alive. They threw him out. I was so ashamed and so was he.'

'When he was thrown out of Harvard it was all hushed up,' Matt said to Hambden. 'They didn't bring criminal charges and he promised to seek professional help.' That much he had learned from the bursar at Harvard, who had checked the records.

'He didn't *need* professional help,' Shirley said bleakly. 'He had me and Mother, and when she died he still had me. He's always had me to look after him.'

'But you couldn't cope, Shirley – you must have realized that when it all began again.'

'I kept giving him medication. I read up on all the drugs, I borrowed them . . .'

'We know,' Matt confirmed. 'And he promised you he would stop, didn't he? But he couldn't. Dr Weaver says it's a compulsion he simply cannot resist. And whenever you were on night duty, no matter what drugs you gave him, he went out. He went out the night Julie Zalinsky was killed. He came across her body and thought it was a sign. He didn't kill her, but he thought he might have. Or maybe should have. Anyway, *he* cut off her hair and added it to the rest of his collection. You know what we found in your basement, Shirley.'

He wished he could forget it, but he never would. Julie Zalinsky's pony-tail, bright and gleaming, had only been the latest addition to Mitch Hasker's gruesome hoard. There was an older hank of bright hair . . . one that might have belonged to Patty Cox, the young girl whose case George had pulled out of the records. There was no way to prove her stepbrother had killed her, now, unless Mitch gave a statement, and no point in doing more than annotating the file. The girls' pony-tails and the animal tails . . . all kept in a carefully crafted cabinet behind a false rear wall that swung wide . . . to reveal the Shadowman's trophies. He'd kept the best – in his mind he'd been the Shadowman, counting coup.

'When Julie and then Clarissa were killed you thought he was the one who'd done it, didn't you?' Weaver asked. 'You thought it was possible, anyway. I think something in you sensed he was getting worse and worse. He nearly killed Mad Mattie Hattie last night, Shirley, nearly scared her to death—'

'He didn't touch her,' Shirley protested.

'Didn't have to, did he? That's not the point,' Weaver said. 'It was in the *town*, not out here in the woods. He's getting careless, he's not sticking to his own rules, Shirley. He's made a brand-new cape to replace the one he lost, it was in the cupboard too. He'd let Laura Brandon see him, then came back to kill her cat because she told him the Shadowman was "pathetic". . . . He was past the point of no return by then.' He glanced at Matt. 'He's only admitted the roaming to me, not the other things, but he swears he didn't kill Julie or Clarissa. I believe him.'

'Yes,' Matt agreed. 'He's innocent of that, anyway.'

'But I love Mitch.' Shirley was weeping now. 'I've always looked after him, protected him, got him the drugs he should have—'

'By stealing them.' Weaver nodded. 'That was bad,

Shirley. He must have known what you were doing, he couldn't have believed they were vitamins, not really. And when he wanted to break out, when the compulsion was too great – he didn't take them.'

'Sometimes I put them in his food . . .' she said faintly, her breath lifting in a cloud above her head.

'But it didn't help, did it? Whenever you were on night duty he roamed the woods in his paraphernalia, killing small animals, sometimes the pets of people he felt had insulted him or ignored him . . . convinced he was the true spirit of his ancestor, avenging himself . . .'

'Oh, God.' Shirley wept.

'I know a good place, Shirley,' Weaver soothed. 'Not far away, so you can visit him whenever you like. They'll treat him well there, let him go on working on his book.'

'Better to write about the Shadowman than to dress up and try to *be* him,' Matt said practically.

After a moment, Shirley spoke in a defeated voice. 'All right.'

Matt and Harlan Weaver breathed out in relief, the vapours circling their heads in the still, clear, frozen afternoon.

Shirley stopped walking. 'Was Mattie . . . very upset?' she asked after a moment.

'At first she was,' Matt replied. 'Nearly had a heart attack when Mitch jumped out from behind that bush in his cloak and wig. She's better now. She'll be all right.'

'Did she recognize Mitch?'

'No. She thought at first it was the ghost of her dead husband.'

'Oh.'

Weaver managed a chuckle. 'She threw a rock at him. "You're not coming back," she hollered, apparently. "I'm having too much fun without you." That's what the neighbour said who heard her.'

'He never meant to hurt her,' Shirley murmured.

'Maybe he did, maybe he didn't,' Matt said. 'Harm gets done, all the same. Letting things happen is as bad as making things happen, sometimes. We all have to be careful of that, Shirley.'

As he spoke, he realized he was talking to himself, too.

Just a reminder, he thought. Just a reminder of what it takes to be a good sheriff.

Solomon, the Biggest Black Cat in the World, sat in the window of Laura's apartment, looking out at the scene below, and sighed. It really was disgusting. Just when he'd nearly caught that mouse in the attic they made him move back here. And Laura was never about any more – always over at the big building fussing around that crabby man who had splashed water all over him.

He washed a paw carefully, then looked out again. Three people were walking round and round the garden – that sheriff person, a tall man and one of the nurses. Suddenly he stiffened. His whiskers curved forward and his ears swivelled.

He pressed closer to the window. There *he* was *again*.

Dancing around in the snow, his feet making no mark, darting in and out between the three people, his grey coat flapping and his dead, empty eyes staring, shaking his fist at the big building and shouting curses that made no sound. He moved through the flowerbeds, the branches visible behind him, the low walls providing no obstacle as he passed through them. The three people ignored him. Almost as if they couldn't see him. It was very strange.

Solomon sighed again and settled down on the window-sill. Humans were funny creatures. They could see if you'd scratched the furniture or made an unfortunate stain on the carpet. But they couldn't see what was perfectly plain in front of their very noses.

Any cat could have told them.

The Shadowman was out there.

Always had been.

Always would be.

# EXCERPTS FROM THE BLACKWATER BAY CHRONICLE

### MOCK DOC ARRESTED IN SHADOWMAN CASE

Today saw the arrest of a physician on the staff of Mountview Clinic for the double murders erroneously attributed to the SHADOWMAN! Full story on page 3.

### HEAD LIBRARIAN RETIRES ON HEALTH GROUNDS

by Emily Granger

Mitchell Hasker, who has been Head Librarian for the past three years, is retiring due to poor health. He will be much missed for his excellent work and warm personality. The Blackwater Bay Historical Society will not be the same organization without him, for he has been its prime mover and guiding light for many years. Hasker, interviewed at his home today, says that when his health improves he will continue his work on the History of Blackwater Bay and the Hasker family's part in it. His sister Shirley, a senior nurse at Mountview Clinic, told us that it shouldn't be too long before Mitch is restored to full health. We wish him well.

### BLACKWATER BAY WINS HOMECOMING GAME

Heckman High does it at last! Our boys are triumphant on the field, trouncing the opposition . . . see Sports Section.

### MOUNTVIEW CLINIC TO EXPAND

Thanks to a substantial investment by Gilliam Enterprises, Mountview Clinic will be partially closed down for six months next summer in order to develop its third floor into new patient accommodation. They will also be adding another operating theatre and expanding their Intensive Care facilities. Another free clinic will begin operating in Blackwater itself some time in the new year, under the guidance of Dr Owen Jenks.

### LOCAL GIRL WINS *STAR TREK* COMPETITION

Debbie Robinson, Head Cheerleader and popular senior at Heckman High, today received news that she had won a free trip to Hollywood and a small part in the new *Star Trek* film . . .

### OVERTONS PLAN AROUND-THE-WORLD CRUISE

Rotary President Don Overton and his wife have decided to take off on their planned world cruise in his 45-foot schooner *Dreamer* at last. 'We have a two-year plan,' Overton told the *Chronicle*. 'We hope to visit every place we have ever wanted to see and take our time about it.' The Overtons, a popular local couple, will be much missed, but we all look foward to the pictures that will be produced by Don, a superb amateur photographer.

### WHAT'S GOING ON HERE?

*Your weekly column on news about town*

by Emily Gibbons

We hear that Deputy George Putnam is romancing our gorgeous new vet. . . . Does she make him purr with delight?

Just Desserts will soon be opening an extension for evening meals with ooh-la-la French cuisine . . .

Margaret Toby has won *another* award for her quilts . . .

Kate Trevorne and her special detective Jack Stryker may

be hearing wedding bells come next June . . . at last . . . and they may not be the only ones! We hear another 'visiting cop' may also be walking down the aisle! Watch this space for further details!

### LOCAL ELECTIONS HOT UP

With election time drawing near, the most hotly contested seat will be that of local County Sheriff. Present incumbent Matt Gabriel will be seeking a return to office, but a new contender in the shape of local developer Jack Armstrong has entered the race. Armstrong claims he will 'shake things up in Blackwater', but Gabriel says experience is what counts in combating crime. His recent success with the Shadowman case gives him a decided edge, but Armstrong has a strong following due to his success in developing the popular new Mall. Get ready for a real battle!